ALSO BY HARRY CONNOLLY

The Way Into Chaos
The Way Into Magic
The Way Into Darkness

Twenty Palaces
Child of Fire
Game of Cages
Circle of Enemies

Spirit of the Century Presents: King Khan

*Bad Little Girls Die Horrible Deaths and Other
Tales of Dark Fantasy*

A KEY,
AN EGG,
AN
UNFORTUNATE
REMARK

Harry Connolly

**RADAR AVE
PRESS**

Cover by Duncan Eagleson

Copy edited by Rose Fox

ISBN: 0-9898284-8-4
ISBN-13: 978-0-9898284-8-2

To every urban fantasy author who has gone before me
and who will come after me, too.

CHAPTER ONE

An Unwelcome Party Guest Catches a Glimpse of Himself

Evening had fallen on Seattle, and there were a great many people going somewhere they didn't want to go. An ER nurse with an aching back, a recent graduate about to ask his father if he could move back in, a middle-aged woman facing another evening of her boyfriend's tedious anime and even more tedious sex—all felt the helpless resignation that comes before an unpleasant, unavoidable task.

Of those thousands of people, none were expecting a warmer welcome than the man standing at Marley Jacob's front gate, and none were more mistaken.

Aloysius Pierce was a man of extraordinary self-regard, especially considering what he'd achieved in life. His education was marked only by his concerted effort to pass with as little effort as possible, and his law career, being run with those same priorities, had foundered. He had a knack for attracting women and then quickly driving them away, and did much the same with his professional clients. Having recently turned thirty, he considered himself a paragon of self-reliance, largely because the only people in his life were as uninterested in community and friendship as he was.

Aloysius possessed an absolute certainty that he would Make His Mark Very Soon Now. All he needed to do was win a few cases in a row, or perhaps just win the right case (his current client had become terse with him, and he could tell their relationship was about to end unhappily). Or he might be introduced to someone influential and be brought into a pivotal role on some sort of project, possibly in the high-tech industry, or

1

filmmaking, or women's clothing. Not that Aloysius had any expertise in those fields—or in anything, really—but he simply couldn't imagine a future for himself that did not include great things.

And why not? He was a good-looking white man, raised in a wealthy family. At least, they'd been wealthy right up until he left for college. He could tell a joke, mix a drink, and convincingly tell a woman she lit up the room just by entering it. Why shouldn't the world give him whatever he wanted?

He believed he was the man who could thaw the infamous Seattle Chill. He was the one who could bring back the Sonics. He was the one who could manage that thing with the monorail, whatever it was. His plans weren't definite, but he was sure they needed to be big. Only then would he get the house, the boat, the bespoke suits from London.

If only Aloysius Pierce had realized that the life he was truly suited for was "glad-handing politician," he might have achieved those things.

On a chilly May evening, he stood at the front gate of his Aunt Marley's urban mansion, uncharacteristically hesitant. Behind him, the street was congested with parked Mercedes, BMWs, and Lexuses, most the color of gold or sable. Every time Aloysius looked at one, he felt as though he'd been cheated somehow.

All the windows were brightly lit, and the din of the party could be heard on the sidewalk. The revelers mingled and laughed within, not realizing a drop of rancid oil was about to land in the froth.

Aloysius couldn't stand Aunt Marley's parties. She knew this and he knew she knew. From the dizzying heights of his own vanity, he was certain that his willingness to endure one of his aunt's soirees would impress upon her the gravity of the favor he intended to ask. With a sigh, he started up the front walk.

Weathers opened the door before Aloysius could ring the bell. As usual. Aloysius greeted him warmly—always be kind to servants, no matter how lowly, was his rule—but the man responded with all the human kindness of a cutlery set. Once again, as usual. Aloysius entered the house, noting with dread the sound of something that might pass for music coming from the front room.

"If you would, sir," Weather said, gesturing toward the end of the entryway. There was a tall stock pot on a table, and beside it stood a young woman wearing nothing but colorful paint.

Aloysius blinked. Despite his imagined quick-wittedness, he needed a moment to take in what he was seeing. The woman was a short, slender blonde with her hair tied up in a frizzy ponytail. She stood with arms akimbo and her chin held high and facing away from him. What he'd first taken for green tattoos or body art turned out to be cash money. The pot on the table beside her was full of papier-mâché glue; guests had dipped bills into the glue before laying them on her. She was slowly being trapped into this pose.

Weathers shut the door firmly and went back to his duties. Not that Aloysius noticed. His body tingled and the whole of his attention was focused on the young woman and, he dimly realized, the broad-shouldered brunette beside her. He was about to ask the second woman to step outside, but before he could embarrass himself, he noticed a holstered Taser under her arm and realized she was a chaperone.

That was fine. Aloysius had operated under more difficult circumstances than this.

He reached for his wallet. He knew better than to show up at one of his aunt's parties without a few bills, although his plan to declare his donation as a way of earning even more goodwill now seemed shaky.

He dipped a twenty into flour water. "What's the cause of the day?"

He'd addressed the chaperone, but it was the model who answered. "We're from the Noon Shadow Arts Collective. We're in danger of losing our studio space, and Ms. Jacobs offered to throw us a benefit."

Aloysius had always considered his own good looks to be something special—simultaneously manly and what he secretly thought of as elfish. But as he side-stepped into her line of sight, the model only glanced at him and looked away.

"Aunt Marley will do that, won't she?" Aloysius let the bill drip into the pot and stirred with his finger. The mention of his relationship to their sponsor didn't earn the spark he'd hoped for: there was no second appraisal, no fluttering eyelashes, no licking of the lips, not even a little smile. She'd seen his face, knew he had money, knew he was related to a great deal of money, and somehow she still wasn't interested.

As though a gauze had been taken from his eyes, Aloysius suddenly realized the model was not as pretty as he'd first thought. Her brown eyes were large but not quite symmetrical, her nose slightly too long, and worst of all, she had the hard, lean strength of an endurance athlete. He didn't like that in a woman.

She must have taken his hesitancy for shyness, because she offered him a distant but kindly smile. In return, he fell in love with her just the tiniest bit, the way he often did with cheerful women he'd decided weren't good enough for him. He laid the twenty on the small of her back—the best parts were already covered with much larger bills—and it felt so nice that he did it twice more.

Why hadn't his aunt told him about this? He would have been the first one at the door.

As he wiped the flour and water from his hands, the model thanked him politely. Aloysius could feel the chaperone watching, and her unfriendly expression spoiled his mood. He spun onto his heel and plunged into the party.

By his aunt's standards, this gathering was almost sedate. The music playing over the speaker system was wholly new to him—he was sure it would turn out to be Sri Lankan trip-hop or something equally outré. By the window a pair of androgynous twins—one dressed in a tweed suit with elbow patches and the other in a diaphanous white dress—talked with an austere older woman in a boxy gray pantsuit. On the couch, a man in a black suit and wingtips was deep in animated conversation with a bodybuilder wearing nothing but a Speedo and, on his back, a modified horse's saddle.

Each and every one of them would have been startled to discover that

Aloysius felt a wave of pity and disdain for them. As he glanced at them, he imagined he could instantly spot their faults. Too much exercise or not enough. Too much money or not enough. Too fashionable. Too conservative. Like a great many unsuccessful people, Aloysius had a reflexive contempt for everyone he met.

Suddenly, all conversation stopped, and even the music hushed. A figure in a tattered black cloak and ghostly white mask glided through the room. It loomed almost eight feet tall and trailed an unearthly chill behind it: the bodybuilder shuddered as it passed. The figure floated through the open French doors onto the balcony and then beyond, the black cloak dragged across the railing like a hanging blanket. Then it disappeared into the night.

The music and conversation resumed. Aloysius scanned the room. Most of Aunt Marley's more unusual guests were in attendance, including the silent and watchful ninety-year-old Guatemalan man with his two burly bodyguards, but she herself was nowhere to be seen. Aloysius wandered into the kitchen, onto the balcony, then into the sun room.

There he found three naked models—Aloysius knew his aunt would refer to them as "nude"—standing on platforms, each with a half-dozen easels set up in a semi-circle around them. Seven guests, all of whom could have come from the same corporate boardroom, struggled to capture the figures in charcoal.

Of course his aunt had set them up right in front of the floor-to-ceiling windows, where any of the neighbors could have seen them. He sighed, wondering if this was a sign of encroaching senility and if it was finally time to file that power of attorney for her estate.

The nearest model was a tall woman, at least fifty years old, who had a scar where her left breast should have been. The second was a small, effeminate man of about the same age. He had a bit of a belly and he'd painted his long, pointed fingernails a sparkling purple.

Beside the third model—a short, dark-haired woman who must have weighed over three hundred pounds—Aunt Marley perched on a stool, struggling to accurately depict the shape of the woman's leg. Aloysius had no interest taking over an easel himself, and carefully pretended not to notice the donation jars set up beside the models.

"Hello, Aloysius," his aunt said without turning to him. Aloysius thought she must have seen his reflection in the darkened window even though she'd never looked up from her canvas. "I didn't expect to see you here. I thought you didn't like my parties."

"It's not that I... I'm sorry, but..."

"It's all right, dear. A person can have a perfectly happy life without ever attending my little events. At least, some reliable friends have told me it's possible, so I guess I believe it. I assume you have a problem?"

"Well, I don't have the problem, Aunt Marley. It's someone else who needs your help, but—" He looked around at the partygoers and disturbingly unashamed models. Their casual confidence had dented his smug disdain, and he wanted to retreat to someplace he could feel good again. Is there anywhere more private where we could talk?"

She sighed, obviously irritated to be dragged away, and turned toward him. Aloysius was once again struck—and not in a happy way—by his aunt's resemblance to his mother. Both had the same long, triangular face and wide brown eyes. The main difference between them was that his mother's hair had turned dull gray and her face had gone dark and pouchy. Aunt Marley, despite being the elder sister and well into her sixties, had the silver hair and complexion of a wealthy woman of leisure. Aloysius's mother had spent her inheritance guzzling chocolate liqueurs, wrecking Italian sports cars, and marrying worthless men. Aunt Marley, with her huge house and crazy parties, was merely eccentric.

She stood. A group of partygoers had come into the room, dragging a few of the dilettante artists from their stools. Marley went to the nearest easel, mounted with a crude charcoal of the model with the painted nails, and marred it with a long ink squiggle drawn with a pen that she took from her pocket. No one saw but Aloysius. "Very well, dear. Let's talk in my study."

She led him upstairs although he knew the way very well. The soft carpet muffled their steps, and the hall had been left dark to discourage wandering guests. Aunt Marley didn't switch the lights on. The darkness made Aloysius feel a little unwelcome but he was certain—absolutely certain—his aunt would not have given that impression deliberately, no matter how it seemed.

At the office door, she waited for him to open it; it was one of her eccentricities that she never touched a doorknob.

The room was soundproofed against the music from downstairs: They might as well have been on a space station for all the noise they heard. Marley crossed to a pair of comfortable chairs and gestured for Aloysius to sit. "Would you like a cup of coffee, dear?"

He glanced at the elaborate Italian coffee machine on the table by the window. It made the best coffee he'd ever tasted, but he fought his usual impulse to indulge himself and declined.

"Thank you!" he said with the effusive display of heartfelt appreciation that was so effective at getting what he wanted from people, "but I'll be fine. It's quite a party you have down there. Those weird life-drawing models are a little outlandish, am I right?" He wasn't sure why he'd said that, but it had bothered him to see them there, naked and unashamed. He certainly wouldn't have posed naked in front of strangers, and he had a body to be proud of.

"They're not outlandish, dear," Marley's tone was disapproving. "And they're not weird. They're the artists this party is meant to help. They're human beings, Aloysius. They look the way human beings look."

Aunt Marley had a way of saying things that made a person feel guilty without really understanding why. "Of course! I mean, I didn't mean to say anything rude, honest."

"I know you didn't mean to be rude." She put a bit more emphasis on the word mean that he would have liked. "What we intend is often beside the point. The artists downstairs are not on display. This isn't an exhibit of curiosities. It's a party. It's a chance to meet and mingle with people outside your usual experience. To expand your horizons. Everyone's horizons, in fact, But then, you've heard this little speech before."

"Sorry."

Few people could squeeze as much smug condescension into an apology as Aloysius. Marley took a deep breath, reminded herself that this was family, and steered the conversation back to the matter at hand. "Who is this person you want me to help?"

Aloysius took a deep breath and leaned toward her. It was time to make his case. "First, I want to say that I know there are certain things Mother told me never to discuss with you."

"For good reason, dear."

"But we're past that, aren't we?" He began talking faster so she wouldn't interrupt. "I know you can do things for people. Unusual things. For instance, White Mask just made an appearance downstairs, and I know it's not a party trick or a special effect. I know that, whatever White Mask is, it's for real... and you could stop it if you wanted."

"Why should I? She doesn't hurt anyone."

"Sure. Okay. But my point is that I know you have a connection to... unusual things. And that you have certain abilities."

"You still haven't told me about the friend you want me to help."

"It's Jenny,"

She didn't react, but he didn't expect her to. "I hope you don't expect me to get in the middle—"

"Oh, no, nothing like that. I know you know about me and her, and maybe you also know that she's stopped returning my calls."

"I guess you should stop calling her, then."

"But she's making a mistake! I know you can help—"

"What do you want me to do, Aloysius? Fire her?"

"No!" he said, although he secretly wondered if Jenny might be forced to come to him for help if she lost her paycheck. Not that his aunt would really do so. Aloysius lowered his voice, trying to keep a gentle tone. "Oh no, I don't want to do anything bad to her. Not at all. You know how I feel."

"You've certainly told me enough times, darling."

He laughed at that, and brushed his hair back. "I guess I have. Okay. So. I know that you... I know you can do things to help people. Tricks."

There was a quiet knock at the door, then Weathers let himself in. "I'm sorry to disturb your meeting, madam, but there is a bit of a row downstairs. One of the guests, a Mr. Caldwell, has discovered that the portrait he was creating has been defaced with a slash of ink, and he has accused his brother-in-law. I'm afraid they might come to blows."

"Hmm," Marley said. "Weathers, inform them that physical violence in my home is unacceptable, then offer to let them work out their competitive streak at the ping-pong table."

"I will do so immediately, madam."

"Some of the other guests will want to gamble on the outcome. Be sure to take their wagers from them."

"Yes, madam."

"... As donations."

Weathers bowed and backed out of the room.

Marley turned back to Aloysius. He was smiling and shaking his head, but her expression was quite pleasant and quite still. "How do you want me to help you?" There was a chilly note in her voice that her nephew did not have the wit to notice.

"I don't! I want you to help Jenny. She doesn't realize what a good thing we could have. I have a great job and I care about her very much, and—"

"But does she care about you?"

Aloysius bit his lip. They both knew the answer to that. "That's how you can help her," he said. "I know you sometimes make potions for people—"

Marley started to stand but Aloysius laid a gentle hand on her forearm. He didn't hold her down, but she let his touch kept her in place all the same. "I know," he pressed on, "you could make a love potion for her."

She settled back and laid her soft, wrinkled hand on Aloysius's. "Are you quite sure you understand what you're asking, dear?"

Aloysius began to realize that Aunt Marley did not truly appreciate the ordeals he was willing to endure to ask this request. Hadn't he come to her party? He leaned back in his chair and laughed with the exasperated air of

9

someone who can't believe he has to state the obvious. "I'm asking you to make her happy!"

"With a rape spell?"

"What?" His grip tightened on her arm. "No, I don't want... that. I want a love potion."

Marley leaned toward him, prompting him to take his hand off her arm. "But dear, that's what love spells and love potions are. Rape magic. I get this too often, I'm sorry to say. Someone will hear a rumor—"

"Aunt Marley... Aunt Marley, no. That's not what I mean at all. I don't want to force her to do anything. I just want her to let me make her happy."

"Dear, it's only love if she chooses you. Do you understand? What you want is to take away her ability to say no. You want her to never deny you anything again."

Aloysius leaned back in his chair. His mouth was open and moving as though he couldn't make the right words come out. Suddenly, being downstairs beside the naked models seemed preferable to being in this room, in this skin, having said what he'd just said. He looked at his aunt as though she'd just slapped him awake. "All I wanted..." He didn't know how to finish that sentence.

"I know what you wanted." Marley laid one hand on his smooth, warm cheek. Her touch was cold and ghostly. "Do you understand who you are?"

"Oh, damn." Aloysius looked down at his trembling hands. "What is wrong with me?"

Marley leaned back in her chair, smiling with relief. "I'm glad you said that, dear. I'm glad you gave the correct response."

It was Aloysius's habit to ignore remarks if he did not know how to respond. "She's not here, is she? I came at night because I thought she'd be gone."

"She isn't here. Shall we?

They stood. Aloysius walked to the door, strangely hyper-aware of his whole body, as though he was paying attention to it for the first time. He opened the door for them both.

A Key, an Egg, an Unfortunate Remark

The music downstairs seemed louder than before. Aloysius didn't want to be down there with them, not again. He felt too small and fragile for crowds and loud music.

At that moment, a middle-aged woman in a scarlet pantsuit raced up the stairs to them. She wore a black eyepatch adorned with a silver skull and crossbones.

"Marley, come and see! Fred and Freddy are playing ping pong, and they're ferocious!" She clutched at Marley's hand.

Marley glanced at Aloysius. He waved at her. "I'll go the back way," he said. "It'll be quieter. Aunt Marley, tell Jenny... I'm sorry to ask this of you, but I don't want to talk to her myself—please tell her I won't bother her anymore."

"I will."

"Thank you. I'll call you."

* * *

Marley let herself be led away, feeling unexpectedly light-hearted.

The scarlet pirate was quite correct: the two men battling at ping pong in the play room were grim and furious, and they played a hard, fast game. Marley asked Weathers for a special bottle out of her private collection and gave each contestant a glass during a break in the game. "For refreshment."

It was a potion, of course, but not a love potion. The effect was quite mild: their physical exertions became pleasurable, and by the end of the match the men were laughing together over a close game well-played. Their wives stared at them with wet, shining eyes; It seemed that the end of their long feud had finally come and both women were on the verge of tears at the prospect.

As the crowd cheered the final point, Marley wandered without purpose —as she often liked to do—to the window. She saw Aloysius standing beside the sundial in her rose garden, absentmindedly stroking it with one hand. He must have been standing out in the chill for quite a while, thinking.

As she watched, he seemed to come to some sort of decision and stalked

11

off along the path toward the front of the house.

She never saw her nephew alive again.

CHAPTER TWO

Breaking Fast in the Usual Way

Marley had her breakfast a little later than usual the next morning. Weathers prepared a bowl of milk-cooked steel-cut oats with a sunny-side egg laid gently over the top; the egg white was perfectly circular, and the trembling yolk lay in the exact geometric center. There were four thin, curled shavings of Italian parmesan near the edge of the bowl at the cardinal points, with the largest at North and each shaving at West, South and East slightly smaller.

With Weathers, everything was done widdershins and everything was done perfectly.

Marley lifted her spoon then set it down again. "Oh, Weathers, it's lovely! It seems a shame to subject it to something as mundane and destructive as eating."

"Thank you, madam," Weathers inclined his head by the barest degree. "However, I must point out that the cook's art is wasted if it is not consumed. Eating is not destruction; it is culmination." He turned toward the back of the house. "Ms. Wu has arrived."

"Oh, good. While I play my meager role in your artistry, she can walk the dog."

When Marley finished, she carried the bowl and spoon to the kitchen. Weathers stood at the cutting board, peeling cloves of garlic. He'd spent the entire night cleaning and it would have been cruel to leave yet another mess for him, even though he would never complain.

Beside him, leaning against the granite countertop, stood Albert. He held a little plastic cup of yogurt in his damaged right hand and peeled off the top with a little grimace of pain. He was Aloysius's half-brother, younger by a dozen years, and he also had their mother's pointed chin and sandy hair. But where Aloysius's hair was limp and floppy, Albert's was short and unruly, and where Aloysius was short and slender, Albert stood six-foot-four and had the build of a linebacker.

Marley set her bowl in the sink and smoothed the lapel of Albert's sport jacket. "Good morning, dear. Another interview today? On a Sunday?"

"And on the seventh day, he bussed tables," Albert said. "Good morning, Aunt Marley. I think this one will go much better."

"Of course it will. I have every confidence in you."

"Afterwards, I have physical therapy at the VA, so I'll be back late." He raised his right hand and flexed the thumb, ring finger and pinkie. They nearly closed into a fist. Well, half a fist.

"I'll make sure Weathers leaves you something in the fridge. But I wish you had come downstairs for my party last night. You might have found something amusing."

"I'm sorry. I wasn't up for talking to strangers about.... Next time."

"That would be wonderful. Would you mind, please?" Albert set down the yogurt and opened the back door for her. She thanked him and went outside.

It was a chilly morning for May in Seattle. The cloying humidity of the night before had given way to a faint blowing mist, and the air held a creeping rawness. Jenny Wu stood by the gazebo, leash in one hand and scooper in the other. Marley's dog snuffled around the edge of the shrubbery, looking for a place she had not already marked as her own.

Once that was cleaned up, Jenny approached the house, looking warily at each window and along the path. Her shoulders were almost touching her ears and she took each step as though she thought a trap door might open beneath her.

"Aloysius isn't here," Marley said. "He's asked me to tell you he won't be bothering you anymore."

"Oh!" Jenny was startled, then a little nervous. "Did you..."

"Did I talk to him? Well, yes, but not the way that makes it sound. Mainly I listened to him, and he listened to himself, too, for the first time in a long while."

Being the sort of person who crossed a room to look out a window whenever someone told her it's raining, Jenny glanced from one side of the house to the other. Then she sighed. "Thank you."

"You're welcome. I wish you had come to my party last night, Jenny. I don't invite you out of politeness, you know! I think you would have had fun and met some interesting people."

"I'm sorry, Ms. Jacobs, but sometimes your parties are a little too interesting for me. Besides, I was afraid you-know-who would be there."

"Hm. You have a point, dear. He did drop by for that conversation, after all. Still we're not going to pretend it's the first of my parties that you've avoided, I hope. I invite you for a reason." Marley took a deep breath and looked around. "I love this time of year, don't you? A brisk wet chill makes me feel so alive! And it makes me appreciate the comforts of the house all the more. Still, it'll be nice to lunch together in the gazebo this summer."

An odd look came over Jenny's face as she opened the kitchen door. After Marley entered, she shooed the dog into his play room, hung the leash by the door and finally noticed Albert. She made a small surprised sound and leaned back to look up at him.

"How's it going?" she asked.

"Hey."

"You must be the visiting nephew I've heard so much about. I'm Jenny." She took a tiny, tentative step forward and raised her hand, stiff-armed, like the minute hand of a clock.

Albert slid away from the counter and crossed the room to shake her hand. "I'm Al Smalls." They didn't break eye contact.

Acting as though he was all alone in the room, Weathers was deboning chicken breasts and placing them in a bowl of salted water. Marley crossed to him and touched his elbow. He glanced at her, then turned his flat,

14

somber gaze toward Albert and Jenny.

"That's some tie you have there," Jenny said, sounding a little nervous and awkward. "The knot is perfect."

"It's a clip-on."

"Ew. Really?"

"No, I'm kidding."

She laughed suddenly, like the bark of a seal, then covered her mouth with her hand. "Damn, you made me do my embarrassing laugh."

For the first time since he'd come to visit, Albert smiled. "You shouldn't be embarrassed. I liked it. I'd like to hear it again."

Jenny flushed a little. "Well, maybe we can arrange that."

"I'll even wear a clip-on tie."

Glancing at the top of his head, Jenny looked ready to run her fingers through his hair. "And maybe we can arrange a haircut for you. A clip-on tie needs a flat top, or—"

But Albert had already turned away from her, his smile gone. He dropped his spoon into the sink with a jarring clatter. "I have to get to that interview." He didn't look at anyone as he went out the door.

Jenny's face was still flushed, but she looked confused as well.

Weathers turned to Marley, and there was the slightest hint of satisfaction and curiosity in his expression. For Weathers, that counted as uncontrolled ebullience. "Madam, thank you." He turned his attention to his cutting board again.

Marley glided over to Jenny and put her arm around the girl's shoulders. "Not to worry, dear. Not to worry."

"I always say the dorkiest thing."

"We all make unfortunate remarks, Jenny dear, and we often don't know it was the wrong thing until it's too late."

Marley's bright blue spring rain coat hung by the door like a stooping servant awaiting a command. In the car port, Jenny let her employer into the back seat of the Town Car before getting behind the wheel.

They went first to the athletic club for Marley's morning yoga class and

Jacuzzi. After that they had lunch, attended a talk on irrigation technologies in developing countries at the downtown library, visited the nearly deserted site of a preschool Marley was having remodeled, took a casual browse of a bookstore that only Jenny knew she owned, and finally indulged in a quick but fruitless tour of an antique store.

In all, a perfectly ordinary Sunday. Marley rode in the back of the Town Car. Jenny drove. Sometimes they chatted amiably. Sometimes Marley read a magazine or stared out the window. Jenny carried the umbrella—bright red today, Jenny had given up hoping for a sensible black one—and opened every door. Marley's hand never fell on a knob or latch.

When they returned to the house, they sat together in the dining room under the glowing chandelier, with Marley at the head of the table. Weathers served them chicken soup with mushroom ravioli, salad, and a small crusty roll on the side. When Jenny had been hired four years earlier, they would talk over their meal, but over time Marley had grown less interested, and now they sat in companionable silence.

At least, right up to the moment Marley laid down her spoon and said "Well?"

Jenny glanced up at her, surprised. "Well what?"

"There's something you've been dying to tell me all day. Are you going to let it out, dear, or are you going to burst?"

Jenny picked up her roll as though she might delay the rest of the conversation with a sizable bite, but she set it back down untouched. "Is it that obvious? Okay. There's really no easy way to say this, so I'm just going to blurt it out. I'm going to graduate school in the fall."

Marley clasped her hands under her chin. "Well that's wonderful, dear! Truly wonderful! Do you need a letter or something? I've always heard schools need letters. Oh! I know an amazing woman who runs a program in the mountains outside of Santa Fe. She's a one hundred percent original thinker and it would be quite educational! You'd be out in nature, working toward your degree, and you wouldn't have to wear a stitch for weeks and weeks. You aren't planning to study snakes, by any chance?"

Jenny's eyes were wide and her lips pursed. "Entertainment Technology, actually. I've already been accepted at Carnegie Mellon."

"Oh. Isn't that in Pittsburgh? Well, I'm sure they have a good program and I guess the rest can't be helped. But you should have told me ages ago, dear. I could have been a help. I'm sure I know someone who could have given you an in."

"I know, Ms. Jacobs. That's why I didn't tell you. I wanted to do it on my own."

"Oh, of course!" Marley jumped out of her chair. Jenny stood, too, and they embraced. "I'm so excited for you!"

"Thank you!"

They parted. Marley noticed Weathers standing in the doorway watching them. "Weathers! Good news! Jenny has just given her notice! How much longer will you be with us, dear?"

"Until the end of July, I think."

"Oh we still have weeks together! Good! That will give us plenty of time to sort out the money."

"You don't have to—"

"Now dear," Marley took Jenny's arm in hers, pinning her close. "You wouldn't let me help you get into college, but you will certainly let me help you attend. My mind is made up! Don't argue, you'll only hurt my feelings."

"Okay, I guess." Jenny was a little relieved and a little overwhelmed. "I'm going to miss you, though."

Marley hugged her again. "I'm going to miss you, too, dear, but I knew you'd be moving on someday. And it's good."

Jenny broke the embrace. There were tears in her eyes. "I need to walk the dog again, and... I'll see you tomorrow morning."

Marley squeezed her hand and let her go. Jenny hurried to the kitchen with Weathers close behind. "Oh, look," Marley said. "I didn't let her finish her soup. Ah, it doesn't matter. Who can eat?"

She bustled into the library and settled in behind her oak roll top desk. First she looked up Carnegie Mellon on her computer to confirm it was in

Pittsburgh. That done, she pored over her paper and electronic contact lists. Surely she knew someone in the area. Jenny had worked for her for four years, and letting her move to a new state without making a few calls was out of the question. The girl needed protection.

* * *

The next morning, Marley asked Weathers to prepare something simple for breakfast. He brought her toast with strawberry jam and coffee. As she forced herself to sip and nibble, Albert walked in. He wore the same jacket and tie as the day before.

"Another interview, dear?"

He looked embarrassed. "I think I'll do better today." He ran his good left hand through his unruly hair.

But Marley barely heard him. "Albert, dear, would you do me a favor? There's a Cheval standing mirror in my office, nearly as tall as you, oval, with a walnut frame. Would you bring it out here, to the dining room?"

"Of course."

Albert was surprised by how much it weighed, but he was quickly learning that rich people liked owning dense, heavy things. Having only the smaller two fingers of his right hand made the mirror difficult to carry, but he arranged it just the way Marley asked. When he was finished, she could stand in the doorway to the library and see into the foyer.

"Wonderful. Now please go down to the basement and get me the fishing line off the shelf by the stairs."

"Fishing line?" Albert said and, receiving no response, fetched it for her. She was letting him live in her house and eat from her pantry; indulging her eccentricities without question was the least he could do in return.

"Thank you," she said as she took it from him. "Weathers?" He stood in the kitchen doorway, awaiting her instructions. She held out a deadbolt key for him. "Go upstairs and move the Scribe computer down to the library, please."

As always, Weather's somber face was inscrutable, but this was the first

18

time Albert had ever seen him hesitate. "Of course, madam," he said, and went to the stairs.

Albert followed Marley into the sitting room. She got down on her knees and tied the fishing line to a chair leg at ankle height. She then strung the line across the floor and tied the other end to the couch leg. She plucked it and it twanged.

"Um, Aunt Marley, is today Booby Trap Day?"

She stood and examined her handiwork. "You have to keep your eyes open if you're going to live here." Weathers strode around the corner with a Macbook in his hand. He stepped over the line without even glancing down. "Like Weathers."

Albert had grown used to a casual joyfulness from his aunt, but right now he could detect none. In fact, she sounded almost nervous. "Are you all right?"

She went to the dining room and sat in her usual chair. "All morning I've had the strangest feeling. Someone is coming, dear, and I'm not going to like it."

Weathers came back into the room. "Detective Lonagan has arrived."

CHAPTER THREE
Good Friends Share Bad News

"This time I'll meet him at the door, Weathers, not in the library." Weathers nodded and started toward the front of the house.

Marley grabbed Albert's undamaged hand and pulled him toward the front of the house. They carefully stepped over the fishing line. "Weathers, has Jenny walked the dog?"

"No, madam," Weathers answered. "Ms. Wu has not yet arrived." Then he opened the door.

Detective Charles Lonagan was a homicide detective for the Seattle Police Department. He was a few years younger than Marley, having celebrated his sixtieth birthday only two weeks earlier, but he looked older. His thinning hair was stark white and his wrinkled, sagging skin gave his face a grouchy, morose look that didn't match his personality. He sometimes consulted with Marley on odd cases—he was one of the few people in Seattle who understood what she did and why—but today was not one of those days.

His longtime partner, Detective Sharon Garcia, entered with him. She was about five foot five with broad shoulders and muscular arms. In her twenties, she'd been what would be politely called curvaceous. Three children and two decades later, she had added forty pounds around her middle and seemed much more comfortable with herself. Garcia knew her partner had a relationship of some kind with Marley, but since no one had ever explained who Marley was or what she did, that relationship was a mystery. Garcia hated mysteries. As far as she was concerned, whenever anyone withheld anything from her—ever—they were up to no good.

"Hello, Ms. Jacobs," Lonagan said. He liked a little formality. "May we come in?"

"Of course," Marley answered. Weathers had already returned to the kitchen. Whatever was going to happen here, it held no interest for him. "Please come in. And hello to you, too, Detective Garcia. I'm sorry I don't see you more often. Let's talk here in the foyer instead of the library. I don't think you've come bearing good news, not if you've brought your partner and that expression."

"It's true. I'm afraid that this time I have some bad news."

"Oh, no. It's Jenny, isn't it?"

Garcia's eyes narrowed. "What makes you say that?"

"She was supposed to be here half an hour ago. Has something happened to her?"

"She's being held for questioning," Lonagan said, "for the murder of your nephew, Aloysius Pierce."

Marley clasped Albert's hand. She did not exclaim, cry, or break down. She only closed her eyes and became very still for ten seconds. When she looked at Lonagan again, Albert and the police detectives both thought she seemed smaller than before. "I suppose you need me to identify his body?"

"No, the medical examiner will take care of that."

"Charles, I insist on seeing him. I won't believe it's really him until I do."

"Oh. Well, of course. After the autopsy, the medical examiner will release the body to a funeral home of your choice. Probably by tomorrow morning. You'll be able to view the body there. For right now, we'd like you to come down to the station to answer a few questions."

"Of course. I'll be happy to help in any way I can."

Albert looked from the detectives to his aunt to Weathers and back at the detectives. Everything he knew about police work came from television, but he was still young enough to think himself well-informed. "Can't she answer questions here? Unless you're planning to charge her..."

Garcia spoke up sharply. "We aren't planning to charge her at this time." In truth, she and Lonagan believed witnesses were more helpful if they could be questioned someplace where they didn't feel comfortable. "However, that's where our equipment is. Doing the interview at the station makes it easier to catch the guilty party."

"It's all right," Marley said. "I prefer it, too."

"Excuse me," Lonagan said, addressing Albert, "but we haven't been introduced."

"Oh! I'm sorry," Marley exclaimed. "My manners. This is Albert, my nephew."

Feeling vaguely as though he was admitting to something he shouldn't, Albert said, "Aloysius was my older brother. I assume you'll want to talk to me, too."

"Thank you for agreeing to come downtown with us," Lonagan said.

Marley laid her hand on her throat. "Er, Charles, you don't really think Jenny..."

"I think of us as friends, Ms. Jacobs." Lonagan's expression made him

21

look annoyed, but his voice was as calm and soothing as a funeral director's.

"So do I."

"Well, I hope you understand that I won't be able to answer any of your questions right now. I wanted to give you the news in person, because we've known each other for so long, but—"

"That's all right," Marley said. "We should start. There's so much to do."

Albert agreed to drive her, so she asked him to walk the dog, too. Ten minutes later, after Marley had changed into a cashmere turtleneck, a cotton sport jacket, and a long cotton skirt, all in black, they went to their cars and drove downtown.

"It doesn't feel right," Albert said.

Marley was searching through her cell for a number. "What doesn't, dear?"

"Me following a police car. It should be the other way around, shouldn't it? I feel like the universe has been reversed."

Marley pressed the phone to her ear. "I know just what you mean, dear. Hello, Frederika. Marley Jacobs here. I have some work for you, I'm afraid to say. Call me when you get this message."

After she hung up, Albert drove in silence for a while. He stared at Marley's reflection in the rear-view mirror, correctly reading her expression as a mixture of worry and guilt.

"I didn't like him."

Marley glanced up, startled. "What was that, dear?"

"Aloysius. I didn't like him." Albert knew his aunt felt the same way, and he hoped it would be easier for her if she knew her feelings were shared.

The look she gave him was still full of worry, but she no longer looked guilty. She looked deeply sad. "No one did, once they got to know him."

The visit to the police station to give their statements took up the whole rest of the day. When had they last seen Aloysius? Were they close? How well did Albert know Jenny Wu? Had he ever driven her car? Was he in Marley's will? Was Aloysius?

As for Marley herself, during a quiet moment she went across James

Street to the King County Correctional Facility. There was a scanner at the front door, an ID check, and limited visiting hours, but Marley, being who she was, knew a trick to get around that. Marley knew quite a few surprising tricks.

The block where she found Jenny was much nicer than what Marley remembered from her own arrests, long ago. There was a large common area, lit by garish but well-shielded fluorescent lights. The walls, doors, and door jambs were brown, yellow and red, like an extremely mellow fast food restaurant. Around the edge of the common area were the cells, and all their doors stood open. A mezzanine added a second floor and a place to look down on the common area.

Jenny was still inside her cell, sitting on the end of her bed. Marley sat beside her, startling her profoundly. "I thought this place would be more crowded."

"Oh! Ms. Jacobs!" She glanced around in a panic, wondering how she could keep herself safe if even her elderly employer could sneak up on her. "How did you get in here?"

"I am a lawyer, dear," Marley non-answered.

"You are?"

Marley tugged at Jenny's orange, government-issued sleeve. "Tell me how you got into this mess."

"I wish I knew! I didn't kill him. I hope you know that."

"I'm glad to hear it. Don't worry. I believe you. What happened after you left my house last night?"

Jenny took a deep breath to compose herself. "I went straight home and made dinner. I made that carrot salad thing I learned from your Miss Harriet. At about nine, my roommate Cissy came home with her boyfriend. I never told you this, but they fight all the time, just arguing and saying awful things to each other. Then, after about two or three hours of this, they..." she glanced over at Marley, unsure how to continue. "They make up. That's even louder than the arguing, if you can believe it. I swear, I can't even live there anymore.

"So I went out. First to the 15th Street, but there was some kind of poetry reading that was completely ugh. So I went to the Purple Dot and ate dim sum really slowly. I stayed until after midnight, when I figured Cissy would be finished with her little routine, then went home to bed. The cops woke me up this morning and put me in handcuffs. I guess they searched Al's phone and found the texts he's been sending me… and the Facebook PMs." Jenny sighed. "And the rest."

"Have they checked out your alibi?"

"I don't know. I try to pay cash at those places because it's better for the wait staff. It was pretty crowded, and the only people I talked to were some tourists. Besides…"

Marley waited for her to continue. Jenny wiped tears from her eyes. "I've already packed a couple of bags for school. I've been so excited to go, but when the detective saw them stacked in the corner… I'm sorry, Ms. Jacobs. I didn't like Aloysius, but I know he was your family and no matter what I wouldn't want anything to happen to someone you care about."

"Thank you, Jenny. As a lawyer, I'm afraid I can't represent you. I just realized I might need to be called as a witness."

Jenny let out her bark of a laugh, then wiped her cheeks. "You just realized that, did you?"

Marley's phone began to play Billie Holiday's "Nice Work If You Can Get It" and she held it to her ear. "Hello, Frederika. I'm just fine, dear, how are you? Wonderful. I'm calling with some trouble, of course, please pretend to be surprised. This time it's my assistant, Jenny Wu. She's at King County Correctional Facility with a murder charge hanging over her. Yes, quite serious, but I think it will be resolved quickly in her favor. Do you have time to look into it today? Wonderful. Let's talk about the details tonight." She hung up.

A hulking woman nearly as tall as Albert shuffled into the doorway. Her mismatched eyes bulged and her frizzy hair stuck out in all directions. "Hey ma'am," she said in a high, strained voice, "can I borrow your phone?"

"Why of course, dear." Marley handed it over. "Be sure to return it when you're done."

The huge woman gave Marley an empty look. "Oh, I definitely will." She shuffled off.

Jenny watched her go. "Good luck getting that back in one piece."

"What do you mean?" Marley slipped her hand into her coat pocket, pulled out her cell phone, then put it back.

"Oh, God, I wish you could do that with me." Jenny curled up, wrapping her arms around her knees and shivering. She looked at the stainless steel toilet in the corner. "I don't think I can do this, Ms. Jacobs. I've only been here a few hours, but I don't think I can stand it. I can't spend the rest of my life in prison, I just can't."

Marley took Jenny's hand in hers. "Don't worry, dear. I have a very sharp lawyer who will help us sort this out, and you'll get your life back. I promise."

"I want that. I want my life back, please. Thank you for coming to visit me."

"I don't know what you mean, dear. I'm not even here. See?"

Marley glanced toward the doorway. Jenny peered out into the common area, trying to see what Marley wanted to show her. When she turned back Marley had vanished.

* * *

Back at police headquarters, Detective Lonagan took a break from interviewing Albert and went into the waiting area to check on Marley. There followed a slight kerfuffle when he saw her casually reading through a copy of the General Offense Report and the patrol officer's Statement on Aloysius's murder, along with printouts of the crime scene photos. Lonagan and Garcia both tried to figure out who had given her a copy—the Photographic Media Envelope had not even been opened yet—but they couldn't. They pushed as far as they could without making an incident out of it, then let it drop.

Marley insisted, in perfect innocence, that she saw them sitting on a chair, recognized her nephew's name, and picked them up. She apologized with all apparent sincerity when she returned the file and Lonagan, at least, seemed ready to believe that she had not bribed anyone for it.

Eventually, the questions had all been answered and the statements taken. Business cards were exchanged, and Albert and Marley were asked to contact Det. Lonagan if they thought of anything else that might be important.

In the SeaPark Garage outside, Detective Garcia was waiting for them beside Marley's Town Car. "Ms. Jacobs, I know my partner likes you. You two have history, and he's consulted with you on certain cases over the years, although God only knows why. So for his sake, I'm going to warn you not to hold anything back from him. Not only would it be bad for you, which I don't particularly care about, but it will look bad for him. He deserves better." She looked directly at Albert. "Do you understand what I'm saying?"

Marley nodded. "I understand. I would never betray your partner's trust, believe me. I think much too highly of him for that."

"Good," Detective Garcia said through clenched teeth. "Because if I find out you've held back so much as a middle initial of someone's name, I'm going to come to your house and cuff you both in front of all your high-society friends. Do you understand what I'm saying?"

"Well, I'd better get myself an interesting hat," Albert said.

Garcia turned her full attention on him, momentarily nonplussed. "Excuse me?" The man didn't look like a crazy, but...

"I'll need an interesting hat to wear, for when you arrest my aunt in front of her friends. Maybe I'll go with a Carmen Miranda thing; Aunt Marley, you might want to consider a propeller beanie, right? Because if you're going to arrest us in front of her friends, with all their camera phones, for the crime of spending all day trying to help you catch my brother's killer, I'll want attractive and unique headwear. For the video."

Garcia folded her arms. "Is that right."

"Right," he added. "Then who'll look like a fool?"

The detective stared at Albert for a moment, trying to decide if making

26

him come back into the station would soothe her annoyance, but she knew it wouldn't. All it would do is waste more of everyone's time. "Get out of here."

Smiling, Marley approached the car. Albert let her into the backseat, and they left.

They arrived home at dinnertime. Miss Harriet had decided to work in the kitchen that day, and they enjoyed peerless Normandy Chicken with brine-boiled potatoes. Albert sat in Jenny's usual place. Afterward, Marley offered to call Aloysius's mother down in California to give her the bad news, but Albert said he wanted to do it himself. He went to his room to make the call, where he stayed behind closed doors for over an hour. That gave Marley plenty of time to check in with Frederika and to carefully examine the extra copies of the General Offense Report, Officer's Statement, and crime scene photos, which had somehow managed to make its way into the Town Car.

Albert returned to the library looking shaken. Marley waved him toward an over-stuffed chair beside her desk. "Are you all right, dear? How did she take it?"

"With scotch." He held up his left hand. It was trembling slightly. He clenched his fist and pressed it against his leg. "And songs. Sad, sad songs."

"Oh no. I hope it wasn't 'Danny Boy?' "

"Danny Boy was just the start. I hung up on her during the second verse of 'Puff the Magic Dragon.' "

"Even I tear up at the end of that one." Marley sighed. "When Daddy died, your mother insisted on a turn at the podium during the funeral. I tried to discourage her, but the rest of the family thought it only fair that she say a few words. What they got instead was a full-throated a cappella version of 'In Dreams.' Maybe it wasn't entirely appropriate, considering the occasion, but her voice always did favor Roy Orbison."

"Yeah," Albert agreed, sinking into a funk, "after she'd had a couple of drinks to loosed up her vocal cords."

Marley knew it was time to change the subject. "One thing, though,

27

Albert. I just have to know: Why did you say what you said to Detective Garcia? About 'attractive and unique headwear'?"

He shrugged. "To be random. To break her rhythm and annoy her a little without being rude. She seems basically okay—and I do want her to find Aloysius's killer, but I had just done everything I could to cooperate and she was still standing on our necks. That wasn't cool. Anyway, she comes across like a straight charger, and few things slow down that sort like the unexpected."

Marley smiled. "It's been a long day, hasn't it?" Albert let out a long breath as he nodded in agreement. "Well, it will be longer still. Let's get to the car."

Albert looked mildly surprised and, before he could stand, Marley was already out of her chair and through the open doorway, heading for the car port. He hurried after her, opened the back passenger door for her, then got behind the wheel. The sun had gone down. "Where are we headed?"

"Goodness!" Marley answered. "I forgot you don't know. We'll be visiting Shady Lawns. Of course Jenny knows where it is, but you aren't her, are you?"

"I'm the one with short hair."

Marley typed something into her phone, and the dashboard GPS came to life. Albert followed the directions to a small building on the northwest slope of Queen Anne hill, tucked between rows of apartment buildings and the SPU campus.

"Pull into the spot marked 'Director,' darling."

He did. "Won't the director be angry?"

"Let's hope not."

He got out and opened the door for her. Together they went to the front of the building. Marley swiped a security card through a reader and a light above the door handle turned green. Albert opened it and stepped back so he could follow Marley inside.

CHAPTER FOUR
Unusual Invalids

The walls had been painted an institutional white, and the vase on the end table was filled with plastic flowers. The older woman with the angry scowl and strangler's hands greeted them in the hall with a curt nod. She wore an old-fashioned collared nurse's blouse and hat, but her shoes were black rubber clogs.

Albert stopped just inside the doorway, suddenly unable to go further.

Marley turned toward him. Her expression was strange; she searched his face as though looking for a sign of something important, but he couldn't imagine what it could be. "Are you all right, dear?"

"Mother spent six months in a place like this once. To sober up. I visited her, once. I must have been six or seven."

"I didn't know. Was it awful?"

"It was like there was a huge machine," he said, "just on the other side of the carpet and wallpaper. Like it was beaming a normal person's thoughts into everyone's head, hoping they'd push out what was already there. That's how it seemed, anyway. I was just a kid."

"Some situations are extremely difficult for people with a lot of imagination, especially when they're young. However, there's no one here who needs to get sober, I promise; this is a place for people who can't get along in the modern world. Besides, you already know my opinion of the way supposedly normal people think. Come along."

His skin tingling, Albert followed Marley down a hallway. They moved by open, empty offices to the entrance of a large common room. The furniture was chrome and leather, and the north wall was all storm glass. It

29

could have offered a lovely terrestrial view of Fremont and Ballard, except the windows were so heavily tinted that only faint gray lights were visible through it. Marley stood silently in the doorway and followed her lead.

At the far end of the room, a woman in an angora sweater and poodle skirt lounged on a couch, flipping through a copy of Vogue. Albert gaped at her. He had expected an elderly person—maybe in a wheelchair—but she couldn't have been older than nineteen and she was so incredibly beautiful it took his breath away. She had huge blue eyes, blonde hair pulled back in a pony tail, and the long, graceful limbs of a dancer.

"What is this supposed to be?" she said as she flipped through the magazine. "Because it's not fashion. It's practically pornography!"

"Don't knock pornography, Betty," a man said as he entered. His long dark hair was carelessly parted in the middle, hanging partway in his face like Jim Morrison. He wore a Nehru jacket and pointy-toed boots with heels, and he was just as gorgeous as the woman in his own way—tall and slender, with wide eyes and mouth and perfect pale skin. "It's very freeing to be comfortable with our bodies and what they can do."

In response, Betty turned the magazine toward him. "Is this what you mean, Neil?"

Neil grimaced at the page she showed him. "Aw, whoa. That's not natural."

"Of course it isn't." A third man entered the room. He looked older than the other two—maybe twenty-five years old—and he wore a double-breasted blue suit with a gray and yellow tie. With wingtips, of all things. His hair was combed straight back and he, of the three of them, was the most tall, slender, pale and beautiful.

"Nothing is natural nowadays," he continued. "Do you see the way they wear their pants? All hanging down with their underwear showing! In my day, we wore belts! Or suspenders!"

"You're right, Clive." Betty said. "What's so awful about a belt?"

Neil shook his shaggy head. "It's the music that bothers me."

"Yes!"

30

"Exactly!"

Neil continued his complaint. "In my day, man, the music was about something. The music kids listen to now..."

Clive broke in: "It's a bunch of noise!"

Betty shook her head. "I don't even understand the lyrics."

The scowling nurse came around the corner with a dark-skinned woman who was no more than four and a half feet tall. She wore a charcoal pantsuit, coke-bottle glasses and running shoes. Her graying hair partly covered her bindi.

"Hello, Naima," Marley said. Everyone startled at the sound of her voice.

"Marley, always a pleasure." Naima had a faint British accent. "Let's talk in my office." She bustled down the hall toward one of the open office doors.

The three tall slender people stood out of their chairs with startling speed. They appeared to be a little nervous, as though Marley might punish them for bad manners. "It's so good to see you, Miss Jacobs," Clive said.

"Hello, darlings," Marley called to them. "Everything well, I trust? How was the museum?"

"Wonderful!" Betty said. The others nodded in agreement. "Miss Jacobs, would you like to come to our picnic on Thursday?"

"Yes!" Neil said. "We'd love to have you."

"Oh, darlings, I don't know. Something serious has come up. Maybe next time?"

The three of them agreed that next time would be fine. Marley thanked them for understanding, then led Albert toward down the hall.

Albert was sure something odd was going on, but he couldn't quite get his mind around it. In a low voice, he asked: "Who are those people?"

"You tell me, dear." She stepped into Naima's office.

"Please sit," Naima told them as she closed the door. They did. "I hope you're visiting because you're impressed by the budget reports I've been submitting."

"If I did that, I'd be here every day. No, I'm afraid there's been trouble."

"Like summer 2007?"

31

"Oh yes. Last night a man had his throat cut. His body was found on the Burke-Gilman trail, just under the Aurora Bridge, lying over a storm drain."

Naima took off her glasses and cleaned them. "And you suspect that not all that blood drained into the canal."

"Naturally."

"This facility has been secure, but I'll check with the staff anyway, just to be sure."

"Naima, the victim was my nephew."

Naima was so startled she dropped her glasses onto the desk, then scrambled to put them back on. "Oh! Oh, no."

Marley was brisk and businesslike. "Oh no, indeed. We're going to be moving quickly on this."

Naima pulled her phone close. "I see. No time to flirt with the beefcake, then. Let me make some calls."

"I'll let you get started." Marley checked her watch and stood. "Excuse us."

Albert opened the office door for her then followed her through the common room down a flight of stairs. The three guests watched Marley—and him—with strangely tense expressions. Clearly, they were charity cases of some kind, afraid of something Marley might do if she were displeased. Evict them? Albert couldn't imagine.

There was a kitchen on the bottom floor, a walk-in fridge and a door leading to a small loading dock. They went into the alley.

A cargo van was parked beside the dock, and a large woman in white coveralls was unlocking and opening the back. She stood over six feet tall, weighed nearly three hundred pounds, and moved like John Wayne. When she saw Marley, she raised both arms in the air in greeting. "Hola, Marley!"

"Hello, Libertad. How is your knee?"

"My knee is just fine now. I am kicking asses one hundred percent."

"Wonderful! Albert, be a dear and handle Libertad's delivery, would you? I need to bend her ear and her schedule is tight."

Albert shrugged, hopped down to the ground, and lifted the hand truck onto the dock. Libertad patted two Styrofoam coolers and said "Straight into the walk-in. And wear this." From her pocket, she took an old pouch on a braided leather cord and tried to hang it around Albert's neck.

"Whoa!" He backed away from her, his nose wrinkling. "What is in that thing and how long has it been dead?"

"This holds necessary things," Libertad said. "You must wear it for your health."

"Thanks, but I'll have a salad later instead." Albert lifted the coolers onto the loading dock, then set the hand truck under them. "Back in a few." He started toward the door.

Alarmed, Libertad looked to Marley, who waved him off with a placid smile. "Hope so."

Once he was inside, Marley took Libertad's hands and helped her onto the dock. They embraced. "I don't see enough of you, my friend."

Libertad nodded in return. "You have so much to do. I understand. And now you have some new problem, I suspect?"

"Yes, dear. I'm afraid so. Has your grandmother heard anything recently? Any new, beautiful, young faces at the Bingo hall?"

"No, Marley, not for months."

Something about the way she answered prompted Marley to move close. "Has anyone come to you about your special deliveries? Has anyone tried to buy from you?"

"Not from me, no, but I got a call today from a man named Sylvester. He works for PSBC and, while they were at Fatima Church Hall yesterday, a man offered him five hundred dollars for three pints, half then and half on delivery. The man gave Sylvester the money and an address, then told him to make the delivery at 10:30 that night."

"Oh dear."

"Yes. Sylvester, he was stupid enough to make the deal, but not so stupid that he kept it. He dropped off the pints at seven, shortly before dark, and decided he did not need the rest of the money too badly. He called me today because he said someone is watching his house."

"May I have his address, dear?" They took out their phones and Libertad transferred the information. "Thank you so much. We really must have dinner together again. It's been too long."

"Yes, but at my place," Libertad said with emphasis. "Isabeau wants to cook for you this time."

Marley smiled and clasped her hands. "Of course, dear. Now let's see what has become of my nephew."

Libertad opened the door to the darkened hallway. They heard low voices, like the murmur of lovers.

Marley put her hands into her pockets and went into the hall. Albert and Betty stood in the corner by the open refrigerator door, close enough to kiss. Albert leaned against the wall, his expression blissful and vacant. Betty laid her hand on his chest and moved her face near his cheek. She whispered something that made him sigh. With her other hand, she pulled her shawl closed.

"Hello, Betty, dear. You know you're not supposed to do that."

Betty brushed her lips against Albert's jaw. "I'm tired of drinking from plastic. I want the feel of a man on my lips."

At a gesture from Marley, Libertad took her hand truck and retreated to the van. "You can drink from a man if you want, dear. You just can't do it here, in my city."

"Or what?" Betty turned away from her victim and hunched her shoulders like a cat about to pounce. Albert stared vaguely at the ceiling. "You won't do anything. You never do anything!"

Marley was still smiling, but her face was downturned and her expression wolfish. "Would you like to guess what I have in my pocket?"

CHAPTER FIVE
A Young Man Discovers A Larger World

"Lint?" Betty asked, her tone challenging and a little unsure. "Nothing?"

"It's a little beam of sunshine, dear. Shall I take it out and show you?"

Like a swarm of startled moths, Betty's confidence fluttered away and deserted her. She glided back, releasing Albert and leaving only a smear of pink lipstick on his throat. "You don't have sunlight in your pocket." Her high, strained voice didn't have the bravado she'd hoped for. "You're nothing but an old woman. A useless old woman! You don't have anything!"

Marley's expression hadn't changed. "You'd be surprised what I carry around, dear. And any time you'd like to start feasting on people again, you just let me know. I'll arrange to have you and your things moved to any city you choose, just like poor Sterling."

"Sterling isn't dead!" Betty couldn't help it. She'd begun to wail. "He's going to visit at Christmas. I have his letter."

Marley sighed. Threatening her charges always made her feel sour. "Dear, that was three years ago."

"Three?" Betty squeaked.

"Yes, dear. Bring today's newspaper to your room and compare the dates. After he left us, Sterling... Well, he was gone before Memorial Day."

Betty slumped against the open fridge door and covered her face with her hands. She didn't sob or shed a tear, but her grief was genuine.

Hasty footsteps squeaked from the hall. Marley took her hand from her pocket as Naima bustled around the corner. "What is going on?!" she demanded. The nurse was close behind.

35

"Betty and I were reminiscing about Sterling, the poor dear."

Clive and Neil loped into the hall like school kids about to see someone get detention. Everyone needed only to glance at Betty—and at Albert, still standing against the wall, entranced—to know what had happened. Naima sighed and took Betty gently by the elbow.

"I'm sorry, Miss Jacobs," Betty said. Her cheeks were dry, but Marley knew her anguish was real. "I shouldn't have said those things. It's just..."

"Don't worry, Betty. I understand. You're under a lot of stress. Take a few days to rest and think things over. I'll visit again so we can talk about what you want for the future. Would that be all right?"

Betty nodded gratefully. Naima and the nurse led her up the stairs. Everyone followed except Marley and, of course, Albert.

Marley pinched him and he came awake. "What's going on?"

"You didn't wear the pouch. Now close the refrigerator so we can go."

He did. Marley didn't follow the others up through the building, so Albert opened the back door for her. They went into the alley. Libertad's van was already gone. Marley led Albert up a set of concrete stairs on the outside of the building.

"Aunt Marley, who were those people? They talked like senior citizens but they looked like they're about my age. And I peeked in the cooler. It was full of bags of blood."

"What do you think they are, dear?"

"Hemophiliacs?"

Marley stopped and turned around. Even though she was several stairs above him, they were eye to eye. "Oh Albert." The disappointment in her voice was unmistakable; Albert was surprised by how much it stung.

Back at the car, Albert let her into the back seat, then got behind the wheel and started the engine. He didn't shift out of park. He just sat there for a moment, his hands in his lap, staring at nothing at all. "I almost died, didn't I?"

"Yes, dear."

"They're vampires."

"Of course they are."

"But the way they talked, like a bunch of crotchety old people..."

"They are old. Clive is over ninety."

"Vampires. Whoa. Vampires! I'm... What about being young forever and going to nightclubs every night?"

"Oh, goodness," Marley said. "Nightclubs."

Albert shut off the engine and placed his trembling hands on the wheel. "I need a moment."

"Take nine or ten moments," Marley said with all sincerity. "They're a good investment."

He took out his phone and opened a game of Tetris. They sat unmoving in the dark car, and the only sounds were the beeps of the game. After about ten minutes, he shut it off and slipped the phone back into his pocket.

"This is a rest home for vampires, and you're paying the bills. You have your own squad of vampires."

Marley sighed. "They're hardly a 'squad', dear, although you're not the first person to make that insinuation. They're my guests."

"They're killers. Aren't they? Aren't vampires killers?"

"Yes, when they have to be. It's how vampires survive."

"Doesn't that make them evil?"

"Albert, until just a few short months ago, you were a soldier. You volunteered for a job where you might have to kill. And I think you did kill."

"Aunt Marley—"

"I'm not criticizing you, and I'm not saying you're evil. Far from it. Risking your life to serve your country is a noble choice. You had your reasons for signing up, for swearing an oath to serve, for taking the uniform and weaponry of our nation at a time when you knew we were fighting overseas. You had your reasons, and I don't question them. I know you well enough to know you're an honorable young man."

Marley sighed, then added: "Besides, I've killed, too. With guns. With knives. With... other weapons. Oh, it was many years ago, when I was a young woman—and I may not have had a uniform or sworn an oath, but I was doing what I thought was right."

Albert looked into the rear view mirror at his aunt. A security light from across the street shone into back window, highlighting her gray hair and casting her face in shadow. He couldn't judge her expression, which made it hard to understand the point she was making. For an uncomfortable moment, he was sure she wanted it that way. "So," he said, "we're no better than them?"

"No, dear; we're worse. Whatever our reasons, good or bad, we chose to kill. Vampires, almost without exception, are victims. They don't get a choice. Picture it: A cab driver, waitress, or other average person is attacked on their way home. Murdered. They awaken in their own grave and suddenly find themselves thirsting for blood. It's not a choice on their part and doesn't have to be justified morally. That's why it's wrong to call them evil."

"And you bring them here, where they can survive on the donated blood Libertad delivers, without killing anyone."

"Yes, dear. Exactly. This is a safe place. For everyone."

"Mother said..." Albert paused, trying to figure a way to approach this subject. "Mother said it wasn't safe to know you. She said you hung around with dangerous people and took crazy risks."

"Your mother and I have a complicated relationship. More than most sisters, I think."

"Mother can make turning on a lamp complicated. She once said you know how to do magic. Not sleight of hand, but the real thing."

"What a thing to say!"

"She was drunk, but... Did Aloysius know about the vampires?"

"He did, and more besides."

"And his murder? Why are you 'going to be moving quickly' on it?"

"To protect what I've built, dear. The way Aloysius was killed suggests a vampire fed on him, which I don't allow. Seattle is my city, and the peace I've created here is still fragile. Always fragile. But it mostly works, and has started to inspire similar projects in other places around the country. Do you see? I'm a role model.

"But there are always those who think violence is the best, most lasting solution. It can be hard to give up old enmities, especially when holding onto them feels like virtue. Sometimes creating peace can earn you as many enemies as starting a war. But if someone out there thinks they can destroy what I've created without paying a price, they're in for quite a shock."

Marley sighed. "Then again, it might just be a new arrival in the city who doesn't know the rules. Or maybe Aloysius was killed for a reason unrelated to me, or no reason at all. It could have been a coincidence that he was stabbed above a storm drain. Whatever happened, I intend to discover the truth, and I'll depend on you to help me."

CHAPTER SIX
Help For Those Who Need It

Albert was sharp enough to recognize the end of a conversation, so he started the car and pulled out of the lot. Marley uploaded Sylvester's address to the car's GPS, and within half an hour they were parked outside a small apartment building ten blocks from the West Seattle bridge.

It had started to rain. Albert grabbed the long red umbrella from its place beside him and stepped out of the car. They had parked on rather narrow tree-lined street, and he couldn't help but feel goosebumps run down his back as he looked around. Vampires are real.

As far as he was concerned, there were too few streetlights and too many oaks blocking their light. The street was heavy with night shadows and there was no one in sight.

His aunt had made clear when he came to stay with her that he was not permitted to carry weapons of any kind—it was her only rule and he'd promised to follow it. The scarred stump where his trigger finger used to be

39

throbbed. If only…

Albert took a deep breath and opened the umbrella. Aunt Marley was no fool, and she traveled the city unarmed. He decided to mimic her courage, wisely reasoning that the guns he'd left behind when he was discharged were probably useless against the undead. He held an umbrella over the door as he opened it.

Marley climbed from the car, looking just as she always did. Was she confident she could deal with a runaway vampire or simply fatalistic? "Thank you, dear. Why don't you wait out here while I speak to him? You look a bit too imposing for the conversation I have in mind, and you've just had a fright."

A fright? Albert nearly laughed. "If you say so." He looked up and down the still, dark street. "Are you sure you'll be all right? I mean, if there's a new arrival in the city…"

"No need to worry about that," Marley said in her usually chipper tone. "You won't be bored, will you?"

"I'll play more Tetris. It's something I learned during my tour; a few minutes of Tetris after a nasty encounter helps prevent nightmares."

"How interesting! I'll have to share that with some friends of mine." With that, Marley marched to the apartment building and pressed the buzzer that said "Bustaverde" next to it. A man's voice came over the scratchy intercom. "Who is it?"

"Libertad sent me," Marley said. "To help."

The door unlocked with a terrible buzz, but Marley didn't move. She pressed the intercom button again and told him there was a problem with the door. Sylvester came downstairs to open it for her.

He was a small, jumpy man with dark hair and an old-fashioned pencil-thin mustache. He'd intended for it to lend him an air of suave sophistication, but it actually made him look like a comical bit player in an old movie—which was a shame, because there was nothing comical about Sylvester's life or the danger he was in.

His face was shiny with sweat and he didn't even try to disguise his surprise at seeing Marley. "She sent you?" he asked, as though it was an accusation. "A little old lady?"

"She did, and aren't you lucky? Now look over my shoulder. Is the person watching you still there?"

He looked over her left shoulder. "Yeah. The Camry. And there's a second one now, too. A Town Car."

"That second one is mine. Let's go inside, shall we?"

He led her up a flight of creaky wooden stairs. The stairwell bulb was dingy and weak, and the plaster walls had dust in all the cracks. His apartment door was so warped he had to lean against it to open and close it.

The apartment smelled of sour milk and the carpet needed to be vacuumed. Sylvester lifted a pile of laundry off the couch and set it on the ottoman. "That's all clean," he said, "but I haven't had time to fold it."

He gestured for Marley to sit in the space he'd just cleared and she did. He flopped into an easy chair, obviously exhausted.

Marley took a shirt off the laundry and began folding it. Startled, Sylvester sat up and joined her.

"I have two jobs," he said. "It was three, but I got fired from the security thing because I couldn't stay awake. That happened just this weekend. It's hard to keep up with things here all alone."

"Alone? Where is your wife?"

Sylvester's left hand closed around the shirt he was holding as though he might squeeze juice from it. With his other hand, he twisted his wedding band. "My wife? What difference does that make?"

"You have a suspicious character watching your home, don't you? Do you think that doesn't affect her?"

"She's away. She's sick."

Marley stopped folding. "You can't lie to me, dear."

"Okay." Sylvester took a deep breath. "She left. Gone. She emptied the bank account on Saturday and took off."

They resumed folding. "Aren't you worried that something has happened to her?"

He was quiet for almost a minute while they worked together. Finally, he said: "She'll be back. I used to worry. I used to worry about all kinds of things, but... She has a problem with gambling. She owns a cleaning company and makes more than I do—when she works—but it's not enough. That's why I...."

"That's why you stole blood from the donation center."

"I could lose my job."

"Yes, dear, and then who would cover your wife's debts?" They were quiet a moment. "You know why the buyer wanted it, don't you?"

They had finished folding the laundry. Sylvester had nothing to do with his hands but stare down at them. "I guess so."

"Where did you drop off the blood?"

Sylvester stood from the chair and took a pencil and slip of paper from his telephone table. He scribbled on it and offered it to Marley. She took it without looking at it.

"Thank you. Your wife is lucky to have someone like you looking out for her, and you're lucky that I don't have you run out of my city. Here's my card. Email me, dear, and I'll connect you with a group that can help you cope with your wife's problem. And if you get another offer like the one you had yesterday, contact me. In fact, I insist on it, for all our sakes."

He took the card she offered him with trembling hands.

Marley's phone rang. She answered. "Yes, Albert?"

"Aunt Marley, there's a guy in a Camry watching your building. And he just started dialing."

"That's interesting," she said, exaggerating her usual dramatic tone. "I wonder who he's calling?"

Not being a fool, Albert took that as a hint. "Why don't I go ask?" He hung up the phone and stepped out of the car.

There was no way for him to sneak up on the Camry, not when both vehicles faced each other on opposite sides of the street. Albert closed the door quietly, crossed to the far curb and strolled casually down the block.

He could see the man's face by the lights of his phone—his head was narrow and his hairline receding. He had a five o'clock shadow over a strong jaw—handsome, but he looked weary. He was forty years old, at least .

As he watched Albert approach, the man in the Camry began to get nervous. Of course he'd noticed the Town Car when it pulled in, but he'd dismissed it when he saw a little old woman get out. Then she'd stood at the door of the apartment building until his target had come to open it; he couldn't imagine any reason for that except that she wanted to be seen with the target. Now her big, baby-faced driver was walking toward the car. "He's coming toward me," he said into the phone. "He looks like he might be a plainclothes cop or something."

A voice from the backseat said: "Oh, he's not a police officer, dear."

The man shrieked and dropped the phone in his mad scramble to turn around. There was a small shadowy figure sitting behind him. His elbow struck the car horn, blaring it accidentally, in his mad rush to get out of the car. He ran into the middle of the street and turned to gape at the back seat of his Camry. It was empty.

"What the hell? What the holy hell?" He let out a stream of curses as he tried to control himself. He'd heard a voice and seen a figure inside his car. He was sure of it. Had it materialized like a ghost or had it been there, lurking and unseen, all day? Whatever courage he'd brought with him had fled. They should never have come to Seattle. Never.

Albert didn't slow his approach as he sized the fellow up: His skinny arms were thick with tattoos, and he was wearing leather pants and a leather vest without a shirt. He even wore a leather dog collar. Before he'd gone to war, Albert might have been intimidated.

Sylvester opened the front door to his apartment building, and Marley slipped by him into the street. She crossed directly to the man in the vest, meeting him in the middle of the street.

"Welcome to Seattle, Kenneth." she said. She extended her hand; he shook it warily. "Although I must say, I find it hard to believe that you and your mistress didn't know you should speak to me before settling in my city."

Kenneth's mouth hung open. "I know who you are!" He jumped into his car and started it up. Marley and Albert stepped back as he peeled out of his parking space.

As the taillights grew smaller in the distance, Marley said: "That poor man. His license and registration seem to have fallen out of his wallet." She held up both pieces of identification. As expected, they were from out of state. This time it was Tennessee.

Albert grinned. "Well then, it's good that we know where to return it."

Marley smiled and laid her hand on his arm. "Aren't we helpful?" she exclaimed. "I'm sure he'd love to talk with us some more."

CHAPTER SEVEN
Philosophies Are Contrasted

The address Sylvester had provided was in the northern end of Capitol Hill, where parking spaces were impossible to find but a shirtless man in a leather vest and dog collar would not earn a second glance.

It was ten-thirty when they drove by Kenneth's home. The house was tiny, small, and shadowy, with a dying garden out front. The Camry had been parked in the driveway, but there were no other spots on the street. Albert had to drive three blocks away and pay for parking at the local supermarket. He held the umbrella while they walked back.

When they were just around the corner from Kenneth's home, Marley said: "Albert, I know you've been trying very hard to get a job. Personally, I think you're an exceptional young man who will find an excellent position, but at the moment I need someone who can help me. I wonder if you would be willing to officially come to work for—"

"Yes."

"— me for a while. Oh, good. But you didn't even ask what the job pays."

"If money was my thing, I wouldn't have enlisted. Will every day be as interesting as this one?"

"I hope not, dear. I have a large family, but not that large. But yes, every day will be interesting, if you are open to it."

"Thank you for asking me."

Marley stopped walking suddenly. She looked around the sidewalk, then lifted a round, flat stone slightly larger than a tea saucer from a nearby yard. She brought it toward a pickup truck—actually, a beautiful, gleaming black F-150 Harley Davidson SuperCrew—parked beside a mailbox and smashed the taillight on the driver's side.

"Aunt Marley! What are you doing?"

"Investing, dear." She replaced the stone carefully on the lawn.

Albert looked around. No one else was in sight and no one seemed to have heard them. Still, smashing a car could get a person shot. "But... they could get a ticket. They could get pulled over by the cops. I'm not going to have to break off antennas and steal hubcaps in this new job, am I?"

Marley knew what he was really thinking: Is my aunt suffering from dementia? Wisely, he held his tongue, making her all the more pleased to have offered him the job. "Stop fussing, Albert, and come along. We're behind schedule."

Something about her body language convinced him to change the subject. "We're going to visit a vampire now, aren't we?"

"Yes, dear."

"Do you think it might have killed Aloysius?"

"She, dear. I heard her voice on Kenneth's phone. Vampires are he or she, just like anyone else. I don't know if she killed him or not. It's a typical vampire style, though, because it gives the authorities an easy explanation for the blood loss."

"You mean, laying his body over the grate of a storm drain? I see that. That makes sense." They turned the corner and approached the house. Albert rolled his shoulders and flexed his hands to loosen them up. "What will you need me to do?"

Marley stopped on the sidewalk in front of the house. By the streetlight, he could see that her expression was unusually somber. "This is important, Albert. I want you to pay careful attention to what I tell you, because this will all fall apart if you don't follow my instructions exactly."

"I understand."

"I hope so, dear, because this is crucial. You must do precisely what I tell you."

"Okay. And what is that?"

"Nothing."

"Nothing?"

"You hold the umbrella, dear, and open the doors, and stand beside me with a polite and pleasant expression. Nothing more. No matter what happens or what you see, that's what I want you to do."

"What if you change your mind? What if you're in danger from, you know, teeth?"

"You'll do only what I ask of you and you'll wait until I've explained what I need in detail, or I'll be forced to fire you. Then you'll have to go back to sitting in office lobbies and empty restaurants with your resume in your lap, desperate for employment that we both know is beneath you, and we don't want that, do we?" She patted his cheek. "Don't look so worried, dear. We're only bearding a vampire in her lair. What could go wrong?"

She turned away then and didn't see her nephew look up toward the night sky, fervently praying that she was joking.

Marley didn't lead Albert to the front door. Instead, they walked around the Camry through the side yard. Albert glanced nervously up at the house —the lights were on, but all the curtains had been drawn. Someone could easily have been watching them through a narrow gap in the cloth.

The backyard was small, about twice the size of Marley's kitchen, but the overgrown trees and bushes blocked most of the light from the street. The far end was as dark as a cave.

"Why hello!" Marley said to the darkness, as though coming upon unexpected guests at her own party. "Imagine discovering all of you back here. What a surprise!"

Someone lurking in the darkness hissed at her to be quiet, making goosebumps run down Albert's back.

"She's one of them!" a man whispered. "A renfield!"

"No, she isn't," a woman said in a clear, low voice. She had a southern accent. "I told you about her, but I didn't expect to run into her so soon."

Stepping out of the impenetrable darkness into the penetrable darkness, the woman revealed herself. She was a black woman in her late 20's, her bare arms corded with muscle and her torso protected by a black tactical vest. She held a sawed-off shotgun, but it was pointed at the ground. Unfortunately, it was the ground right by Marley's feet.

"Nora, isn't it?" Marley said, seemingly unperturbed by the weapon. "Welcome to Seattle, Nora. Now please go home."

Two others stepped out of the darkness behind her. One was a tiny blonde woman with a loaded crossbow in her hands. The other was a black man, almost as tall and broad as Albert, holding a katana in one hand and a huge revolver in the other. The two of them looked just old enough to buy a beer, which meant they had a few months on Albert. "I don't take orders from you," Nora said.

"This is my city. You must have heard that things don't work that way here." Marley gestured toward their weapons. "No murders allowed."

"Told you: renfield," the man said, his voice surprisingly deep.

"No," Nora said. "She's something else."

The man cocked his revolver.

Albert, feeling increasingly jumpy about facing off with armed unfriendlies, shifted his stance as though about to scoop his aunt up and sprint through the gate with her. Marley froze him in place with a glance. Then she turned back to Nora. "I'm going to offer the people inside the house the same deal I'm offering you, right now. You can stay in Seattle and live in peace, or you can go home. I don't allow murder in my city."

The big man leaned forward. "That thing in there can't be murdered. It's already dead."

If he expected Marley to be intimidated but he was disappointed. "She can talk and think, Nelson. She can laugh and cry. I'd say that was good evidence of life. It's true that she has problems—"

"Problems!" the little blonde spat out. All three spoke with southern accents.

"But we don't execute people for that."

"She must be senile," the little blonde said.

"There's no need to be rude, Audrey."

Audrey's blue eyes were flat. "If you've heard of me, you should know what I do to people like you."

"I haven't heard of you," Marley said. "But I can see you."

The big man turned to Nora. "Why are we talking to her? Why don't we just—"

Nora looked over Marley and Albert's shoulder toward the house. "It's already too late."

Everyone glanced up at the house. Kenneth stared wide-eyed at them through a parted curtain, then hurried back out of sight.

Marley heard a rustle and a heavy thump behind her. She turned to see that Albert had taken Nelson to the ground. The katana lay in the grass and Nelson's heavy revolver was in Albert's left hand, barrel pressed just behind Nelson's left ear.

"Albert!" She exclaimed. "You let that young man up!"

"Yeah, Albert," the blond woman said, aiming her crossbow at him. "Let him up."

Albert felt strangely calm now that he was holding a weapon again. After so much disconcerting strangeness, being armed felt like returning to a safe place, even if that safety was an illusion. He gave Audrey a cool look. "You shoot me with that crossbow and I'll break it over your head."

"We need to go," Nora said. She had her shotgun trained on Albert but wasn't enthusiastic about it.

Audrey licked her lips. "I think I can—"

"They know we're here!" Nora interrupted. "Without the element of

48

surprise, we have to pull back. You know it!" She lowered her weapon. "Let him go, Albert. I'm only going to ask once."

"Yes, Albert," Marley said. "Immediately."

Albert shrugged and stepped back. Nelson rolled to his feet, katana back in hand. Albert kept the pistol aimed at him.

Nora grabbed Nelson's elbow and pulled him away, but she never looked away from Marley. "Ma'am, I was raised to respect my elders," she said, "so I'm not going to say what I'm thinking right now. But a thing just like the one in there killed my cousin. Maybe you don't know this, but when those things hunt, it's often a black man or woman that turns up missing the next day. If you think I'm going to walk away from that creature, you're mistaken."

She stepped back into the bushes, disappearing into the darkness. Nelson and Audrey did the same.

Marley glared up at her nephew. "Never again, Albert."

"He was creeping up on us!"

"Albert!" She yanked the revolver from his hand and threw it into the bushes.

"Aw."

But his aunt didn't want to hear it. "Never. Again. Now turn around." Marley moved her arms away from her body. "Show your empty hands."

Albert did as he was told just as the back door swung open. Kenneth lunged through, a double-barreled shotgun in his hands.

"We're unarmed!" Marley yelled.

"You're trespassing!"

"I came here to return your license and registration—you dropped them, you know."

"No, I didn't," Kenneth said. He moved to touch his pocket, presumably to search his wallet, then thought better of it and returned his hand to his weapon. "Who are those people you were talking to?"

"I assumed they were guests of yours. I heard voices in the back yard and thought it might be you, so I went around the side to say hello. May we

49

come in? I have your ID here in my pocket and I'd like to have a visit with your mistress. I suspect she and I have much to talk about."

Kenneth stood in the doorway, biting his lip for a moment, then waved them forward with the barrel of his shotgun. He'd learned to never, ever invite strangers into the house unless they were desperate for a private feeding place, but this woman had appeared inside his car. Better to invite her than let her force her way in whenever she wanted. Besides: "She wants to speak to you, too."

In a low voice, Marley said: "Be nice, Albert."

Albert hurried forward, putting himself between his aunt and the gun. "I want to give my notice," he said.

"Oh, very funny," Marley said. "Although you'd still have lasted longer on the job than some."

CHAPTER EIGHT
The Misery of Being Ageless and Unchanging

They went inside, with Kenneth leading them through the house as he backed up. The kitchen had been painted landlord white years ago but never touched up since, and the cabinet doors were dingy and crooked. Except for a single dirty dish, fork and glass in the sink, it looked like it was still waiting for renters to move in. Kenneth backed them into the empty dining room, the bare wooden floors creaking under their feet, and nodded his head toward the front room.

The living room was small but comfortable: It had even been decorated. The furniture was sparse, just two chairs and one loveseat, but they were covered with red velvet. Between them sat a black maple coffee table with six silver candlesticks all messy with melted wax. The black velvet drapes were too long for the windows, but they had rarely fit any of the homes where they had been hung.

In all, everything had an intentionally gloomy look about it and an unintentionally shabby one. Kenneth gestured toward the loveseat. Marley thanked him and sat, placing the license and registration on the coffee table. Albert stood beside her.

Kenneth went into the dining room and opened a wooden door. It made a noise like an old time radio sound effect. Beyond it, there was nothing but a set of stairs leading down into darkness. They heard the heavy clump of approaching footsteps and soon, Kenneth's "mistress" swept into the room.

She was dressed all in black leather, with high heels, heavy eyeliner and teased, dyed black hair. She entered with full confidence, utterly in command of the room and herself. Perhaps she was not quite as tall and slender as the vampires at the rest home, and perhaps her wide, catlike eyes and broad mouth were less pronounced, but she was as beautiful as any airbrushed magazine model. "You must be Marley Jacobs." Her voice was low and seductive. "Please call me Spire."

"Wonderful!" Marley said with complete sincerity. "I've never heard that name before. How original."

Spire eased herself into the larger of the two velvet chairs as though it was a throne. Kenneth started toward the other chair, but noticing Albert was on his feet, stood behind Spire. He held the barrel of the shotgun so it covered both Marley and Albert at once, but was knowledgeable enough to understand trigger discipline.

Albert began to breathe heavily. Beads of sweat stood out on his forehead and he struggled to hold himself still. A man with a gun could make a situation turn bad very quickly, well before his aunt could explain what she wanted in detail. He tried to convince himself that she knew what she was doing, but he had the sneaking suspicion that he'd survived Afghanistan just to die in Seattle.

Spire seemed amused by them. "You realize the risk you take by coming here, don't you? I know you fancy yourself 'Protector of Seattle' but should you really have come here, to the center of my power, before I've even fed for the night?"

Marley was as calm and friendly as if they were sitting in a crowded cafe. "Oh, vampires don't have centers of power. Stop teasing. And, considering my role as protector of this city, as you call it, I feel it's important to visit notable new residents."

Spire leaned forward with a predator's smile. "Do you really think you can protect this city from someone like me?"

"Protect the city from you? Oh, darling, I don't think you understand. I'm here to protect you."

Spire laughed. "Is. That. So."

"I'm not here to threaten you, dear. Far from it. I'm here to welcome you to my city, and to help you live a long and comfortable life."

Spire turned to Kenneth with a chilly smile on her face. "She's here to welcome me," she told him, and gestured for him to sit. He did, but he didn't put away the shotgun. "How kind of you, Marley. But I don't need any help from you. I've already lived a long and comfortable life."

"Have you?"

"Of course."

"How old are you, dear?"

"I'll be three hundred thirty-five next Halloween."

"What a wonderful day for a vampire's birthday! But you can't lie to me, dear."

Spire's amused expression vanished. "What did you just say?" Her voice was low and dangerous. Kenneth leaned forward, laying his finger over the trigger.

"Spire, I just told you that you can't lie to me. No one can. How old were you when you were turned? Eighteen?"

The vampire watched Marley through narrowed eyes. "Nineteen."

"Ah. And judging by the changes to your face and form, I'd say it happened, what, twenty-four years ago? Twenty-five?" Spire glanced away. "Dear, you aren't even as old as I am. But you are reaching a dangerous stage for vampires. You need to live a secret life, yes, but you are becoming more beautiful every day. More graceful, more perfect. I'll bet you already attract a lot of attention. The last place you lived... Where was that?"

Kenneth was so startled to hear his thoughts mirrored in Marley's words that he blurted out the answer: "Minneapolis."

"Thank you, Kenneth. Minneapolis. I'm sure you had reached a point where too many people knew who you were, even if they didn't realize what you were. You couldn't slip away anonymously from a crowded place with a victim because everyone was watching you. It became difficult, yes?"

Spire's self-assured smile had returned, but it didn't touch her eyes. "I'm a careful predator."

"How careful can you be if every head turns when you enter a room? I'm sure you already know that vampire hunters have already started to recognize you."

"Maybe you should pay a visit to the hunters, then."

Marley sat back and folded her hands on her lap. "I just did, dear, in your back yard."

Kenneth leapt out of his chair, nearly dropping his weapon. "What?" He ran to the front window to peek through the curtains. He moved to the next window, then the next.

Spire stirred in her seat, watching Kenneth uncertainly. For the first time, she looked unsure what to do.

"Don't worry." Marley said. "I sent them away. Come back, Kenneth, it's safe enough for now, come back." He did, warily. He still held tight to his shotgun, but it was now aimed at the ceiling. "If they don't take my advice, they'll get a visit from the police. Personally, I consider vampire hunters murderers, and I don't believe in solving problems with murder." Marley sighed. She looked completely composed, even as Spire became more agitated. "Our problem is, everyone is a potential hunter. When all mortal eyes turn toward you, it's only a matter of time before someone realizes what you are. There's no avoiding it, Spire.

"They stake out your home at night," Marley continued, "to make sure. To convince themselves. They come for you in the early morning hours.

They usually start by shooting your helper," Marley nodded at Kenneth, "although sometimes they stab or beat them to death. Then they stake you in your coffin and drag you into the sun. And often, they record the whole thing on camcorders and post it on the internet."

Spire's perfect brow furrowed ever so slightly. "They do what?"

"They post it online," Marley said. "Usually it's because they want to expose the Secret Vampire Threat to the world, or some such foolishness. Sometimes they do it because people record themselves doing everything nowadays. The ones who wear masks and post anonymously are slightly harder to catch, but most don't bother. Surely you've seen the videos?"

Spire shot an accusing look at Kenneth, as though he had been hiding something from her. He said: "I've shown them to you." There was nothing defensive in his tone. He merely sounded tired.

"Of course he has, dear. Don't blame him. Let me demonstrate something." She took her phone from her pocket and held it up. "Do you know what this is?"

Spire stared at it blankly, then looked away and waved one long hand dismissively. "Of course I do. You're wasting my time."

"Oh Spire, haven't I told you that you can't lie to me? This is my telephone. Kenneth has one, too. Show her, dear."

Kenneth reluctantly took out his phone and held it in his palm. Spire looked as though she thought he'd conspired against her.

"Spire, when Kenneth called you about us tonight, did you think he was using a pay phone? Because there are very few pay phones any more. They've all been taken out. And do you see that plastic case over there?" Marley pointed to a small end table with a closed laptop on it. "That's a modern computer. That's probably how Kenneth showed you those hunter videos I was telling you about."

"Shut up," Spire said. "You shut up."

"I can't do that, dear. Even if you were very careful with your feeding and never killed your victims, you would give yourself away. Best case scenario: you'd end up loaded into a U-Haul truck like luggage—again—fleeing across the country. Maybe you'd get a visit from the police. Worst case scenario: hunters break into the house while you're sleeping. Your life is not the only one that needs to be protected, it's Kenneth's, too. And let's not forget about the lives of those hunters who, in their ignorance and fear, take matters into their own hands. The ones who survive often spend the rest of their lives in prison."

Spire couldn't bear to hear another word. She lunged forward. Marley's hand flashed to the pocket of her jacket. In one motion, she hooked her thumb into the opening and pulled it wide.

Warm orange light shone out of the gap. Spire screamed in agony and terror, then fell back, hands in front of her face. She collapsed into her chair and curled up in the fetal position.

After that scream, Albert expected the vampire to be burned or scarred by the light, but her beautiful face was still flawless.

Kenneth rushed to check on her. "You're okay," he said, reassuring himself as much as her. She let him lower her hands. "You're okay."

Spire didn't respond to him. Turning slowly back in her seat, her hands gripped the arm rests so tightly her knuckles were white. Her voice was tight with fear and rage. To Marley, she said: "You're nothing! You're an old woman. The world is finished with you, but here you are, daring to... I should kill you."

"No!" Kenneth said. "No, Spire, love, listen to her."

Spire spun toward him, shocked. Before either of them could speak, Marley started talking again.

"Yes, dear. Listen to me. Do you know the life expectancy of a vampire 'in the wild'? Sixty years, if you include the time before they turned. That's all. And you're almost 55."

"Sixty? I don't believe you.

"The world is getting increasingly difficult to manage, isn't it? Do you know who the president is, dear? Because it's not Ronald Reagan."

"Hah! I know it's his vice-president, George Bush!"

Kenneth looked at the floor, embarrassed.

Marley's expression became sympathetic, and her voice was gentle. "No, dear, not for more than twenty years. I'm willing to bet that it's becoming harder and harder to cover for these little slips, and they're becoming more noticeable. Isn't that right, Kenneth?"

Kenneth's voice was glum. "Yes."

"Ken!" Spire looked frightened and betrayed. "Ken, don't!"

Kenneth turned to Marley. "Every time I show her a video on YouTube, she's surprised and delighted. She calls fifteen-year-old music 'the new thing.' Some things she can remember, but when I tell her who's president, or the latest with gay marriage, or... She forgets so much when she sleeps."

"It's getting hard on you, isn't it, Kenneth?"

"I'm afraid for her," he said, speaking louder than he intended. "At first we could laugh it off, like she was joking, but Vice-President Bush? How do I explain that away? I want to keep her safe, but I can't just lock her away from the world."

"Because you love her."

"Yes," he said. His eyes brimmed with tears. "Always."

Marley turned back to Spire. "Do you see him, dear? Doesn't he look tired? He's aging, too. Haven't you offered to turn him and make him young forever like you?"

"Yes!" Spire said, her voice raw, vulnerable and honest, "but he's worried about us. He says we can't find a daylight servant to keep us safe."

"Oh, Spire, please. As beautiful as you are, in your fantastic clothes, you couldn't find a pretty young thing to watch over you in exchange for the promise of eternal life? How absurd!

"The truth is—and I'm sorry, Kenneth, for putting you in a difficult position—that he doesn't want to be a vampire. He has realized it's a curse to be ageless and unchanging. To him, you've become a beautiful invalid, and he's exhausted from taking care of you."

Kenneth sniffled, then stood suddenly and went into the other room. He set the shotgun on a table by the window then began to weep quietly. No one spoke for a moment.

A Key, an Egg, an Unfortunate Remark

Spire looked at Marley. All her composure and authority was gone. "I know you're right. I know it. I try to pretend to be current, but sometimes things slip out. I remember some things from day to day, but to me the world is just the same as when I was turned. I had no idea it was so hard on him." She stood and started toward him.

"Darling, one moment." Marley gestured toward the seat. Spire sat again. "Give him a little time, if you would. What's your given name, dear?"

"Susannah."

"Oh, that's beautiful, too. Let me ask you, Spire, has Kenneth been with you all this time? Ever since you were turned?" She nodded. "He must love you very much. That's an astonishingly long time for a companion to stay with a vampire. I think we'll have to find a place for both of you."

"A place?"

"I have a home, dear, right here in the city, where vampires live in privacy and safety. You won't be able to drink from the population any more —it's not safe and it's not acceptable, even for a careful predator who tries her best not to kill—but you will be fed and comfortable, and you'll have people like yourself to talk to."

"I have money," Spire said. "I can afford it."

"Keep your money, dear. It's my role in life to protect this city, and I'm happy to offer you a place. I'm sure we can find Kenneth a job there, if he wants one, so you can be together."

There was silence for a while as Spire considered it. Kenneth entered the room again. He'd wiped his cheeks dry but his eyes were red. He knelt beside her chair.

Spire laid her hand on his. "Did you hear? What should we do?"

"The day after we left Minnesota, Lagerfeld and three of his buddies burned our house down. Ecks texted… wrote to tell me about it. It was just like Memphis, but we hadn't even been there six months. We've only been here three days, and already they've caught up to us. Is it Lagerfeld again? The Memphis crew? Those frat bros from Purdue? I don't know how much longer I can keep you safe."

Spire turned to Marley. "What if I hate it?"

"You won't be a prisoner," Marley assured her. "If you want to leave, or you want to hunt in the wild again, I'll provide a moving truck to take you to any other city in the country."

Spire understood. "I accept."

Marley made a call. Within thirty minutes, Naima and three helpers were packing up Spire's and Kenneth's things. The nurse arrived shortly after with a small cooler full of blood packs. With everything in hand, Marley and Albert went out to the car.

"Damn," Marley said.

Albert was surprised. "Are you disappointed? Because I thought that was amazing."

She patted his hand. "Thank you, dear. I'm not disappointed about the two of them. Not at all. It's just that I can't get Jenny out of jail because I still don't know who killed your brother. It certainly wasn't those two. Spire had fresh packs of blood delivered, and she was expecting Sylvester to be her evening meal. Besides, dressed like that she would do her feeding among others like her. She wouldn't have gone near Aloysius and he wouldn't have gone near her, not unless she was quite desperate."

"Could there be another vampire in town that we don't know about?"

"I wish I could say yes," Marley answered. "It would make things so much simpler. But I'm afraid that your brother was murdered, and I can't help but think it was done in a way designed to misdirect me."

"What's next?"

Marley's phone rang. To her great surprise, it was Weathers on the line. "Madam," he said without any exchange of pleasantries, "there is a squad of armed gunman preparing to assault the house."

Marley hung up the phone without responding. "Come along, Albert. It's time to go home."

CHAPTER NINE
Another Visit from Unwelcome Guests

Marley was chatty on the way home. Her initial disappointment at realizing Spire was not involved in her nephew's death had evaporated, and Albert thought she seemed positively chipper. He assumed the phone call had been good news, which showed just how little he understood his aunt. When they were five blocks from the house, she asked him to park at the curb.

He did. "What next?"

"Shush for a few minutes, dear. I have something to prepare back here. Be as silent and still as you can."

Albert stared through the windshield at the neighborhood around him. The houses were large and well-cared for, the landscapes sculpted, the gutters clean. He looked them over for several minutes, one by one, taking in the placid lawns and comfortable-looking glow coming from a few of the windows. "Huh."

"Hmm?" Marley said absentmindedly.

"This neighborhood, and these houses—they're not, you know, for rich people, but they're for the almost rich. Cardiologist-rich, maybe. I don't know. Maybe that's rich, too. Anyway, I was looking at them, thinking that I will never have a house like these in a neighborhood like this. But that's okay, because I know there are vampires in the world, and none of these people do, and that's pretty freaking amazing." He was quiet a moment. "They don't know, do they?"

"Oh my, no. Not if I'm doing my job correctly, they don't. Let's get out of the car now."

Albert climbed out of the car and opened the door for Marley on the curb side. She climbed out with a tiny green thermos in her hand, then gestured for Albert to sit on the hood and bend low. He did. She dipped her finger into the thermos lid and began drawing a shape on Albert's forehead.

"Remember when I asked you to be quiet for a moment? Well, I'm glad you didn't listen, because it's important to be reminded how amazing the life we lead is. Of course, if you'd distracted me so severely that I'd made a mistake while preparing this spell, the car would have filled with a living gas that would have devoured us down to our bones. Aren't we lucky that didn't happen?"

"Oh," Albert said. "Um, yes, that's very lucky, and I'm sorry. I really need to learn to do what you tell me."

"Finished! Stand, please, and hold this mirror." He did. Marley drew a shape on her own forehead. "I've practiced more with the mirror than doing it on other people. Next you'll ask me what the spell does."

"That was my plan."

"Invisibility, of a sort. It will make people look away rather than look at us, and they won't realize they're doing it. Let's move quickly, though, because the effect will vanish when this stuff dries. Good thing it's a humid night."

Albert followed her down the sidewalk. "Really? That's... That's fantastic! I mean... wow."

"I feel the same way, even after all these years," Marley assured him.

"I don't even have to go naked, right?"

"Not unless you really, really want to."

"Couldn't we have put it on the car, though, and just driven into the garage?"

Marley made a disappointed little harrumph. Albert was slowly beginning to realize that he shouldn't make her do that. "If we were utterly mad, yes," she said. "Personally, I have no intention of driving on city streets in a car that no one else can see to avoid. We'll also have to be extremely careful crossing the streets; drivers won't yield to invisible pedestrians."

A Key, an Egg, an Unfortunate Remark

"Good point, good point. Wait. Why are you sneaking into your own house?"

"A surprise party, dear."

"Are we really invisible? Okay, um, forget I asked that. I'm not going to make you tell me the same things over and over. Mother was right, wasn't she? You can do magic. Damn, I wish we'd had invisibility over in Afghanistan."

"It wouldn't have been practical, Albert. The effect only lasts a few minutes—fifteen or twenty at the most—and the ingredients cost a little over $40,000."

"What?"

"And that's not from government contractors, either. Besides, not only does an error in preparing the salve summon the living gas, but one mistake in drawing the spell would strike the recipient stone dead. Think of the congressional investigations!"

Albert made a little choking noise and his hand moved involuntarily toward his forehead to wipe it clean, but he stopped himself in time.

They didn't say anything more after that. Marley kept up a quick pace, which Albert liked. Across the street from Marley's house, two house-painter vans were parked against the curb. She glanced at them, but it was just a glance. The front gate stood partway open. "Don't touch, Albert. They might not be able to look at us, but they will certainly see a gate opening on its own."

Marley slipped through the opening. Albert followed. He glanced up at the house, expecting to see brightly-lit windows—he knew the sort of parties his aunt threw—but everything looked dark. "Who's the party for?" he whispered. "I don't have a present."

"You're not meant to. Once again I'm going to ask you to do nothing without my explicit instruction."

"Okay. Werewolves?"

"What, dear?" Marley said as they hustled up the walk, then diverted to the path that led to the back door.

"Is it werewolves this time? Do I need a gun with silver bullets or something?"

Marley stopped and looked up at his face, searching his expression for a sign that he was simply making a terrible joke. "Oh, Albert."

"What? It was vampires earlier, so..."

Marley exhaled loudly, letting her disappointment show. Then she went up the back stairs and pressed the doorbell.

Weathers opened the interior door a few moments later, but he looked all around the yard, unable to see who had rung the bell. "Open the door please, Weathers," Marley said. He did, swinging the storm door wide and standing silhouetted in the light from the kitchen. Marley and Albert entered the house.

Marley drew a finger across the clear, shining oil on her forehead and somehow, although Albert had been able to see her the whole time, he knew she became fully visible again. Marley reached high up and smeared her finger through the mark on his face, too.

"Ah," Weathers said, pleased to see them both. He shut the door.

"How many are they?"

"Ten, madam. There are two stationed by the gazebo, and two others at the edge of the garden. The rest are stationed out front in the vans. I believe they are all human."

"Ah well. Everything has to be difficult, doesn't it?"

"Yes, madam."

"Has Miss Harriet gone home?"

"Yes, madam. An hour ago."

"Good. I suspect two out front will stay behind to drive the vans, which means four will enter the house. Does that sound right, Albert?"

"What? The painting vans? You mean four painters?" He asked, rattled. Marley loved parties, everyone knew that. But why were they talking as though they were in danger?

Then Marley confirmed all her nephew's worst fears. "Home invaders, dear. They're our party guests, and what a surprise it will be when they find out I'm the one organizing things, not them. I do love parties."

Weathers nodded. "Yes, madam."

"If there are so many of them, it means that someone is taking me seriously—as they should—and they're probably well-trained. That's why I'm asking for your opinion, Albert. You were in Afghanistan. Didn't you have to break into people's homes?"

"We didn't break in." His voice was tight and his face felt hot. His injury began to throb. Wasn't his war supposed to be over? "We acted under orders..." His hands roamed over his body, checking for equipment he didn't carry any more.

Marley had pushed him too far and too quickly, and she knew it. "It's all right, dear. It's all right. We're not going to confront them."

"What are we going to do, then? Do we have any weapons? Can we call the police?"

Out of concern for her nephew's anxiety, she pretended the first two questions hadn't been asked. "We could, dear, but we won't. Weathers, would you make sure the proper doors are left open?"

Weathers bowed and went into the library. Marley crossed into the dining room, then went through the open doors into the huge living room. Albert trailed behind her. Both of them stepped over the fishing wire.

"You know, if I had armed men outside my house, I'd be nervous. I might even be slightly anxious. In fact, I think I'm feeling a little anxious right now."

"I hope you aren't doubting me, dear," Marley said over her shoulder. "But never mind. It's difficult the first couple of times, but you get used to it. Besides, you shouldn't assume!" Marley went to the front window in the corner and threw the curtains open. "Weathers, remember that time it was a squad of armed women?"

"That was before my time, madam." Weather said from the other room.

Albert rushed forward. "Aunt Marley, get out of the window!"

She stopped him with a wave of her hand, switched a reading lamp on, then stepped away from the glass. "I know, dear. A lighted window on a dark night makes for a tempting target. Still, I had to let them know I was home, and I wasn't visible long enough for one of them to shoot me."

"It would have been long enough for me," Albert said seriously.

Marley noticed that Albert's damaged right hand was clenched and trembling. "Ah," she said, laying her hand on his arm. "There's always something new to learn. Thank you. I'll remember that for next time. Now get into the library, please."

Albert backed away from her, moving through the open doors into the dining room. After glancing at himself in the standing mirror he'd moved just that morning, he crossed the hall into the library.

Weathers dropped a coiled power cord into Albert's pocket, then laid a laptop computer into his hand. "Will you be able to carry this, sir, without closing the top? Madam's instructions were quite specific that it not be put to sleep."

Albert glanced at it; a line of text advanced across the screen but before he could look closely Weathers diverted his attention to the corner of the room.

A trap door stood open at the far end of the library. Albert edged toward it. It led down into darkness, with only a metal ladder along one side. "Is this a sewer thing? Because I'm wearing regular shoes."

"I understand the injury to your hand is quite debilitating," Weathers said without showing the slightest interest in Albert's question. "Can you carry the laptop down the ladder without closing it?"

Albert glanced at Marley, who stood in the library door with her back to him. He cradled the computer in the crook of his right hand. With his index and middle finger gone, he could only hold it with his two smaller fingers—both of which still hurt when he bent them. It wasn't impossible. "No problem."

An explosion shook the front of the house. The walls shuddered and books fell from the shelves. Albert could suddenly smell apricot orchards, smoke from a black powder IED, and Afghani dust. He shook them away. Only memories, he told himself.

Weathers, as always, was unperturbed. "Then you'd better start down now, sir."

CHAPTER TEN
Things of Value Are Preserved

Just inside the doorway to the library, Marley looked into the standing mirror. It was perfectly placed to let her see the front door, which had just been refashioned into a cloud of smoke and flying splinters. It was going to be one of those nights, for everyone.

Something about the size of a plum landed on the floor with a metallic clunk. Marley laid a hand over her eyes, blocking the sudden flash of light. When she looked again, she saw four men in black tactical gear rushing into her home, Heckler and Koch MP5's held to their cheeks.

"Gentlemen!" she called, "welcome—"

A spray of gunfire interrupted her, shattering her image in mirror and punching through the mahogany breakfront behind it. The sound of gunfire lit a yearning inside Marley's chest, as it sometimes did, for the long ago days when she was the one with the gun. With all that power. But of course she had turned her back on all of that.

She turned and hurried toward the trap door. Back out in the main part of the house, she heard a clatter of falling bodies and a second rattle of gunfire. A man cried out in pain. Someone had been shot.

Marley's yearning for the feel of a gun evaporated like a drop of water on a hot skillet. In fact, she almost rushed into the living room to apologize for the fishing line—she hadn't known it was for that, after all—and to offer first aid.

But she didn't want to be murdered, either, so she waved at Albert to start down the ladder. He did. Weathers draped a canvas bag over her shoulder, then held her hand as she started down herself. An orange-furred Pomeranian popped its head out of the bag, looking alert and excited.

"Take care, madam," Weather said as he lowered the trap door.

"Not coming, Weathers?"

"I should like to stay to observe, if you don't mind." There was a sudden explosion from the kitchen. A plume of distinctive white smoke billowed into the room.

"All right, then. No eating," Marley told him.

The trap door clicked shut, leaving them in utter darkness. Marley threw a switch and a dim column of bare bulbs illuminated the shaft.

Albert started to climb again. "We're not going to leave him up there!"

"It'll be all right, Albert. I've told Weathers not to kill anyone."

"But..."

"Keep moving, dear. We're much too busy to stand on a ladder and chat."

Albert started downward again, carefully cradling the laptop and quickly switching his left hand from one rung to the next. They descended perhaps forty feet that way, and just as Albert began to suspect that they were going to pass through the core of the earth, they reached a small round concrete room.

There was a little table and some chairs, a shelf with canned goods on it, and two coat racks. On one hung two heavy ski jackets with pairs of fur-lined boots beneath, and the other held two lined raincoats over rubber boots. They were prepared for all-weather evacuation.

"Ah, well," Marley said. She was a little breathless as she reached the bottom of the ladder. "Just a moment before we move on." She gestured toward a deadbolted door behind them, then collapsed into a chair. The dog popped its head out of the canvas bag again and Marley scritched it behind the ears. "I'm sorry to say that these coats, boots, and things are fitted for Jenny. I don't have anything in your size."

Albert realized that his hands were shaking, and not from the effort of climbing down the ladder. He'd faced armed gunman before, obviously, but never alone and never unarmed. How had his aunt gotten into this mess?

A Key, an Egg, an Unfortunate Remark

He set the computer on the table and sat across from her, making a deliberate effort to match his aunt's composure. "No cross-dressing for me, then. Aunt Marley, what do you think is happening up there?"

Marley removed a tablet computer from a little case, swiped the screen and read the display. "Apparently they're burning down my house."

"But—"

"It's all right, dear. As I'm sure you've realized by now, Weathers isn't a human being, poor dear. He'll be just fine."

"Well, okay. Good. But... your invisibility thing... spell, I mean. Your invisibility spell would have given me plenty of time to take care of these guys. I could have taken one of their guns, or even a knife from your kitchen, and—" Marley held up her hand. She didn't want to hear it. "They shot at you! The spell cost what? Forty grand? Your house is worth at least a million dollars!"

"Well above that, actually."

"Why didn't you tell me? I could have saved your house and all your things. I would have been happy to do it."

"Happy to kill them?" Marley's voice had become high and tight. "For a million-dollar house? Is that the price for a human life? Ten human lives?"

Albert's whole body grew hot with anger. He laid his good hand on the place where his right index and middle finger used to be, which was still tender even after all these months. In a tightly-controlled voice, he said: "Don't talk to me as though I don't know..."

Marley sighed. Her own anger had passed—holding onto it had become difficult as she got older—and now she was merely tired. "I'm sorry, Albert. That was condescending of me; you deserve better. If there's anyone in my life right now who understands the cost of taking a life, it's you. Please accept my apologies, dear."

He took a deep breath and looked around their little concrete room. He also reminded himself why they had fled to this underground bunker. "Forget it. It's a tough moment."

"True, but that's no excuse. I will say this, though: Every life is sacred to me. I could have stopped those men myself, but one of them might have died. That's not a risk I'm willing to take. The house can be remade, but a person can't. My things... well, it's only money."

Albert wisely held his tongue at that.

"I need you to understand this," Marley said. "I need you to see who you are, and who I am, too."

"Some things are worth fighting and dying for."

Marley tried another tactic. "Albert, I know I can be an insufferable know-it-all sometimes and I know I can be difficult to put up with. But you'll just have to accept that I really do know what I'm doing, most of the time. Well, some of the time. Well, all right, often I'm just trying to do what seems best at the moment."

"Like everybody."

"Hah! That would be a nice thought if it were true, but it's not. I'm sorry, but I simply don't believe that everyone is trying to do what's best in any given moment. I've seen too much of the world for that. Too much habit. Too much blind tradition. Too much fear of change and loss. Too little willingness to make something new. You see, it's not just that I've built something in this city that works without murder or grief—that works without any violence at all. It's that I'm building on it and expanding it, when I can."

"And I respect that," Albert said tonelessly.

"But I can't do it alone. I can barely get by in my regular life alone. I need help, and I'd like that help to come from you, even if I make things difficult sometimes."

"Okay," Albert said. "I'll help. I want to help. But for the future, let's skip the part where you tell me that I don't understand the price of violence. Because I do, and I have my own ideas about when that price is worth paying."

"I understand," Marley said, in a knowing way that made him feel uneasy.

"Will Weathers be able to stop the gunmen upstairs?"

A Key, an Egg, an Unfortunate Remark

"Oh, he won't even try," Marley said. "Weather's interests are not the same as ours. He'll observe the things that interest him and ignore the rest. The idea that he should save the house or stop the gunmen would be utterly foreign to him."

By this point, Albert was genuinely anxious to know just what Weathers was, if he wasn't a human being. However, Marley didn't seem willing to explain it, so he changed the subject. He pointed at the laptop half-closed on the table beside him. "Of all the things to save from the house, why this laptop? Nowadays, you can back up everything on it to a remote location called 'the future.' "

Marley slapped her hands onto her thighs and stood. "Let's get somewhere safe and we can go into it in detail."

Albert threw the locks on the door and heaved it open, revealing a long, dimly lit passageway. "You need an underground monorail to take you from station to station."

"Haven't you seen the movies? It's the criminal masterminds who get rail transit in their hideouts. The good guys have to hoof it."

They went down the long passage together. The very long passage. Albert estimated that it was at least the length of a football field, but in fact he'd underestimated. Finally, after what seemed a respectful delay, he said: "When you said Weathers wasn't..." Albert searched for the right words. "Is he a werewolf?"

"Oh my, no. I told you he wasn't human. Werewolves are most definitely human."

"Like vampires? Now I guess I understand why you were so upset about my silver bullet remark. But what is Weathers, then? I'm dying to know."

Marley made him regret asking the question immediately. "First I'm going to ask some questions of you: Who were those men? Why did they attack the house?"

Albert stopped suddenly. "Well, it's not one of your crazy parties. You said they were home invaders. Thieves."

"Home invaders don't station gunman at the back of the house to shoot people who try to flee; they burst in through all the doors at once. They don't enter the house in a team of four, all clumped together and aiming their weapons in different directions. They don't use white phosphorus."

"White phosphorus!" They started walking again. "You're describing military tactics."

"That's what I thought, too. If I were forced to guess, I'd say they were professional killers hired to murder everyone in the house. What does that tell you?"

"You're not as popular as I thought?"

Marley laughed. "I'm positively despised in some circles."

"They probably don't want to steal something from you, since they already set the house on fire. Most likely, they just wanted to kill us all. Unless it was something they could grab quickly."

"I don't think so. There's nothing available for a quick grab in my home."

"And I don't think it's Nora and her crew," he added, pleasing Marley greatly. Jenny—and more than a few of her other assistants—would have assumed Nelson was the lead hunter simply because he was male. It was a pleasant change of pace to have an assistant who could see things clearly. "They didn't have the gear, the training, or the manpower. Actually, you know what they could have planned to grab? Weathers. What if someone wanted to kidnap him, since he's not, you know, normal?"

"Don't say normal, dear. It makes you sound like a... well, just don't. And there's no need to worry about Weathers, I promise you. He's a demon."

Albert stopped short a second time. He stared at Marley with his least attractive expression: open-mouthed shock. "What?"

"If you keep stopping, we're never going to get to the end of this tunnel." They started again. Peering ahead, Albert could see a door at the far end. "Yes, he's a demon, but that doesn't mean he's damned, or he comes from hell, or even that he's evil. He certainly doesn't go around tempting people to sin."

"Right." Albert said, wryly. "That would be devils, not demons."

"Very good, Albert!" Marley's dog barked once as though in

congratulations.

"Aunt Marley, I was joking."

"Sometimes a single joke can contain more truth than a whole newspaper. Anyway, he's a being from an alternate place. Not evil or good, but utterly alien. He's come here to learn about narrative and interrelation."

"Narrative? You mean, stories?"

"He's fascinated by the way people relate to each other and how they pare back sensory details to understand the universe. It's tremendously interesting to him and he's more than happy to be my servant if he can be exposed to human narrative."

"Like soap operas in the middle of the day."

"Yes. Too bad they're being canceled. They've been very useful to me over the years. But those gunmen can't kidnap Weathers. They might offer him a bargain, which he would only take if it didn't conflict with his bargain with me. More likely, when they point their guns at him, he won't be there any more."

Albert nodded, taking that in. "And when you told him 'No eating'?"

"Oh, look, here we are at the door." Marley laid her thumb on a sensor pad. The door clicked, then slowly swung open. Albert was startled to see that it was nearly an inch thick, made of steel and swung open smoothly and quietly. The other side was faced with plasterboard.

Marley entered the room beyond. It was a basement, small and functional but not fancy, with a thin coat of dust everywhere. She led Albert upstairs; the basement door had been nailed open.

In the dining room, Marley yanked a white cloth off the table and directed him to set the laptop there.

But Albert didn't notice. He was looking around the place. There were white cloths over everything, but this was clearly a nice, middle-class house: not very large, with ordinary furniture that could be acquired from a mall furniture store.

"To the table, please," Marley said, with unnecessary sharpness. "I don't want the battery to run down too much. What's the power level?"

Albert glanced at the upper corner. "Ninety-one percent."

Marley wasn't reassured. "Plug it in, plug it in."

Albert uncoiled the power cord and plugged the laptop into a wall socket. Then he squinted at the screen.

"Aunt Marley..." he paused a moment. "Is this a speech to text program?"

"I should hope it does more than that. This computer has a spirit attached to it—I call it Scribe—and it's writing my biography."

"What?"

"Take a look."

Albert studied the screen, once again making that unattractive expression of open-mouthed shock. Properly chastened by the text on the screen, he closed his mouth. "It's not just taking down what we say," He made the hand signals for Attention, Look out, and Rally, then stopped just as things became tedious, "but what we do. And it's kind of snotty. How?"

"I told you," Marley said quickly, hoping that criticism would pass unremarked. "It's writing my biography. I summoned a spirit—and because I know you'll ask, they're not the same thing as demons or devils. I call it Scribe. It writes down pretty much everything I do, within certain guidelines."

"What about me?" Albert asked, becoming alarmed for no sensible reason at all. "I'm in here, too."

"You're part of my life, dear. Don't worry, I've asked Scribe not to get too deep into people's thoughts, because that's rude. It also has a knack for leaving out unimportant detail. That's why I'm going to put it to rest and do a little reading while you get a couple of cans of soup from the pantry and make us a midnight snack. Beef barley, I think. It's been too long since I ate."

"Well, all right." Staring warily at an utterly inert and harmless computer, Albert retreated into the kitchen.

Marley sat in front of the laptop. "Scribe, give me three asterisks."

* * *

"Scribe, please start again."

Albert wisely waited until Marley had set her computer aside before putting a steaming bowl of soup in front of her. "Did you find anything?"

"Yes," Marley said. "And it's very annoying."

CHAPTER ELEVEN
Old Lives and High Scores

Albert sat opposite her with his own bowl. "How so?"

"Well, I don't exert much control over Scribe," Marley said, wisely. "It knows to leave out bathroom time and boring things, but otherwise it records events as it sees fit. And that's fine. But sometimes I wish I could set a buzzer beside it so it could alert me when it has a flash of the future."

"It can see into the future?"

"Yes, but only in limited ways, and only sporadically. Still, sometimes I think it's deliberately trying to infuriate me," she said unfairly. Marley turned the computer toward her nephew. "Look at the last three paragraphs of this chapter."

Albert read aloud from the screen. "As the crowd cheered the final point, Marley wandered without purpose—as she often liked to do—to the window. She saw Aloysius standing beside the sundial in her rose garden, his hand absent-mindedly stroking the surface. He must have been standing out in the chill for quite a while, thinking.

As she watched, he seemed to come to some sort of decision and stalked off along the path toward the front of the house.

She never saw her nephew alive again. Seriously?"

"I wish it were a joke."

"Aunt Marley, wait a second: Did this computer really record the last time you saw Aloysius alive? This is from your party the other night?"

Marley directed her aggravation away from the blameless text toward her nephew. "Albert, do try to keep up. Things are frustrating enough as it is. Think how much trouble I could have saved if I'd known about that last sentence."

"But if you'd saved him, the sentence wouldn't be there, right?" Albert asked, displaying a surprising capacity for cleverness.

"Don't be tiresome," Marley snapped again. "Eat your soup."

They ate in silence, Marley's spoon clattering irritably against the edge of her bowl. Her cell phone rang several times, but she ignored it; she didn't even glance at the number to see who it was. Albert scrunched himself down as small as he could manage and ate as quietly as he could, a habit he'd learned in his mother's kitchen and thought he'd shed when he enlisted. Luckily for him, he didn't even notice the return of those old behaviors because he was entirely focused on keeping his mind a blank so his aunt would not be able to read his thoughts on her laptop.

He was still hungry when they'd finished, but Marley collected the bowls and dropped them into the sink with a clatter. "It's time to get some sleep. The next police interview is going to waste several hours, so we should get an early start."

They went upstairs. There were no doors on the bedrooms or the bathroom, only curtains. Marley pointed toward a back bedroom where Albert found some men's clothes, but of course they were all too small. He stripped down and lay in bed, trying to catalog all the ways his life had changed since breakfast. It had been a long Monday.

In the master bedroom, Marley changed into a sleeping robe and opened the window to blow out the stale air, at the same time wishing she could do that with her thoughts and habits. She, too, lay in bed for a long time before she slept, but she spent the night in bitter self-recrimination, trying to figure out how she could have gotten so lazy and distracted that she'd let Aloysius lose his life. The blame, she was sure, lay solely with her, and she did not try to find fault with anyone else. Not the victim of the crime. Not the one who'd committed it.

They slept until ten the next morning, much later than either had

74

planned. Albert opened cans of roast beef hash and fried them in a skillet while Marley went through her texts and, of all things, her voice mail. "Weathers is fine," she announced.

Then she started making outgoing calls. First, she called Frederika, her lawyer, giving explicit instructions to contact the police and arrange a time to meet with them about the home invasion and arson. Then she called to arrange a new car. Then she called two friends who'd left worried messages —leaving voice mails, of all things—letting them know she hadn't been home when the fire started and would they please let others know? That she had to meet with the police later made an excellent excuse. After that she made a call to her financial advisor, letting him know about the fire. He immediately got to work on the insurance and her alternate living arrangements. She hung up when Albert placed a gigantic plate of hash in front of her.

"One of the messages was from Jenny's parents," Marley said. "They're in town, from China."

Albert set forks on the table, hoping his aunt wouldn't make him learn to fold linen napkins into crowns. "That was fast. She was just arrested yesterday."

"I don't think they're here for that. They called because she didn't pick them up at the airport and no one is at her apartment. They're looking for her and worried."

Albert remembered Jenny's laugh. He barely knew the girl and he liked her. "Are you going to meet with them?"

"Oh, God," Marley said. "We have so much to do today and we're already getting a late start. And what can I do? Tell them to call the police? If they're resourceful at all, they'll have already done that in the..." She glanced at her phone. "Thirteen hours since they left that message. I'm just going to assume they've already helped themselves as much as I could have. And truly, how would they prefer I spend my time, holding their hands or exonerating their daughter?"

Albert was startled to hear his aunt brush off someone else's concerns in such a brusque manner. It seemed quite unlike her. In fact, he'd seen so much magic the day before that he half-suspected the change in her personality had come from some sort of spell. "But... if they're Jenny's family... I mean, I don't really know her that well, but she seemed cool. Should we—"

The look Marley gave him was frank and pitiless. "Albert, I know you were struck by her—who wouldn't be?—but assuming we can figure a way to have Jenny released from prison, she'll be leaving shortly to go to school on the other side of the country. So any interest you might have in her beyond the platonic is wasted energy."

Albert was surprised by how much that stung, although he didn't yet have the self-awareness to understand why. "I see your point," he said without much enthusiasm.

"But you'll ignore my point anyway, correct? Never mind. I know what young men are like. Here." She took out her phone and tapped the display a couple of times. "Do you want to see?" Marley handed the phone to him. There was a video already loaded. He pressed play and watched his aunt's house burn for a minute and a half. Every window had flames roaring out of them.

"That feels weird to watch," he said. "And awful. I'm sorry your home burned down. That's..."

"I know." Marley stirred her hash with her fork. "We're getting a late start," she said, "but we needed the sleep. And we'll have to get you a change of clothes."

Albert's fork stopped halfway to his mouth. "All my clothes are burned up. And my books. And my X-Box. Jesus, I lost all my progress on all my games."

"Well, I can't replace your high scores, but I can certainly get you a suit. That will be our first stop, of course. Then we'll see about Aloysius."

Once their meal was finished, they cleaned and dried the dishes, then put everything back into the cabinet. There was a knock at the door. Albert opened it to reveal a tall, slender, elegant black woman. "Oh! Hello," he said.

A Key, an Egg, an Unfortunate Remark

She was as gorgeous as the vampires, and he found it difficult not to stare.

Marley rushed forward to embrace her. "Hello, Ubeh. Have you brought the car I requested?"

Ubeh's French accent startled poor Albert, making his pink skin flush. "Good morning, Ms. Jacobs! I do. Here are the keys." Ubeh offered them to Albert. "For you, I presume."

"Thank you," he said as he took them. "It's nice to drive a different car every day."

"Albert." Marley looked displeased. "If they know my house they know my car. We're switching for your safety as well as mine."

"I was joking!" Albert said. He turned to Ubeh. "I tell jokes."

Ubeh didn't seem impressed or amused. "I brought you a Volvo this time, Ms. Jacobs. It is nondescript but comfortable and it doesn't have the awful sight-line problems of so many Japanese models."

"Thank you, dear."

"And I'm so sorry to hear about your house last night. Is there anything else I can do?"

"Not at the moment, but thank you. It's time we were off."

Their first stop was a trip to Nordstrom for new clothes. Albert had spent the previous day in his interview suit—in fact, those were the only clothes he had left. But while he would have liked to buy a stack of faded jeans and long sleeve pullovers, his aunt picked out five black button-down shirts, two black vests, and five black suit pants. Work clothes for a man in mourning. He also picked up a pair of pajamas, new underwear and socks, and two pairs of faded jeans. The bill was higher than he would have liked, but his aunt ordered him not to fuss and assured him that her insurance plan with the ruinous premiums would cover all of it.

He expected the next stop to be the police station, but Marley wanted to visit a funeral home first.

The director was a serene, soft-spoken young woman who insisted that the body was not ready for viewing yet, but Marley persisted. She asked Albert to wait at the far end of the room and examined Aloysius's body with a monocle she took from her pocket.

Finished, she sighed, thanked the director, and led Albert out to the street.

"It's really him," she said. Albert was startled to think there had been a chance that it wasn't. Then Marley said it was time to stop by Aloysius's office.

"Is it safe for us to be out on the streets?" Albert asked. He'd spent the entire morning on edge, expecting a pair of painting vans to cut them off on the road. It was one thing to keep a watchful eye, but that was no guarantee of safety. "Whoever tried to kill you last night might—" He'd intended to say: ...might be expecting you to appear at certain places, but Marley interrupted him.

"I can't just cower at home, can I? Besides, now that we know for sure that Aloysius was indeed killed and that it wasn't a vampire, we don't have any choice but to start digging into his life."

If Albert couldn't get her to stay home, he hoped to convince her to go someplace relatively safe. "Aren't the police waiting for us?" Albert said.

"We have an appointment, dear, and we'll be going with my attorney. We're victims, not suspects, and we don't know anything anyway, do we?"

"Well, I certainly don't," Albert said, and that was that.

CHAPTER TWELVE
Betwixt the Saddle and the Ground

Aloysius's office was on the third floor of a squat brick office building in Belltown, just a block and a half from the Pacific Science Center. The lobby directory listed them as SPG Attorneys at Law, but the door to their offices had Shankley, Pierce, & Grabbleton painted on the front.

Albert let Marley into the waiting room. The phone at the receptionist's desk was ringing, but the receptionist herself ignored it. She stared into space, her watery, red-rimmed eyes vacant.

"Hello, dear."

Marley's voice seemed to awaken her. She held up an index finger, then pressed a button on her phone. "SPG Associates," she said into her headset. "One moment please." She pressed another button, then turned to Marley. "Can I help you?" she asked, punctuating the question with a wet sniff.

"My name is Marley Jacobs. I am... well, I was Aloysius Pierce's aunt."

"Oooo!" the receptionist exclaimed. Her arms shot out and she leaped out of her chair. The coiled phone cord reached its limit and snapped her headset off her head, yanking it under the desk. Arms still upraised, she bustled around the desk, her clunky shoes making her stutterstep, then embraced Marley. "Ooo ooo ooo! I'msosorryisn'tthisawful?"

Marley gave Albert a startled look. "Er, yes indeed," she said, patting the woman's back. "Just terrible. May I see his office?"

"I'm afraid not," a new voice said. All three of them turned to a bronzed woman standing by an open office door. She was in her mid-forties, but her hair had gone prematurely silver, giving her the look of an older woman. She wore a gray pantsuit and had the toned muscles of someone with the money and time for a gym membership. "The police have asked everyone to stay out of that room until they've had a chance to go through it."

Albert surprised himself by saying: "But it's already been a day and a half! Maybe you should send them a Facebook invite, so they're absolutely sure that they're welcome."

"They're busy with other things," the woman said. She gave Albert a stoic, measuring stare that he was too inexperienced to recognize as casual interest. "Plus, I don't think they're worried about finding new suspects; they're so happy with their current one."

"Too happy, I should think," Marley said. "Can you spare me a little time? I'd like to ask a few questions about Aloysius."

She sighed and looked at her watch. "Why not? Billable hours are overrated." She stepped into her office, revealing the name Shankley on the door. Marley and Albert followed.

It was nicely furnished, but not large. The leather chairs were a little worn and the oak desk slightly scuffed but everything was tidily arranged. "Are you going to be Al's Miss Marple?"

Marley smiled. "Oh, I shouldn't think so. I don't have her brain, Ms. Shankley."

"Call me Inez." She gestured toward the chairs. Marley and Albert sat while Inez went behind her desk.

"That's an unusual name for someone so young," Marley said.

Inez tilted her head and offered a crooked smile. "Funny how names get that association, isn't it? I can't wait for 2070, when everyone thinks of 'Hunter,' 'Tyler,' and 'Dakota' as old people's names. Anyway, I was named after a family member who did something important many years ago, although I'm sure I don't remember what it was. It does make it difficult to bring in new clients, though."

"I'm sure. Please call me Marley, and the first thing I need to ask you is if I can have access to Aloysius's computer files. I brought a travel drive with me. I'd like to look through his currently active cases—"

"I'm sorry," Inez answered. "Truly. But I can't do that. The police asked us not to share the information and Al's clients deserve confidentiality."

"I am an attorney myself."

"And I suspect you're working for his accused murderer. She was your employee?" Marley nodded, surprised to be facing someone who knew so much. "The police will get around to requesting all this material, and her defense team—whether that's you or not—can get it from them. Sorry."

"Well," Marley said, "I can't say I'm not disappointed, but this isn't unexpected, either." She opened her purse and fished around inside of it. "What was your relationship to Aloysius?"

"Actually, can I jump in here with a question? Why do you use his full name? I'm pretty sure he hated it. Around here we called him 'Al.' But... did you have something against him?"

"My name is Albert," Albert said helpfully. "I was his brother. I have other brothers named Alan and Alsace, sisters named Alia, Alice and Allyson, and so on."

Inez was startled to discover that Aloysius had any family at all, let alone a large one. "Really? You add 'and so on' to the end of that? Well."

Albert shrugged. Marley took a glass vial from her purse and pulled the stopper out of it. "What does this smell like to you?"

Inez accepted it and took a whiff. "Cinnamon." She handed it back. "There's a certain resemblance," she said, examining Albert with that same stoic expression. "Not in attitude, but in your color and around the eyes."

"Yes," Marley said. "My sister certainly leaves her mark. What was your relationship with Aloysius?" Marley handed the travel drive to Inez.

Inez spun in her chair and plugged the drive into her desktop computer. "Our relationship was professional and sexual. Oh, don't make that face, Albert. I don't mean that he paid me for sex. We shared an office lease, a computer network, and a barely competent receptionist, and we consulted with each other occasionally—well, he sometimes asked my advice. It never went the other way unless I wanted to flatter him a little. We didn't share clients. That was the extent of our professional relationship." She began copying files onto the travel drive. "Outside the office, our relationship was sexual, not romantic or personal. Oh, hi, Stan. Did you finish with Mr. Nguyen already?"

Marley and Albert turned to see Stan in the doorway. He was a fat man with a graying crewcut. His flushed red face suggested he was ill in some way and his grey herringbone suit coat was slightly frayed at the cuffs. He strolled into the crowded office with the shoulders-back posture of a man with a lot of belly to counter-balance. "Yes, he's gone." His voice had a simpering quality that made everything he say slightly theatrical. "What is this you're saying about Al?"

"That he and I were lovers, off and on, for years."

Stan huffed. "That's ridic— Really?"

"Yes, Stan. Sorry to keep it a secret from you, but Al insisted."

"You can't be seriou— You are, aren't you? You and him? Oh, God, that explains so much." He covered his face with his hand and walked out of the room.

Inez looked after him, bemused. "He'll spend half the afternoon trying to decide if he has the right to be angry, then tomorrow everything will be normal again. Back to Al... Aloysius: I hope you don't think me callous, but he wasn't particularly important to me. I am not in a place in my life right now where I want a romantic entanglement, but I am a physical person. Al was discreet, capable, not too creepy, and he followed the rules."

"What were the rules?" Marley asked.

"I instigate our liaisons, not him. He went elsewhere if he was feeling anxious. No dating or other romance. We met only at my place and he wasn't allowed to spend the night. And finally, we weren't finished until I was finished. You'd be surprised how hard it can be to find a man willing to live up to that last rule."

"No, I wouldn't," Marley said. "When was the last time you were together?"

"Three nights ago, the night before he was killed. Although I should call it evening because he was out by nine PM. One more thing: we were under a... well, I'd call it a 'trial separation' if we were together in any meaningful sense. He sent me an email on the morning he was killed, explaining that he needed to put our liaisons on hold for a while."

"An email? The two of you share an office. He couldn't have spoken to you personally?"

Marley's sympathetic outrage didn't have its intended effect on Inez, who merely shrugged. "We handled all our sexual arrangements through emails and texts. Besides, I received the message at home; it was Sunday morning, after all. I didn't object to his request and he knew I wouldn't. Ah, here you are."

The files had finished copying onto Marley's drive.

"You know why I'm telling you this, I hope?" Inez asked.

"Because you don't want it to look as though you have something to hide."

"Exactly. And I don't. I used to be ashamed of the way I felt about this sort of thing—my boredom with dating and the trappings of romance, my preference for solitude, my love of quiet. I used to think that made me abnormal—and my friends would not stop pushing me into blind dates, of all things. Then one day I suffered a cramp while I was swimming in Lake Washington and barely made it to dry land. I don't know if either of you has ever had a close brush with death..." Marley and Albert nodded mildly, encouraging her to continue. "It puts things in perspective. Suddenly, I decided not to feel like that any more. I'm a free adult. I'm not hurting anyone, and anyone who objects to my private life doesn't deserve to be part of it."

Inez ejected the drive and handed it to Marley. "Did he have a password?" Marley asked.

"Of course!" Inez scribbled something on a post-it and passed it to Marley. "Start with the spreadsheet file in the root directory. Active cases have an 'O' for 'Open' in the appropriate column. It's all pretty obvious."

"Thank you." Marley dropped everything in to her purse. "Has anything strange happened in the last few weeks? Threatening calls or arguments in the office? Did Aloysius's manner seem unusual?"

"Well, yes, to that last one. Stan had been down in California taking depositions last week. The Sunday Al was killed was Stan's first day back in the office and they had some sort of argument. Sherilynne might know what it was about; I was at home."

"What sort of argument? A serious one?"

"They always sound serious, but they never are, if you know what I mean. Oh, and before you get the idea that Stan might be the killer, it's pretty much impossible. He gets easily winded and has tremendous difficulty lifting his hands above his shoulders. It's some sort of ailment he has, but I'm sure I don't know what it is."

"What about Aloysius's friends? Did he have any arguments with them that he told you about?"

"Well..." Inez glanced back and forth between Marley and Albert, wondering for the first time if they knew Aloysius at all. "I don't want to speak badly of your nephew so soon after he died…"

"But…" Marley prompted.

"Okay. As near as I could tell, Aloysius didn't have any friends." Inez shrugged uncomfortably. "I spoke to him about it—teased him, really—but he had no interest in friends. I don't think he knew what to do with one. He liked money and sex, he liked being around new people sometimes, but I think he saw friendly companionship as a waste of time."

Marley sighed. "Thank you for answering all my questions, dear, but I really wish you would give me a copy of his computer files."

Inez turned her palms toward the ceiling. "I know, but I'm afraid it would be impossible."

"Ah, well. May we call on you again if I have any questions?"

"Of course. Please let me know when the service is going to be held."

They went into the outer office. The receptionist was staring at her computer screen with glazed eyes. Marley walked up to her and laid a gentle hand on her shoulder. A quick glance showed that she was reading up on eco-friendly funeral arrangements.

"Tell me, Sherilynne—it's Sherilynne, isn't it?"

"Yes. I'm so sorry—"

"Thank you, dear. Did my nephew seem different on that last day before he was killed?"

"Well, yes. I haven't had a chance to speak to the police about it yet, but he did. Do you think I should email the detective in charge to let him know?"

"That depends, dear. How did he seem different?"

"He was softer. He'd always been very alpha male," Sherilynne said, her weak eyes becoming dreamy at the thought. "Kinda unyielding and sharp toward other people. Very masculine. He always believed in himself, you know? But that day he seemed almost… guilt-ridden."

"That's not a word I expected to hear you use. What makes you say that?"

"Well, he called me into his office and told me he was going to try to find me a new job somewhere else. He said I deserved better."

"Did he say he wanted to bring your relationship into the open?"

Sherilynne glanced at Albert and lowered her voice. "He told you about us?"

"No, dear, but it's plain for anyone to see. Did he promise to start seeing you openly?"

"Well, he didn't come right out and say that, but I think so," Sherilynne said, sharing for the first time one of the many lies she told herself. "It was no good for us to be sneaking around and I'm positive that's why he was going to help me find work somewhere else. For propriety."

"When did you see him last?"

"When he left the office for the day." She gasped and her hand flew to her mouth. "Do you think I was the last to see him alive?"

"Only if you were the one who killed him. Is Mr. Grabbleton still in?"

Sherilynne's phone rang, but she ignored it. "No, he had to run out."

"What about the argument that morning?"

"They argued all the time. It was part of Al's personality; even though Stan is a really nice guy and super smart, Al had an alpha's instinct to control and dominate beta males. So they weren't exactly friends. You know."

"I understand, dear, but I'm curious what exactly they were arguing about that morning."

"Stan was angry about something being missing from his office. They argued about that all the time, and it was really unfair of Stan to blame Al every time he lost his umbrella or whatever. Anyway, the odd thing was that Al actually apologized. I mean, I was as surprised as anyone could be, but it happened right in front of my eyes! Al just said 'I'm sorry, Stan, I'll make things right' or whatever. It was exactly what I'd been suggesting he do, so it was, wow, shocker."

"Where did Stan go? I'd like to talk to him."

"I don't know, I'm sorry. I can only take messages for him and ask him to get back to you." She had to raise her voice to be heard over the ringing phone. "I can forward an appointment request, if you like."

"Please do, dear, and thank you. We need to move along, now."

Albert opened the office door and they stepped through it. Sherilynne called out to them over the ringing phone: "Let me know if you need help with the arrangements! I'm very good at that sort of thing!"

Albert pressed the elevator button to head down. "Aloysius really had a lot of women going, didn't he?"

"Apparently so, even if he did seem to be breaking things off with them. And yet, he was still mooning over Jenny."

"Probably because she didn't want him. Some guys fixate on things they can't have and don't show any respect for the things they do have."

"They're not things, dear. They're women."

Albert flushed. "Er, sorry. I didn't mean anything by it."

"I know it's a common turn of phrase, but personally I find it distasteful. Still, your insight is probably correct." The elevator doors opened. Marley and Albert got on and rode down to the lobby. "I wish I knew where Stan Grabbleton went. I'd like to speak with him, too."

"So what's next?"

"That's a good question. We have some time before we speak to the police and there's still a great deal of work to be done; this is still the early stages of the investigation."

"We don't even know who did it yet."

Albert meant it as a joke, but his aunt said: "Exactly! We need to keep turning over rocks, as they say. I'd like to search Aloysius's house. I'd like to go over his files. And I'd like to speak with Stan Grabbleton."

"Speaking of which... as an employee of yours, maybe it's not my place to ask, but what you did upstairs—with the vial you asked Inez Shankley to smell and the computer files—that was magic, right? Another magic spell?"

"Barely. Like most of what I do, it's mostly trickery."

"Trickery?"

"I tricked her into giving us those files."

Albert couldn't help feel disappointed. "When you put it that way, it's way less appealing."

Marley laid her hand on Albert's arm and made him bend low so she could kiss his cheek. "I've been grumpy with you all morning, haven't I? Come on. Let's break into your brother's house and I'll explain why."

CHAPTER THIRTEEN
A Thorough Search of Feelings and Domiciles

Albert took to the collection of clues eagerly. Inez, he was sure, was their most likely suspect. Yes, she'd played it cool, but what if it was an act? Also, Albert suspected Stan and Aloysius were involved in some sort of swindle. Why else would they argue all the time? Because it certainly didn't have anything to do with alpha males. Albert had known his brother fairly well, and there was nothing "alpha" about him.

"Different people see different things," Marley told him. "Quite a few of them see exactly what they want to see."

"That makes sense," Albert said, wondering if Marley's remark was also some kind of lesson in magic. "Still, even if they're not super-successful, they're still lawyers. If Stan wanted Aloysius dead, he wouldn't have to raise his arms over his shoulder. He'd only have to reach as high as his wallet. And if Aloysius apologized sincerely, it might have been too late. The hitman might have already been hired."

"Or it was Sherilynne," Marley offered.

Albert suspected she was joking, but he answered seriously. "She should be a suspect, too. He was giving her the brush-off, and she might have found out about Inez."

"And Jenny."

"And Jenny," Albert said, feeling more judgmental about it than he had a right to. And he knew he didn't have the right, and shook the feeling off. "And who knows how many others. She acted like she didn't understand that he was giving her the boot, but maybe she did. Why do you think he apologized to Stan?"

Marley looked out the window, seeing the city zip by without paying much attention. "Maybe he wanted to play a new role."

Aloysius's house was nestled on a tree-lined street on the southeastern side of Queen Anne Hill. It wasn't a new house, but the swing on the front porch and pale blue drapes in the windows gave it a comfortable air. Albert pulled in to the empty parking slot, then double-checked the address. He'd expected to find something tacky, like plastic flamingoes in the front yard.

"I wonder where his car is." Marley said.

Albert let her out of the backseat and they went onto the front porch together. Albert looked all around them; if there was anyplace the gunmen from last night might lie in wait for them, it was here. He didn't see anything suspicious and could only hope it was because there wasn't anything so see. "I hope he gave you a key, Aunt Marley, because he sure didn't give one to me."

Marley shrugged. "I never asked for one. Hmm." Marley went to the swing and ran her hand along the wooden slats. Finding nothing, she did the same along the back. "Ah!" She pulled a key out of a key holder.

"He kept a key on his front porch?"

"And in the first place we looked, too." Marley gave the key to Albert, and they went inside.

The house was simply furnished, with IKEA chairs and tables placed in vague clusters, as though Aloysius knew they were supposed to go together but didn't understand why. None of the colors complemented each other and the walls were cracked and peeling like student rental housing.

Albert typically felt a thrill when he found a reason to look down on his older brother, but this was just depressing. "This place is like a 'before' picture on one of those house-flipping shows. Was he underwater on his mortgage?"

"He never asked me for money, and I suspect he would have."

Albert looked around, trying to dredge up a charitable feeling. It wasn't easy. "What are we looking for? Suitcases full of drugs? Pickled human limbs? Boy band posters?"

"I have no idea. I never was much good at the investigative side of things. But I did learn one thing the hard way: put these on before you touch anything else." Marley gave him a pair of latex gloves.

They went through the house together. Nothing seemed to be disturbed. If the place had been searched already, it had been done carefully and neatly. They didn't find anything unusual in the downstairs except a cabinet full of Cookie Crisp cereal. The refrigerator had nothing in it but leftover take out cashew chicken and a carton of milk. The only cooking utensil in the whole kitchen was a quart-size Pyrex gravy separator.

Marley led the way upstairs. All the doors stood open. Feeling clever, Albert went to check the bathroom medicine cabinet while Marley went into the front bedroom.

"Well!" she said quite loudly. "This isn't good!"

Albert ran to her, thrilled at the prospect of a fresh clue, but what he discovered confounded him. Aloysius's narrow, iron-framed bed was set in the exact center of the room and an elaborately designed circle had been painted onto the floor around it. There was even a pentacle with a number of runes and glyphs written inside and outside it. Marley bent low to examine it closely.

"Oh..." Albert was momentarily at a loss for words. He was glad they had another clue, but a bit crestfallen that he didn't know how to decipher it. "This is magic, right? Was he summoning something into his bed? Is this why all those women..."

"No, dear," Marley said, distracted. "I doubt he would bring women here. This is a circle of protection."

"Can you tell what it's supposed to protect against?"

"Judging by these marks, everything."

She moved to the window and began searching along the jamb. Albert moved close to her. "This is what you do, right? Magic? Did he learn it from you?"

"Certainly not!" Marley took offense at the idea that she would teach anything to a person like Aloysius. "And this is absolutely not what I do. This is a very basic, very crude sort of craft. Crude, blunt and obvious. Ah, here it is." Up near the top of the window, where the drapes were heaviest, was another circle—this one about the size of a poker chip—with a glyph inside. "Albert, dear, check every..."

Marley's voice trailed off as she slowly turned around. For a moment, Albert thought she'd heard voices downstairs. He had a sudden vision of himself being fingerprinted and photographed like the criminals he'd seen on television. Then she gestured toward the closet. "Open that, please."

Albert shrugged and crossed the room, moving as quietly as he could. He wasn't sure why he was sneaking up on a closet door, but something in his aunt's manner suggested it. He grabbed the handle in his good left hand and yanked it open.

The closet was full of a great many of the usual things—shirts and sport coats hanging on the rod, a tie rack, nice black leather shoes, not-so-nice black fabric luggage—and one unusual thing: a woman.

She was in her mid-thirties, pale-skinned, with a weak chin, a mass of curly black hair, and thick spectacles. She stared wide-eyed up at Albert, terrified.

To his embarrassment, Albert's first thought was a clue! The curly-haired woman was obviously terrified, and he foolishly thought a joke would put her at ease. "Well well," he said. "I've freed a hostage."

She thrust a pudgy hand at him, fingers splayed, and there was a flash of light and a crack of electricity. Albert felt heat blossom against his chest just as a tremendous force lifted him off his feet and flung him back onto his half-brother's bed.

"I want to talk to her, Albert!" Marley said imperiously.

The woman had already staggered to the door, and his aunt made no move to intercept her, so Albert forced himself to stand. His muscles were stiff, but he didn't seem to have any third-degree burns. He lumbered into the hallway like Frankenstein's monster.

The woman had reached the top of the stairs, where she clung to a post as though it was the only thing keeping her upright. Whatever she'd done, it had taken a toll on her, too.

She spotted him and stumbled down the stairs, her thin sandals clop-clop-clopping. Albert lunged forward, feeling his strength and agility returning quickly.

He vaulted over the railing onto the bottom step. The curly-haired woman stumbled on the landing and backed away, looking trapped. She lifted her hand again.

"Be cool!" Albert said. "We're not going to hurt you, so just be cool!"

"Zoe!" Marley called. "Dear, you left your rather large purse in the closet." She appeared the top of the stairs with a shapeless plaid cloth handbag in her hands. "Why don't we talk downstairs? Would that be all right?"

Zoe looked at Albert, then at the bag in Marley's hands, then at Albert again, trying to decide what risks would be worth taking.

"Hey," Albert said. "Let's just talk." He stepped backward into the living room, opening a path for her.

Zoe sighed and slumped down the stairs. Marley followed. Within moments, the three of them were perched on pressboard chairs, watching each other with evident discomfort. Albert checked the front of his shirt and was glad to see there were no visible burns. Marley seemed lost in thought. Zoe took a lanyard from her pocket and hung it around her neck. Screwed onto the end was a wooden disk with a pentacle carved into it. When she looked at them again, with her pinched face and squinting eyes, she looked like a mole newly emerged from her burrow.

"So—" Marley began.

"I don't have to tell you a thing, you old bag!" Zoe said savagely. "And if either of you tries to do anything to me, I'll tear off your balls!"

Whatever advantage she'd hoped her aggressive posture to earn never materialized. Albert looked as though he wanted to reassure her somehow, and Marley was as placid as a statue.

"Dear, do you know who I am?"

Zoe didn't seem to want to answer that question, but she couldn't resist. "Yes," she blurted out. Tears began to run down her cheeks.

"Why were you hiding in my nephew's closet?"

"It's not fair," Zoe whined. "Aly cost me everything. I lost my job, my apartment, my plan for the future.... I was going to be rich! Now I can't even find a friend who'll put me up, because he cost me all of those, too. I just came here for..."

"For what, dear?"

"Something that belongs to me."

Marley asked, "What is it?" But Zoe wouldn't elaborate. She just sat there with tears streaming down her cheeks. "Albert, get Zoe a glass of water, would you?"

Albert lunged out of his chair, went into the kitchen and returned with a tall glass of water. He'd even put ice in it. When he returned, Marley was still trying to get Zoe to explain why she was in the house. The young woman wrapped her arms around her shoulders and stared down at her dirty feet. She wouldn't even accept the glass.

"Here," Albert said, his voice soothing. "Drink it. It'll make you feel better."

Zoe took the glass and threw it, smashing it against the fireplace hearth.

"Well," Albert said, "we know she didn't break in because she was thirsty."

"I'm not stealing anything," Zoe snapped, aggravated because no one was as upset as she thought they should be.

"Of course not," Marley said, while Albert returned to his seat beside her. "You're only here to pick up something that belongs to you. Right?"

"Yes!"

"Something you left here?"

Zoe laughed bitterly. "Something Aly took. God, he was the worst boyfriend ever! And I should know, I've had some real winners. I just want what's mine, and then I'll go. Just let me look for it alone."

"Dear—"

"Don't try to threaten me!" Zoe's resentment had turned nasty again. "You're not supposed to be here either, so if you get me arrested you'll get yourself arrested, too!"

"He was my only brother," Albert lied. Any qualms he might have had about being unkind to her had shattered with that glass. "And he didn't have any kids. This house and everything in it is mine now."

"Then why are you wearing those gloves?" she asked with childish triumph.

"As a courtesy to the police!" Albert answered. "So no, I'm not trespassing and no, I'm not letting you rummage through my late brother's things unsupervised."

"But it's mine!" Zoe whined.

"What's yours?" Marley asked. "Tell us."

Zoe sighed again. She looked around the room as though taking one last opportunity to find what she needed. "A book. A leather-bound journal. It's the only valuable thing I own, and Aly slept with me just so he could take it. But he said I could have it back! He called me to apologize and he said he'd arrange a time to return it at the end of the week."

"When did he call you, dear?"

"Sunday afternoon."

Marley and Albert glanced at each other in recognition—Sunday had been a big day for poor Aloysius—but Zoe was sure that glance was really about her. She was sure they knew all about her book.

With a shrug, Marley said: "We haven't found anything like that here, but if we do—"

Absolutely certain they were lying to her, Zoe grabbed the carved wooden disk at the end of her lanyard, holding the rim in her thumb and forefinger as though making an "OK" gesture. She made a fist with her other hand, pressed it against her temple, and grimaced in furious concentration.

"Surrender to my will! Surrender to my will! Surrender surrender surrender —"

There was a hiss that sounded like rain on red hot metal and the wooden disk began to glow. Out of habit, Albert reached for a weapon he no longer carried, and his whole body shuddered in anticipation of something even worse than the shock he'd received upstairs. Maybe if he ripped the lanyard from her neck...

Marley leaned forward and blew on Zoe as though she were a birthday candle. The glow and the hiss both dissipated, leaving Zoe looking shocked and frightened.

"Zoe." Marley's voice wasn't sharp, wasn't angry, wasn't anything, really, but it captured the other woman's attention. "You should know better than to try that sort of thing with me."

Zoe let her fists fall into her lap. "I knew it!" she screamed, venting her helpless rage. Then she stood and stomped out the front door.

Marley went to the front window and watched her make her way down the front steps. There was another symbol carved on the top of the window sill. "Albert, please check every window in the house for a mark like this one. Make note of which ones don't have it, if any. And be thorough; this is important."

Albert opened his mouth as though he wanted to talk over the encounter they'd just had, but wisely went to work instead. Marley returned to the bedroom and sat in a chair in a corner, staring at the bed and the circle beneath it, carefully thinking about nothing at all.

Then, after a long while, she noticed something odd. She moved toward the foot of the bed and got down on her knees to run her fingertips over one of the marks. The floor board beneath it wobbled. Marley pried up a tiny section of floor no larger than a credit card.

"What have you found?" Albert asked as he returned to the room.

"I noticed that one of the symbols was different from the others," Marley said. "The others are protective marks, but this one is for secrecy. And what was it hiding?" From the hole in the floor, she pulled a key ring jangling

94

with at least a dozen keys.

"Now we can access the Gym Locker... of Doom!"

"Wouldn't that simplify things! Of course we'll have to try every lock in this house first. We'll also check his office when we get a chance. What did you find?"

"Every window has a mark," Albert said, "even the ones in the basement. Every door, too. They're just below the top hinge, where the door lies flush against the jam."

"Thank you, dear."

"Does this mean something was after him?"

"I'm not sure, dear. These marks aren't fresh. Look at the way the paint is wearing away right there. The marks still retain their potency, but he made them at least a year ago. They'll need refreshing soon. But he was worried about someone who could do magic."

"Is that why Zoe's whammy-jammy didn't do anything to us?"

"Partly. It's perfectly possible the marks were there to protect him from her. In fact, it seems like the most likely explanation. For now."

"So he was in danger from magic, but it wasn't new."

"And he didn't tell me about it. I must tell you, Albert, this whole affair is annoying me to no end. Scribe gave me warning about your brother's death —"

"— Half-brother."

"Half, excuse me—if only I'd had the wit to check it. And now I discover that he's erected supernatural protections without my knowledge. It's not just my city we're talking about, it's my family, too. How can I defend against a danger I don't know about? And I like to think I would have known, if..."

She didn't want to finish that sentence, so Albert did it for her. "If he hadn't been such a creep." Marley didn't respond. "I know. Is it wrong to stand in the guy's house after his death and talk about what a jerk he was? Because so what? I didn't like him and he knew it. I'm sure he knew you didn't like him, either. I'm pretty sure he thought of himself as a great guy, and anyone who disagreed could..." Albert paused and considered his audience. "… could get lost. Truth is, I don't think that sort of thing mattered to him. He was always good at getting what he wanted from people and he never gave away more than he had to. Just like Mother."

"You're right, dear. Of course you're right."

"But it sure sounds like he had a come-to-Jesus moment just before he died, doesn't it?"

Marley went to the window and looked out. For this next part of the conversation, she didn't want to see Albert's face. "That might have been my doing. He came to me late Saturday, the night before he died—straight from Inez's bed, it seems. I told him what I thought about him and he seemed a little startled. Most of us like to think of ourselves as essentially good—even when deep down we know we're not—and Aloysius must have thought he was fooling the people around him as thoroughly as he was fooling himself. I was harsh with him and caught him off guard, as I meant to. He must have done a little self-examination and resolved to be a better person."

Albert was puzzled by her tone. "That can't be a bad thing, can it?"

"It is if it got him killed, dear."

They searched the house a while longer, but all they found was a small safe in the upstairs office. It had dust on the dial. Albert searched the desk more carefully, finding a slip of paper taped to the bottom of a drawer. The numbers on the slip proved to be the combination. Albert found only one thing inside: a leather-bound journal with a handful of magical symbols and instructions written in a cramped, careful hand. "Here it is," he said. "Zoe's book."

Marley snatched it from him and shut it.

"Aunt Marley, I'm guessing we're not going to be returning that book to her."

"Oh my goodness, no. Not with that personality. I think that's all, Albert. Best we go." She closed the safe and turned the dial so the dusty side was up.

Albert led her to the front door and let her out. She slid the key back into the key holder. Albert scanned the surrounding cars and houses, but there was no sign of danger.

"We learned something here, right?" Albert asked once they were back in the car. "I'd like to think we're making a little progress as we go from place to place. What's next on the list?"

"You have questions for me, don't you?"

"I do, but I'd rather be driving somewhere specific while I ask them."

"Then let's go back to the burned house. I want to look at the ruins before I speak with the police about it."

Albert started the car and pulled into the road. "What exactly was that circle in Aloysius's room supposed to protect him from?"

CHAPTER FOURTEEN
Explanations, Both Official and Not

Despite herself, Marley was pleased. Albert had shown admirable restraint in waiting this long to broach this subject, and he'd started with a specific question. For the first time in many years, she found herself happy to have this conversation.

"Aloysius's circle was there to protect him from things that aren't real, dear, and things that don't believe they're real."

"So... nothing? It couldn't protect him from anything?"

"No, dear, from things that aren't real."

"But if something isn't real, it doesn't exist."

"That's not true. Some of the very best things in the world are not real."

"Like my winning lottery ticket and super-hot heiress girlfriend?"

Marley pretended she hadn't heard that entirely predictable response. "You can't put a piece of mercy into your pocket, can you? You can't hang a sheet of kindness on your wall. You can't really measure out an ounce of prevention. But despite the fact that they're not real, they have powerful effects on our lives."

"Okay, I guess. But the circle around his bed... would it really have protected him?"

"Well, yes. It was full of another unreal thing: magic."

"So, magic isn't real."

"No, it's not. And that makes it very powerful."

Albert rolled his eyes. "You're deliberately being confusing, aren't you?"

"I'm answering your questions, Albert."

He was about to make a joke about one hand clapping, but stopped himself. His aunt had said jokes sometimes reveal the truth, but he didn't want to risk annoying her. "You're saying I need better questions." He navigated traffic in silence for a moment, wishing he was smart enough to see the point his aunt was making. "Are those vampires real? Wait... That's not what I want to ask. Something about them is fake, but the effect it has on them is powerful. Am I getting this right?"

"Not fake, dear. Never fake. Simply not part of the real world. Vampirism is a curse, and like any curse, you'll never touch it or see it or measure it in any way. You'll only ever see its effects."

"What about the invisibility potion? And the vial of stuff you made Inez sniff?"

"I didn't make her. I asked her. But never mind that for the moment. I know certain tricks to create things that aren't real. A willingness to help, for one. A keen interest in someone's own shoelaces, for another. A false version of my own voice on the phone."

"And a false voice on the phone can relay important information, right?"

"Or offer comfort where it's needed."

"So magic is not real but it can do things. The circle around Aloysius's bed was a pretend barrier with real-world effects."

Marley was secretly pleased. "Yes, dear. The problem with Aloysius's circle, though, is that it tried to be as real as possible, and that made it very weak magic."

He didn't know how to respond to that. They reached a stop sign just around the corner from Marley's home. Albert looked into the rear view mirror. His aunt seemed very small and he thought about all the doors he opened for her. "Aunt Marley, do you have a curse on you?"

She smiled at him. "We are all cursed in one way or another, dear."

Albert could recognize the end of a conversation better than most. He drove through the intersection and went around the curving road until Marley's property was in view.

At some point during the day there must have been lookiloos on the sidewalk, but it was late enough that they'd moved on. Albert parked the Volvo at the curb and opened the door for Marley. Together they went up the front walk to the gate.

The air carried the sweetness of woodsmoke, spoiled by the sharp acrid scent of burned plastic. Albert coughed a little as the breeze turned the stink toward him.

The building had burned down to its foundations. Even the chimneys had collapsed. The sight of it made him suddenly angry, and he clenched his fists at his side.

Marley laid a hand on his. "Don't get worked up, dear. It'll be our turn soon. Let's get some lunch. That way our blood sugar will be nice and high when we speak to the police."

They turned toward their car and were startled to see a man and woman walking toward them. They were dressed in sky blue jackets over canary yellow shirts and pants. The woman appeared to be about forty, and the man about fifteen years older—their shoes and hair styles suggested they had money, but both looked ragged with worry.

"Excuse me," the woman said with a slight Arkansas accent. "Are you Marley Jacobs?"

Marley stepped forward and clasped her hands. "I am. You must be Jenny's parents."

"I am Wu Cheng-Lun," the woman said. "This is my husband, Wu Huan-Yu."

"A pleasure, I'm sure. I'm sorry I haven't returned your call before, but as you can see I've been a little busy."

Jenny's father stared past them at the burned building. "Our daughter did not meet us at the airport yesterday. None of her friends can tell us where she is. The party was supposed to be tonight—"

"I'm sorry," Marley interjected. "What was that? A party?"

Cheng-Lun answered, "My husband has turned sixty. We celebrated traditionally with our family back in Guiyang, but Jenny wanted to throw a birthday party for us here, with all of our old colleagues from the university."

"A party!" Marley said, her expression strangely blank. "With university people!" She turned to her nephew and clutched his arm. "Albert. Jenny was going to throw a party but I didn't know about it."

Albert took hold Marley's hand. "Aunt Marley," he said in as gentle a tone as he could, "one moment, okay?" He turned to Huan-Yu and Cheng-Lun. "I'm sorry no one met you. If we'd known you were coming, we would have arranged something."

Huan-Yu still hadn't looked away from the burned building. "We called all the hospitals..."

"Jenny hasn't been hurt," Albert said quickly. "She wasn't even here when this happened." He waved at the property behind him. "I'm surprised none of her friends told you, but, well, Jenny's been arrested. For murder."

Cheng-Lun gasped and covered her mouth in shock, and Huan-Yu actually staggered as he clutched at his wife's arm.

"I'm sorry!" Albert said, cursing himself for his bluntness. "There's probably a gentler way to give you that news, but... look, it's just a temporary thing. We know she didn't do it. It'll just take a while to clear up."

"A party, Albert," Marley said. Albert was astonished to realize his aunt had entered a strange fugue state. "A party!"

Albert bent low to speak quietly to her. "Um, Aunt Marley, this particular moment isn't about you. Hold on a minute, okay?"

"They can't do this!" Huan-Yu snapped. "Jenny is an American citizen. We come from China, but she was born here!"

"Sure," Albert said, correctly guessing that discussing the subject of Jenny's citizenship would be unproductive and awkward.

A Key, an Egg, an Unfortunate Remark

Cheng-Lun squeezed her husband's hand. "We have money for her defense."

Albert nodded. "My aunt has already... one moment." He turned to Marley. She was staring off down the street, her gaze fixed on something very far away. "Do you still have Detective Lonagan's card? Aunt Marley?"

He touched her elbow and she snapped back to reality. "Oh yes! Yes I do." She reached into her purse and pulled out the card.

Albert took it from her and gave it to Cheng-Lun. "This is the officer in charge of the case."

"Thank you very much," she said. "We must go."

"We'll do what we can to help," Albert said, but Jenny's parents glanced at Marley before they turned away. They were not impressed.

"Albert," Marley said urgently, tugging at the lapel of his jacket. "Albert, Albert, she betrayed me. Jenny betrayed me. A party, Albert! Full of university people! Do you know how interesting university people can be!"

"Aunt Marley—"

"Not just because they're experts in their fields, which is wonderful, but because they're also the pettiest, bitchiest, most vindictive back-stabbers in the world. I love university parties, Albert; they're so diverting!"

"Aunt Marley, I'm sure—"

There was no stopping Marley, not on this subject. "But Jenny organized a party and she didn't tell me. I invited her to every party I ever threw—and that's no small number—but she left me out! Why would she do that, Albert? Why?"

Marley looked up into Albert's eyes, and he realized, instinctively, that this was not a question he should answer. Not ever. "I have no idea," he lied. "Maybe we should talk to her about it after we get her out of jail. We are still going to get her out of jail, aren't we? And find Aloysius's real killer?"

Marley took a moment to think about that, then she sighed. "Yes. Of course, yes, we're going to do the right thing. Of course."

He offered her his arm. "Are you all right?"

She slipped her hand into the crook of his elbow. The honest concern in his voice helped her regain her composure. "It must seem perverse to you that I'm so upset about this, but losing my home was not one-tenth as painful as finding out that Jenny.... Those social engagements are important, Albert. Sometimes I think they're the only thing that keeps me going. But never mind. Of course we'll get Jenny out of prison, and of course I will do everything for her that I promised. Of course I will."

Albert let her into the back seat of the car and got behind the wheel. They drove in silence, while Albert tried to decide whether he should apologize for hiding in his room the previous Saturday night.

They had lunch at a little Italian restaurant near the local elementary school. Marley ran into some friends of hers, which meant Albert ate a plate of cheese ravioli at the counter while his aunt and her friends chatted and laughed over inconsequential things. It was a mini-party all on its own. Just as the bill was coming, an elderly couple wandered into the restaurant and asked Marley about the fire.

That was the end of the fun. Marley's lunch companions were shocked, but Marley assured them that everything was fine, no one was hurt and she didn't need any help. She lingered just long enough to put them at ease, then stood to leave. Albert took his cue and led the way to the car.

"Ah, well," Marley said once they were safely in the car. She was almost back to her old self. "It was fun while it lasted."

The visit to the police station was shorter but more contentious than before. Frederika was already there. Marley insisted that it was "unnecessary to the point of silliness" to have a lawyer present for this, but Frederika refused to leave. Albert strongly suspected they were putting on a little show for the detectives, mainly because his aunt gave in. Of course he was right.

There were different detectives this time, and the questions were pointed but polite. Marley explained that the men had broken in, that she and Albert had escaped from the house, and that they'd only found out the next day that it had been burned down. No one had been hurt and she didn't know if anything had been stolen. She didn't keep much money in the house, although she did have art and books worth thousands of dollars. Yes, it was all insured and the insurer will fax over a list. No, she didn't have financial issues, quite the opposite, here's the business card for the firm that handles her investments and such.

What she didn't have was a list of enemies to give them. Frederika was outraged at the suggestion that the home invasion and arson was somehow Marley's fault, or that she might have done something to deserve all this.

That derailed the conversation for several minutes as detectives insisted these were routine questions and they had to be asked. Marley assured them she understood completely and to just go right ahead with whatever they wanted to ask. She was sure she'd heard worse in her time.

Next they began to ask questions about Aloysius: Had he asked Marley for money? Had he seemed nervous or distracted lately? Had he brought new people to the house?

Frederika became increasingly aggravated, pointing out that Marley had already gone through all of this only the day before. She wanted to know if the police ever shared notes, and why did they have to cover this ground yet again, and what exactly was Marley being accused of?

At that point, the detectives decided they had what they needed and would call if they had additional questions. Frederika made it clear they should contact Ms. Jacobs only through her.

The outgoing chief of police was waiting in the hall. He thought all this was terrible, terrible, and his department was going to do their best to get to the bottom of it. Marley thanked him by his first name—they knew each other well—but Albert had the distinct impression she wanted to escape. Before he could think of a way to help her slip away from all these cops, the mayor arrived.

Twenty minutes later, while Frederika lead Albert and Marley through the SeaPark building, Marley said: "That's the downside of helping other people: they want to help you in return."

"Marley," Frederika said, her voice slightly too loud and far too pushy. "Do me a favor, please? Do not speak with any government officials at all unless I'm present. Just don't. You have my number, you contact me any time one of these bastards calls or knocks on your door. I don't care if they're your best friends or blood relatives, I want to be there to keep them honest. Okay?"

"It's okay, dear. I promise."

Slightly mollified, Frederika harrumphed, climbed into her car and pulled away. Albert waited until she was out of earshot to say "She's... um..."

"Good to have in your corner," Marley finished diplomatically.

"That's just what I was going to say." They crossed the parking lot to the Volvo.

Marley stopped ten feet from the car. Albert stopped a few paces after. "Forget something?" he asked.

She stared at the back bumper, goosebumps running down her back. "It was fun to have lunch with all those people, wasn't it? Let's go for a walk. I feel like walking. I'd like to have people around. Better yet, let's take a bus to my neighborhood library."

Albert came and stood beside her, stooping low to stare at the back bumper at the same angle. Whatever his aunt was seeing, he couldn't see it. "Is there something wrong with the car?"

"Yes, I think there is. Don't ask me what. However, I think it would be best if we made different arrangements for the moment. Shall we take a walk?"

CHAPTER FIFTEEN
Seeking Out Coincidences

Albert led the way out of the garage and down to Third Avenue, where they could catch west-bound buses. The big downtown library was just two blocks away, but Marley wanted distance. Albert suddenly got the idea that there was a bomb on her car, maybe a big one.

But Aunt Marley would have warned someone about that sort of thing, he assumed.

They boarded a bus at the start of the afternoon rush hour and just happened to sit across from a very casual acquaintance of Marley's, the owner of a travel agency who was usually open to the occasional chat at the cafe. Her name was Elaine and, after a few pleasantries, she asked after Aloysius.

"I'm surprised, Elaine. I didn't think you knew him."

"Oh, he came to my house for his work a few times. Did you know I donate office space to an environmental group?"

"No, I didn't."

"Well, they're an odd group—and sometimes they don't smell very nice —but their intentions are excellent. They've been working on some sort of preservation project somewhere. Not that I pay much attention to them anymore."

For a moment, Albert was convinced his aunt had arranged this meeting for his benefit, but that didn't make any sense. Why would she bother? And yet, they had abandoned the car and run into someone who knew Aloysius. Just by chance.

If this was a trick, Marley played her part perfectly. "How interesting, dear. What business did Aloysius have with them?"

"He's met with them a few times about a development project. They've been protesting by filing court papers and sneaking onto some construction site or whatever it is they do, and he was trying to convince them to stay away."

"Was it working?"

"I think so. They're long on process, my little activists are. They like to discuss things endlessly. I guess he offered them a different patch of land on the other side of Cedar River Watershed—I listened in one time. His approach was mostly carrot with a little bit of stick, and that always works best with these people. Trying to intimidate them turns them into heroes of the revolution, you know. Riles them up, sometimes to the point where they might actually consider taking action."

"Beyond filing court papers, you mean?"

"Yes. Didn't you know any of this?"

"No, honestly, I didn't know what he was working on."

"Well that's funny," Elaine said. "He said he had his current client because of you. I assumed he meant that you referred your friends to him." When Elaine wanted to drop a hint, she wasn't subtle about it.

However, Marley wasn't about to have that conversation. "You know he's been killed, don't you?"

Elaine reeled back, shocked. "He has? How?"

"He was murdered. Two nights ago. His body was dumped on the Burke-Gilman trail."

"Oh my God. Did they catch the man who did it?"

Marley shook her head. Without quite understanding why, she decided not to mention Jenny. "They don't even know where to start, as far as I can tell."

"Well that's awful!" Elaine said, her thoughts in a whirl. "Oh, God. Oh, my gosh! Oh, sweetie, I'm so sorry."

"Thank you. Let me ask you, Elaine, just between us: did any of the activists in particular dislike him?"

"Oh, Marley, none of them could have committed murder. They're vegans; they won't even take honey from a beehive. I have to keep my butter tray in a drawer or they lecture me about it. They wouldn't take a human life."

"Well," said Marley, nodding as though that was the most convincing argument in the world. "That's nice."

Elaine pulled the cord and got off at the next stop, all the while promising to keep in touch. It was several more miles before Marley pulled the cord, getting off the bus just across the street from the local library.

The main branch downtown was ten stories of beautifully deconstructivist glass and steel, with a huge bank of computer terminals filling a large portion of the fifth floor. The Magnolia neighborhood branch, by comparison, was about the size of a cozy restaurant. After exchanging pleasantries with the staff behind the desk, Marley settled herself at one of the computer stations, inserted her travel drive into a USB slot and began perusing the files Inez had copied for her.

Having nothing to do, Albert stood beside her for a minute or two, watching the librarians do their work. It occurred to him that he had not yet bothered to get a library card and he suddenly felt like a trespasser. His aunt, meanwhile, slowly clicked through one file after another. Finally, he couldn't hold it in any longer. "How does it look?"

"Even more straightforward than I'd hoped," Marley answered. "His itinerary is quite clear and apparently the poor dear had only one active client. He didn't only lack for friends, I guess. Here." She placed a handful of quarters into palm. "Feed these to the printer, dear. I'm going to make hard copies."

Marley printed up ten pages. Albert wasn't sure if he was supposed to look at them but he couldn't resist. Aloysius's client was Evelyn Thomas of Thomas & Gunderson. On the day he was killed, Sunday, he'd started the day at his office, then—

"Time to go, Albert."

He folded the pages. The library had automatic door openers, but Marley didn't go near the buttons that activated them. He held the door for her and together they went down to the curb.

"Are we walking..." He couldn't say the word home. It still didn't feel right.

"No, we're going back downtown. I ordered a cab on the computer."

"Okay."

"Don't worry, Albert. Even if you're not driving, I'll need you to accompany me."

"My doorknob-turning skills are legendary."

Marley glanced up at him. "Not getting bored, are you?"

Albert was honestly surprised. "Why, because no one has tried to kill us all day? I'm in favor of that. Unless there really was a bomb on the Volvo."

"I'm pretty sure there wasn't."

"Glad to hear it." He glanced around the street, looking for painters' vans or suspicious characters, especially ones with automatic rifles. There was nothing to see, but it was still day. Maybe the killers came out at night. "No, I'm not bored in the least."

"That's too bad," Marley said sincerely. "I'm not overly fond of boredom, but I prefer it to all this drama."

"So…" Albert was suddenly uncomfortable with the question he'd been dying to ask for more than half an hour. "So, did you cast a spell to make Elaine run into you?"

"Of course not, Albert. How could you even suggest such a thing? Did you see me cast a spell? Draw on the floor or chant some sort of pseudo-Latin nonsense?"

"No," Albert said carefully, "because that would have weakened it, right? It would have weakened the magic. But you did something that dredged up this new lead."

"I acted on a feeling that we should do something other than what we were about to do," Marley explained. "Those feelings can be quite fruitful, I find. Occasionally, if one has the training and aptitude, one must seek out coincidences."

If anyone else in the world had said that to Albert, he would have laughed at them. To his aunt, he said, "Where are we going next?"

"We need to visit the people on this list. This one here," she pointed at a name on the itinerary but Albert wasn't quick enough to read it, "would be best to visit at sunset, because he's a ghost. In the meantime, I want to talk to Evelyn Thomas."

A dozen questions swirled through Albert's thoughts, but he wasn't yet sure which were good ones, so he held them back. Marley was glad. He glanced at his watch. "It's already ten to five."

"Good point." She took out her phone and dialed. "Hello, dear. I'd like a few minutes to talk to Evelyn Thomas before she goes home for the evening. Yes, tonight." There was a pause. "I understand that, dear. Tell her it's Marley

Jacobs on the line and see if she'll make time for me." There was a longer delay. "Wonderful! I'm on my way down there now." She hung up the phone.

Albert grinned at her. "There are advantages to being you."

"Indeed there are. Evelyn bid for the rebuild on my house when it was burned down last time. Her plans were... interesting. I think she wanted to create a home for a minotaur, while I wanted a home for me." The cab arrived. "Ah, here we are."

The offices of Thomas & Gunderson were on First Avenue, just a few blocks south of the Pike Place Market. When the elevator doors opened, Marley led Albert into the darkest reception area he'd ever seen. The receptionist sat in a pool of light at the far end of the lobby, and only three small spotlights shone on tiny works of art on the walls. The urge to blurt out that they'd entered a cave was strong, but the weird lighting made him reluctant to speak. He leaned close to one of the framed images; it was a black and white photo of a lonely, blasted tree.

As they approached the desk, they saw that the receptionist was filling out a paper time sheet for a temp agency. She finished a grid and stood hurriedly. "Marley Jacobs? Please come this way." They went through the door behind her desk into a brightly lit hallway. The walls had been painted a frosty blue above huge, looming silhouettes. Albert stared at the figures as he passed, wondering who in their right minds would want these lunging nightmares on their office walls. He also thought it was cool as hell. None of the offices had doors on them, and none were empty.

Evelyn Thomas's office was, naturally, at the end of the hall. The receptionist knocked twice then opened the door. "Thank you, dear," Marley said as she glided into the room.

Evelyn Thomas was almost Marley's age, but she was taller and had a CrossFit muscularity to her. Her hair had also turned silver but she wore it in a fashionable bob. Her suit was as white as snow, which matched the color of the long-haired cat purring in her lap.

"Marley! I apologize for not getting up, but as you can see I'm playing hostess for the moment." She gestured helplessly toward the cat.

The glass-top table beside her lay beneath a warm spotlight, like a darkened stage waiting for a singer. There was another pool of light on a bare desk in the far corner and a third on a couch place beneath a framed section of blueprint. There seemed to be nothing else in the room worth shining a light on.

Evelyn gestured to one of the other chairs around the glass table. Marley sat. Albert stood nearby, just inside the pool of light.

"Of course, Evelyn. There's no need to disturb such a fine beast, especially after business hours."

"Business hours never end for some of us, as I'm sure you can understand."

"Er, yes, I guess you're correct. How has business been?"

"Slower than I would like, but not as disastrous as it could be, considering the economy these last few years. It makes me wish Thea were still alive to help me run the place." Thea Gunderson was the co-founder of the company that still bore her name, even though she'd died some years before. Neither Albert nor Marley recognized the name, but Evelyn didn't notice. She was the sort of person who believed events that were important in her life would be notable to everyone.

Evelyn regarded Marley closely as she stroked her cat. "And I assume you have been just humming along, then?"

"I have my little projects." Marley waved her hand vaguely. "Do you know why I've come?"

CHAPTER SIXTEEN
An Awful Plan Is Revealed

The look Evelyn gave to Marley was remarkably similar to her cat's: the casual disinterest of a predator with a full belly.

A Key, an Egg, an Unfortunate Remark

"I would love to think you have a job for us," Evelyn said without evident enthusiasm, "but I realize that's a long shot. Much more likely is that you want to speak to me about your recently deceased nephew, Aloysius Pierce, and the work he was doing for me."

"Indeed I do. You seem to have been his only active client."

"Then I guess times were even harder for him than for us. He certainly did an excellent job, though. Very attentive, though if I was the only client. … Please accept my condolences, by the way. Aloysius told me that you and he were not exactly close—I'll confess that I'd hoped hiring him would give me an inside track to one of your 'little projects,' but he quickly disabused me of that notion. Still, he was a good lawyer. Very attentive, as I said. I hope it hasn't been too great a shock."

Marley sighed. "Thank you. It's the complicated family relationships that make grief the hardest. One doesn't always know what one should do or how one should behave."

"Ah," Evelyn responded. She had no idea how to respond to that and quickly moved on. "Tell me, do you know the young woman who did it?"

"Did what, dear?" Marley asked more in surprise than curiosity. She knew what but she hadn't expected Evelyn to turn the conversation that way so suddenly.

"Killed him, of course. I understand the police caught her the very next day."

Marley's gaze was steady. She was beginning to suspect Evelyn's own mind was a home for a minotaur. It was time to change the subject. "Yes, I know her. What was Aloysius working on?"

Evelyn hesitated, then shrugged. "All right then. It's not like it was a secret." She rubbed her face against the space behind the cat's right ear, then set him on the floor. "I'm afraid we'll have to be cutting your cuddles short, Mr. Fur." She stood. "Through here, Marley."

Striding out of the spotlight into the darkness, Evelyn pushed against the wall. A large section swung open without the click of a door latch or the squeak of a hinge.

This room beyond was flooded with light; Marley and Albert felt a sudden rush of relief as they followed Evelyn into it. In the center of the room stood a single large table with a tiny diorama of the Seattle waterfront. On the right edge was the Pike Place Market. On the left was the P-I Building, with its globe on top. Between the P-I Building and a huge piece of blue glass meant to represent Elliott Bay was Myrtle Edwards Park.

The space between those landmarks was unrecognizable. Instead of the actual grid of streets and buildings, there was a strange warren of hexagonal buildings in alternating rows of four or five, like the Dungeons and Dragons sheets Albert's squad buddies had sometimes gathered around, except these had a sliver of space between them.

Each hexagonal building was seven stories tall, topped with a glass roof and connected to one another by glass-covered bridges. The whole complex stretched from Broad Street to Lenora, turning Belltown and the waterfront into something closely resembling a beehive-shaped factory for robot workers.

Marley stared at it, astonished and a little queasy. "What, exactly, am I looking at?"

"This is my dream," Evelyn said simply. "The city of the future, a space designed for humans to live comfortably and productively. Notice the glass ceilings on the buildings for upper level park land. The glass-covered provides a way for people to travel without exposing themselves to the—" Evelyn gave a little shudder. "—the rain.

"There are living spaces inside," she continued, "a level for offices, shops and parks, and even a parking garage below. Each building has a promenade on the top level, allowing people to walk or bike wherever they like."

"They look like beehives," Albert said without considering how it would sound.

Evelyn didn't take offense. "That's a common misperception," she said smoothly, being impervious to insult. "These buildings will be the pinnacle of green architecture. Human waste would be processed to provide natural gas for supplemental heat and electricity with no adverse smell or sanitation worries. The frames holding the glass panes would double as solar panels—"

"It's a grand design," Marley said doubtfully. "But who would live there?"

"Not many, at first," Evelyn said. "The early residents would be people who dream of the future, of living cleanly and productively in a more comfortable environment. Early adopters. But once others saw how pleasant, effective, and efficient it was—much better than the haphazard way people live now—I believe there would be a waiting list as long as the city census report to move in."

Marley bent low to peer through the dome of the nearest hexagon. "It all seems very... designed."

"That's what we need more of in this world: design. Conscious choices. Sensible order. Not a system where a few grab as much as they can, then parcel it out bit by bit to the only newcomers with the resources to buy in. The homes we live in today are designed to accommodate building materials of three hundred years ago simply because it's traditional and expected. Look at this."

Evelyn removed the top of one of the buildings and set it on a small table. "See inside here? These would be the living areas."

Albert and Marley peered inside. It looked like one of those tilt maze games, where the player rolled a ball bearing along a path while avoiding a number of holes. "The most expensive units would be along the outer rim, of course, where the views are. But notice the floors: they're angled slightly toward the hub of the building."

"The floors aren't even?" Albert asked.

"The world isn't even," Evelyn countered. "It isn't natural to live on a flat, level surface. Our bodies weren't built for it. A home built on a gentle incline is comforting to the human psyche on a deep, deep level, and most people wouldn't even be aware of it unless they had tacky wheeled furniture, God forbid."

"It's certainly a visionary idea," Marley said, keeping her tone as neutral as possible. She'd nearly called it interesting, but even Evelyn could have seen through that. "This is what Aloysius was working on?"

"Yes. What you see here is the most ambitious version of the plan. We showed a smaller version to city leaders when the Sculpture Park was being planned."

"Sculpture Park? But that was years ago!"

"Sometimes a dream takes years." Evelyn stared down at the model city as though it was a delicious birthday cake and she couldn't wait to blow out the candles. "I pitched the project to the city council and mayor's office when the Sculpture Park was being planned. This is art people can live in. Of course it couldn't have been built on this scale, covering so many blocks —I couldn't expect that sort of imagination from politicians.—but I thought a two-three-two grid would have been enough to demonstrate the soundness of the plan. Unfortunately..."

"That required more land than had been set aside for the park."

Evelyn bared her teeth. "Exactly, Marley. It would have required more land—land currently dedicated to ugly condos and rat-trap waterfront restaurants. Eyesores. Boils on the most public face of the city. But they were privately owned, and the politicians didn't have the balls to lead the way to a new and better world by invoking eminent domain. Doesn't fit within the parameters of the current project, they said."

She spoke with a raw intensity that showed her disappointment and resentment was still fresh. "But you never gave up," Marley prodded.

"And I never will, Marley. Not on this. Not on human beings. I love people, and I want them to live in a way that will make their lives satisfying. That's why the vast majority of the profit this firm brings in goes to this dream. So... what do you think?" Evelyn asked the question the way a cult leader might check a new recruit for sudden enlightenment.

For once, Marley was at a loss for words. "The novelty of it is overwhelming," she finally said. "I'm afraid this old brain isn't used to being exposed to such radical ideas."

Evelyn laid a hand on Marley's. "Think about it. Please do think about it. I could use a partner like you, someone with influence."

"Is that what Aloysius was doing for you? Looking for partners?"

A Key, an Egg, an Unfortunate Remark

Evelyn replaced the top of the display. "Indeed he was, unofficially. He was quite the salesman, in his way. He drew up contracts, negotiated sales, and tried to find leverage for me. Really, he went above and beyond." As she said this last sentence, she gently caressed the upper edge of the nearest hexagon. "He was a believer."

"Did you hear about any troubles he might have had? Any negotiations that turned contentious? Something like that?"

"If there were, he didn't tell me about them," Evelyn said. "And he would have. He was a bit of a talker."

"He was, wasn't he? Thank you for your time, Evelyn. I have to admit I'm not a believer myself, but it's certainly an interesting idea." Marley smiled to cover her slip up: she'd called the project interesting after all.

But Evelyn had entered a serene state where she was either oblivious or impervious to such remarks. "It's new, I know," she said, "but if you think about it, it makes an awful lot of sense. You'll think about it?"

"How could I not?"

Evelyn was pleased. "Oh, good. So many people have closed minds, it seems."

"Did Aloysius keep an office here? Are there any personal possessions in a desk or something?"

Evelyn laid her hand on Marley's elbow in a gesture that she intended to be comforting. The change she'd undergone while describing her life's work, from brisk, chilly businesswoman to dreamy-eyed believer, was quite startling. "I'm sorry, but no. He brought everything with him when he came and took it all when he went. Marley, I should have said this before, but I truly am sorry for your loss."

That was the cue for them to leave. "Thank you," Marley said. Evelyn escorted them to the elevator and bid goodbye to them warmly.

After the elevator doors closed, they were silent for a few seconds. Finally, Albert said: "That was, er..."

"Odd. Very odd. Somehow, Aloysius was paying his bills by working on that woman's dead project."

"Undead project," Albert offered. "She doesn't know when to put a stake in it." Albert realized this was a careless turn of phrase and hurried the conversation along before his aunt could scold him again. "When did the Sculpture Park open?"

"It was 2007," Marley answered, politely ignoring Albert's faux pas. "I attended, of course. The planning for it took years before that. It was always meant to be an art park, not an apartment complex."

"I'm guessing she wants to force it into whatever she wants it to be. Anyway, what's next? Ghost?"

"It's so hard to know which item on the to-do list will be fruitful, isn't it? That's the problem with so many endeavors. Well, we do need to speak with Elaine and her activist friends. I know you've been anxious to meet a werewolf—"

Albert's blood ran cold. "Actually—"

"And in this city, a group of environmental advocates is a good place to stumble on one. But the sun will be down soon, so we should visit the ghost first," The doors opened and they went out into the street. The sun was sinking low over the mountains across the Puget Sound. "Let's go down to the waterfront. Ubeh should have a new car for us."

Ubeh, looking as beautiful as ever, was waiting for them in a Starbucks on the ground floor of a waterfront hotel. The place was otherwise empty, but the baristas stood behind the counter, unselfconsciously staring at her. "Ms. Jacobs! I came as soon as I got your email."

"I hope you weren't waiting too long, dear."

"Not at all. In fact, it was a delight to just sit for a while with a book and a cup of coffee. My children rarely leave me with any time of my own. But Ms. Jacobs, I must ask: was there something wrong with the Volvo?"

"Not at all, dear. It's just that I sometimes have a bad feeling about things."

Ubeh shrugged. "If you have a bad feeling about one of our cars, of course we will be happy to replace it." She placed the keys in Albert's outstretched hand and he wisely decided not to make a joke of it, not that he could think of one at the moment. "I'm afraid I don't have any more European cars available. This one will be Japanese."

Marley and Albert thanked her, then let themselves be led outside to a black Lexus. Albert opened the door for Marley and she climbed in. She reached up and took Ubeh's hand. "Keep in mind, dear, that my bad feelings often turn out to have a basis in fact."

"Of course."

"Albert, West Seattle, please."

Marley sent the address to the car GPS, and Albert followed the directions, driving across the West Seattle bridge to a condo building on an east-facing slope above Salty's Restaurant. He pulled into a visitor space in the parking lot and let his aunt out of the car.

New condos, which littered Seattle from one end to the other, were almost always built from the same boring palette: burgundy, charcoal, and light grey. However, this building was at least two decades old and was ugly in a less fashionable way, being as flat and square as a gigantic children's block. The exterior was a dingy brown and the windows, strangely, were recessed somewhat, giving the structure a swollen look. Worst of all, the panes had been tinted, apparently in the belief that Seattle wasn't dim and gloomy enough. Still, it was no one's idea of a setting for a proper haunting.

So Marley nearly laughed aloud when her nephew turned to her with a puzzled expression and said, "A haunted condo?"

CHAPTER SEVENTEEN
Yep, a Haunted Condo

"Yes, exactly."

Albert didn't try to hide his disappointment. "That just doesn't seem right. Ghosts are supposed to be in an old mansion, you know? Or an

117

asylum somewhere. Someplace old and secluded with cracked plaster and overgrown weeds. Somewhere something terrible happened."

"Albert! I had no idea you were such a romantic! There are many types of ghosts, you know. Some ride the bus every day and go to work in offices. Some sit in cars on the highways, stopping and starting endlessly. Some linger in institutions, whiling away the hours in familiar places, thinking the same thoughts over and over."

"You make it sound like the city's full of them."

"There are more than you think, but most of them are harmlessly taking up space." Marley glanced at a Geo Metro parked at the far end of the lot. "Albert, dear, open the trunk of the Lexus. Quickly, please."

He did. There was a case of bottled water in the back, along with a bundle of tools and a duffel bag that was padlocked shut.

Marley rummaged in her purse. "Just a water bottle, please."

Albert broke the plastic covering and retrieved one. "Do they stock all your cars this way?"

Marley didn't look up from her purse. "Ubeh is more than a pretty face. Ah!" She retrieved a little billfold and took out an American Express gift card and an envelope perfectly sized for it. The card went into the envelope. Marley wrote FOR YOU on the outside. "Dear, put this under the windshield wiper of that Geo Metro. The water bottle goes on the hood beside it."

Flummoxed, Albert stood with the bottle and envelope. "Does giving gifts help with the ghost?"

"Albert! Quickly! The sun is setting."

Marley turned and started toward the door. The Metro was in the other direction, and Albert had a bad feeling about leaving his aunt alone for long. He sprinted across the lot, left the things his aunt had given him in the way she'd instructed, and ran back.

He thought back to the moment when he'd accepted Marley's offer of employment and she'd immediately smashed that taillight. Was she paying back the owner of that truck? Paying forward to someone else?

A Key, an Egg, an Unfortunate Remark

That reminded him to glance around again, in case the gunmen were nearby. They weren't. Maybe, if they were really lucky, the gunmen were done with them.

She didn't glance up when he caught up with her, and he found himself back on their original topic of conversation.

"I'm guessing ghosts aren't shimmering see-through wraiths, then."

"Life just isn't that easy."

They had reached the pitted concrete steps that lead up to the front door. What Albert could see through the smeary glass panels was nothing more than a cramped, bland, boring entry hall. Nothing spooky about it. "So what do they look like? I mean, how can I tell if I'm talking to a ghost?"

"Ghosts are trapped in the past, Albert. They'll do the same thing over and over, think the same thoughts, return to all the same places. Nothing enrages a ghost like a change in their environment, even a change for the better. So if you meet someone who only listens to decades-old music, who says the same things all the time, or who gives directions by referring to landmarks that have been long since torn down, you're probably dealing with a ghost."

"But... living people do that, too, not just dead people."

After scrutinizing the aluminum panel beside the door, Marley pressed the buzzer for the marketing office. "Oh, you don't have to be dead to be a ghost. But the one we'll be talking to today certainly is."

On the other side of the glass door, an inner door swung open and a woman lunged toward them, turned the deadbolt lock and yanked the front door open. She was just under forty, dressed in a wrinkled lavender suit with scuffed black shoes. Her hair was as pale as sand and the fluorescent lights of the entry hall highlighted the flyaway strands that had escaped her ponytail. She looked like she needed a solid month of good sleep. "Hello! How can I help you?" she asked in a desperate, breathy voice.

"I'm in the market, dear, and I'm hopeful about the view." Marley gestured into the building as though they could all see the office buildings and looming harbor cranes of Seattle through the faded wallpaper.

"Of course! Of course. Please come in. I have some excellent opportunities for you."

Marley breezed past her toward the elevators. "Wonderful. I'd like to look at the penthouse, please."

"Er, I'm afraid that unit isn't available. The owner currently lives there."

"I seem to have been mistaken about your openings. How about the floor below? That would be the..."

The saleswoman finished that sentence reluctantly. "Eleventh. Actually, I have a very interesting unit on the fourth floor—"

"Not the eleventh? I'd heard that whole floor was open. Was I misinformed again?"

"Well, no."

"Why don't you want to show the eleventh? Does the owner upstairs walk around in lead boots or something?"

The eager look in the salewoman's eye faded as she answered. "No. I'll be happy to show you those units."

"Thank you, dear. Albert?" He pressed the button for the elevator.

The woman took a nametag with magnetic backing from her pocket and attached it to her lapel. "I'm Natalie. Pleased to meet you."

Marley didn't want to risk being recognized—which didn't happen often, but still—so she pretended to miss the opportunity to introduce herself. "It must be a difficult job, selling condos in this economy," she said politely.

Natalie didn't answer. She stared up at the display above the elevator door, counting the numbers. Her expression was slack and her complexion pasty.

Once inside, Natalie tried to rally her mood. She started her sales spiel, working hard to put an upbeat lilt in her voice. Despite her efforts, she lacked sincerity and Marley cut her off.

"Do you get a lot of prospective buyers? A lot of visitors?"

"Why yes. The last person to come here was some sort of TV producer."

Marley and Albert exchanged a look. "Really? What did he look like? Slender? Sandy hair?"

A Key, an Egg, an Unfortunate Remark

"It was a she," Natalie answered. "Dark hair. She looked like she was just out of high school, to be honest. She ran off midway through my tour."

"Oh, how unusual."

"I wish," Natalie said, not quite low enough to pass unheard. The doors opened and she remembered herself. "The eleventh floor is completely vacant at the moment. The rooms are quiet—" A sudden wave of cold made them all shiver. "Well. Ha ha. I'll have to ask Ludmilla to adjust the thermostat. You said you wanted a view of Elliott Bay? Come this way—"

"Natalie," Marley said, as though about to break some bad news. "Dear. You know we aren't going to be buying a unit, don't you?"

Natalie glanced from Marley to Albert and back again. "I— I—"

Marley laid a gentle arm on her shoulder. "This building is haunted, isn't it?"

Natalie burst into tears.

"Here now, let's go this way." Marley led her to the nearest unit. Natalie's hand trembled too much to fit the key in the lock; Albert took it from her and opened the door for them both. Marley walked Natalie inside.

It was a nice space, and if Albert had ever had an interest in a condo, he would have considered it—if not for the sense of foreboding that seemed to come from everywhere at once. He switched on the lamps. The gave off a dim, unhealthy light.

There was a couch in the living room that faced the bay windows and beyond that, downtown Seattle. Marley eased Natalie onto it. "Each unit comes with a mocha cotton couch and matching loveseat," Natalie said, her voice sounding strained. Then she laughed. Then she started crying again.

"Take it easy, dear. We'll get you back downstairs in a few minutes. Have you seen the ghost yourself?"

"No." Talking about it seemed to make her feel better, and she got control of herself as she went on. "No, I've never seen a wispy human figure or heard voices. Just... him, upstairs, and whatever he has with him. God, sometimes it seems like half the people who live in this building are nearly dead themselves, me included. And the other half make me check the locks on my windows and doors every night before I go to sleep." She clutched Marley's arm suddenly. "You seem like nice people; you should get out of here! You shouldn't be in a place like this!"

"We'll go soon enough. Do you know anything about my nephew, Aloysius Pierce? He was here just last week. Sandy hair? Pointy chin? He probably made a pass at you."

"Oh him! I remember him. He represented some development project or other, I think. The owner would never sell any of his properties, though. Never."

"Did he come here often? Think carefully, dear. He was my nephew and I'm terribly concerned."

"Just once. I liked him. He was flirtatious. I like it when people are nice to me. The owner..."

"The owner didn't want to see him again, right?"

"That's right."

"Can you take us upstairs? I want to drop in."

"I can't. I'm sorry. Rules."

"We'll be going upstairs for a visit anyway. Thank you, Natalie. You can head back to your office now."

They went back to the hall and eased Natalie onto the elevator. She looked a little confused as the doors closed, and waved at Marley and Albert. They waved back.

"To the stairs!" Marley exclaimed.

"I'm a little confused," Albert admitted. "The guy still owns property, even after he's dead?"

"Ghosts don't always know they're dead, and often the people around them don't know either."

"Huh. That explains that smelly guy who sits next to me in Starbucks." Albert tried the door. "It's locked."

"Try one of the keys you got from Natalie."

Albert held up the key ring in his left hand and gaped at it. "I could have sworn I gave this back to her."

"She thinks you did, too. Hurry up, please."

It turned out to be the third key he tried. The lock snapped back and the door swung open into a dimly-lit stairwell. Marley stepped inside and looked up at the landing above.

"Oh my," she said. "Who do you think that is?"

Albert saw the body, too, and vaulted up the stairs two at a time toward it. She was a young woman, slightly older than Albert himself, thick-bodied and dark-haired. She was dressed in fashionably muted earth tones, and beside her lay an open backpack with personal gadgets—Alphasmart, cell phone, empty water bottle, energy bar wrappers, tablet computer, and a few other items he didn't recognize—almost spilling out. She had curled herself into a corner of the landing, as though hiding there.

"She has a pulse," Albert said. "Do you think she fell down the stairs?"

"She didn't fall, dear. She curled up here on her own. We appear to have found where Natalie's TV producer ran off to." Marley shined a flashlight into her face. The woman's eyes were closed and seemed a little sunken. Her lips were white and cracked. "She's dehydrated."

The woman's eyes opened. "Quiet," she croaked, her voice barely above a whisper. "He'll hear you."

"We're going to get you out of here, Kara. Can you stand?"

The woman shook her head, but Albert was unclear whether that meant she couldn't stand or didn't want to. It didn't matter to Marley. She took the backpack and waved at Albert to take the woman. He scooped her up and carried her down the stairs.

Marley scowled and waved him off when he tried to give her Natalie's key ring, so he had to unlock the stairwell door without putting down the woman, then do it again for the condo unit. Marley squeezed past him and waved at the couch, dropping the backpack beside it. As he set the woman down, she moaned with pain.

Marley emerged from the kitchen with a tall glass of water. "Tiny sips, dear." She put the glass to the woman's lips and helped her drink. "Tiny tiny sips. Too much at once isn't safe."

"Quiet," the young woman said again. "He'll hear you. Quiet, he'll hear you. Quiet, he'll—" Marley gave her another drink.

There was a company name on the backpack. Albert straightened the material so he could read it. "Haunt Hunters. Hey! I like that show!"

CHAPTER EIGHTEEN
Things Could Be Much Nicer Than They Are

It took some time, but eventually the producer regained her senses. Marley kept pressing the glass of water on her, and she kept sipping.

"How long have you been here, dear?"

Before she answered, the woman took out her cell and looked at the display. "Two days? Only two days? God, I thought it was a week."

"I'm sure it felt that way. My name is Marley and this is Albert."

"I'm Kara." She held up her hands. They were trembling.

"Nice to meet you, Kara. What brings you here?"

Marley let her voice grow louder, and as she expected, Kara shuddered. "Quiet, he'll..." She stopped, then was silent a moment while she cleared her thoughts. It wasn't easy; it felt as if there was someone else in there, someone vicious. "I'm here because my bosses received a tip about a haunted building. I'm supposed to check it out. God, it sure checks out."

"Who sent in the tip?"

Kara waved one trembling hand in an attempt to be casual and worldly. "Some creepy lawyer guy. He met me at the airport, actually, early on Sunday, and showed me the building. Tried to press me for drinks, too."

"But he wasn't your type, was he?"

Kara gave Marley a wary look. It occurred to her that Marley had not just come upon her by chance and Kara began to suspect she'd been set up somehow. "Right. I returned after dark..." She trailed off, shuddering again.

Marley took one of Kara's hands into her own. "You discovered that this haunting is the real thing."

Kara's mouth was dry again. She took another small sip. "I did. I really, really did. Oh God, I've been offline for two days. I'm probably so fired." She began dialing.

Marley caught Albert's attention and jerked her head toward the kitchen. They retreated into a spacious kitchen unit with granite counters and glasstop stove to give Kara privacy for her call.

"I've been watching her show since my tour ended," Albert said. "I didn't think they investigated the real thing."

"They don't," Marley answered. "Thank goodness. They mostly point night vision cameras at themselves or occasionally a stray raccoon, then work themselves into a tizzy. They've come into my territory twice, and both times they didn't get anywhere near the actual ghost of a dead person."

"Which saved you the bother of running them off, I'm guessing."

"Absolutely correct," Marley answered. "But that's not the important thing here."

Albert nodded. "No. The important thing is that Aloysius called these people in. He wanted the ghost upstairs to be featured on a TV show."

"No, dear," Marley said patiently. "He wanted the TV show people to put the ghost to rest. That's how they end every episode, after all."

"That's right! I forgot about that. Then the properties would pass on to someone else, someone who isn't determined to hold on to everything, as Natalie said."

"I think so. I think Evelyn wanted to buy up some valuable real estate, and our friend upstairs was in her way."

"Aunt Marley, why did he turn to these TV people? Why didn't he come to you?"

Marley sighed and looked out the window, wondering if this was the reason her nephew was dead: he didn't think he could come to her for help. "Because he believed I wouldn't do a thing about it, and I understand why he thought so. I have a live-and-let-live attitude about my city. If a person is going about their daily activities without hurting anyone, what do I care if they're dead or not?"

"It's hurting Natalie, though. And Kara."

"Yes, Albert, exactly. This particular ghost is doing harm. And if Natalie is correct that this haunting is drawing bad people toward this building, then it absolutely must be put to rest. Human evil combines with the supernatural in truly awful ways."

"Are we going to have an exorcism? Like in that old movie?"

"It's looking that way, but no, it won't be like any movie you ever saw. And really, Albert, it's not an 'old' movie unless it's older than I am."

Kara stepped into the doorway, politely clearing her throat. She'd slung her backpack on. "I'm not fired, if you can believe it. I sure can't. They were actually worried about me and my boss was going to call the police if I hadn't checked in by morning. They're also not going to send a production team up here. They cancelled. Apparently, this isn't the first time they... I'm catching the next flight back."

"No, you aren't!" Marley exclaimed. "You're still woozy and weak, aren't you?"

"Well—"

"I won't hear another word about it. This is a haunting and you have had a ghost's thoughts in your head. That's no small thing. You need to purge them. If you don't do it quickly, you might never be free. You go downstairs and tell Natalie that the two of you need a decent dinner. She'll know a place. Comfort food, dear, that's what you need, along with lots of water and no alcohol. Honestly, getting on a plane with nothing but airport food and a back of salty pretzels... I shudder to think of it. Run along now, I'd come with you myself to check on you but it's getting late. Run along!"

Kara was about to respond but instead she turned and headed for the door. She still felt a little woozy, and obviously she didn't have to catch the very next flight. Once she opened the door to leave the unit, she found the strength to run for the elevators.

In answer to Albert's expression, Marley said, "Oh, she'll be fine."

"I'm sure she will, but… 'Run along'? That really works?"

"On a young woman? It does for me. I wouldn't suggest you try it." Marley glanced at her phone. Sunset was nearly over, and so was the advantage it gave. "Shall we make another attempt at the stairs?"

They did. The landing was empty but for a few coins that had fallen from Kara's pockets. Marley made sure to pick up every one, then count them carefully: there were three pennies, two nickels and three quarters in total. Marley jingled them between her cupped hands happily.

"Rich people love their money," Albert said. He thought he sounded too sharp and was about to apologize but Marley only laughed.

"Indeed we do."

To their surprise, the landing at the top of the stairs was furnished. There was no carpet, but there was a small loveseat, end table, and standing floor lamp against the wall. A platinum-colored princess phone sat on the end table.

Albert stood beside the phone, staring at it. "Do we call? Because I'm pretty sure I'd turn into a girl the moment I touched that."

"You should be so lucky. No need to challenge your masculine self-image, dear. Calling would just create an additional opportunity for someone to tell us no. Let's put the key in the door and see what happens.

The deadbolt lock above the knob was different from the others in the building: it was plated with silver. Albert found a likely key and unlocked it on the first try.

The door creaked as it swung open onto a dark hallway. Finally, Albert had his spooky sound effect, although he took much less pleasure in it than he would if it had come through the speakers of his television. Marley shook the jingling coin in her hands again, and the sound seemed to cut through the gloom, echoing like a cough in a church.

"Hello? Mr. Quigley? Amos Quigley?" Marley slipped past Albert and walked down the darkened hall.

The hair on the back of Albert's neck stood on end. "Maybe I should go first," he whispered.

127

"Oh, hush."

Marley reached the end of the hall, then turned left. A huge empty room lay before them. The furniture was all leather, chrome, and glass, as chilly and impersonal as a sidewalk in winter. Through the windows that made up the entire eastern wall, the clouds glowed pink and blue, and the glass sides of the downtown Seattle skyscrapers flashed as fading rays of sunlight reflected off them into the room.

In the very center of the room, seated in a low-backed chair, staring at the fading light, was an old man. All they could see was the back of him, and the wisps of gray hair neatly combed across his balding head.

Marley and Albert walked slowly into the room. "Amos Quigley?" Marley said again. "I've come to talk to you about something of great importance."

"Gold," was all he said in response. The room was so still that dust moats seemed to hang in the air, unmoving. Marley and Albert circled around him far enough that they could see his long, beakish nose and shadowed eyes. His skin was very pale. "Gold."

"I wonder," Marley said slowly and carefully, "if we could take a moment of your time."

"Everyone takes," he mumbled. His voice was low and raw like an old engine grinding its broken gears. "Everyone thinks they can dip their looter hand in. Everyone has their projects. Everyone think I should give away my own money, money that doesn't even have any real value."

Each word out of his mouth filled Marley and Albert with exhaustion and despair. The room darkened and his voice took on the droning quality of a thoughtless, senseless machine. "They put a printing press in the basement of the Federal Reserve and gave them all the ink they could ever want. My own money loses value every day. Every day. The only sensible choice is to put gold behind it. Nail dollars to real gold. Nail dollars to nail dollars to nail dollars to…"

Albert staggered. The ghost's empty, irrational droning sucked the vitality out of him—his knees went weak and his mind began to go blank.

A Key, an Egg, an Unfortunate Remark

His heart beat slower and slower with each passing moment—Albert could feel it fading—and he realized that he was in the unique position of feeling himself slow down while terror overtook his thoughts.

"Mr. Quigley," Marley broke in. Her face was pale, too, but beneath the misery and fatigue, she managed to focus. "I want to talk to you about a man's death."

Quigley began to shout. "Inflation is government-sponsored robbery and—"

Marley shook her hands, jangling the coins inside. Quigley immediately fell silent and tilted his head.

"I thought that might break through to you." She jangled them again. The old man's head turned toward her slightly, and the miasma of life-stealing despair lifted slightly.

A floor lamp on a timer switched on suddenly, startling Marley so much that she dropped the coins. She cried "Albert!" and they both fell to their knees to find them again.

"August fifteenth, 1971, was the worst day in history," Quigley said as he turned his attention—or what passed for attention with someone like him—back toward the window. Albert found it impossible to hold his head up. His forehead fell against the carpet, his nose mashing against a nickel.

"Albert, get up." Marley's voice was strained. She jangled the coins, causing Quigley to interrupt his monologue again. He looked in Marley's direction without seeming to see her. "Get up right now."

"I'm sorry," Albert said, although he didn't lift his head off the floor.

"Everyone takes," Quigley said.

"I'm not here to take," Marley said. "I'm here to invest. Would you like some money?" The mood in the room suddenly changed from a dismal, irrational despair to a vicious avarice. "Yes," Marley said. "That's changed things, hasn't it?"

She stepped toward Quigley, a coin in her hand. "How would you like a nice, shiny quarter?" Quigley's face lit up as though all his dreams had come true. He turned over his palm and let Marley place the coin in it.

"More."

Marley stepped back, holding a penny up where he could see it. Albert struggled to his feet, then staggered toward his aunt. He still harbored a vague hope of protecting her somehow, which demonstrated both his fine intentions and his inability to judge his own strengths.

"I have more for you," Marley said. She glided closer to him. Quigley opened his hand again—the quarter was gone. Marley gave him the penny. He closed his hand over it, then opened it again. The penny was gone.

"More."

Marley held up another quarter. She moved toward him, making sure that Quigley's eyes were on it. Then she stepped back. "Someone came to visit you recently. A slender man with light-colored hair wanted to buy one of your properties, but—"

"Never sell," Quigley said. His whole body began to grow darker as though he was absorbing light. "Mine. Never sell."

Marley moved toward him again as though about to give him the quarter, but then stopped. Quigley stopped talking and the darkness around him stopped expanding. "Of course you'd never sell. Of course you said no. But what I need to know is this..." Marley held the quarter closer to him. "What property did he want to acquire? Was it this one?"

Quigley stared at the money, his entire self given over to his raw yearning for it. The room felt like the inside of a tiger's cage. Albert would not have been surprised to see the old man turn into an alligator and snap the coin from Marley's hand with his long jaws.

Then Quigley looked up at Marley. For the first time, he seemed to genuinely see her there, and it was awful. "Why do you want to know?"

"Because," Marley answered, swaying slightly under the old man's terrible gaze, "banana Wilberforce transmit the cabbage ticket."

Quigley nodded wisely, as though thinking this over carefully, then said: "Waterfront chowder restaurant. Near the Unocal brownfield."

Marley placed the quarter in his palm, then another penny, then a nickel. She held up the last quarter, then pocketed it. Quigley's eyes never turned away from her as she side-stepped around him toward the door.

Marley grabbed Albert's elbow and pulled him after her. "Thank you, Mr. Quigley," she said. "We'll see ourselves out." Then she hustled her nephew toward the exit.

Albert opened the door and they rushed into the stairwell. Albert nearly collapsed onto the loveseat, but Marley steered him away from it. They hustled down the stairs into the eleventh floor hallway. Albert stood unsteadily in the dingy light his gaze fixed on the door to the room where they'd taken Natalie and Kara. "Can we—"

"No, dear. No lying down. Think what happened to poor Kara. Now come push this elevator button."

A few minutes later they had hung Natalie's key ring on the outside of her office door and stumbled into the clean night air.

"Oh, my Lord," Marley said. "I never dreamed things had gotten so bad. Quigley has got to go."

CHAPTER NINETEEN
Prioritizing Is the Key to Success

"I'm sorry," Albert said. "I was useless in there."

He collapsed against the hood of their car, letting his cheek rest against the cool metal hood. Marley came over and patted his head. "Well, of course, dear. I wouldn't expect you to be much help against that sort of ghost. Not yet. Still, better to encounter one with me than all alone. Now, a word of advice: you're going to feel like cursing just now. Don't. Profanity only makes things worse."

"Okay then: I feel fudging awful."

Marley laughed. It was only a little laugh, but it surprised her nonetheless. "You can drive, can't you? Of course you can. Let's get out of

131

here and visit a nice restaurant. We need fortifying and I'm afraid only chowder will do."

There were seafood places at the bottom of the hill but Marley didn't want to risk another conversation with Natalie or Kara. For his part, Albert was happy to put as much distance between himself and Amos Quigley as possible. Eventually they drove all the way around the bay and pulled in at a seafood place across the street from the Sculpture Park.

Albert parked in the gravel lot and helped his aunt from the car. He was still deeply shaken but did his best not to show it. "This place is a little rundown compared to your usual."

Marley walked away from the restaurant entrance, stepped between two cement blocks used to keep cars from encroaching on the train tracks, then stooped to pick up a stone about the size of an apricot. She turned it over in her hand as though she'd expected to find a message written on it, then suddenly threw it over her shoulder.

It soared in a high, narrow arc and fell onto the windshield of a black SUV, making a small spider-web crack low on the passenger side.

"Aunt Marley, what are you doing?" Albert looked around nervously, but no one had seen them. He looked at the SUV, hoping against hope that the cracked glass would magically vanish. Unfortunately, the laws of the universe did not violate themselves for his sake, nor did time flow backwards. The windshield was broken. Albert knew that, if that were his car, he would be furious.

Oblivious to his concern, Marley started toward the door. "I like to eat in a variety of places, dear. And I hear their chowder is something special." Still, she looked a little dubious as Albert opened the door.

The chairs and benches were made of rough wood, scarred from years of ill-treatment and the tables were not much better. The booths were mostly empty and poorly lit. When the maitre d arrived, Marley asked to be seated near a family with children.

The waitress and Albert both were startled when Marley informed them they would be starting with dessert and ordered two dishes of ice cream.

A Key, an Egg, an Unfortunate Remark

"There's an extra ten dollars in it for you if you can have them here in three minutes."

She did, and they both tucked in immediately. "Oh yeah," Albert said. "This is just what I needed." They forced themselves to eat slowly and savor their food, even though their encounter with Quigley had left them ravenous.

When the waitress returned, they ordered entrees and clam chowder. "I can see why the TV people called the producer back to L.A.," Albert said after she left. "It's fun to watch the investigators on the show wander through spooky, decrepit buildings and freak out in the dark, but dealing with that Quigley dude wouldn't have been fun at all. It was all..."

"It was misery," Marley said. "Misery and stale, irrational ideas that drain the vitality, creativity, and joy out of people. Don't get me wrong; there are contented ghosts out there, breezing through their days thinking the same old thoughts and doing the same old things without harm to anyone, but some are desperately unhappy and frighteningly irrational."

"And not all of them are dead."

"That's what 'undead' means, dear. Dead but not dead. If you're going to stand astride the line between life and death, it doesn't much matter which side you came from."

Albert's scalp tingled. He had let himself fall into a routine almost as soon as he'd settled into his aunt's home: job interview in the morning, work out in the afternoon, video games through the evening. He hadn't even tried to contact his old friends from high school, not for weeks. He remembered Weathers stepping over the fishing line Marley had tied in her living room; Weathers must have seen everything as though it was new, every time he saw it. Albert didn't think he could manage that, but he resolved to never let himself become one of those undead, not even a happy one. He didn't want to be anything like Quigley.

"But Quigley was extremely dead," Marley said reassuringly. Her nephew would have been disconcerted to discover just how easily she could read his expressions. "He's just about at the farthest, nastiest end of the bell curve."

"And we're going back there to deal with him."

Marley sighed. "We are, but not right away. I already knew he was there but hadn't realized he'd gotten so... intense. Still, Aloysius's murder has to be our top priority. As troublesome as Quigley has become, the mystery surrounding my nephew takes precedence."

"Still, ghosts and vampires... It's not like the movies, is it?"

"Has Hollywood misinformed you?" She laughed, but it was a pleasant sound. "Do you think forensics examiners have labs with glass walls and atmospheric blue lights. Do you think they run DNA tests on every piece of evidence for every crime, with the results coming back that same afternoon? Do you think doctors charge into operating rooms shouting 'Stop! You've misdiagnosed that patient!'"

Albert grinned sheepishly. "Point taken."

"People don't want to see the real thing, because it's often so dreary. There's so much grief and unhappiness, and entertainment is meant to be fun."

"In that case, let me ask one more thing."

"I won't be ready to work on the task at hand until our food arrives, so please do."

"Thank you. And thank you for letting me ask so many questions. Okay. Here we go: What's the craziest secret about the supernatural here in Seattle? What would really blow my mind?"

"Albert, those are two very different questions. The craziest secret is that our city is very ordinary in terms of the supernatural powers here. But what would probably blow your mind the most is..." she paused for dramatic effect, "that there's a dragon in Puget Sound."

For a moment, Albert didn't move or think or do anything at all. A dragon? As much as he feared the animal teeth and claws of a werewolf, a huge creature like.... He tried to convince himself he'd misheard. "Um, a... what?"

"A dragon, dear."

"Like a real St. George-on-a-horse dragon?"

"Oh, please! Saint George." She said the name with genuine distaste. Just like that, Marley was angry and snappish again. "The only dragon you can kill with a sharp stick is a little baby one. And you don't condone killing babies, do you?"

"Absolutely not," Albert said promptly.

"Hmf." Marley knew she'd let her temper get away from her. The effect of Quigley's power had still not given way; she needed that chowder. "Anyway, dragons are quite powerful and mysterious creatures. Wondrous, dangerous, and thrilling."

"So, if I got a scuba suit, then, and dove into the deepest parts of the Sound, would I see, like, scales the size of trash can lids?"

Marley gave him a shrewd look. "Now it's my turn to ask a question: what do you think you'd see?"

He fell quiet and thought about it for a moment. The waitress arrived with their food and he didn't answer until she'd arranged everything and left. "Magic becomes less powerful when it becomes real, yes? And dragons are very powerful—"

"—Possibly the most powerful things in the world."

"Which would mean that wherever I looked, I wouldn't find it, because it isn't real, even though it's most definitely there."

"Oh, what a joy you are to me, Albert. You have no idea how nice it is to talk with a man who listens."

As they ate, their moods began to improve. When the waitress returned to ask if everything was all right, Marley ordered ginger ale for the both of them, and that also turned out to be just the right thing.

Their meal was nearly finished when a woman across the room began to scream. Everyone leaped up to see what was going on. A young mother had jumped up onto the seat of her booth, and she was holding her two-year-old over her head.

Albert moved around Marley toward the commotion. "I'll check this—"

"Oh my God!" A man said. "It's a rat!" He had a military haircut and biceps that could have landed him on the cover of a fitness magazine. He

135

snatched up a big suitcase from his own booth and ran for the door.

"Ah well," Marley said. She threw a handful of twenties on the table and sedately joined the herd of fleeing customers.

The manager stood by the door, pleading with people not to go, for all the good it did him. Marley patted his arm as she went out and assured him that she'd left money for the bill on the table. He thanked her sincerely.

Just before the door closed behind them, they heard a woman's high-pitched voice shout "Again, Rocky? Again!"

They walked across the parking lot. Albert looked around guiltily for the SUV his aunt had damaged, but it had already left the lot. "That was gross."

"Oh, stop," Marley scolded him. "There was nothing wrong with our food, except for all the salt and heavy cream." She turned and looked across the street toward the Sculpture Park. Night had fallen but the park was lit up. "So. Shall we take a walk?"

Her phone rang. There was a low hissing voice on the line. "Danger," it said. "You will die. You will in danger. You will have fear and have pain. You will in danger."

Marley's response was chipper. "Why thank you, dear, for letting me know. I'll be right over." She hung up the phone.

"Albert, let's get the car. We'll have to take a detour from our so-called investigation. I think it's time to introduce you to one of the more colorful residents of my city."

CHAPTER TWENTY
"We Like Kitties"

At Marley's instruction, Albert found a parking space in a small corporate campus on the south side of the ship canal, then he and Marley walked along the trail toward Lake Union. The was getting late, but there were still joggers on the path—most of them students—and a few couples braving the late chill to sit by the water.

Now that night had fallen, Albert's paranoia shifted into high gear. The path was poorly lit and filled with greenery. If a vampire was going to swoop down on them, this would be a likely place for them to do it. Not that he could really picture Betty, Clive, or Spire actually swooping, but the thought was in his head and there was no dislodging it.

Worse, the canal on their left cut off retreat from that direction, and the path itself was an effective bottleneck. If those gunmen made another try for Marley, Albert would be unable to protect her. They certainly couldn't swim to safety.

Marley was utterly untroubled by such thoughts as she led Albert to the underside of the Fremont Bridge. The trail was cramped, with chain link fencing on the canal side and an extremely steep, overgrown hill on the other. Worse, as far as Albert was concerned, was that the bridge above blocked almost all of the light from the streets above.

Marley stood on the path and called: "Hello, Fremont Bridge!"

Something rustled in the bushes on the hill, making the hair on Albert's neck stand straight up. He started to move in front of his aunt to guard her, but stopped himself. She'd made it pretty clear that she didn't want him to be her bodyguard. "We're going to talk to a bridge?"

"No, dear. A troll." Albert thought immediately of the Fremont Troll, a statue tucked under the northern end of the Aurora Bridge. It was little more than a huge trollish face, with one hand laid over a stone Volkswagon. Albert's heart began to race. "Trolls don't have names of their own," Marley continued, "so they take the name of the connection they live under. Isn't that right, Fremont Bridge?"

"Yes, Marley Jacobs." The low, hissing voice came from the bushes, and Albert jumped back.

"It's all right, Albert. Fremont Bridge, would you come out a bit so I can introduce you? There are no people nearby."

"Yes, Marley Jacobs." A long-fingered hand emerged from the bushes.

The arm it was attached to was also long and frighteningly slender. Then the body slid into the faintly-reflected streetlights, and Albert could see the whole thing.

It was smaller than he expected, about the size of an underweight twelve-year-old boy. Its arms were as long as an orangutan's and its feet were another set of hands. He thought it looked like it was built for snatching prey from hiding, and he was right.

It was the face that disturbed Albert most. It was like the edge of a pillow, rectangular but rounded off, and wrinkled like ruined leather. It had no eyes that he could see, just two nostril holes it could close and open, and a lipless mouth full of tiny, sharp piranha teeth. Albert felt a strange hollow chill in the pit of his stomach and he had to squelch the urge to grab his aunt and carry her back to the car.

"Fremont Bridge, this is Albert Smalls."

The little troll made a sound like it was clearing its throat, which Albert immediately recognized as laughter. "What part of you is small?" it asked. "You seem large to me. Too large for climbing."

"I think the smallest part of me," Albert said carefully, "is my knowledge of trolls. You don't look much like your statue."

Marley grimaced and waved furtively at Albert, trying to back him off the subject, but it was too late.

"Not my statue! I never make statue! No one make statue of me! Statue is horrible and insulting! Statue has eyes."

"I'm very sorry," Albert said, his mind racing through all the possible things he could say to make things right. "It must be obvious how little I know about trolls, since I've just insulted you when I meant to compliment you."

The little creature considered this a moment. "I understand. I take a compliment instead. Your meaning smells strongly to me now."

"Fremont Bridge, why did you think I was in danger?"

The troll curled its hands in front of its chest. "Marley Jacobs, you stood in place that will be destroyed. You go there and then will you die. If you die, who will bring new batteries for my phone?"

"Too true. Do you know what sort of danger it is?"

"Place will be destroyed. Marley Jacobs die. Batteries die. No more Candy Crush Saga."

"We must avoid that, if we can. Thank you for the warning. How have you been?"

"Lonely."

"Oh, good. I'm very happy for you."

Albert spoke up: "I just realized that the murder took place just across the canal. Two nights ago."

The troll uncurled its legs, rising upward as though it was a marionette and someone was pulling invisible strings. "Fremont Bridge never murder. Fremont Bridge keeps to its deal. Never break. Likes batteries. Likes delicious birds and rats. Likes kitties."

"Yes, of course. We like kitties, too, in our way," Marley explained. "But we're not asking if you ate him, dear, only if you witnessed his murder."

It looked mildly confused. "Why do you care about someone else's prey?"

"He was my brother," Albert said.

"Connection," Marley interjected. "We're connected to him."

"That is a strong smell to me now. Humans have many confusing connections. I am disappointing to you, Albert Smalls, because I did not witness this killing, only the activity that came after. I was in my invisible place hiding from burning light for many hours. When I woke, the dark had come long before and the prey you are connected with had been discovered. Many people. Flashing lights."

"Ah," Marley said. "Thank you. Do you need anything? A new battery?"

"Battery is fine for now but I would like more kitties. I am bored eating rats and crows."

"How about a fish, instead? A nice, long, fresh salmon?"

It clasped its hands together in delight, made that laughing sound once more, then sprang against the side of the bridge support, scrambled up the vertical face with astonishing speed and grace, then crawled along upside down until it vanished on the underside of the bridge.

Marley took Albert's elbow and they began to walk back to the car. "Dear, I suppose you're curious about trolls, now?"

"Hell yes, but you've been answering my questions all day, and I'm working for you. I don't want to be a pest."

"If I think you've become a pest, you'll know. I don't suffer in silence, believe me. I'm glad you asked it about the murder. I'd never have thought of it."

"For all the good it did."

"It's important to ask! Feel free to do it again."

"What did he mean by 'invisible place'?"

"I made a special bag for him. It's completely invisible."

"You can do that? Then—"

"I didn't use one for us for several reasons. They're very difficult to move. They're very difficult to move around in. They're also very dark. They're collapsed-mine-shaft-a-mile-down dark."

"They are?"

"These bags are invisible, dear. That means no light gets inside. And that's fine for a troll—it doesn't have light where it comes from and it doesn't much like it. But for a human being it's deeply disturbing. It's like punishment."

"Where does he—it, I mean, come from?"

"I don't know. Trolls are an interesting problem. The rumor is that some fool was trying to open a connection to another place, and screwed up so badly that he brought trolls into our world. They're spread out over the whole globe and the whole of human history. When a new bridge—a new connection between places—is built over water, one of the trolls, summoned so very many years ago, appears beneath it."

"Is there no way to send them back?"

"It's beyond my abilities. Besides, they don't want to go. I've spoken to a dozen trolls in my lifetime, and they all fear returning to their home, although none of them remember why."

"Okay. It's not rude to call a troll 'it'?"

"They prefer it. They take as much offense at being told they have genitalia as they do at being told they have eyes."

"And he's... it's lonely?"

"Every troll is lonely. They seem happiest that way. I don't think they like their own kind much. They live beneath bridges and they don't want to have any other kind of connections."

"It's still early," Albert said. He looked down at his phone. "Earlyish. Where to next?"

"Home. We still haven't spoken with everyone yet, and we won't be able to until the morning. We still have a lot to learn about the work Aloysius was doing and his sudden change of personality."

They got into the car and began to drive home. After several blocks, Marley said, "Albert, dear, who do you think is following us in that car?"

CHAPTER TWENTY-ONE
Bitter Accusations Politely Made

Albert glanced into the rear view mirror but couldn't see anything except headlights. "No clue. What would you like me to do?"

"I'm sending the address of the nearest Dick's to the GPS. If it's still open when we get there, pull into their drive-through."

The hamburger place was still open and the drive through only had two other cars in it. After Albert got into line, he watched the trailing car—a Civic—get in line behind them. The headlights still prevented him from seeing much detail, but he could tell it was a compact car, painted blue.

"Let me out, dear," Marley said. With the motor running, he climbed from the car and opened her door. She climbed out.

"What do you want me to do, Aunt Marley?"

"Order something off the menu. The fries are quite good." She walked toward the restaurant entrance. Albert closed the back door, glanced at the blue compact—the driver was searching for something in the glove compartment, conveniently shielding his face from view—and got behind the wheel again. He watched his aunt rap gently on the glass door until one of the customers stood out of his chair and opened it for her.

After that, Albert lost sight of her. He felt a bit nervous until he remembered that, in all the dangers they'd faced so far, he'd been largely useless. Aunt Marley had handled them almost without effort; the only worthwhile contribution he'd made was by carrying things, pulling on doorknobs, and driving the car.

Albert couldn't bring himself to feel embarrassed about it. His aunt had introduced him to a new world, and he was still learning the rules.

He asked for a large order of fries that he didn't want, paid, then pulled up to the window to pick them up. Marley was standing there, behind the counter, looking into a monitor. She frowned and spoke to the woman in a paper cap. As the woman handed Albert his order, she said: "Your aunt wants you to park out front."

He did, shutting off the engine and rushing to the building to open the door for Marley. Together, they walked over to the Lexus. "I don't recognize him," Marley said. "I wonder whether he's someone you know?"

Albert and Marley both watched the man in the Civic drive around the corner of the building, creeping along at barely a mile an hour. He saw them looking directly at him and, after a moment's indecision, sighed and shrugged. He turned the wheel hard, pulling into a spot three spaces over from their Lexus.

"Don't freak out," he said as he climbed from his Civic. He held up both hands to show he was only carrying a take out bag. "There's no reason to get all freaked out."

He was a short man, maybe five-foot-four, with a sizable belly and a neatly-trimmed beard. His clothes were tidy but so nondescript they were

142

barely noticeable. He opened his long coat and reached inside.

Albert immediately crouched and stepped forward, adrenaline surging. "It's all right, Albert," Marley said, stopping him. "Isn't it, dear?"

The driver stared at them, his mouth hanging open, wondering if things were about to get violent. "Just getting a business card."

"I don't need one," Marley said. "You're a private investigator, aren't you?"

He sighed. "I knew I shouldn't have gotten into line behind you, but the fries here are so good—even if they do rip you off by charging for ketchup. Oh, well. Give me a moment to contact my client."

"Just what I was going to suggest, dear."

The investigator set the bag on top of his car and made a call. Judging from the part of the conversation they could hear, his client wasn't happy. The man said "I do not know that," at least a dozen times before finally asking if Albert was in the police or military.

"Military," he answered.

The man repeated that into the phone. "I am good at my job, but I'm not invisible. Someone who has been trained can spot me, and that's what happened."

Albert did not have the chance to explain that wasn't at all what happened, because the man immediately said, "Would you like to meet with my client tomorrow? I can arrange something in my office for, say, ten?"

"Oh, I don't think so," Marley said. "My days are much too busy for that. If your client wants to meet with me, she can come here, right now. I'll give her thirty minutes."

The private investigator relayed that message and winced at the response. Then he hung up his phone. "She's on her way," he said, with a distinct lack of enthusiasm.

Marley asked what it was like to be a private investigator, and he rolled his eyes before starting a litany of his woes, from the weight he'd gained after sitting all day to clients who won't pay their bills. Albert offered him a second bag of fries when his first was finished—which he accepted with both guilt and gratitude—and he finally introduced himself as Kevin Fletcher.

Eventually, a pearl-colored Seville pulled into the lot and a woman climbed from behind the wheel. Her expression was carefully neutral, and it clearly required great effort to keep it that way. Luckily for her, she had a lot of practice pretending to be calm and rational. As she passed Kevin, she said: "I certainly hope I will not be seeing a bill from you."

"Oh, you'll be getting a bill," he snapped back. "And you'll pay it, too." Then he folded his arms and leaned against his car, scowling.

She turned her back on him and found herself facing Marley. Suddenly, she seemed unsure what to do next. "My name is Celeste Salkin."

"I know who you are, dear."

"I would prefer," she began, sounding brittle, "that you not refer to me with that word, or any other term of endearment."

"I like to keep my conversations friendly, but I suppose that's too much to expect for the moment."

"Much too much. I suppose you're wondering why I had you followed."

Silence.

"Well?" Marley prompted, becoming annoyed. Celeste hesitated. During the drive over, she'd planned and practiced what she wanted to say, but suddenly she didn't have the courage for any of it. Worse, she couldn't think up something that did not require courage. "Oh, come on," Marley finally said. "It's late and we're all standing out in this chilly parking lot. This is no time for cold feet."

"I think your nephew was selling drugs," Celeste blurted.

"Do you, now? And what makes you believe that?"

"Never you mind. I just do. And I know he was murdered and my... I'm concerned about the... I know you're up to something."

"Up to something! Well, how perceptive you are, Celeste. Of course I'm up to something. Someone murdered my nephew! Should I sit at home and cry?"

"I'm sure I wouldn't know what steps you would have to take."

A Key, an Egg, an Unfortunate Remark

Marley peered at Celeste's pinched, disapproving expressions, trying to understand where this was all going. Albert was surprised to see his aunt looking confused, so he leaned down to Marley's ear and said, "She thinks you were helping Aloysius." When that was clear enough, he added, "Sell drugs."

His voice was quiet, but not so quiet that Celeste and Kevin couldn't hear. Celeste's expression turned a little more self-righteous, as though being understood was the same as being proven right.

Marley took hold of Albert's arm as if to hold herself steady, then laughed long and loud. Kevin fought the urge to laugh with her and Celeste began to look a little sick. Marley finally caught her breath. "And to think I was actually worried about this!"

"Laugh if you must," Celeste said primly, "but your nephew was murdered and right after that your house was burned to the ground. And I know about you and your parties!"

"How could you know about my parties, dear, when you've never been to one? I invited you once or twice, didn't I? After that lovely summer picnic Marjorie threw? But you never even RSVP'ed and I took the hint. Now I'm dying to know what you heard that kept you away." Marley couldn't hide her delight. "Was it something salacious?"

In the long drive to this meeting, the one thing Celeste had not imagined was that Marley would laugh at her. "I don't think—"

"No, no! Enough of that!" Marley said. "What did you hear that kept you away from my parties? Tell me."

For a few moments, Celeste was still taken aback, but when she spoke it was with the conviction of someone finally airing a long-held grievance. "I heard about your yoga event."

"Oh, yes, that was a benefit for earthquake victims, I believe. What of it?" Marley had thought that gathering had been rather tame, but perhaps there had been an incident no one told her about... if such a thing was even possible.

"Well, what I heard was that it was partner yoga," Celeste said with

145

distaste. "You made people, some practically strangers to each other, get together and touch each other."

After a lingering moment of astonishment, Marley's delight evaporated, leaving only sadness. "Yes, Celeste. Fully-clothed human beings touched each other in a platonic way. Thank goodness you stayed away. I'm sure it would have been hideous for you."

"I don't need to go to parties," Celeste said. "I have my daily schedule: my trips to the gym and my reading routine and—"

"You didn't go to the police," Marley interrupted, sounded even sadder. "Who do you think Aloysius was selling drugs to? Not your children. At the picnic you told me they're all grown up and living on the east coast now, I remember. So... your husband?"

Celeste stood there, silently grinding her teeth. Marley stepped toward her, but she stepped away.

"Celeste, of course I'm not selling drugs, at my parties or anywhere else. I do want to talk to... George, was it?"

"Oh no you don't." Celeste's voice was suddenly loud. "You keep away from him. Otherwise I might have to start talking to people about what I know."

"Celeste, I'm not your enemy and I don't mean any harm to you or your family, so before you start spreading rumors you might want to call your lawyer. Ask her what it will cost you to lose a slander case. Try to get a dollar amount. Then you can decide how you want to proceed."

Celeste didn't like that idea. "You can try to pretend all you like, but I'm on to you and soon everyone will be. Keep away from my husband." She turned and marched back to her car, climbed in and drove away.

Marley turned to Kevin. "I'm sorry to have caused you any trouble. You may have a hard time getting your fee from her now."

Kevin shrugged. "That's what collection agencies are for." Rubbing his chin thoughtfully, he said: "So, is it true that you can hook me up with—"

"No."

The flat finality of her tone was extraordinarily convincing. "Okay! All right! Fair enough. You folks have a nice night." He also got into his car and drove away.

When he was out of sight, Marley took out her phone and made a call. "Frederika, when you get this in the morning—Wednesday morning—I'd like you to do me a favor. Dig up George Salkin's phone number or email or something and contact him for me. It appears that he had a relationship with Aloysius, and I'd like to step in and help him." She hung up. "There's yet another person to check out. This list is supposed to be getting shorter, not longer."

Albert opened the door and let her into the car, then got behind the wheel. "Home?"

"Home."

They pulled into traffic. Albert glanced into the rearview mirror at his aunt. "She's another ghost."

Marley sighed. "She is, but she doesn't have to be. There must be a way to draw her out. I'll put my mind to it later."

"Another name for the list of people to save, huh?"

Marley looked at his expression in the rear view mirror. For once, she was unsure what he was thinking.. "Very much so."

CHAPTER TWENTY-TWO
Chains Forged in Life

When they woke Wednesday morning, they found Weathers in the kitchen, brewing coffee. Marley asked him to prepare a hearty breakfast; she had a lot of people to see that day and her appetite was fierce.

She first placed a call to Elaine, discovered that the environmentalists she hosted would be arriving soon, and made arrangements to meet with them. Before the call was even finished, another came in from a number she didn't recognize. It was George Salkin, and he wanted to meet with Marley immediately, wherever she was.

Unwilling to let him know where she was living now, Marley proposed alternate plans to meet him at a coffee shop beside the Fisherman's Terminal.

An hour later, Albert opened the door of the cafe for his aunt, and a trim, sixty-ish man in a pale green polo shirt and cream-colored dockers hurried toward them. "Marley Jacobs! George Salkin. Of course I recognize you—we have an awful lot of friends in common—but isn't it strange that we don't know each other?" He was grinning a thousand-watt smile, but it couldn't disguise the calculating look in his eyes. Albert disliked him immediately.

Marley was well-practiced at hiding her own dislike. "I suppose this is our chance to remedy that, don't you think? I'm just sorry it has to be under such terrible circumstances."

"Ah. Yes. Please accept my condolences."

"Thank you."

"There's a private room back here that I reserved for us. Can I get you a coffee?"

"No need." She went to the counter, ordered a single tall latte with a sprinkle of nutmeg, then paid. Albert ordered a regular coffee, and waited for the order to be ready while George led Marley to the little conference room at the back of the cafe.

Then he closed the door.

While Albert stood anxiously at the counter, waiting to rejoin his aunt, Marley graciously let George pull her chair back for her, then smiled when he sat beside her and made an excuse to touch her hand. He hoped they could be good friends, and he leaned forward as he spoke, holding her gaze in his. Marley noticed he wasn't wearing a wedding ring.

Albert pushed open the door and set Marley's coffee beside her. "Thank you, dear. Shut the door, would you? The three of us have a lot to discuss."

"Three?" George said, looking put out. "Well, okay. I mean, that will be

148

fine. It's just that I have to talk about something sensitive..."

"Business arrangements often are."

"But not illegal, I swear."

"Of course not. But Aloysius is gone and you want to continue to do business. Well, I called you because I want to help. So I'm going to ask you some questions, and if you want even a chance to continue your business arrangement, you'll answer honestly."

"Well, all right. I guess your first question is going to be what I paid him."

"Not at all. I want to know what he was selling you."

George put his hands on the arm of his chair, intending to stand and walk out of the room. If the boy's aunt didn't even know the product, how could she take over deliveries? Still, he hesitated. He wanted it. He really, really wanted it. "Okay. It was a special drink. A smoothie, really. It made me feel confident and... and persuasive."

Marley seemed to understand immediately. "Ah. It was white and chalky, I'm assuming? But slightly sweet?"

"Yes!" George's smile became bright and hopeful. She knew what the boy was selling after all. In fact, it almost sounded as though there might be other products on offer. He would have to remember to ask about them later. "Yes, I have a big negotiation coming up, and I was relying on this week's delivery—"

"When did he make deliveries to you?"

"Er, today was the day. Every Wednesday morning at ten-thirty sharp. He was very punctual."

Marley nodded. "I understand completely. You realize there won't be a delivery today. I know what he was giving you but he didn't get it from me. That's why I don't have any prepared."

George licked his lips. His charming manner was starting to crack. "Sure. I understand. I guess."

"Do you know who was preparing these smoothies for Aloysius?"

"No clue. I assumed it was something the boy put together. He was a clever kid, your nephew."

"He never mentioned any names?" George shook his head. "Not Zoe?"

"He didn't. Sorry. When I said I assumed he was making the smoothies, I mean that's the impression he gave. He wanted me to think it was something he made." George licked his lips and rubbed his mouth. This wasn't going as well as he'd hoped. "Are you sure you don't have any smoothie for me? It's just that the real estate market has been difficult this past year. Business-wise. I've hard a hard time making the deals I used to."

"An awful lot of people are in the same situation, I think."

"Sure, sure. But I've come to rely on that smoothie. For my confidence."

"And persuasion," Marley said, with a note of disapproval. "You rely on it because it lets you talk people into deals they wouldn't normally agree to. You can make them buy properties they don't need at prices that don't make sense. Of course that solves your problems, but it only adds to theirs."

George looked as though he'd just been insulted. "I paid your nephew ten thousand dollars a dose."

Marley stood, and so did Albert. "Is that all? You were getting off cheap. For the sorts of deals you were making, he could have gotten twice that. Maybe more. Not that it matters. You've had your last 'smoothie,' I think."

"Why don't you sit back down?" George asked, smiling. He opened his jacket to reveal a small belt holster with an even smaller black pistol.

"Be still, Albert," Marley said, just as he tensed up. "All right, George. We'll sit and we'll talk a bit more. But what I really want is for you to give me that weapon so I can get on with my day. Then I want you to go home and tell Celeste everything you've been up to."

Goosebumps ran down Albert's back as George laid his hand on his thigh, inches from that little Beretta. There were more than a few options if the old guy decided to draw, but none were good. The best they could hope for was that he'd take George down without being fatally shot.

George smiled. "Why don't you sit down?" His stillness suggested that he was in control of the conversation and entirely comfortable with his threat of violence.

Marley sat, then patted Albert's chair. He settled down, letting his weight rest forward, ready to spring.

George put his hand on his gun. "Don't, son."

Marley opened her bag. "He won't do anything," she said confidently. "He knows better. So, you want more of the potions Aloysius was selling you?"

"I do indeed."

"Hm. Tell me, does this smell familiar to you?"

She handed him the same vial she'd given to Inez. He took it warily, then sniffed at it. "Not really. This smells like good chocolate. Aloysius's smoothies were like drinking a chalky curry sauce with syrup mixed in."

He returned the vial. Marley lifted it to the light, shook it, then frowned and shrugged. Empty. "In that case, I'll need to research his recipe."

George sighed, then stood, then set his holstered weapon on the table between them. "You do that. Just remember that I'm a man of influence in this town. The path to long term happiness in this burg passes through Doing-What-I-Say-Ville."

He left. Marley wrapped George's gun in a bit of newspaper, and they dropped it into the trash on the way out.

In the car, Albert said, "What's Celeste going to say when he tells her what he's been up to?"

Marley took a sip of her latte. "They really do make a delicious cup of coffee, don't they?"

CHAPTER TWENTY-THREE
The Fellowship of the Couch

Marley sent Elaine's address to the GPS. It was well to the north of them, and traffic was at a standstill because the Ballard Bridge was up. By

151

the time they arrived, it was late enough in the morning that there was plenty of street parking.

Marley rang the front doorbell, and Elaine came out to meet her all covered with flour. They hugged briefly, despite Elaine's protests, and Marley stepped back without a speck on her black blazer. Elaine directed them to a path around the side of the house that went down to the alley level, explaining that the office didn't have a connecting door into the house.

"Office" was a grandiose name for a small studio apartment just behind the garage. The entrance was at the bottom of a steep flight of concrete stairs, and the McMansion next door cut off most of the meager Seattle sunlight. Mounted on the wall, above a worn doorbell, was a plastic sleeve with a single sheet of laser printer paper inside. On the sheet, in large, outlined letters, was PEOPLE'S WORLD NATURE EDUCATORIUM, DISTRICT 1.

"Classy," Albert said.

Marley knocked. "I assume there's no district two, or any other number, for that matter."

She'd barely finished her sentence before the door swung open, revealing a short, wiry man with a wiry grey ponytail. His beard was almost a foot long but it didn't hide his bright, wide smile. "Speak, friend, and enter!"

"Mellon." Albert's answer came from the books but his pronunciation was copied from the movie.

The wiry hippie laughed aloud. "Well! It's been a long time since someone gave the correct response to that call. I like you already. Call me Merry."

The door swung wide, revealing a small dinette table with dinged green metal chairs around it, all clearly scavenged from someone's dumpster. A tattered map of Seattle's bike trails hung on the opposite wall. Another printed sheet of paper hung above the kitchenette; it read THIS KITCHEN IS CRUELTY-FREE. The room smelled like armpits and bong water.

Merry gestured toward the three people seated around the table. The pale, shapeless Asian woman was introduced as Hsing. She was about

Merry's age and she looked at Marley and Albert as though she wasn't quite sure if they were real. The woman beside her was only a few years younger, but had the body of an triathlete. Her thin, straight brown hair framed an utterly humorless expression; her name was Janet. Last was Philip, a very young guy with a wispy beard and black hair he wore in a ponytail.

Marley stood before them with her hands clasped in front of her. "I assume you all know why I'm visiting you."

"Because of your nephew," Hsing answered, her voice almost as droning as Amos Quigley's had been. "Aloysius Pierce. It's so terrible what happened, but at least he's gone to bathe in the love of Jesus."

"Er, thank you."

"I know why she's here," Janet said, her expression stony. "She's come here to accuse us of his murder."

"Now that's not true!" Marley shook her finger. "You don't even believe that yourself. You can't lie to me!"

"No, I don't believe it." Janet admitted to a lie with the same self-righteous stoicism she used when accusing someone of lying. "But I had to shock the others. They're too trusting. I don't want them pouring their hearts out to some wealthy capitalist with a sob story."

Marley didn't even blink. "I'm not interested in the contents of their hearts, liquid or otherwise. I am interested in why he was meeting with you, and what you thought of him."

"We hated him," Janet said with that same cold certainty.

"I don't 'hate' anyone," Hsing interjected. "That goes against my faith. I loved him."

"I didn't hate the dude, either," Merry added, "but I didn't trust him. I wished him the same spiritual peace and universal love that I would wish on anyone, but he didn't give us a lot of reasons to like him."

"He was a fornicator," Hsing said. Merry and Philip looked embarrassed.

No one seemed to want to expand on that, so Marley said, "I assume he wasn't representing you." She knew that wasn't true, but it was an effective goad.

153

Merry, Hsing, and Philip laughed. "No," Merry said. "He was an errand boy for the corporatist/developer complex."

Janet stared into Albert's face. "Like so many are."

"We've been opposing a certain development site out at the Cedar River —"

"All of our drinking water comes from there, you know!" Hsing cut in, her voice suddenly very loud.

Marley nodded kindly to her. "Not all, but I do know about the area."

Merry cleared his throat. "Well, they somehow got a permit to excavate on the site. Somehow."

"Not to mention," Hsing said, her voice becoming more angry and strained, "that land is supposed to be preserved! Not to mention that their equipment has been digging beyond the permitted area! Not to mention—"

A loud, persistent beeping interrupted her. She removed a kitchen timer from her pocket and shut it off. Then she pushed her chair back. Merry stood and pulled his chair out of her way to let her head toward the bathroom. "You be sure to turn on the fan, now."

She went into the room without a response, shut the door and turned on the exhaust. Everyone but Janet looked uncomfortable. Within seconds, they could hear the flick of a lighter and the sound of bubbling water. The nasty-sweet stink of marijuana smoke came through the door.

"You have to understand," Merry, said apologetically. "The timer is to reduce her usage. She's trying to cut back."

"So," Marley said, "I assume you were trying to block the development project?"

"We know quite a few ways to make our voices heard," Janet said. "All of them legal."

"And I know a couple of judges who listen with an open mind," Merry said, "as long as the paperwork is done correctly. We have our ways. But Aloysius wanted us to lay off. What's more, he offered a deal: If we left his boss's project alone, he would sign over a larger plot of land to us, to be turned into a preserve. It was right on a migration zone. A really great opportunity."

"But it was all talk," Janet said.

Merry sighed. "She's right. It was all talk. He kept telling us the paperwork was being put together while the watershed site was being ravaged, and then he stopped taking our calls as soon as our guy on the scene said—"

"So you see," Janet broke in, "we did have reason to want him killed."

"I suppose you did," Marley said thoughtfully.

"But we didn't do it."

"And what about you, Philip? Do you have anything to add?"

The young man was startled by Marley's unexpected attention. "Me? Um..."

Janet stood. Her chair slid back, caught on the edge of the carpet and toppled onto the floor. She made no move to pick it up. "I'm going out to the van. Philip, come with me."

Philip blushed bright red. He opened his mouth as though to say something, but then he stood and followed her outside.

"Well!" Merry said, clapping his hands and rubbing them together. "That was productive, but I don't think we can get much further today. What do you say we arrange another meeting for... Monday. We can make a list of agenda items regarding your nephew and what you need to accomplish in that arena, and we can spitball some ideas."

"Thank you so much," Marley said, "but I don't think that will be necessary. I'll be in touch if there's anything further."

She turned toward the door. Albert took the hint and opened it for her. Together they went up the front stairs and met Elaine in the garden where she was pulling weeds. "How were they?" she asked.

"They're quite a collection of characters," Marley answered. "Why do you let them use that apartment, dear?"

"Taxes, partly," Elaine pulled off her gloves and wiped a bit of sweat from her nose. "It does me good to rent that unit, but I don't like the idea of someone living there. My little hippies are a nice compromise. Besides, occasionally they do some good."

"Did you ever hear them argue?"

"Them? Never. Oh, do you mean when Aloysius was visiting? You know, at first he was nearly frantic to get them to leave his precious project alone. He even threatened to call the drug squad or whatever they call it, but I... convinced him not to."

Elaine's hesitation when choosing that last verb was all the hint Marley needed. "Elaine! You and Aloysius?"

"Well, why not? It's been years since Lee ran off with a younger woman. Why can't I have some fun? But it was only the once, and not exactly worth writing songs about. But no, I never heard them argue, and as I said, I don't think they would do anything to your Aloysius."

They clasped hands and promised to do lunch, then Albert and Marley went back to the car.

"Do you see that van, Albert?"

She nodded at a windowless blue van with rust marks along the bottom. Someone had painted clouds along the top of the panels, with a single sun beam shining downward as though the advancing rust was rocky ground. Its springs squeaked as it gently rocked. "I don't want to see it," Albert said. "I mean, I really really don't want to, but that has to be them, doesn't it?"

"I think so, too. Let's pull the car a little closer."

They did, parking across the street and down the block just a little bit. Within twenty minutes, the back doors of the van swung open. Janet and Philip climbed out, both looking a little flushed. Janet marched directly back toward the studio, but Philip loitered a bit, glancing furtively up and down the block as though he thought someone might be pointing a camera at him.

"Albert, flash the headlights, please."

Albert did, and Philip came toward the car with a certain weary resignation. Albert got out and opened the back door for him, but Philip hesitated. He was used to doing what he was told, but it occurred to him that he was about to be kidnapped, maybe. Did he really want to be so cooperative? He thought he ought to make the big guy behind him wrestle

156

him into the car or something.

"Oh, don't be like that, dear, you're perfectly safe with me." Marley patted the seat beside her. With a shrug, Philip climbed in. Albert got behind the wheel. "Would you like us to drop you somewhere, dear, or stay here?"

Philip said, "Stay here." He felt he was incriminating himself with his own words and suddenly found he couldn't speak. "Uh…"

"Oh, you don't have to make any explanations to me, Philip. There's nothing surprising about you and Janet. I imagine she's very intense, but not much fun."

"I wanted to do some good in the world," Philip responded. He was ready to say anything to avoid talking about Janet with this adorable old woman. "I wanted to make a difference, to learn how to fight for the environment and social justice, but it's pretty rare that we actually do anything. Mostly we just talk and talk and talk."

"Philip, who is the fifth member of your group? Who is the 'guy on the scene' that Janet didn't want me to hear about?"

"I shouldn't really talk about that. I'm not supposed to."

"That's backwards, dear, and you know it. You are supposed to talk about it, but the others don't want you to."

Philip didn't say anything for a few seconds. "There's an old cabin out by the development site. It's not supposed to be there, any more than the trucks and such, but it's there, and we have a… friend who lives there illegally. He watches over things for us."

"And why aren't you supposed to talk about him? Because he's a squatter?"

"No," Philip said. "He's dangerous. He's killed people, I think."

Marley took out her phone and opened up a map of the Cedar River area. "Show me where the cabin is, dear." She offered it to him. "We're going up there, and we need to know where it is so we can avoid it."

Philip hesitated but, like the obedient boy he is, he marked the general area on the map. It felt to him as though he'd already gone too far and he didn't want to say anything else, so he got out of the car. Before he shut the door, he said: "But I really do think you should stay away from there. This guy, he's not always in control of himself. He's really, really dangerous."

Marley gave him a calm look. "No worries, dear. Little old ladies never want to do anything dangerous."

CHAPTER TWENTY-FOUR
The Un-Recruitment Drive

Albert watched Philip, with his spindly, hunched shoulders and his long, bird-like neck, walk back to the office. "Jesus, is everybody getting some but me?"

"And me," Marley answered. "But you're right, it hardly seems fair, what with spring in the air and so on and so forth."

"It wasn't just spring, not with Aloysius. Did the guy hit on every woman he saw? Successfully?"

"It's starting to seem that way, but don't be too surprised, dear. Aloysius was confident and manipulative. Guess what that will get you?"

Albert didn't give the obvious one-word answer. "But he was so skeevy. Why would—"

"Careful, dear. You don't want to become one of those men who whine about women's taste in men. That's a quick route to Jerkville."

Albert glanced into the rear view mirror at her. "Jerkville?"

"Creep Town."

"Isn't that where Aloysius lived?"

"All right then, Masturbation City."

"Okay, Aunt Marley, now I'm officially uncomfortable."

She laughed, and he laughed a little, too. "Now you know how I feel, dear, considering how the conversation was going."

"Ah. Sorry."

"It's all right," she said. "As long as you don't become one of those pathetic men who complain about women hating 'nice guys' or something."

"You're the boss."

"What did you think about the activists?"

"I think it was a waste of time to visit them. It's hard to believe they would be a threat to anyone," Albert answered, grateful for the change of subject. "They seem like useless relics."

"Useless they may be—or perhaps I should say 'ineffectual'—but they aren't relics, dear."

"I wasn't talking about their age, Aunt Marley. I was talking about the whole peace and love, tree-hugging thing."

"I knew exactly what you meant. It's easy to make fun of a cultural moment a few decades after it has passed. It's easy to point out the indulgence and hypocrisy. What's harder is criticizing your own time and your own assumptions. What's more, I may not sneak bong hits in the bathroom, but I still hold to certain values—"

"I'm sorry," Albert interrupted. "I keep sticking my foot in my mouth, don't I?"

"Did I get a little testy? I guess I did. Let's forget all that. It does seem strange to me that Evelyn would have Aloysius working on a project all the way out in the Cedar River area while he was working on her downtown development plans. Or do you think it's all the same thing? Or do you think he had another client off the books who had him handling something else? You know, Aloysius's schedule had every Wednesday morning—the whole thing—blocked off for 'Errands' with no other details. I thought he was picking up dry cleaning and going to the grocery, but now I know he was delivering magic potions for someone else, possibly Zoe—unless he stole her spell book so he could make the potions himself, cutting her out. Also, it wouldn't have taken him all morning to make that one delivery. What else was he doing with that time? Was he selling or delivering potions to other people we don't know about yet?"

Albert sighed. The whole thing seemed like a confused muddle and he hated muddles. "Good questions."

"And I tend to agree with Elaine that her activists are unlikely suspects. Janet strikes me as someone who would commit murder, but she wouldn't waste her time on an 'errand boy,' as they called Aloysius. But what would their 'dangerous friend' do if he came into the city? Then we have to consider all the women he slept with: Zoe and Inez and Elaine and—"

"Elaine doesn't seem like the murdering type, does she?"

"You didn't know her when her husband ran off. She… actually, everyone has a hidden side. Anyone can be driven to the edge if they're desperate enough. Except me, of course." Albert wasn't sure if his aunt was joking, and before he could figure it out, she began to talk again. "Your brother—excuse me, half-brother—led a complicated life. We're going to have to keep digging."

"Are we going up there to look at the site and meet the 'dangerous' hippie in the cabin?" Albert flexed his damaged hand; he didn't put much stock in Philip's assessment of who was dangerous or not.

"We are indeed, but not right away. If, as Merry said, the construction crew is gone, I think we can deal with other things first. I would really like to know who else Aloysius was selling charisma potions to, and what the keys on the key ring open, and—"

"And who sent the men that burned down your house," Albert said. "And who killed Aloysius."

"Albert, dear, look in your side-view mirror. We have some good news coming our way."

A tall man with the muscles of a body builder strolled down the sidewalk toward them, and Albert could tell he was coming straight for the car. It was Nelson, the vampire hunter Albert had knocked to the ground in the backyard of Spire's house.

Marley rolled down her window. Albert took this as a sign to sit tight. Still, even though Nelson's hands were empty, he felt vulnerable; his hands trembled and his stomach felt tight.

"Hello, dear," Marley said out her window. "I have been waiting for you to approach. What can I do for you?"

"Can we talk?" Nelson asked.

"Of course! Over a cup of coffee? There's a cafe down the street."

"To be honest, ma'am, I was hoping for someplace more private."

"Oh, this is the perfect place, trust me." Marley gave him directions but promised to wait long enough for him to follow their car in his gleaming black pickup truck. Ten minutes later, they had parked and gotten into line. Marley ordered green tea, Albert ordered another black coffee, and Nelson paid for all of them.

He insisted on a table away from the windows. They ended up sitting next to the entrance to the unisex bathroom.

"I'm the one who wanted to talk, so I guess I should start," Nelson said. He had a short, broad nose, a heavy jaw, and very dark skin. He was also much younger than Albert first thought, maybe seventeen or eighteen. Albert couldn't help wondering who he would turn out to be sleeping with. "I'm just not sure where."

"Start with why you want to leave your little group. That's why you came, isn't it?"

Nelson rubbed his mouth nervously. "Well, yes, it is. I don't mean any disrespect to Nora. She's a hero to me. Honestly, she is."

"But you're becoming increasingly uncomfortable with the choices she's making. And with Audrey."

Nelson sighed. "How did you know?"

"I've seen it before, many times. No matter how much you dehumanize your enemy—"

"Oh my enemy isn't human," Nelson cut in. "My enemies are dead things. Sins against God. Ma'am, I don't have any problem with..." He lowered his voice, "killing vampires."

Albert cut in: "Then what is the problem?"

"It's the helpers. The renfields."

"Oh, please," Marley said, "I suppose I qualify as a 'renfield' in your eyes?"

Nelson nodded. "You both do. And... I don't like what we do to them. To people like you."

Albert cut in: "You kill them."

Nelson nodded again. "Nora says they're accomplices to murder. The law makes every accomplice to a crime just as guilty as the person who commits it, so why shouldn't we follow the same rules? And sometimes they're dangerous."

"They are," Marley said. "They try very hard to protect their loved ones."

"But what if they're coerced?" Nelson said. "What if they're under the control of the thing and can't help themselves? I can understand using force to get past them, tase them, maybe, to subdue them quickly, but what if they'd be glad to be freed after the vampire is put down?"

Marley's voice was sly when she said, "And what if you could leave them alive at the scene of the murder, with their prints all over the murder weapon, right?"

"No!" Nelson was genuinely surprised by the suggestion. "I mean, that's not how we do our thing."

Albert didn't like the way this conversation was going. "I'm not under anyone's control, especially not a vampire's."

"How would you know?" Nelson countered. "You're doing things that seem perfectly sensible to you, am I right? But you're protecting monsters. Does that seem like the sort of thing a sensible person would do?"

Marley was smiling. "Maybe a sensible person wouldn't, but I would."

"See? Ma'am, I know you moved that vampire we were after, and I won't pretend I wasn't angry about it. I was and I still am. We've been after it for nearly two years, for some killings it did back home, and we were so close to finishing."

Albert couldn't hide his surprise. "Two years? Dude, how old were you when you got sucked into all this?"

Nelson suddenly looked very tired. "My best friend's father was killed by a vampire when I was fourteen. He didn't believe me when I told him—he thought I'd lost my mind—but I believed it. Nora tried to keep me out of the hunt, but I had a mind of my own."

"And she thought it would be safer to train you than let you run loose on your own."

"Yeah. She called me 'Robin' until I hit my growth spurt."

"Growth spurt!" Albert almost laughed. "Nelson, how old are you?"

Nelson didn't like that question, but he answered it anyway. "I just turned seventeen."

Albert turned to Marley as though Nelson's age was a problem she could fix. "That's too young, right? Hell, I'm too young for all this, and I served overseas. You shouldn't be doing this, dude. You should be entering bodybuilding contests or something."

Nelson shrugged. "It's hard, living on the road. I can't get the right tone on my lower back."

Albert nodded. "Backs are tough."

"You said you were angry," Marley interrupted. She watched Nelson's expression carefully. "Were the others angry, too?"

"I don't think they get angry anymore."

Marley's only response was to nod. It was the answer she'd expected. "Well, I'm glad you're only planning to tase us rather than shoot us, but I'm sure you didn't come here to tell me that."

"No, I didn't. Like I said, I'm planning to leave Nora's group for good, and to leave the city, too, but it wouldn't be right if I didn't warn you first. Nora has found the nest you've been keeping here in Seattle. She's planning a raid that will kill them all, and both of you, too."

CHAPTER TWENTY-FIVE
The Trojan Phone

"It's certainly nice of you to warn us," Marley said. "Of course you realize the... nest, as you call it, is really more of a rest home, and it has staff, too? And that the vampires living there agree to never hunt and feed on humans again? You realize that I've found a non-violent solution to the conflict?"

"For as long as that lasts."

"I have to admit, I'm not a fan of permanent solutions to peoples' problems. Not when that solution is killing them."

"I hear you. We may not agree on everything, but I don't want you or the people working at the nest to get hurt. I'm here to avoid all that. And more."

"What do you mean?"

"I want to give you this."

Nelson reached into his back pocket and took out a battered iPhone, which he set on the table between them.

Marley looked at him expectantly. "I have a phone, dear."

"This is Nora's. She doesn't know I have it—I palmed it in Iowa as we were leaving a restaurant by the highway. It's locked with a password, though, and I can't get at it. Maybe you two aren't, you know, computer experts or whatever, but I figure you can afford to hire one."

Marley didn't move to touch it. "And what would I do with Nora's phone?"

Nelson didn't answer for a long while. "She's killing people. People. It's wrong and it has to stop. I can't do it, not by myself. But you can. She's got a database in there, and a calendar with all our travel, and... who knows what else? She put her whole life there."

"That's a lot to trust me with."

"Trust?" Nelson leaned back in his chair and rubbed his face. "I don't see it that way, I guess. This a burden I can't carry any more, and I don't want to get caught with it, and I can't do anything with it anyway. Who else can I send it to, the cops? They wouldn't believe me and wouldn't do anything about it."

"But I will."

"Lord, I hope you will. I hope you will understand that, whatever you think of Nora, she's trying to do what's right." Nelson took a deep breath. "I should get back." He stood and so did Marley and Albert. Nelson gently took Marley's hand in both of his. "Thank you for listening. Please do what's right, and God bless." He released her and offered his hand to Albert. "No hard feelings?"

Albert shook his hand and Nelson hurried out the door. Marley waited for him to pass in front of the windows, then gathered her jacket. "Let's move quickly."

Albert hurried to open the door for her, as someone behind the counter called out a thank-you-and-come-again to their retreating backs. They walked quickly to their car, and Albert felt strangely attuned to his aunt. Her body language was different, and he kept his mouth shut.

Once they were in the car and moving again, Albert asked where they should go next. Marley directed him to a grocery store on West Dravus, then asked: "What did you think of him?"

"Fourteen!" Albert exclaimed. "Jesus. I like him and sort of admire him, too. I wish I hadn't knocked him down the other night. I don't trust him, though. It's possible he's telling the truth, isn't it?"

"Yes, it is," Marley answered. "I'm not sure what to believe, but I don't think I can leave my guests and staff in harm's way."

They drove all the way to supermarket in silence, then parked at the edge of the lot. When Albert let Marley out of the back seat, she turned away from the store and started down the sidewalk, moving toward the Magnolia hill. Albert walked beside her, watching for Nelson's truck, in case he was following them. He had to raise his voice over the sound of passing traffic. "What do you think about decoding the password?"

"It's easier than most people think," Marley answered, raising her voice, too. She handed him the iPhone. "Hold this. The real question is finding someone trustworthy with the skills and time to do it right away. I'd love to get it done today. But who can I find to come to our safe house? Who can I trust?"

As they walked, she began emptying her jacket pockets, collecting a tissue pack, swiss army knife, baggie of M&Ms, a pair of pens, and a tiny notepad, which she dumped into Albert's other hand. He had to trap them against his chest to keep them from spilling onto the sidewalk and into the blackberry bramble beside him.

The sidewalk passed over the Interbay train yard. "Time to go," Marley said, as a freight train rumbled beneath them. "Take me home, Albert, but remember to drive slowly. You know how frightened I get when you drive so fast."

She slipped off her jacket, slid the phone into the inside pocket, then wrapped the jacket around it. Once she had it wadded up, she dropped it into an open freight car full of what looked like scrap metal. The black jacket slid down into the refuse and disappeared as the train rolled northward.

"Well!" Marley said, relieved to be rid of the phone. "That was insulting."

A chill breeze blew from the bay to the south, moving along the train tracks like a river through a ravine. Albert shrugged off his jacket and wrapped it around his aunt's shoulders. "You think they had the GPS turned on?"

"Thank you, dear. If they were smart, they were listening in, too. Who did they think they were dealing with? Nelson was doing quite well until he gave me that phone."

Albert looked at her sideways as they walked back to the car. "You never once told him he couldn't lie to you."

"I didn't, did I? You know, I believe much of what he said. He truly is uncomfortable killing vampire companions. The term renfield is deeply foolish. The character may have been in Dracula's power, but he also warned the humans several times. Why would you murder an agent in your enemy's camp? Hmph. Nora's people impress me less every time we meet. And here I thought the visit would be good news—that we were stirring things up enough that trouble was coming to find us! But no. The plain fact is that they're a distraction and we are much too busy to deal with them."

"And they were trying to spook you into revealing the location of your guests."

166

A Key, an Egg, an Unfortunate Remark

"Exactly."

"Now they're going to follow that train out of town."

"For a while, at least. Still." Marley took out her phone and dialed a number that wasn't on her speed dial. "Naima, dear, I'd like to see about planning a vacation. Maybe someplace sunny." She hung up. "I can't be too careful. I expect Nora and Nelson will be upset when they realize they've been had, but that's how this game is played. Let's head back to the house for real. I want to know who Aloysius was visiting during his Wednesday morning 'errands.'"

At the house, they discovered that Miss Harriet had decided to work that day and had prepared turkey and cranberry sauce sandwiches for them. Marley ate while she reviewed Aloysius's files, giving special attention to his rather large contact list. After an hour, she had a list of ten names similar to George Salkin: older, well-off local businessmen who were not mentioned elsewhere in the files. Aloysius had never billed them, served papers on them, or written up contracts for them.

The first one she called was a man she knew slightly; he'd attended a few of her parties the year before, but upon discovering that she was unlikely to invest in pet food factories in China, he fell away from her social circle. His name was Harold Dixon. It only took a moment for the man's assistant to put her call through, and when Harold greeted her by saying how glad he was that she had changed her mind about investing with him, the urge to order her broker to transfer funds was so strong she felt light-headed.

She kept her resolve. When she asked about Aloysius, Harold became wary. Marley explained her relationship to him and inquired about today's delivery.

Harold told her everything was fine, asked her not to call again and hung up. Marley stood shakily and staggered into the corner of her office.

Albert, who had been sitting across from her, rushed to her side. "Are you all right? You're very pale."

"I thought I was ready," Marley told him in a quiet voice. "I expect him to have a charisma charm running when I called, but it's so much stronger

167

than I thought it would be."

"Do you need anything? A glass of water?"

"A little hot tea, I think. With sugar."

From the doorway, Weathers said: "Immediately, madam." He stalked toward the kitchen.

"Most charisma magic is weak stuff," Marley said as Albert helped her back to her chair. "Just knowing about it is all the counter-spell you need, usually. The effects are supposed to be subtle or...."

Albert finished her sentence: "Or when the effect wears off, the victim will realize what happened."

"Well, they don't usually realize it, because very, very few people in the world believe in magic. Mostly, they feel resentment and they do their damnedest to get out of whatever silly arrangement they've gotten into. Even if there's an ironclad contract... well, let's just say it's better to have a subtle effect that leaves you with a mostly willing business partner than someone who feels trapped." Marley stopped to rub her eyes. "Using the phone cuts out all the visual parts of the charm."

"But it was powerful anyway."

"Indeed it was! Who ever delivered this week's dose—and I assume Mr. Harold Dixon just took it—gave him a doozy."

She waited for Weathers to bring the tea, then sat quietly sipping at it. When she felt sufficiently revived, she called the next name on the list, another real estate agent. This one was willing to stay on the phone long enough to express his condolences on the death of Marley's nephew, even if he sounded distracted while he said it. He also let her know in no uncertain terms that this week's delivery had gone fine, as always.

She called four more before giving up. The last call was blocked by a developer's executive assistant, who informed Marley that she knew exactly why she was calling and had been instructed not to put the call through, then hung up on her.

The calls had left Marley rattled enough that she lost her temper. "The nerve! I should go down there straight away—"

"No, you shouldn't," Albert said. "As your nephew, I respectfully request that you not go near any of those people. Not while they have these spells on them. As your driver, I respectfully decline to drive you."

"Is that so? I could call a cab, you know." She waved her hand at him. "Oh never mind. Of course you're right. Thank you. Well, it seems clear that Salkind is the only one who didn't get this week's delivery. I wonder why."

"Probably because Aloysius was skimming some and selling it on the side."

"I—I do believe you're right, Albert. How clever of you."

As Albert felt a flush of pride, Marley's phone rang. Caller ID showed it was her attorney, Frederika, on the line, and the first thing she said was: "Marley, do you have an alibi for last night? Around 9PM?"

CHAPTER TWENTY-SIX
Honesty Is the Most Dangerous Trick of All

Frederika explained that Inez Shankley had filed a police report about a break-in at her office and she'd named Marley as her main suspect. Marley told Frederika about the meeting in the parking lot and gave her Kevin's name, then asked to meet outside the SPG Associate's law office.

Frederika got there first. Knowing her client well—and being too energetic to wait—she rushed forward and yanked open the back door of the Lexus before Albert could even turn off the engine.

"I've already spoken with the private investigator and he's happy to sign an affidavit, so your alibi is set. I think he's hoping to get some work out of me. How do you want to proceed, Marley? We can get a court order to make her back off, or we could just straight up sue her. I don't know Shankley personally, but I know of her. I could kick her ass in court."

"There will be no ass-kicking! Not today. Today we'll just talk. Nicely."

"I can do nice," Frederika said as she violently wrenched open the front door. Feeling useless, Albert hurried to keep up.

The reception area was a mess. Files had been pulled from their cabinets and strewn across the carpet. Sherilynne wasn't behind the reception desk; she was bent low in the corner, picking up loose sheets of paper and dropping them, all disordered, into baskets. She grumbled and sniffled as she worked. The phone rang. She stamped across the room and answered it with the handset.

Inez Shankley's door was open, so Marley started toward it. Inez was quicker, though, blocking the doorway before they could get close.

"Inez," Marley said. "What happened here?"

Inez smiled cynically. "You don't know?"

"Be careful," Frederika interrupted.

"I'm always careful," Inez said smoothly. She turned to Marley. "I lock my doors and set my alarm every night before I leave. That's how careful I am."

"Inez." Marley's voice was flat and firm. "Whatever happened here, I'm sure you know I had nothing to do with it. I mean, really."

"You came here asking to see his office and his files, didn't you? And that very same night someone broke into the former and stole the latter. That's a remarkable coincidence, don't you think?"

"Inez, does your computer network track access to the files?"

"Yes, it does. It logs when the files were accessed, who did it, and when. All I'd need to do is contact my admin service—"

"Do that, would you please? For the time—Albert, when were we here in the office yesterday? About ten-thirty?"

Before he could answer, Inez spoke up: "It was nine-fifty-five to ten-twenty."

"Oh good. Check those times, dear. We'll wait here."

Inez looked suspicious but she went into her office and closed the door.

Marley turned to Sherilynne, who had hung up the phone and now stood staring at a drift of paper in the corner of the room. "Is Stan in, dear?

I've been wanting to speak with him."

Sherilynne moaned, a sound part ghostly misery, part grieving beluga whale. Then she tilted her head back to stare at the ceiling. The phone rang, but she made no move to answer it.

Marley took her gently by the elbow and steered her toward a little set of chairs that were clearly supposed to be a waiting area. They sat together.

Frederika moved to the door to look out into the street, ready to throw her body at any approaching police officers, if Inez made the mistake of calling them. Albert edged toward the desk; the ringing phone bothered him more than he wanted to admit, and he wondered what would happen if he answered it and took a message.

"He meant something to me, too, you know," Sherilynne said. "And now what do I have? No boyfriend. A job where no one likes me. And I'm not even invited to the funeral!"

She began to cry in earnest while Marley sat beside her and patted her hand. The phone finally stopped ringing, and Albert stared at his shoes, wishing he had something he could do.

"Sherilynne, dear," Marley said, trying to break in between gasping sobs. "Dear. No one has been invited to the funeral yet. No arrangements have been made."

That broke through to her. "None? But it's already Wednesday!"

"He was murdered, dear. We're not in any rush. Give Albert your contact information and we'll make sure you know the time and date."

"Oh my gosh," she said, wiping her eyes. "Oh my gosh, I will." She stood and made a beeline to the desk. The phone started ringing again but she ignored it. She picked up her purse, rummaged inside for a pen and Post-it, then scribbled down her contact information.

Albert accepted it from her and put it in his pocket. He'd barely pulled his hand out again when she flung herself at him, throwing her arms around him and squeezing his floating ribs painfully. Then she went to Marley, bent over and gave her a big, awkward hug, which Marley felt obliged to reciprocate.

After that, Sherilynne sniffled and pivoted toward Frederika, who held up one hand and said, "No."

Sherilynne stopped as if poleaxed. Marley laid a gentle hand on the weeping woman's shoulder. "Is Stan in his office?" she asked again. "I would like to speak with him."

"I'll email him to let him know."

"Has he been in today?"

"No, he hasn't been in to the office since you were here last."

"I see. Is that unusual?"

"A little. He usually tells me where he is. Should I have him call you?"

"If you would, please, I'd be grateful. Also, you should probably polish up your résumé."

Sherilynne sighed. The phone started ringing again, and this time she moved to answer it.

Inez yanked her office door open. "For God's sake, would someone answer the—" She stopped as she saw Sherilynne put on her headset. Then she turned to Marley. "Would you come into my office, please?"

Marley did, with Frederika and Albert. This time, Frederika took the chair beside Marley, leaving Albert to stand by the door.

"I've discovered something alarming," Inez said. "According to my admin service, the last time anyone has accessed Al's files was yesterday, from this computer. While you were in this office."

"That's right, dear. You copied them onto a travel drive for me, then passed them across the desk."

"I don't remember that."

Frederika huffed in disbelief, and Inez's response was sharp.

"I mean it. I truly don't remember doing that. I told you I couldn't share the files with you."

"You did say that," Albert said. "You told us you couldn't copy the files, but you were copying them onto my aunt's thumb drive as you said it." He felt strange dealing in this half-truth. If he wasn't complicit in the trick they'd played on Inez, he certainly was now. Also, he suddenly felt connected to his aunt in a new and unexpected way.

Inez gaped at him. "Why would I do that?"

"Well, I thought you were doing that thing where you say 'No one is allowed to have extra dessert' while you give your buddy a second slice of cake. I thought you wanted to give it to us on the sneak."

"It's true, dear." Marley said. "The files came from your own hand, and if I'd known you were on autopilot…. In any event, you can see I had no reason to break in here and search your office; your computer records show that you yourself gave me what I asked for already."

"Unless," Inez countered, "what you were looking for wasn't in the files." She made a sour face. "No. Forget that. I'm only saying that because I'm embarrassed."

Marley was sympathetic. "Well of course you are! You're an intelligent woman who did something you wish you hadn't. Believe me when I say that I sympathize."

Inez met her gaze evenly. "Then I'm going to play on that sympathy and ask you to delete those files. Please."

Marley took the travel drive from her purse and held it up. "There are copies on my computer which I'll delete when I'm at home, but there's something I want in return. I have questions I need answered."

Inez looked wary. "What are they?"

"What happened here last night? And what was Aloysius really up to?"

Inez arranged the pencils in her pencil jar so they were perfectly spaced. "Al was falling behind. He only had the one client—a big one with a lot of stupid errands for him to run—but I happen to know he was having trouble with some of those errands. He was also having trouble paying his bills in a timely manner. His share of the office dues were late last month, again." She pressed a button on her phone. "Sherilynne, would you bring in April's office balance sheets, please, assuming they're in some sort of order." She released the button. "Luckily, we didn't have the phone or electricity shut off, and Al was able to cover the past due charges. I certainly wasn't going to pay his share, considering our relationsh… God, I just realized…" Inez pushed her chair back. "The police found his car. Did you hear that?"

"No, I didn't. How did you?"

"Um, from a friend. Anyway, they found his car under the viaduct. It had been torn apart—all the upholstery was slashed. Someone must have searched it."

Sherilynne bustled into the room with a manila folder in her hand. "They were in my desk and they weren't touched."

Inez accepted them. "Oh, good." Sherilynne sniffled. Inez looked at her closely, noting her red, puffy eyes. "Are you going to be all right?"

"I just miss him," she answered. "I'm sad he's gone."

Inez sighed. "I am, too." Inez reached up and took Sherilynne's hand. They clasped hands kindly for a moment, then broke off.

"That's all right," Marley said. "I don't need to see the balance sheets. What about the break in? It was to search Aloysius's office, wasn't it?"

"Boy," Sherilynne said. "Stan really went way too far this time."

Everyone fell silent as all eyes turned to her. Frederika stood out of her chair. "Are you saying Stan Grabbleton did this?"

Inez dropped her head into her hands. When she spoke, the kindness of their shared grief was gone. "For God's sake, Sherilynne, how could you say something so stupid? Do you really think Stan cut the wires of his own office alarm system and threw a bunch of his own files all over the floor?"

Sherilynne looked around uncertainly. "No?"

"No!" Inez shouted.

"But why did you think it was Stan?" Marley asked.

"Think carefully how you answer," Inez told her.

The phone began to ring out in the reception area. Sherilynne stood nervously looking from face to face. For the first time in several weeks, she wished she could rush off to answer a call. "Well, Al told me a couple of times that Stan had gone through his desk. He would never say why, only that he'd done it."

Marley turned to Inez, but Inez spoke up first. "Those boys had their problems, but I wasn't part of that. You'll have to speak to Stan about it, because I have nothing to say on the subject."

"What about the break-in in general?" Marley asked.

Inez sighed. "Judging by the looks of things, I don't think they found what they were looking for." The phone in the reception area was still ringing. "Sherilynne, would you please go out and pick that up?"

Sherilynne was glad to be sent out of the room, but she went slowly enough to have time to complain. "I already have a full-time job and you want me to pick up and sort the files, too. You really should hire a temp for this!"

"If I hire a temp," Inez said, her voice rising, "It will be so someone answers our phone!"

"Call the police," Frederika said. "I want my client off their radar in the next fifteen minutes."

"Of course," Inez said, letting her embarrassment turn into irritation.

"What about Stan?" Marley asked. "I'd like to speak with him." Inez could only apologize and suggest they talk to Sherilynne about that.

Marley was finished. Albert led the way to the exit, holding the door for both Marley and Frederika. He followed them to the sidewalk and down the block. Frederika had a habit of standing very close and looking at the ground as she spoke, and she spoke very quickly in her incredibly abrasive voice. He decided she must be a fantastic lawyer because there was no other reason to put up with her.

"Jenny is cracking up under the stress," Frederika was saying. "She's asked to see you several times and loses her temper when I tell her to be patient. She's a sharp kid, but a little spoiled. I think she needs someone to come hold her hand and pet her hair."

"Someone like me, you mean."

"And her parents are even worse. Jenny isn't allowed to call me every half-hour, but those two... I keep telling them to visit their daughter in jail, but they won't go near the place. I think they're afraid they'll be locked up, too, just because they're Chinese.

Albert glanced out into the street. A black SUV rounded the corner too quickly. Something about it raised the hairs on the back of his neck. Then he noticed the spider-web crack low on the passenger side windshield.

"I'm worried that Jenny will start talking to the police without me," Frederika was saying. "She doesn't know anything about the murder—you're right, I think, she wasn't involved, but—"

The SUV swerved across the median, heading straight toward them.

CHAPTER TWENTY-SEVEN
Pebbles and the Snatching Thereof

Albert acted without thought; he lunged forward, bending low, and wrapped an arm around each woman's waist. Marley gasped in surprise, but Frederika shrieked and struggled. He lifted them both, pinning them against his chest, and began to run.

The SUV turned harder, angling toward them. Albert wasn't going to reach the cover of the nearest parked car in time. He lunged toward the wall of the building, hoping the extra distance between him and their attacker might give him an extra stride.

They were right against the brick building when the SUV veered off, tires screeching. Frederika, who was closest to it, shrieked directly into Albert's ear. There was a brief scrape of a fender, and the vehicle bounced over the curb and swerved back into traffic.

Albert didn't stop running.

"Dear, that's enough," Marley said. "You can put us down."

"What if they have guns?" he said, his voice too loud. His brain was full of static, fearful thoughts, along with the sounds of a Taliban ambush he had barely survived the year before. "What if they circle around the block?"

"Well, they won't catch us by surprise again, will they? Come on, now. That's enough. Put us down."

A Key, an Egg, an Unfortunate Remark

Albert let his pace slow, the adrenaline rush draining out of him. A sudden flood of sweat ran down his face. He stopped beside Marley's car and set both women down, but he held on to Frederika's elbow with a trembling hand. "I heard you cry out. Are you all right?"

"No, I'm not all right!" she snapped. "Look at this heel!" She lifted her foot to show that the high heel had been snapped off her shoe. "My God, look at that. Ruined!"

"Frederika, dear, Albert just saved both our lives."

She seemed to consider that for a moment, then resentfully said, "I suppose so. I don't much like being grabbed from behind, though."

"Neither do I," Marley said, "but I'm quite happy to make an exception this one time. Thank you, dear."

"You're welcome. You're not hurt?"

"Not at all. How about you? You didn't strain your back, did you? Do you need to play a little Tetris?"

"What?" Frederika cut in. "What's this about Tetris? I love Tetris."

Albert managed a smile. He wiped the sweat from his eyebrows with a trembling hand. "I think I'm fine. Upsetting, though, isn't it?"

Frederika laughed. "I'll say! And quick! I didn't have any warning at all."

Marley laid a gentle hand on Frederika's shoulder. "I'll be sure to check in with Jenny as soon as I can. You get back to the office. And thank you for coming along."

"For all the good I did you," Frederika muttered.

"Now stop that. You kept Inez honest, as I knew you would. Keep me up to date, please."

"Of course." Frederika wobbled off to her car.

Albert looked up and down the street. "I guess they're not coming back. And they must have had a spotter, but I didn't think to look for one until it was too late."

"A spotter? What do you mean?"

"The SUV was going pretty fast and this is a short block. Unless it was doing forty-mile-an-hour circles through the neighborhood, I don't see how they could have timed it that well, unless they had someone watching to let them know we'd left the building and were about to round the corner. But that didn't occur to me right away, and they got away before it did."

"Well don't beat yourself up about it, Albert. I thought you did just fine saving my life. That's not something Jenny could have done. Thank you."

"You're welcome. God, I've been paranoid as hell waiting for those guys to take another shot, and they still caught me off guard."

Marley looked down at her Lexus with reluctance. "Let's go to the waterfront, shall we? I feel like looking out over the dragon's lair."

Albert opened the door to let her in, then climbed behind the wheel. "Any place in particular?" he asked, and tapped the GPS.

"Not this time. Let's just drive and see what we find."

He pulled into traffic. There were no SUVs evident in front or behind him, but he was feeling more vigilant than he had since he'd returned to the U.S., even more so than after the home invasion.

"They could have killed us," Marley said. "The driver and whoever he was working for, he had us right against the wall."

"Yeah, he did."

"Do you think he was only trying to frighten us?"

"I wish he was; he could call it a success and go home. No, I think he was trying to run us down. But if he'd crushed us against the building, he'd have disabled his vehicle, too. Whoever he is, he wasn't on a suicide run."

"Well! I'm going to consider that reassuring."

They drove in silence for a block or two. Finally, Albert said, "I felt bad for Inez."

"So did I, to be honest. I hated to truth to her like that, but lawyers can cause an awful lot of trouble when they set their minds to it. I couldn't have her suing me."

"We tricked her," Albert said, "and she took the blame. It felt sketchy and I feel a little ashamed."

"Thank you for saying 'we,' dear, even though it was me and only me that tricked her. And yes, it was sketchy. I do sketchy things sometimes, but always for a good cause. At least, I tell myself it's a good cause, the same way we all do. Even George Salkin, with his awful smoothies, thought he had a good cause."

"But that guy was ripping people off to make himself rich, so screw him. Your good cause is the real thing."

"Thank you, dear. Let me know if your assessment changes."

Albert pulled onto Broad Street, heading toward the water. It bothered him that his aunt was taking all the blame on herself, as though he wasn't right there with her, making his own choices. "Another thing: Aunt Marley, I said 'we' because I'm working for you and with you, and you're getting my one-hundred-percent commitment. And if that means we are going to deceive two women who are grieving harder for my dead half-brother than I ever will, then I'm going to have to own that."

Smiling, Marley said, "How about right here, Albert?"

They'd just turned onto Alaskan Way, and Marley pointed to a spot between Pier 70 and the Victoria Clipper building. A "For Lease" sign was hung in the nearest darkened window. Glancing back at the sign for the Clipper, Albert saw a long line of people filing in to board. He'd always wanted to visit Canada. If that's where they were headed, it was okay with him.

He pulled in, let Marley out of the back seat, then bought a parking meter sticker for the car. At Marley's instruction, he took a thick brown towel from the trunk. Then he and Marley turned north, strolling toward Myrtle Edwards Park.

Albert nodded up the hill. "We keep ending up here." Just across the street—and the train tracks—was the cheap seafood restaurant where they'd eaten after meeting Amos Quigley; it had since been closed for health code violations. He could see the sign from here.

"Indeed we do. I keep feeling we'll discover some vital clue here."

The Art Museum's Sculpture Park was attached to this end of Myrtle Edwards Park, and they could see a huge, bare, metal tree up the hill. Beyond the fountain, a ramp led up to the exhibits, but Marley turned away from them and chose the concrete walkway beside the water.

The first benches they found were sculptures—they looked like gunmetal sea shells with a seat pinched out of one side. Marley frowned and shook her head at them. "The bay is too deep for the piers to stick straight out from the waterfront, so they're all angled to the north. Let's keep going so we'll have a view of the water instead of all this aluminum and glass. Oh! This is new!"

She walked toward a tall, misshapen white pillar. Albert had no idea what it was until they came around to the other side. It was a huge, elongated face, staring out into the Sound. Marley stood and admired it in silence. Albert joined her, wondering what it was supposed to make him feel.

Eventually, they went farther into the park, reaching a place where the bike and pedestrian trails met. "Ah," Marley said, then crossed the bike trail toward a low wall. Albert wiped part of it dry and they sat. Their view was obscured partly by blowing mists—unusual, so late in the spring—and partly by the steel railing in front of them, but it was still nice. Joggers and bicyclists passed on the trail, and they occasionally heard the ringing of little bells.

"We're very exposed here," Albert said.

"We are, but I think we'll be safe for a bit." Marley took out her phone and handed it to Albert. "There's something I want you to do. Our GPS keeps a log of all the places we visit. I want you to call this number on the speed dial—"

"The one labeled GPS?"

"Yes, clever, aren't I? You'll sign in automatically. Download the log file to my phone, then delete it from the device. Just follow the menu, it's pretty self-explanatory."

"All right." Albert lifted his finger to poke at the speed dial, but Marley stopped him.

"But not yet."

He lowered his hand. "When do you want me to do it?"

"Later. When it seems right."

"When it seems right? Is this a hazing? Because if so I have could give you some tips—"

"No, dear. It's more like asking you to snatch the pebbles from my hand."

Albert hesitated, but only for a moment. "You know, I've heard people say that before but I honestly have no idea what it means."

Marley laughed. "I'm sorry, Albert. It's from before your time, I think. Listen, I have something to take care of or I'd do this myself. But do you remember the moment you realized that SUV was dangerous? It was moving too fast, right? But that wasn't all, was it?"

"No, that wasn't all."

"I've felt it too, in my time: a strange sort of understanding that doesn't seem to come from anything in particular, but which nonetheless informs you about the world." She waved toward the phone. "A time will come when calling the car's GPS will seem like the right thing to do. You won't know why, in all likelihood, but you'll feel it. Call then."

"Will I learn some vital clue if I do it at just the right time?"

"I genuinely have no idea what will happen."

Albert held the phone in his lap, staring down at the numbers. Did it seem like a good time to call right now? He didn't feel anything about it in particular, except that he didn't like to leave work undone. Better to finish things right away.

Still, he knew that wasn't what his aunt was talking about.

He turned to ask her a question, but she was gone.

CHAPTER TWENTY-EIGHT
The Harsh Glare of Adversity

Jenny Wu stood against the wall near the entrance to her cell. She looked and felt grimy, had dark circles under her eyes, and had chewed her lower lip to the point that it bled continuously into her mouth. Her face was downcast but she kept a constant vigil; there wasn't much she could do if the other prisoners started to threaten and tease her again, but she wanted to see them coming.

"Jenny, dear, why are you—"

Jenny shrieked in surprise. It was a high, loud, echoing sound that startled everyone in the holding cell to silence. Everyone turned to look at Jenny and Marley, with Jenny in the doorway and Marley just inside the cell.

"... Standing here in the corner?" Marley finished.

"Ms. Jacobs, how did you get in here?"

"The same way I always do. Come, dear." They sat at the edge of the cot.

Out in the common area, a fireplug of a woman with a crooked, acne-scarred face stalked toward them. "Hey! I didn't give either of you permission to sit."

Marley smiled at her. "Carol, I'm so happy to have found you right away. Here, I've brought you a note from your little girls."

Marley took a folded sheet of paper from her pocket and handed it to Carol. "You know my daughters?" Carol said, at once confused, amazed, and suspicious. She unfolded the blank sheet of paper and began moving her lips as she read it.

"Jenny, haven't you been arraigned yet?"

"My lawyer says the prosecutor put it off until Monday. I don't think I can last until then, Ms. Jacobs, I really don't."

"It seems more crowded in here, doesn't it?"

"That only means there are more people to notice me. Isn't there something you can do?"

"Your parents came to see me." Marley's voice was uncharacteristically flat and toneless.

"Oh," Jenny answered. Marley's blank expression confused and alarmed her. "My father's western birthday is Friday, so they're visiting."

"You're throwing him a birthday party."

"Not from prison, I'm not! Why are we even talking about... Is there some way you can get me out of here?"

"I'm trying, dear, but the judge has to set bail before I can pay it. Also, it's been difficult to find out the truth about Aloysius's murder. He was living a more complicated life than I ever suspected."

"Ms. Jacobs—"

"Let me ask you—sorry, dear, but I must cut in, I really am pressed and this is important—how was he doing for money?"

"He was struggling," Jenny answered. "Except when he wasn't. Once he took me to a little sandwich shop followed by a free art gallery tour. The next week it was dinner at Lola's. When he had it, he spent it, but I don't think he had it as often as he would've liked."

"Did he talk about it?"

"I certainly didn't bring it up. He only said one thing, which was that the hardest thing about being a lawyer was getting his clients to pay his bill. I don't think practicing law was everything he'd expected it would be."

"Thank you for that, dear. He never talked about people who were unhappy with him? Never said he was worried about losing a client?"

"Not to me. We only went out a few times and we never got very close. We never even did more than kiss. I don't even know why he chased after me the way he did."

"It's been suggested to me that he chased you because you didn't want him and I suspect that's right. I also suspect that, if you'd slept with him, he'd have gone away when you told him to go."

"Really? God! If I'd known that—"

"You never went to his house, did you?"

"No. He never offered so I didn't have to turn him down."

"Did he ever seem nervous or frightened? Did he ever seem as though he thought he was being followed?"

"I've thought about that a lot. I've gone over it again and again, but there really isn't anything. He never seemed concerned with anything except himself and what other people thought of him. Ms. Jacobs, please, I heard about the condition of his body."

"What's that, dear?"

"That he was drained of blood."

"Oh?"

"Was it... was it one of yours?"

"No, dear. I checked that very carefully. First thing, in fact."

"Well, maybe a new one who just came to town? Could that be it?"

"We did have a new arrival, but it wasn't her. I checked her out, too."

Jenny became exasperated. "But are you sure? You can't really be completely sure!"

"I'm sure, Jenny. You know me well enough to know that."

"But it sounds like something one of your... things would do."

Marley was startled by that. Things? It wasn't like Jenny to talk that way. "It was meant to, dear."

"The police should know! They might want to interview them."

Marley gave Jenny the same even stare she'd just given Carol. "We both know that police attention would be a death sentence for them."

"You know what else has the death sentence? Washington State! This state. You know that, don't you? I'm facing lethal injection for a crime I didn't commit, while your 'guests' live in luxury, with a nurse to turn down their beds. I've never killed anyone, but they have."

"They had nothing to do with Aloysius's death."

"We don't know what really happened to Aloysius! The police have decided I'm the one they should charge and they aren't going beyond that. And Ms. Jacobs, we both know that, as amazing as you are, you aren't a detective."

"Yes, I certainly know that."

"So what hope is there for me, really? People go to prison every day for crimes they didn't commit. We know that. And your guests, they're still killers; you know they are. Even if they haven't killed anyone since they met you, they killed people before. A lot of people. And anyway, how can you be sure none of them were involved? Really really sure?"

"Jenny—"

A Key, an Egg, an Unfortunate Remark

"They're not even really alive! God! How can you protect them over me? I mean, I really am grateful for your help because I could never have afforded a lawyer like Frederika on my own, and my parents are talking about selling their house and emptying their accounts to help pay for my defense—my dad does genetic research on rural communities, of all things, and my mom teaches at a small medical school. They're not rich. So I really mean it when I say I'm grateful, really! But your 'guests' are dead and they've already killed people. Are they ever going to be punished for what they did? No, it has to be me. I have to be punished for something I didn't even do, and I have my whole life ahead of me."

Marley sighed, looked down at the floor, and shook her head. When she looked up again, her expression was icy cold. "Jenny, I have to tell you, I've been where you are. Yes, it's true, I have. I was looking at murder charges, and I was terrified. Sitting hour after hour, thinking too much and doing too little, the fear builds until you're desperate to make a deal."

"Oh Ms. Jacobs—"

"But I will tell you this, Jenny dear: I love you, because I think you're a wonderful young woman with a lot to give the world, and I'm going to move heaven and earth to find out who really killed my nephew, so that you can move on and live a good life—"

"I appreciate that, but—"

"But! If you send the police after my guests, I'll ruin you. Do you see Carol over there, reading a blank sheet of paper over and over because she thinks it's a note from her children? I can do the same to anyone—detective, lawyer, judge, psychologist—until they're ready to testify—honestly, mind you, as far as they know—that you're convinced Aloysius was killed by vampires. My guests will already be in a new safe house and you'll be all over the cable news networks. I'll still find out the truth about Aloysius's murder and I'll make sure you're set free, but by then you'll be infamous."

Jenny looked down at the floor and sniffled.

"Don't cry, Jenny. I'm giving you the chance to avoid the mistake I once made, a mistake I'm still paying for. Be strong and endure; you can't get

185

through this ordeal by playing to your weaknesses. Stay strong, and when we clear your name, I'll throw you and your parents a little party."

When she spoke, Jenny's voice was small. "I sit here, hour after hour, no one tells me anything and nothing gets better, and now you tell me you're choosing them over me."

"Oh my goodness," Marley said quietly. "I thought you understood me better than that. I don't choose one person over another. Never ever again, dear."

Jenny wiped away her tears and discovered she was alone on the bench.

* * *

Sitting on the park bench by the water, Albert suddenly had a strange feeling: The perfect moment to call his aunt's GPS had arrived. He marveled at his inexplicable certainty as he took the phone from his pocket; the movement felt as natural as scratching his nose.

He lifted the phone and pressed the speed dial.

Out on the street, hundreds of feet away, the Lexus he'd been driving exploded.

CHAPTER TWENTY-NINE
Marley's Cunning Non-Plan

"Oh, wonderful," Marley said. "No one was hurt."

Albert was on his belly on the damp grass. When the shock wave had hit him, he'd followed its momentum onto the ground. He lifted his head and saw his aunt sitting on the low wall again, as though she'd never left. The urge to grab her hand and pull her down beside him was incredible.

Instead, he crouched, putting himself between her and the source of the explosion. "What was that? What just happened?"

186

A Key, an Egg, an Unfortunate Remark

"You have to ask? Someone put a bomb in our car."

He spun toward her suddenly. For the first time, Marley saw a look of honest anger on her nephew's face. "And you didn't tell me?"

"But I didn't know, dear! Honestly, I didn't." She clasped his hands and moved her face close to his. Albert let her hold onto him. "I told you I didn't know. I only knew that something was wrong with the GPS and that I shouldn't call it. I didn't know why."

"But you knew there was something!"

"Yes," she said. Albert pulled his hands out of hers, and Marley was startled that such a small rebuke would sting so much. "It's true. I knew something significant would happen, but I never dreamed it would be this."

There were no gun shots. No screams. Albert dared to stand upright and look around. He missed his M4 so much even though he knew it wouldn't be any use. He didn't even have a trigger finger anymore. He couldn't see anyone nearby. "Aunt Marley, you sat me down here and gave me your phone and told me to... What if I'd been standing beside the car when I called? What if... what if a mother with a baby stroller..."

Marley patted the spot beside her. "Albert, dear, take some deep breaths. Do you need to play your Tetris?"

"No, I don't want to play my f..." He stopped and stood staring out at the water. The slow churn of the waves was calming, for some reason. It made him feel insignificant. He sat on the bench. "This isn't my first car bomb."

"I wouldn't expect it to be."

"No one was hurt this time." He said it with a certainty that he shouldn't have trusted. He had no reason to believe it. He hadn't examined the scene —He hadn't even gone near it.

Still, he knew.

Marley laid her hand on his. "You did well."

It suddenly occurred to him that this had been a test. A test he might have failed. "Am I just a stone you throw over your shoulder? Some crazy, random thing you toss out into the world with no idea what it will break?"

She sighed, patted his hand, and turned to look out over the water. "I'd have thought you understood by now, dear. I thought you were paying attention."

"What am I missing?"

"Me. You're missing me. Let me ask you something: How did it feel when you pressed that speed dial button?"

Albert looked back at the burning car. Sirens grew louder. He didn't want to answer because he thought the answer he was about to give would make him sound like a bad person. "It felt right. It felt like exactly the perfect thing to do at the time."

"You had a moment of certitude."

"Yes, exactly. It was like water flowing down a hill."

Marley tightened her grip on his hand. "First, let me say that certitude is a very dangerous thing. It feels so powerful that it can drive people to do awful, awful things. Certitude is powerful magic, yes, but it can also be a curse, especially if you let unexamined bias substitute for mindfulness. Certitude has to be balanced with sensible self-doubt and an open mind or you risk all sorts of terrible things."

"Okay," Albert said warily. "I've had my moment of certitude and you've warned me about it. But Aunt Marley, you always seem utterly certain that what you're doing is correct. You smash taillights and—"

"Of course I do, dear. And that's magic. It's almost the most powerful magic there is, because it's barely magic at all. But there's something about it you haven't picked up on yet."

"What's that?"

She folded her hands in her lap, then sat up straight and proud. "I don't have any idea what I'm doing."

Sirens screaming, a police car skidded to a halt at the edge of the park, a respectful distance from the burning Lexus. More police cars approached. A woman in a minivan packed with kids parked across the street and leaned out the drivers window, video taping the fire with her phone.

Albert turned toward his aunt. He had heard what she'd said, but it didn't register. "I'm sorry? What was that?"

"It's true. I don't know why I do these things. When I asked you to call the GPS with my phone, I didn't know a bomb would go off any more than you did. Asking you to make that call seemed like the right thing to do at the time. The same is true with that stone in that parking lot." Marley nodded toward the shuttered restaurant. "I just saw it there and had a feeling about it. And can I just say how much I love the phrase 'like water flowing down hill'? This feeling has been with me for decades, and I've never been able to describe it so perfectly! You did it on your first try. Very good, Albert."

"So you threw the stone onto that windshield—"

"I didn't know the stone would crack that windshield, any more than I knew I would recognize that same crack on the SUV that tried to run us down a while ago. I'm sure you recognized it, too."

"I did."

"I just knew I should throw it, so I did."

"And you gave me the phone because it seemed right?"

"Exactly! And it worked out all right. The bomb went off without hurting anyone, although I think a few windows might be broken."

Albert stood on the wall and looked toward the street. The glass had been blown out of both windows on the street side. The windows across the street in the restaurant were broken, too. Whoever planted that bomb had been too smart to overdo it.

He turned back to her. "It would have been better to call the cops, Aunt Marley. They would have sent a bomb squad over, and they might have gotten... I don't know, evidence off it without wrecking everything and scaring the hell out of everyone. You know a car bomb is going to make our lives very complicated, right?"

He still didn't understand. That was too bad, because Marley couldn't explain it any more plainly than she had. Perhaps he would understand better when the adrenaline rush from the explosion wore off. For now, Marley brushed him off with a flick of her wrist. "Could have been, might have been. Oh, look. A policeman is coming this way. I suppose we should talk to him."

She stood and strolled toward the approaching officer, who was still at least thirty yards away. Albert followed. "What about the taillight on that truck?"

"I'm not sure. I don't always discover the effects of the things I do. I wish I did. So who can say? Excuse me, officer! Excuse me! If I can just say, that was my car."

As Albert predicted, things became complicated after that. Marley and Albert spent a great deal of time answering the same questions several times from several different authority figures. They produced their ID several times as well, to be scrutinized by several different pairs of eyes.

Ubeh arrived after a short while. The police interviewed her briefly, then she managed to approach Marley. "Oh, Ms. Jacobs, this is a nightmare! What has happened?"

"Someone tried to kill me, dear. How did you get here so quickly?"

"I live in a condo just over there." Ubeh pointed uphill to a squarish brown building above the park. "I rushed right down when I got the call. No one was hurt then? Thank goodness."

"Yes, it was only the car. And I'll be needing a new one."

"Oh!" Ubeh turned toward the fire. Fire engines had finally started to fight the blaze. "But that one is destroyed! I can't get you a new car, Ms. Jacobs. It's company policy. I'm so sorry."

"Now don't fret, dear. It sounds like a sensible policy to me, considering."

"But I feel as though I have betrayed you! Here this awful thing happens, and I can't help you at all."

"Dear, you certainly can help us. About that Volvo…"

"Oh, yes! Our mechanic found a tracking device on it this morning. He suspects it was placed there by the police."

"He's probably correct, dear, but you should call him right away to let him know about this."

Ubeh's eyes widened and her phone was in her hand a moment later. Her thumbs moved over the keypad with surprising speed. "My boss, Carolina, will receive a text before a phone call, but just in case..." Text sent, Ubeh dialed a number and pressed the phone to her ear.

Before the other party picked up, a pair of detectives interrupted. "Excuse me," one of them said to Ubeh. "May I see your ID?"

"Of course. Is there something... Carolina? Did you get my text? It's not a joke. Clear the building right away."

"Ma'am," the detective said, more sternly. Ubeh dropped her phone in her purse, then took out her drivers license. The detectives looked it over, then ordered her to accompany them to a waiting car.

"Wait a minute," Marley said, "She—"

Albert caught her elbow. "Call a lawyer for her. Right away."

Ubeh was patted down by a female officer, then put into the back of a car. Marley took out her phone as the car pulled away. "And I was hoping to leave Frederika out of this."

Not ten minutes later, Detective Lonagan pushed through the crowd. Detective Garcia followed in his wake. "Marley!" he called. "My God, what is going on with you? Are you all right?"

"I'm fine, thank you. I've just had a fright is all."

"First your house and now this... what have you been doing?"

"Not a thing!"

Garcia stepped forward, put one hand one Albert's chest and pushed. He didn't resist, allowing himself to be shoved back. "That's a lie. You've been digging into the murder of Aloysius Pierce. I know you have."

"Nonsense." Marley said. "My nephew has been killed, and it turns out that I don't know anything about his life. I don't even know who to contact about the funeral. I didn't know who his friends are, or who he worked with. My own nephew, a stranger to me! His mother will be arriving soon, and I have no idea what I'll say to her."

"Besides," Albert interjected, "we know you don't believe the attack on my aunt's home or this car bombing have anything to do with Aloysius's death."

"You know that, huh?" Garcia said, squaring off with him belligerently.

"How do you know that?"

"You're still holding Jenny Wu, aren't you? Or maybe you think she planted this car bomb while she was sitting in prison, using her psychic powers."

"Or maybe she wasn't acting alone," Garcia responded. She turned to Marley. "Is Jenny Wu named in your will?"

"Sharon," Lonagan interjected, "this isn't the time or the place."

"No, Charlie, I think this question deserves an answer, and I want to hear it from her own mouth." She turned to Marley. "Was Jenny Wu named as a beneficiary in your will?"

Marley laid her hand on her throat as though she was surprised. "Will? Me? I'm going to live forever."

Garcia narrowed her eyes. "Ms. Jacobs, I'm going to have to ask you to come to the station with me to answer some questions."

Marley shrugged. "If you're going to arrest me, I'm prepared to sit silently in an interview room while I wait for my attorney. Otherwise, I'll be happy to ask that same attorney to make an appointment to answer any questions openly and frankly. Of course I want to get to the bottom of these ugly attempts on my life, but wouldn't it be better for you to collect all of your forensic evidence or whatever first? I've seen the television shows."

"That's your right, Marley," Lonagan cut in. He was clearly worried for her; unfortunately, that worry expressed itself as an urge to take charge, in the most condescending way possible. "We don't want to make things harder on you than they have to be. I'd like to arrange for an officer to take you home."

"Thank you," Marley said, "but I don't want that. Albert will see me home safely enough."

"Mar—Ms. Jacobs, if someone is trying to kill you—"

She interrupted him, speaking in a foolish tone that was not like her at all. "Your officer isn't going to be able to do a better job than my Albert. He served in Afghanistan, you know."

Lonagan and Garcia turned skeptical looks toward Albert. Embarrassed, he glanced down at his shoes. Did she have to put on this embarrassing performance now?

"So I don't think I have anything to worry about! Come along, Albert. Oh, and Detective Lonagan, thank you for your concern. I appreciate it very much."

Lonagan led Marley and Albert through the crowd, all the while trying to convince them to accept a ride. Marley, however, was adamant that it wasn't necessary, and the frivolous way she insisted made Albert feel increasingly awkward, as though she was putting on a show to convince Lonagan she was silly and clueless. The detective had never known her to act this way, and no matter how confused her behavior made him, eventually he had to reluctantly let her walk away.

The police had blocked traffic turning from Western onto Alaskan Way, and a crowd of pedestrians—who seem to have appeared out of thin air—streamed toward the scene. Albert and Marley pushed their way through the crowd in the other direction.

"That Detective Lonagan sure was worried about you," Albert said.

"Yes, I noticed that, too."

"Really worried," he said, with extra meaning.

Apparently, Albert needed to lighten the mood. "I'm not against the idea of a happy romp in the sack with a willing admirer, Albert," Marley said. "But he's not my type."

"Oh. I thought women were into cops." Marley gave him a look. "Or not. Is that why you were doing that whole 'My nephew is a soldier' thing? To back him off? Because that was embarrassing."

"It wasn't only to discourage him. I also wanted to get out of there before Homeland Security showed up. Being an older, wealthy, well-connected white woman is a helpful thing with the local authorities, but I don't want to test it with federal police. Besides, police officers carry guns, pepper spray, batons—and they tend to ignore people who tell them to Put that away. We have enough trouble without adding weapons."

Albert shrugged. "At least we know what Fremont Bridge was talking about when he said this was a dangerous area."

A taxi was parked against the curb, the driver leaning on the hood eating a fast food sub. He looked like an amateur bodybuilder. "Excuse me," he said to them. "What happened down there?"

Albert got a bad vibe from the guy, but Marley was pleasant when she answered. "Some sort of fire. Tell me, are you engaged?"

The driver wrapped up his sandwich and moved toward the driver's door. "Tell me where you want to go." He got behind the wheel quickly.

Marley smiled at Albert. "Aren't we fortunate?" He opened the back door for her and she slid into the seat. He shut her door and, as he passed behind the back bumper to open the door on the other side, the taxi driver stepped on the gas and swerved into traffic.

Albert stood in the gutter and watched his aunt being kidnapped.

CHAPTER THIRTY
A Pretend Conversation

The cab driver glanced into his rear view mirror. He'd expected his passenger to panic when he'd pulled into traffic. He liked to see a little fear; it made the next part so much easier. Instead, she looked utterly composed. He wondered if she wasn't a little senile.

"Lady, you and I are going to have a conversation. If it's friendly and polite, and I hear the things I want to hear, maybe you'll come out of it without any broken bones. Get me?"

Marley glanced at the cabbie license. The name read RICHARD KINGLOVSKI. "I 'get you', Dominic, but you don't have to be so rude about it."

Startled to hear his own name, Dominic swerved suddenly in his lane, almost colliding with another car. "Throw your purse into the front seat!" he said harshly. "Now."

Marley sighed and did as he asked. Dominic opened it and dumped it out. He tossed her phone out the window, then ran his hand over the other items, glancing at them when traffic allowed. Whatever he was looking for, he didn't find it. "How did you know my name?"

"Don't ask, dear, you won't like the answer."

* * *

Back on the sidewalk, Albert sprinted after them, lunging off the curb when the crowd of lookiloos got too thick. His only hope was that the cab would catch the red light.

It didn't. It breezed south through the intersection, heading up Western Avenue toward the highway—if they even got on the highway; it was possible they would head toward the waterfront ferries, or into a warehouse in Georgetown, or they might turn north toward Lake Union and from there they might head east or north.

Albert pushed his way back onto the sidewalk. It would be humiliating to return to Lonagan and Garcia after his aunt had said He served in Afghanistan, you know in that proud, silly, little old lady voice, but he didn't have a choice. "Dammit!"

"Hush, Albert."

Albert cried out and spun around, nearly colliding with a chubby couple in full bicycle gear. His Aunt Marley was standing against a streetlight, her eyes shut tight and her fingers in her ears.

"Aunt Marley! You're safe!"

"Albert, hush! I'm trying to concentrate."

* * *

Dominic sneered into the rear view mirror. "Concentrate? What you should concentrate on is making me happy. If I don't get what I want, it's gonna get ugly for you."

"Yes, yes, I hear you. Dominic, I must know: How is that fellow who

195

injured himself in my home? The one who tripped and shot himself in the leg? I didn't get close enough to discover his name, so I have to ask this way. Is he all right? I'm honestly concerned, you know. I had no idea my little fishing line would lead to a gunshot wound; if I had, I wouldn't have set it up. That's just an awful thing."

Dominic didn't respond. He stared into the thinning traffic on 99 South, his face grim. "I get it," he said, finally. "You know who I am. I get it."

"I'm not being coy, dear. I'm never coy. I'm truly concerned about your friend."

"He's not my friend."

"Then your teammate? Squadmate? What should I call him?"

"You shouldn't be talking about him at all! You should be talking about yourself."

"But I talk about myself all the time! I'm quite good at it and I'm sure I'll be doing it again soon. To get back to your friend, I know you didn't take him to a hospital, because the police haven't—Oh my goodness! He didn't die, did he?"

"No, he didn't."

"Oh! Thank goodness! I'm so glad. I haven't harmed anyone physically in many years, and even though I didn't directly—"

"Shut up, lady. I mean it. Jesus, maybe I should shoot you just to get your damn attention."

"Well, you were nice enough to answer my question, so we should focus on your concerns now," Marley said. "You wanted something from me. What was it again?"

"Don't play games with me! You know what I'm looking for."

"Is this how we're going to do this? Because I'm already bored. Listen, young man, I'm happy to take a little ride with you and talk about whatever plan your employer is putting into action—"

"Who says I have an employer?"

"Don't play games with me, Dominic. There's a plan in motion, I can feel it the way someone with a nervous stomach gets sick on a roller coaster. I don't know what that plan is, yet, but it's already cost the life of my nephew."

"Things don't have to get bloodier," Dominic interjected. "If you're smart, you'll give me what I want and this can all be over."

"Oh no. It will all be over very soon, yes indeed, but it will end because I'm going to end it. You won't tell me what you're looking for or who you're working for, dear? That's fine. You just tell your employer that whatever this plan is, no more lives are going to be lost. You all should quit now. Or else."

"That's it!" Dominic swerved onto an exit ramp and raced down to the street. There was no traffic on the road below, and he pulled to the curb, brakes screeching, beside one of the massive concrete supports for the highway above. "Nobody tells me or else! Nobody!"

He drew his brand new Springfield XD-S—at last, a chance to shoot someone!—as he turned around. He wasn't supposed to kill the old woman, but his employer never said anything about shooting off a finger or two.

But she wasn't there. She'd vanished from the back of his car like a ghost.

* * *

"Albert, turn around."

He did. His aunt stood on the sidewalk, surrounded by people flooding toward the explosion. Albert moved close so they could talk without anyone passing between them. "What just happened? I swear I saw you get in that taxi—have you been here the whole time?"

"What a question to ask! Of course I've been here. Couldn't you see me? I'll be disappointed if you say no."

"I'm going to have to disappoint you, then, because I was freaking out. You got in the car, then you were beside me, telling me to be quiet, then I couldn't see you anywhere. It made me feel like a Flatlander."

"Oh, well," Marley said, moving against traffic toward Belltown. Albert followed. "And you did so well with the bomb, too."

"That was magic, wasn't it?" Albert asked, keeping his voice low. "You created something unreal—a copy of yourself."

"Yes of course, dear, but telling me this now is almost like backsliding."

Albert stopped walking. "Oh. Can't we call it a review instead?"

Marley took out her phone and started dialing. "I didn't learn as much from him as I would have liked, but it appears they believe I have something they want."

"Like Aloysius's files? Or his key ring?"

"I don't think so. Dominic—that's the name of the man who tried to kidnap me—emptied my purse onto the front seat. The key ring was right there, but he didn't take notice of it. And of course they broke into the office and stole his files last night—Hello? I'd like to order a taxi." Marley finished the call and then hung up. "Unless..." She thought a moment. "Unless he was looking for a specific key ring and thought this wasn't it. Something with a particular chain or charm on it?"

"No, I don't think so, Aunt Marley. If he was looking for any key at all, he would have taken all of them to sort out later."

"You're right, Albert, I know you're right. Now I'm the one being disappointing. Oh look, here's our cab. How prompt."

"Are you getting in this one?"

"Absolutely," she said. "Since Ubeh can't lease us any more cars, we should buy one. Let's get something with a high clearance, something a little rugged. I think it's time we went up to the cabin, met the 'guy on the scene,' and saw this plot of land Aloysius was so concerned about."

Albert opened the door for her. "You mean, the really, really dangerous guy on the scene? The one who maybe killed people?"

But Marley was already in the cab and didn't answer.

"Well," Albert said as he hustled to get in the other side. "That'll be a nice change of pace."

CHAPTER THIRTY-ONE
Sincerety Is Key. If You Can Fake That...

Marley amazed Albert by walking onto a used car lot and walking off with a title to a Jeep Cherokee only twenty minutes later. She gave him the keys, he opened the door for her, and they drove off the lot.

She asked for quiet on the drive so they rode in silence, although this time she did not use the time to create any potions. She simply sat and looked out the window, speaking only when she needed to give directions.

Albert didn't think consciously about the people who had come to his aunt's house to burn it down, or about the conversations they'd had. He did his best to think about nothing at all except the road and the traffic, and how much he missed the GPS with his aunt's information on it.

He hoped that, by turning his attention to other things, his subconscious would churn over everything that had happened in the last few day and present him with a sudden realization that would make everything fall into place. Then he would realize who had killed Aloysius and why.

It didn't happen. Instead he followed Aunt Marley's directions toward I-90 and North Bend, driving through the evening twilight until it turned to night. Eventually, he parked beside a turnoff and shut down the engine. The sign in front of him indicated that a quick right would lead to the Cedar River Watershed Education Center, but his aunt sat silently in the backseat and, remembering what she said about living gasses devouring them to their bones, Albert sat quietly, clearing his mind.

Suddenly, everything around him seemed to go fuzzy. The Jeep Cherokee became indistinct and the steering wheel felt slippery in his grip. He himself began to feel cloudy, as though the boundaries between himself and the universe were breaking down. He wondered if it was safe to interrupt whatever his aunt was doing to tell her he was having a stroke.

"There!" she said suddenly. "That was complicated, but I think it will last until sunrise. Let's pull in to the center now."

The ignition key was difficult to grasp, like picking up cold gravy with a baseball glove. "Did you put a brain-damage spell on me?"

"Not quite and thank you for helping. I'm afraid we're going to have to break into the watershed, and we're going to have to play a trick on the workers to do it. Go ahead, Steve."

The engine started, and Albert carefully steered the car around the corner into the parking lot of the Education Center. If he focused on what he was doing and who he wasn't—Steve, a municipal employee with important business on the far side of that gate—the car was much easier to manage. He drove toward the gate as if he'd always known it was there and stopped in front of it.

He found it unlocked, which his real self knew was a clever trick of his aunt's but which annoyed his pretend self Steve to the point that he mentally composed an angry report he would never write to a supervisor he didn't have. Albert drove through, stopped again, then closed the gates. He locked the padlock out of a habit his pretend self thought he had, and felt a little ashamed as he climbed back into the Cherokee.

"I locked us in," he admitted sheepishly, the car seeming to go indistinct again.

"I should think so," Marley said in a voice that was very different from her usual pleasant tone. Albert felt suddenly reassured about his role; his pretend self solidified around him, and they drove down the hill toward the water

The roads were rough and crooked, with trees close by on both sides. It took all his attention to drive safely. Rattlesnake Lake was behind them; they were moving away from the public tourist spaces past the administration buildings, alongside the powerhouse, penstocks and toward the Masonry Dam. Albert had never seen any of this before, but Steve knew this was the major source of water and power for the Puget Sound area.

Albert began to feel agitated, as though he'd stumbled into an operating room mid-surgery. The risk of being caught—

"Albert, dear," Marley said, suddenly sounding like herself again, "you've been such a help to me these past few days, and you've been doing so well, too. But if you can't handle playing a little trick like this one, I'm going to have to find someone else to drive me."

Albert's real self blushed. Why was he trying to make water flow uphill? "I'm sorry," he said. "Let me get my head in the game." He reminded himself why he was here, and that he was playing a simple trick. He centered himself, letting his pretend persona waft off him like perfume. Suddenly he felt more in control of himself, of their shared trick, and of the car he was driving.

Marley directed him toward the bridge that separated the Masonry Pool from Chester Morse Lake. They passed two women in uniform working in the dark by the side of the road, but the women didn't do more than glance at them. Marley's trick was indeed working.

Except for a pump station, they'd left all municipal power and water installations behind them to the west. Albert followed the twisting road along the southern edge of the lake, always taking the turns Marley indicated.

Finally, as the waters narrowed to a river, Marley indicated Albert should pull over. He shut off the car and let her out into the road. There was no rain but the mountains all around them blocked off all city and street light. The woods were dark and Albert's eyes hadn't adjusted yet.

"Is this the place where the construction crews were?"

"No, dear." She held up her phone; there was a little pin stuck in a map and the label for it read PHILIP'S DANGEROUS MAN. "We should talk to him first, don't you think?"

Marley held the phone up before her as though taking a measure, then marched off the road into the woods.

Albert rushed after her, trying to blink his eyes to make them adjust to

201

the darkness faster. Marley didn't stumble once. It must have been that she'd ridden in the backseat without lighted dials or headlights, so her eyes were better prepared for the darkness beneath the canopy. At least, that's what he told himself. If she was walking so confidently because of magic—or even just certitude—he would never keep up.

The trees were thick here and their branches so densely intertwined that the ground below was bare of everything except fallen, rotting branches—nudum, Steve informed him. His pretend self seemed much smarter than he was.

After about seventy-five yards they came to a dilapidated old cabin set at the edge of a tiny meadow. Marley took an LED flashlight from her pocket and lit it up. The cabin was one story high, made of weather-beaten wood and shattered glass. The roof couldn't have kept out the rain any more than the walls could have kept out the wind. A bit of blue plastic was visible through the broken window.

"You know, Albert, in some cultures it's considered rude to knock on someone's front door. Interrupts what they're doing, you know. It's much more polite to stand outside and wait to be noticed."

It began to rain. "We're not going to do that here, are we?"

"We just did. If no one responded to my light shining in their windows —which isn't terribly nice but I am a nervous little old lady after all—there's no one here to respond. Let's try the door in case they've gone to sleep. Life in the country, you know."

Marley stepped onto the porch and Albert followed, half-expecting to fall through the floorboards. He didn't. Marley gestured for him to try the doorknob. Albert had a terrible feeling about it, but he did. The knob turned and the door opened half an inch, but a hook held it shut.

"Hey!"

They turned toward the voice and saw that a man had entered the tiny clearing. Marley shone her flashlight on him. He dropped the small stack of wood he was carrying to shield his watery eyes. He was middle-aged and balding, with torn, filthy clothes and a modest pot belly. "Oh, hello—"

Marley said pleasantly, stepping off the edge of the porch.

She didn't get a chance to say more. "This is my place!" the man shouted. His voice grew rougher—like a growl—with every word. "This is mine!"

With astonishing speed, white hair sprouted all over his body, he grew taller and more stooped, his jaws extending outward like a snout, and long, wicked fangs unfolding from his gums like the fangs of a snake.

Fear ran down Albert's back like ice water. The transformation had finished before he realized it had begun. The dumpy, balding man had changed into a powerful, hairy one—with clawed hands and the head of a wolf.

The werewolf leaned forward and growled. It was a sinister, vicious sound. Then it started toward them.

CHAPTER THIRTY-TWO
An Uncomfortably Large Dose of Nature

Albert leaped from the porch in front of his aunt. There was a part of him that didn't believe it, that was sure the transformation he'd just seen was a trick, like ones his aunt used. He sidestepped and the thing changed direction toward him, jaws wide and drooling, clawed hands outstretched.

An even smaller voice inside him thought: Your disbelief is going to get you killed.

It lunged at him, arms outstretched, and Albert's training took over. He threw his weight backwards, brought his hands up, caught the creature by its wrists—that wiry fur isn't a costume, this is a real damn werewolf—and rolled onto his back. He brought his foot up, planted it on the creature's stomach and, its garbage breath hot on his face, he kicked.

The werewolf was big, but it wasn't so big that Albert couldn't throw it around. It flew over him onto the wet grass.

203

Textbook. Albert had always thought that move was as ridiculous as Captain Kirk, and that practicing it had been a waste of time, but it had gone off perfectly. He hadn't even needed to think about it, and part of him was convinced he could not have done that again if he had a hundred chances. His old DI was going to get one hell of a thank-you card, assuming Albert lived through the night.

With that thought, Albert panicked. While the werewolf was still tumbling in the mud, he did a kip to regain his feet, then he grabbed his aunt around the middle—while she was bending down, for some reason— and threw his shoulder against the cabin door, bursting the hook from the jamb.

Marley gasped in surprise. "Albert! Stop!"

But he wasn't listening. He swept her into the darkened room. His hand fell on a chair even before his conscious mind realized it was there, and he kicked the door shut, then jammed the chair beneath the knob.

"Albert, put me down this instant!"

The chair turned out to be an old cafeteria chair, made of steel pipes. It was sturdier than he would've expected and thank you lord for that.

It was too far to run to the car, not in the dark with tree branches and roots he couldn't even see. Albert's back was covered with gooseflesh and sweat ran down the side of his face. His breathing was rapid and shallow; he knew he needed to take control of his fear but they needed to get someplace safe first. Was there some way he could hold the creature off in the cabin? Some weapon he could use? A back door?

The room was so dark he could only see the shapes of the windows, which were starlit grey against impenetrable black. "Do we need silver?" Albert gasped.

"Albert! Put. Me. Down."

"Where's your flashlight?" he nearly shouted at her. "We need to find some sort of weapon to hold it off! Do we need silver?"

The door rattled and bucked, and the werewolf snarled and roared on the far side of it.

A Key, an Egg, an Unfortunate Remark

The hair on the back of Albert's neck stood on end, but his aunt only sounded aggravated. With him.

"What we need is for you to put me down! Honestly!"

He did. He moved to the far wall but there was no back door, just a pair of windows with jagged glass along the frames. The monster outside still roared as it battered against the door. Albert's stomach was in knots and sweat kept pouring his face. "I can lower you out the window, and we can circle around to the car—

"You want to sneak by a werewolf, Albert? In the woods? At night? Please."

He rounded on her, fear and desperation pouring out of him. "Then what do we do?"

The floor board beneath the back legs of the steel chair cracked. The chair slid an inch beneath and the door swung open slightly. The noise of the monster snarling and slashing its claws against the door was astonishingly loud.

Marley wagged her finger at Albert. "What we do not do is carry me around like a flour sack. I realize you did exactly that once before and saved my life from the driver of that car, and I'm grateful for that, dear—"

The door bent open just enough that the werewolf could force its snout through. It snarled and clashed its massive teeth in animal rage. "Aunt Marley, please."

"But I can't have you slinging me under your arm every time you feel a little frightened!"

The floorboard broke and the chair slid down into the crawl space below the house. The door itself began to batter against it, smashing back and forth against the jam and the chair. The werewolf's frenzy reached a pitch, and the slamming of the door echoed in the cabin like thunder.

Albert had never been more terrified in his life. The idea that he was about to be torn apart by fangs and claws made him want to jump out of his skin. He couldn't understand why Aunt Marley seemed so calm. Had she lost her mind? Was he talking to a copy of her, sent with him into danger on one of her impulses?

No. Albert took a deep breath. Whatever his aunt might do, she wouldn't do that. And he couldn't lose control of himself. Not now.

He smashed a broken pane with his elbow and shouted. "Keep running until you reach the treeline!"

The snarling and battering against the door suddenly stopped, and the creature withdrew. Through the darkened windows, they could see a flash of white as the werewolf raced around the house.

"I'm sorry," Albert said, his voice still quavering. "I'm kinda freaking out right now. Werewolves freak me out."

"Thank you," Marley said. She sounded uncharacteristically prim. "And it's perfectly understandable that you're afraid! Once again you can get through this just fine if you're willing to do exactly what I say."

"All right."

"Give me your hand."

Albert lowered her onto the floor so she was lying on her back. She patted the spot beside her and he dropped to the rough, splintered wood. Marley flipped on her powerful little flashlight and rolled it into the corner so they were lit by the reflected light.

When he returned, the werewolf crashed against the door like a shotgun blast. Splinters bounced against their faces. "Hands over head," Marley said, raising her voice to be heard over the wild screams, snarls and bangs of the shattering door. "Heels to butt."

Albert did as he was told, leaving his throat, chest, and belly exposed. Sweat soaked his shirt and his hands trembled uncontrollably. The door finally broke apart, and he suddenly realized that his aunt was between him and the werewolf; shame ran through him and he fought the urge to jump up and throw a futile punch.

The werewolf charged forward, open jaws rushing at Marley's throat. Then it stopped, just inches away. It backed up a step, then lunged toward her belly. Again it stopped only inches away.

It circled around their feet, drool sloughing off its gaping jaws. It looked huge in the dim light—it's going to tear us apart—and Albert closed his eyes so he wouldn't have to look at it.

Except that only made things worse. He opened just in time to see gaping jaws rushing at his face.

They looked four feet wide—large enough to swallow his whole head—but again they stopped short of breaking his skin. Hot spit and stinking breath struck his face, and Albert felt his whole body quivering. He was a larger meal than Aunt Marley, and younger, too. It was only right that he become the thing's first course. He waited to feel teeth tearing into him.

But the werewolf only roared. Then, apparently not getting the reaction it expected, backed away.

Marley and Albert watched it move toward the far end of the cabin and squat on a battered old sofa beneath the slanted blue tarp strung near the ceiling. It looked at them both and, with the speed of a changing TV channel, the werewolf disappeared and the man appeared.

He put his face in his hands and cried.

CHAPTER THIRTY-THREE
The Egg Revealed

The man ran through the door into the night, sobbing.

"Darn it," Marley said. "I ruin so many nice outfits doing this work. Help me up, Albert."

Albert rolled to his knees and helped his aunt stand. Marley brushed off her clothes, then had Albert turn around so she could brush him off, too. "Oh, it's no use. Why can't we run into these poor souls somewhere nice and clean, like a kitchen showroom or something? Would you grab my flashlight for me, dear?"

"Of course," Albert said, and did it. His sweat-soaked clothes were ice-

207

cold against his skin and he felt queasy. "You know, I've been in firefights before. I've run from cover with the enemy shooting from all around because... because I had to. Once, I ran into a burning building. But I have never been so scared in my whole life as I was just then."

"You were the one who was excited to meet a werewolf."

"Aunt Marley, I never actually said... you're going to keep torturing me over this, aren't you?"

She smiled. "You bet I am."

Albert laughed. It felt really good to laugh. "Why didn't the werewolf kill us? Is it because I'm not delicious? Because I'm pretty sure I'm completely delicious."

"It's because he's part wolf. Wolves don't attack human beings, Albert; a werewolf will only attack you if you run from it like prey or if you challenge it."

"We surrendered to it."

"More than that, we acknowledged its dominance by baring our bellies. Even if the human inside the creature hated us with a murderous passion, the wolf's instinct would have stayed his hand. It recognized kinship with us and accepted our submission."

"That's better than the Geneva Convention, I guess."

"Albert, you already know what animal is the most dangerous to other human beings."

"Lots of them: sharks, bears, tigers, hippos—"

"Yes, but only in relatively small numbers. The most dangerous animal to human beings is always going to be other human beings."

"Oh. Well. That I know."

"I know you do, dear, better than most."

It occurred to Albert that they were still standing in the cabin, and that his aunt was certainly waiting for him to be ready to leave. He wasn't.

"Can I just say that your 'most dangerous' question wasn't fair, because I thought you meant animals people transform into."

"Yes, dear, I'm very tricky; I think we've established that. And while I've

208

heard of weresharks and weretigers, I've never heard of werehippos. But the world is large and life is short. It's possible they exist and I don't know about it."

Albert exhaled slowly, burning off the last of his adrenaline. "Personally, I'd rather see werehumans—people who transform into decent human beings."

It wasn't terribly funny, but Marley laughed anyway out of a welcome camaraderie. "Are you under the impression that I'm testing you, Albert?"

"Constantly."

"The first time I saw a werewolf, dear, I went absolutely mad with fear. I'll tell you about it sometime, if I get the chance."

"Okay. I gotta say, not that I'd ever want to meet one, but a wereshark sounds cool."

With that, Albert was ready. He led his aunt through the open doorway into the night. The balding man sat on a fallen log a little off to the left, still weeping.

Marley approached him. "It's not as bad as all that, dear. No one was hurt. You can stop crying now, unless you feel you really need it."

"It's hard to stop," the man said. "And I could have killed you. I could have killed you both!"

Marley turned to Albert. "Werewolves tend to have very strong emotions and have a hard time controlling themselves." She crouched in front of the man. "My name is Marley and this is Albert. What's your name?"

"Francis."

"Nice to meet you, Francis."

He looked up at them. "Nice to meet you, too. Both of you. I'm sorry for almost killing you."

"Apology accepted. Francis, do you like being a werewolf?"

"No! I hate it!"

"Truly? Knowing you can change doesn't give you a feeling of power? You don't feel like an action hero, strong and fast and filled with animal magnetism? No benefits at all?"

Francis looked at Marley a little uncertainly. "Benefits?" He laid his hand on his belly. "I've lost some weight over the last few months. The wolf eats a lot of squirrels. It's like Super Atkins."

"I imagine so."

"I hate it out here. Camping is something you should do for a weekend with your kids. Not eleven months! And... and..." Whatever Francis wanted to say, he couldn't.

Albert said it for him: "You've killed people."

"I couldn't help it!" Francis sobbed. "I didn't want to, but I don't have that kind of control over it. It's in control of me." Tears began to run down his face again. "But I'm ready. Now that I've finished the job I came to do, I think I'm finally ready for... for my cure."

He glanced back at the cabin. Marley seemed to understand. "Show it to me."

He led them back inside but stopped just past the doorway. He stared into the corner but didn't approach any closer. Marley turned on her flashlight and retrieved a little steel box, painted blue, sitting on a folded cloth. The corners were rusty, and it squeaked when she opened it.

There was a revolver inside. She picked it up, let the cylinder fall open, and took out the single bullet inside.

"Oh, Kemosabe," she said dryly. The bullet went into her pocket and she tossed the empty gun to Albert.

"I need that!" Francis said. "That's my only way out of this!"

"Don't be silly, dear. There are six or seven different cures for lycanthropy, depending. Whoever sold you this bullet was taking the easy way out."

"Really?" Francis said, stunned. "A real, true cure?"

"Very much so. And don't get yourself all worked up over it, please. I don't want to lie down on this floor again."

He began taking deep breaths. "Of course, of course."

"Now, what was this job you had come here to do?"

Francis explained that the People's World Nature Educatorium had set

210

him up in the cabin last winter. Merry was his cousin and, after Francis's "condition" started, he'd turned to Merry for advice, correctly guessing that his cousin would have read numerous books on the subject.

Unfortunately, they were all novels. Merry explained that Francis had been given a great gift and was now living close to nature. The whole group admired him, it seemed, and one even tried to convince him to bite her.

"Janet?" Marley said.

"Yeah. I didn't do it, obviously. She's scary enough without the fangs. Anyway, they were sure there was an illegal construction site up here that was dangerously close to the water table, so they asked me to move up here and keep an eye on things while they filed a petition with the court or something."

Marley laid her hand on his arm. "Show me the site."

Francis suggested they leave the car behind and the flashlight off, because he thought a light moving through the trees would summon a bunch of Homeland Security goons who'd drag him off to Guantanamo Bay. They slipped out of the cabin and followed a deer trail through the woods.

"Who gave you the gun and silver bullet, dear?"

"Some guy. A lawyer. He sought me out a few weeks ago after I sugared a couple of gas tanks. To be honest, I think he knew what I was right away, although he was really really careful. A few days later he came back again..."

"And he gave you the gun?"

"He tried to act all sympathetic, but he wasn't very good at it. It was pretty clear I was just an obstacle to be swept aside. Not that I turned it down. Along with the gun, he brought pictures of my wife. And my two kids."

"Jesus," Albert blurted out. "You had to leave your kids behind?"

"Yes, of course! Do you know how infuriating kids can be? I wouldn't have lasted three days at home; I'd have killed them all. I had to go away."

Marley sighed. "I can't imagine how hard that must be."

Francis stopped and turned toward them. A strong wind was blowing through the trees, and the rain clouds had parted, leaving the moon space to shine between the clouds. "Are you being straight with me? Can you really offer me a cure, or is this just a trick to get me to help you?"

"A trick?" Marley exclaimed. "Me? Oh, Francis, do I look like someone in the habit of playing tricks on people?"

"No, you don't."

"Well, you're wrong." Marley said. "I trick people all the time! Lie to them, too. At the moment, though, I'm telling the truth. For one thing, a werewolf who feels betrayed can be an absolute horror. For another, I don't want to; it would be too cruel. Tell me how you got your condition."

"It was in an airport bathroom in Phoenix... don't get that look, it wasn't like that."

"What look?" Albert protested. "I don't look."

"This guy splashed me at the sink and wouldn't apologize. We had words and he lost control. Then, ta-daa!"

"Did he look like a real wolf?"

"I can't tell a wolf from a big dog," Francis said. "Still."

Marley continued patiently. "I mean, did he look like a hairy wolf man, the way you were, or did he go on all four paws?"

"Paws," Francis said. "I go on all fours sometimes, too, when I'm hunting."

"Ah, I see. Well, the good news is that your cure is not even particularly difficult."

"It's not?"

"The bad news," Marley continued, "is that it's expensive."

"How expensive?"

"Very. Even I think it's expensive, and I'm rich. I couldn't do it for you as a charity. It would have to be a loan, and you'd have to come to work for me to pay it off."

"What kind of work?" Francis asked suspiciously.

"Albert, tell Francis what we do."

"Travel the world, capture spies, rescue sexy countesses, avert nuclear war—"

A Key, an Egg, an Unfortunate Remark

"Countesses!" Marley exclaimed. "Don't you wish. No jokes, Albert, dear. It's too dark out here for jokes."

"Sorry. I'm still a little tense. What we do is help people like him."

"How very succinct, dear. Perfect."

Francis looked at them hopefully. "I... will it really work? Because I want it more than anything and if it doesn't work I'll lose my mind."

"It'll work," Marley assured him. "If it doesn't..." She handed him the silver bullet. "Now let's get a move on, please. It's been a long day and I'm an old woman."

They had to hike along the trail for more than a mile; luckily the rain had already stopped and the intermittent starlight was bright enough that no one tripped. Their eyes had adjusted to the dim light by the time Francis pointed through a break in the trees toward the riverbank and said, "Down there."

Marley and Albert took the lead moving down the slope into a small clearing. The trees here had been cut down and stacked just at the river bank twenty yards down the slope. The muddy ground was cris-crossed with tread marks and the side of the hill had been gouged many times by shovels.

Albert moved close to the hill. "Was this hill dug out by hand?"

"Yeah," Francis answered. "They had other big equipment, but work on the side of the hill was done carefully and slowly. I overheard some of the workmen discussing a NAGRA site, but I wasn't fooled. Merry was convinced there was going to be a condo here or something, but that never made sense to me and I never saw any evidence of it. Just the dig and a little ferry barge to carry away whatever they found."

"Oh no," Marley said suddenly. She had walked farther along the path than the others and could see something beyond the curve of the hill. Albert and Francis rushed toward her just as she turned on the flashlight.

"Don't—!" Francis began, but he quickly fell silent.

The hill had been dug deeper here. Marley played the flashlight across the mud. At the edges there were the sharp, irregular marks of a shovel and the even grooves that would be left by a stiff broom, but most of the

213

depression was a large, smooth, concave surface, nearly five feet from shovel mark to shovel mark and narrower at one end than the other.

Marley knew that shape. A huge egg had once been buried here.

"What's that?" Albert said, pointing to the sole imperfection in the smoothly curved mud wall. Marley shone her light on it. "It looks like the impression of a heavy chain."

Marley looked behind her at the river flowing just down the slope, then she turned to Francis. "When did they take all this equipment away? When did they close up the dig?"

"Recently. Late Friday, I guess."

Marley turned back to the curving depression in the hillside and shut off her flashlight. It was nothing but shadow now, but she stared at it.

"Oh, Albert, this is so much worse that I feared. We have to get back to the city right away."

CHAPTER THIRTY-FOUR
The Recrimination Game

Marley took the revolver from Albert and gave it to Francis. "If you don't hear from me within the week, I'm most likely dead. I'm sorry to give you hope for this cure and then abandon you this way, but this is an emergency."

Francis accepted the gun from her. "What is going on? What's happening here?"

"Even if I had time to explain it, Francis, I wouldn't. We have to go."

Francis caught her elbow. "Please! I want to help!"

Marley smiled at him in a kindly way and laid her hand on his dirty cheek. "Thank you, but no. You're a werewolf, dear. You can't even help yourself."

A Key, an Egg, an Unfortunate Remark

Francis led them back to the cabin, and they left him there with his gun and silver bullet while they hurried to their car. Albert turned the car around and, riding inside of Marley's trick like an astronaut in a rocket, he raced along the trails to the gate—which had somehow been unlocked again—then out into North Bend.

The streets were empty. He followed the signs to the highway. Marley's trick, whatever it was, seemed to evaporate off of him and the car. "What was that, Aunt Marley? A big boulder with a chain around it?"

"It was too smooth to be a boulder, don't you think, dear? And besides, I can't talk about that, not quite yet, so please don't ask right now." She took out her phone. She had a voicemail message, of all things.

Marley pressed the phone to her ear and listened. The call was from Libertad's sister, Felicidad. Marley had to play it twice, because the woman was crying so hard she could not speak clearly, but Marley understood the gist of it: Libertad had been admitted to Harborview Medical Center with a gunshot wound to her back.

Marley told Albert to drive directly to the hospital, but not to break the speed limit. She had a bad feeling about the highways, and the night.

Albert, reading her mood clearly, fell silent. Within the hour, they'd parked in the lot at Harborview and made their way to the Emergency Room.

Marley hung back, letting Albert trigger the radar that opened the door. They walked along a wall of clouded glass and rounded the corner into the waiting area.

It was quiet, even for a Wednesday, except for the fifteen people clustered at one end. Some sat and wept, some paced, some stood around the group as if guarding it. They spoke to each other in soft, soothing Spanish.

Libertad's sister spotted them and broke away from the group to greet them. "Marley, thank you for coming, it's so late."

"Of course I came. Libertad is my friend. How is she?"

"They expect her to survive, Mother Mary bless us all, but they're concerned about her arm. She might lose it."

"Oh no!"

"They're doing their best for her."

"And this is the best place for her. The doctors here are excellent at this sort of thing. Do they have her insurance information? Because I have it all right here on my phone."

Felicidad laid her hand on Marley's arm. "Thank you, but they already have it from her knee operation. Unless something has changed...?"

"Nothing has. Where is Isabeau?

"On her way."

"Felicidad, what happened?"

"It was nine o'clock. She was working, making a delivery or something, whatever it is she does for you...?"

"And?" Marley asked, breezing by the implied question.

"A black pickup truck pulled up and someone shot her from the window with a shotgun. A drive by at very close range. Libertad ducked at the last instant, which saved her life, but what did she do for you? All she would tell her family is that she drove a delivery truck, but she was a trained medical assistant. She could have gotten a better job than truck driver! What did you have her do that was so dangerous?"

Felicidad's tone changed as she began asking questions, becoming more urgent and accusatory. "Nothing bad, I assure you," Marley said.

"Then tell me what it is! Why is it a secret? Why is someone shooting at her?"

"It's a secret because it has to be. Libertad understands. If she hasn't told you, you'll have to trust her. I'm sorry. I know it's frustrating."

Felicidad gave Marley a disgusted look. Just like that, they had become enemies. "You think you can do whatever you want with other peoples' lives. You think you can just decide because you have money! I know her truck was full of blood. Blood! The police know it, too. What do you say to that?"

"What are you doing?" Libertad's mother Esme had joined them. She wagged her finger at Felicidad. "Libertad is a good woman and Marley is her friend. You should treat her with respect."

A Key, an Egg, an Unfortunate Remark

"Mama—"

"Htt!" Esme said, which was enough to settle the subject, apparently. "Marley, it's good to see you again. Libertad likes you very much."

"I consider her my friend, too."

"You didn't do anything to get my daughter shot, did you?"

"Oh, I sincerely hope not."

Marley noticed Albert staring into the far corner of the room and turned to follow his gaze. There, sitting all alone, was Phillip.

Libertad's family moved closer to them. One of the men, a short, muscular man with a salt and pepper mustache, said, "Gunmen broke into your house the other day, didn't they? They burned it down."

Esme and the others gaped at Marley open-mouthed. "Is that true?"

"It is, I'm afraid. And the car bomb on the waterfront this afternoon was another attempt to kill me."

There was a general uproar at this, and the whole family moved away from Marley as though she was radioactive.

Felicidad's voice cut through the commotion. "That's why you come in here with a bodyguard? Did my sister know about all this?"

"Of course she did. And this isn't a bodyguard; he's my nephew, Albert, who drives for me."

Everyone looked at Albert, and he felt the ought to say something that wasn't a joke. "I only met Libertad once, but I like her. I hope she comes through okay."

The man with the mustache pointed toward Albert's right hand with his chin. "What happened to your hand?"

Albert held it up, at once self-conscious about it and determined not to be give in to the urge to hide it. "I made a bad decision. And I should probably point out that I haven't actually done any bodyguarding."

Felicidad didn't think much of that. "Maybe you should have been with Libertad, then. She's the one who needed you." This time, no one scolded her.

Esme leaned forward, clasped Marley's fingers in her own chilly, fragile

217

hands, and said, "Mother Mary watch over you."

It was a dismissal, and Marley led Albert away from the family as they drew toward each other. Philip was still sitting alone in a corner, staring at his hands. Marley sat on one of the steel and fake leather chairs beside him, and Albert sat beside her.

"Oh!" Philip said, startled.

"What brings you here, Philip? Not feeling poorly, I hope?"

"No, ma'am," he said. "I..."

"What happened? Come along, dear. Don't hold it in. Tell me."

Philip rubbed his nose and looked up at the ceiling. "Someone shot at one of our Educatorium meetings. Janet was hurt."

"What?" Marley clutched at his arm. "When did this happen?"

"Just as the evening meeting was starting, around six-thirty or so? Merry had just arrived—late, as usual—and we'd sat down to start our planning session, when bullets started coming through the wall."

"How do you mean?"

"You're super-interested in this, aren't you?"

"It's not idle curiosity, dear. Did you see who shot at you?"

"No. The shooter was in the alley. He had some kind of machine gun—I don't know much about firearms—and he shot through the garage door and the dry wall into our room. And now I'm saying words like shooter like I'm a character on a TV show."

"Was Janet the only one hurt?"

"No one was hurt. The bullets went right along the top of the wall over our heads. But before the shots had even stopped, Janet had jumped up and run out the door to see who was shooting at us. She saw a vehicle pulling away, and someone inside fired a second... volley? I guess? We found her lying on the patio with blood all over her. God, I thought she'd been shot in the throat, but a couple of shotgun pellets had passed through her jaw."

"It must have been terrifying."

"She'll be okay. The police questioned all of us about a black pickup with a broken taillight, but I can't imagine who that could be. I mean, why would anyone even bother with our group? We never do anything!"

Marley kept her expression calm. "I can't imagine either."

"She doesn't have insurance, of course, because the government said she had to get it and God forbid she would ever... but I guess they're used to that here. I didn't realize."

"Have you been here the whole time?"

"She won't see me," Philip said. "I don't even want to see her, but I came down here because she doesn't have any family on the West Coast, and I thought I ought to. But she doesn't want me to visit. I don't..." He sighed. "I don't think she sees me as a human being."

Marley patted his hand. "Having met her, I'd say it's possible she doesn't see anyone as a human being."

"I'm over it," Philip said with finality. "I'm sitting here out of a sense of duty, but I don't even like her. She sure doesn't like me. I'm sick of the whole scene. You know, when I first signed up with the Educatorium, I thought we would be doing some good in the world, you know? I thought I would be learning how to take action, stand up to the corrupt powers of the world."

"But you're not?"

"Mostly we plan future meetings. Hsing always has 'reservations' about anything we plan, and Merry always lets her postpone a protest until we can talk it over more. Filing court papers, sure, but actual protest? It's never the right time."

"That doesn't sound like Janet at all."

Philip held his breath for a moment. "No. It doesn't. She tried to convince us to take action, to destroy some machinery or set fire to something, but she could never overcome Hsing's basic inertia. Janet did things on her own."

"Like what?"

"I never found out. Sometimes she'd disappear for a few days and she'd come back looking all smug, and we were sure she'd been out there doing. I even approached her separately to get her to take me along, but she never would. She just took me..."

Bitterness and embarrassment cut off the end of that sentence, so Marley finished it for him. "To her bed. You became lovers."

Philip snorted. "Except 'lovers' has the word 'love' in it."

Albert broke in. "Where was she last Sunday night?"

"Is that the night that lawyer was killed?"

Albert nodded.

"You know, not long ago I would have said she couldn't have done it. She couldn't have murdered someone. Now I'm not so sure. She has this way of looking at you as if you're a smear on a pane of glass, and she can't wait to wipe you away. Anyway, I don't know where she was. She wasn't with me. She didn't show up for any meetings for, like, a week. The one you crashed was her first day back. She didn't say where she went. Never does."

Marley tried to keep her tone light. "What makes you think she went somewhere?"

"That's usually what happened. She'd vanish and no one would know why or where." He rubbed his hands on his pants. "But you know what? I'm done with all of it." He tugged at his hemp shirt as though he wanted to strip it off and throw it in the trash right that moment. "I'm going to reinvent myself. Do you think I could go emo? It suits the way things have been going for me lately, and I could really pull off that look."

Marley smiled at him. "How old are you, dear?"

"Twenty-two."

"You're old enough to become whatever you want to be."

Philip liked that answer. He stood, slung his pack over his shoulder, and headed for the exit.

"We'd better get going, too, Albert. I feel a conversation with the police coming close, and I don't want that. Not yet."

They went out to the car. Marley didn't want to return home. Weathers would certainly feed the dog but he would never walk it, and there would almost certainly be a mess to clean in the morning. Still, she didn't feel safe returning there.

Marley picked a downtown hotel at random and checked them in.

Albert, thinking about Felicidad's remark about being his aunt's bodyguard, asked if it would be best for them to share a room just in case they were found anyway, but Marley brushed the suggestion aside. She hadn't hired him to stand between her and danger.

They took adjoining rooms. Not only did Albert lock and latch his aunt's door, he jammed a chair beneath the knob. "Call if you need me?"

"Absolutely, I will," Marley answered. "Albert, did you notice? About the pickup truck?"

He nodded. "A shotgun blast from a pickup truck with a broken taillight? Is that why you had the urge to break it? So we would know it was Nora's crew coming after Libertad and those hippies?"

"I don't know. It does help us tell them apart from the SUV with the broken windshield that almost ran us down and, I think, was the source of the rats in that seafood restaurant."

"The guys in the SUV are moving against Amos Quigley, trying to take his property. And Nora's crew has started striking out at the people you meet as if you're a gangster."

For the first time Albert could remember, Marley looked startled. "A gangster, Albert?"

"As if," he said quickly. "Obviously you're not one. But you have an organization, and the ones on the street, or that you meet with in public, are going to be targets."

Marley went to the window and looked out over the city. "I have been a gangster, of a sort," she said. "Long ago, we had factions. We skulked and killed in secret. I didn't expect Nora to escalate things so quickly."

"I was surprised, too." He edged toward the door. "It was unfair of Felicidad to say that to you."

"What do you mean, dear?"

"When she said you thought you could do whatever you want with other people's lives just because you have money."

She turned back to him, her face very pale. She'd never looked so sad. "But Albert, I do that all the time. I wave money in front of people, make my arguments, and convince them do what I say. I needed a driver and hired you, didn't I, when you were anxious for a job? Haven't you felt the breath of a vampire on your throat, suffered a ghost's despair, driven a car with a bomb attached to it, and exposed your belly to a werewolf? I needed your help and I dragged you into it with the promise of a paycheck, didn't I?"

Her voice sounded strained, and Albert knew it wasn't just the late hour. "Libertad and I both know the risks. We could quit if we wanted to. And I don't know about your other employees, but I'd be willing to help you out even if you weren't paying me. Not that I want you to cancel my check."

"I wouldn't even if you asked, dear. And thank you."

"You're welcome. We sure have a lot of suspects, don't we?"

"Do we?"

Albert hadn't expected that response. "I think so. Nora and her people are here, in town, and they're willing to do violence. We may not have a motive to tie them to Aloysius but we can't count them out. Janet hated him because he was working on Evelyn's project. Stan hated him because he acted like an asshole. Zoe hated him because he slept with her and stole her little book of spells. He was selling something he shouldn't have to George, and George's wife was seriously hacked off about it. Whoever supplied him with those potions might have found out he was skimming. His only client, Evelyn, seemed to like him but maybe he told her that her project was nuts and she flipped out. Besides, I don't like her. He was sleeping with both Inez and Sherilynne at work, which can't be a good idea, not to mention Elaine..."

"Do you think Elaine's a suspect now?" Marley was genuinely surprised. "I thought you said she wasn't the type."

"You were the one who said she had a temper. But yeah, everyone he slept with, pissed off, or worked against is a suspect, as far as I'm concerned. Why?"

"Oh, no reason."

"Aunt Marley, do you know who cut my brother's throat?"

She gave him a very frank look. "No, Albert. In all honesty, I do not know who cut his throat. Now get some sleep. In the morning we need to buy some new clothes and find Stan. Something tells me he's much more important than he seems."

"All right," Albert said. "Good night."

He shut the adjoining door, then locked, latched, and propped a chair against the exterior door to his own room. It was almost two thirty in the morning. As he undressed and got into bed, he thought about the frank and honest look his aunt had given him as she said she didn't know who had killed Aloysius. He also remembered her telling him that honesty was the most dangerous trick you could play on someone.

He couldn't figure out what it all meant.

CHAPTER THIRTY-FIVE
Door, Opened

The front desk called them both at six o'clock the next morning. Marley awoke feeling refreshed and alert, if a little sore from the previous night's hike. After this mess was all cleared up, she would need to book an hour with her sports massage person soonest.

Albert had a harder time of it. He wasn't sore from the long woodland trek, but he was dry-mouthed and weary from lack of sleep. He wasn't a soldier anymore; couldn't he press the snooze button, metaphorically speaking? He glanced at the phone, wondering how he could arrange another call, and fell back to sleep.

"You're up, aren't you, Albert?"

He jolted awake, throwing off the covers. His aunt's voice seemed to come from only inches away—he could have sworn he felt her breath on his ear—but his room was empty and the connecting door still shut. Another one of her tricks. "God, that is cruel. Cruel!"

The bathroom sink had wrapped cups beside the faucet, and he filled one with tap water and drank it down, over and over. Then he showered and dressed. His black suit jacket was a mess, but there was nothing he could do about it. Just as he was tying his shoes, his aunt knocked softly on the connecting door.

He opened it for her.

"Good morning, Albert. I trust you slept well?"

"Yes, but not enough."

"That's a problem of the young. You have so much life, but you spend too much of it dreaming."

"You know, a real chauffeur would answer that with Yes, madumb in a weary voice."

"You're my assistant, Albert, not my chauffeur. That's why I haven't bought you a hat."

He went to the bathroom, wet his fingers, and ran it through his unruly blond hair. It didn't look good—he knew that—but his aunt hadn't complained and he didn't care. He was going to grow it out. "We find Stan today?"

"First we find some food, then we find some clean clothes. Then we find Stan."

They rode the elevator to the hotel restaurant. Albert ordered yogurt and granola with fruit on the side, claiming his stomach wasn't ready for anything heavier. Marley ordered a bowl of corn flakes with a hard-boiled egg and toast. "I have the feeling it's going to be a big day."

"Do you ever have small days?" Albert asked as the waitress set coffee in front of them.

Marley found three messages on her phone. The first was from Weathers, informing her that, as of midnight, a pair of men had parked on the street in a van to surveil her safe house. Marley shared that news with Albert, explaining that it had only been a matter of time.

The second was from Naima, letting Marley know about the attack on Libertad. The information she shared was identical to what Marley had learned the night before from the family. Naima also said the facility had three days' supply and could go for another six days on pig blood, but even that was pushing it, especially with a new resident. They would need to resume shipments before that time, and Libertad would not be back at work by then. Naima was already searching for a fill-in, but if Marley had any ideas, she'd be glad to hear them.

The third was from Frederika. She'd visited Ubeh in jail, as requested, just long enough to tell her not to talk to anyone without a lawyer present. Then she'd declared she could not represent her and suggested Ubeh engage another attorney. Finally, she explained that she had a lead on Stan, and please give her a call back.

"Well!" Marley dialed and held the phone to her ear. "Frederika sounds almost annoyed with me."

"She did nearly get killed yesterday," Albert pointed out. "That makes some people tense."

"We both know that very well," Marley said, then turned her attention to the phone. "Frederika! Good morning to you. How are you, dear?" Marley put extra sugar into every word. "Oh, I'm so glad. Albert and I are just enjoying a little breakfast out, before we start our day. At the Brasserie Margeaux. No, I've never been here before, either, but that's sort of the point, what with the recent attempts on my life."

They talked a while, then Marley hung up just as the food arrived. "She says Stan Grabbleton doesn't want to speak to us except through an attorney."

"Does he think we're cops?" Albert asked, stirring his food together.

"He seems to think that we're trying to pin Aloysius's murder on someone other than Jenny, and he's not eager to be a 'fall guy.' If you can believe he used that term."

"From his perspective, he has a point, I guess."

"Frederika decided to hire our private detective friend to look for him, and he already has a hit. Apparently, we're meeting him here in two hours and then heading to Portland."

"Cool. I like Portland."

They had nearly finished their meal when the restaurant door swung open with great force and Evelyn Thomas rushed in. Her silver hair looked the same as it had in her office and she was again dressed completely in white. The large white handbag under her arm was open and the head of her long-haired white cat peeked out.

"Oh, wonderful," Marley sighed.

Evelyn scanned the room, saw Marley, and rushed toward her. "Marley! Oh, it's good to see you! What a surprise! I was just walking by, thinking about you, and there you were."

"That is an amazing coincidence," Marley replied sweetly, "but I'm afraid we were just about to leave."

"Hello, Alan," Evelyn said. She pulled out a chair and sat down. "Mind if I join you? How have you been?"

"Rushed," Marley answered curtly. "How goes your project?"

"The habitat? Oh, I've just about given up on it," Evelyn said with a melancholy sigh.

"Really? I'm surprised to hear that. I thought it was your life dream."

She let out a regretful, and theatrical, sigh. "There's no support for it from the local powers-that-be. After our conversation, well, I feel I should move on to other, more modest dreams."

"Well. That sounds awful."

"Marley, I've been meaning to ask you: Did Aloysius give you anything to hold? Did he store something in your home or—I don't know—a safe deposit box?"

"What do you mean, Evelyn? What sort of thing?"

"He was my attorney, and I asked him to store certain documents for me, things I didn't feel safe keeping in my office, what with my temp receptionist. I'm in a very competitive business, after all, and it can be especially hard for a woman. I'm sure I don't have to tell you that."

"What makes you think he'd give them to me?"

"To be honest, I don't think he would, but I've spoken to the police about it, and they don't have anything like it in their evidence files. No one seems to know. Really, I've just about exhausted every avenue; I only come to you because I don't have anywhere else to turn."

"Well, it's awfully lucky that you've found me. Aloysius did occasionally ask me to keep things for him—we were not very close, you know, but still…. What did these documents look like?"

Evelyn's face became excited, but before she could speak the waitress returned to the table. "How was everyth—Excuse me," she said to Evelyn, "but you can't bring a cat into the restaurant."

"Oh why don't you… go count your tips!" Evelyn snapped. It wasn't the most devastating thing she could have said, but it was the nastiest thing she dared with Marley sitting right beside her. The waitress dropped the check and marched away.

Albert gaped at her. When Evelyn spoke to Marley again, her tone was much sweeter. "You can see that I'm desperate. It was a sheet of paper, cream-colored and thick like stationery. There were numbers written on it in brown ink, hand-written."

Marley seemed thoughtful. "Numbers?"

"Two dozen of them, arranged in a sort of spiral."

Marley made a regretful but insincere shrug of her shoulders. "I'm sorry, but he never gave me anything like that. I had a box of old Christmas cards he gave me years ago when he went to law school but never took back, and a carton of promotional key chains, if you can believe it, but nothing like what you're describing. And all of that was destroyed in the fire, anyway."

Evelyn stared into Marley's face. It was clear she was disappointed, and it was also clear she thought Marley was lying.

Marley waited to see what she would do. Whatever it was, she knew it would reveal something important. It was impossible to guess what that something might be, but she could feel it like an overfull balloon about to burst.

"Well," Evelyn said uncertainly. She absent-mindedly scratched much too hard at her cat's ears. "Well, I guess it can't be helped, even though the fire wouldn't have… anyway."

227

Was that all? Disappointed, Marley signed the check, adding extra to the tip along with a note of apology for the behavior of their unwelcome guest. "Albert, it's time to visit the clothing store."

She stood. Albert and Evelyn stood as well. As they made their way to the door, Evelyn said, "Can I drop you somewhere?" then took out her phone and dialed. She held it to her ear as Albert pushed open the door.

"No thank you," Marley answered, stepping aside so Albert could release the door. It swung shut behind her.

A van rounded the corner so fast the tires squealed. Albert turned toward it. The side door slid open before the driver applied the brakes. Albert had no time to react. Three men in black hoods, all aiming MP5s at them, stepped out just as the van shrieked to a stop.

"They found me again!" Evelyn yelled.

"No," Marley announced as the gunmen came toward them. This was happening too fast. "Albert! Grab hold of Evelyn!"

Albert, who had been moving to shield his aunt with his body, grabbed Evelyn's wrist. The closest gunman was shouting at them, right index finger already on the trigger, left hand reaching for the lapel of Albert's jacket. Marley grabbed Albert's thick bicep, laid her hand on the restaurant door handle behind them, and yanked it open.

CHAPTER THIRTY-SIX
An Unexpected View

There was no sensation of movement, not for any of them. Instead, it seemed that the entire world swirled around them like leaves in a whirlwind. Then it stopped.

Sunlight blinded Albert, and a chill breeze blew on his face. He saw sky, and a black iron fence, and dark gray stone. They were no longer standing outside the restaurant; they were up high, somehow. He could feel the unexpected altitude. He gasped, as shocked as if someone had poured a cold beer on his head. Evelyn shrieked and jumped back, almost breaking out of his grip.

Marley stumbled into someone—where ever they'd appeared, they were surrounded by people. "Oh!" she exclaimed. "How clumsy of me!" Marley's hand still clutched the door handle behind her. She released it, offering a silent prayer of gratitude to the great powers of the universe. They'd come here. Well, it could certainly have been worse. Much worse.

"What's going on?" Evelyn shouted. "Where am I?"

The crowd moved away from them, not that there was much space to move on the narrow, concrete deck. A man in a cap and a long red doorman's coat stepped up to Evelyn and said, in a very gentle voice, "Are you all right, madam?"

"I don't know where I am!" she said, sounding panicky. "I don't know how I got here!"

Marley kept her tone neutral. "I'm sorry for the commotion. She's with us and... well, she hasn't had an episode like this in a long time. Come here, Evelyn."

Albert realized he was gripping Evelyn's wrist too tightly; he let go. She staggered away from him, bumping the man in the doorman's coat. Her eyes were wild, but she fought to take control of herself; it wouldn't do to have a public freak out in front of so many people. It simply wouldn't do.

Marley put her hand around Evelyn's shoulders and led her toward the low wall and high iron safety fence at the edge of the deck. "Look out there, Evelyn. Look. You know where we are, don't you? What do you see?"

"It's... it looks like Manhattan."

"We're in Manhattan, yes. And you know where we're standing?"

Evelyn looked back at the building. "Is this the Empire State Building?"

Marley winked at the man in the long coat and cap and he moved away. "It is," she said, her voice low. "I heard you say those gunmen had found you, but I suspect they won't look here. And it's such a beautiful spring day! May in New York City! How wonderful."

Albert crowded close to listen in. Evelyn trembled. There was no way to retreat without creating a fuss, and she didn't dare to that. "What did you do to me?" she whispered. "How did you do this?"

Marley kept her voice low. "My dear Evelyn, many years ago, I did something terrible. I hurt someone for no other reason than to further my own ends, and that someone hurt me back."

Evelyn's eyes were wide and her whisper was harsh with fear. "What are you talking about?"

"I'm cursed, dear."

Evelyn stepped back and bumped into Albert. She glanced at him, half expecting him to pull a gun or throw a punch.

Marley gently took her hand. "I'm telling you this for a reason. I didn't bring you along to 'save' you from gunmen who were never any real threat to you. Evelyn, dear, I know more than you realize."

Evelyn felt the first little twinge of nausea. "I don't know what you're talking about."

Marley looked her straight in the eye. "Do you understand who you are?" Evelyn quailed under her gaze but didn't respond. "No answer to that? Let me go further, then: I have been where you are, dear. I have. There have been times in my life when I was ready to do anything to achieve my goals, and anything is what I did. Terrible things, Evelyn. Now I'm cursed, and trying to do the right thing with my life, but I could just as easily have been killed. I could have spent eternity in darkness and misery, dragging my chains behind me. This whole business of yours—"

"I don't know what you're talking about," Evelyn whispered harshly, doubling down on her denial. "The only business I'm in is development. Buildings. Architecture. That's my only business."

"Humankind is our business," Marley said, her voice smooth and and gentle. "The common welfare..."

Evelyn didn't want to hear any more. She wrenched her hand free of Marley's and lurched toward the door. Albert was close behind. As she

230

swung it open, it struck Albert on the hip, blocking her exit.

"You're the one," Albert said, staring down at her. "You killed my brother, or you had him killed. Why?"

Evelyn didn't answer. She strained at the door, and Albert let himself be pushed aside. She fled into the building, presumably toward the elevators.

Albert turned to his aunt, who sighed and looked through the security fence at the city below. "It's beautiful, isn't it? Not the way nature is beautiful, but utterly wonderful in its own way. People are capable of amazing things, when they want to be."

"Excuse me." They turned to see that the man in the long coat had returned. "Will she be all right doing down alone?"

"Thank you for your concern, but yes, she'll be fine. She's much more capable than your brief glimpse of her makes her seem. Unfortunately."

He nodded and faded back into the crowd, unsatisfied but unwilling to press further.

"How long have you known?" Albert demanded.

Marley looked up at him and Albert was startled to see a note of fear in her expression. What did she think he would do? Abandon her?

All she said was, "Let's get out of this crowd."

"Aunt Marley—"

"Evelyn is already on her way back home. Do you want her to find that number key before we do? We're in a hurry, Albert. Now open that door, dear. Please."

He opened the door and let her pass through. They rode the elevator to the eightieth floor, then another down to lobby. The lobby interior was breathtakingly beautiful and, despite her protests that they were in a hurry, Marley paused to admire it. Then they stepped out onto the sidewalk.

Albert felt strangely unmoored from his own life. It was invigorating. "I've never been to New York before."

Marley took his elbow and they began walking toward the corner. Pedestrians streamed around them. "I have, obviously. Several times."

"Why did you say 'obviously?' " Marley gave him a look. "Okay. You're cursed, somehow. You never open doors for yourself, and the one time you did you came through the other side of the country. And because you said obviously it must mean that it's a door you've opened before. Is that the curse? That every door you open takes you through a door you opened sometime in your past?"

She smiled up at him proudly. "Exactly so."

"That... that must suck. Is it in some kind of order? Random?"

"I believe it's random, but you must understand that's only the fourth time I've tried it since the curse was laid on me. I'm not exactly experimenting with it to work out all the nuances. There are some doors I've opened that I would never want to open again."

"What, like the door to hell?"

That didn't get a response.

"... Er, Aunt Marley, I was being sarcastic. I thought you'd laugh or something and... I don't know, tell me you were talking about a nuclear reactor or something."

But she didn't want to talk about doors to hell. "I did once jump out of a Cessna at four thousand feet. I had a parachute at the time, of course."

"You mean the three of us could have fallen out of the sky without a parachute?"

"We all die, dear, but which would you prefer: to be tortured to death in a dank warehouse by Evelyn's hired creeps, or with a gorgeous aerial view of the Utah desert in spring time?"

"You make me almost grateful."

"Besides! With all the doors I've opened in my life. What are the odds?"

"But Aunt Marley, couldn't you have thrown one of your decoys at them, and let them take that instead of you?"

"Possibly, Albert, I could have done that for myself, even with so little preparation, but I couldn't have created one for you, too, and you couldn't have done it for yourself. Now hush while I make a call." Marley dialed and introduced herself. She needed two tickets, she explained, to get her from JFK to Portland as quickly as possible. Portland, Oregon, thank you, and please forward the particulars by email. She wanted to be in the air by noon, and if a flight couldn't be booked She hung up. "Let's try to hail a cab."

That turned out to be surprisingly easy. Marley turned, raised her arm, and a cab pulled to the curb. Once safely settled into the backseat, Marley typed out a message to Frederika, then sent it.

The cab driver turned out to be an effusive talker, which pleased Marley to no end. They chatted happily about the city, travel arrangements, where Marley and Albert had come from, the driver's relatives who lived on the West Coast, and numerous other subjects, from theater to moon bases.

The drive itself went so quickly, it was as if traffic had been magically cleared for their convenience. So, it seemed like an exquisitely short time later that he was dropping them off at their charter company. Their plane was in the air a few minutes before noon, and the pilot announced that strong winds would almost certainly shorten the six-hour flight time.

Albert glanced around the cabin, a little incredulous. He thought he was accustomed to his wealth, but sitting in a swiveling chair in a small jet—holding just the two of them—made him feel like a character in a movie.

"Aren't you going to ask?" Marley prompted.

"Don't I ask you enough questions?" Albert responded.

"And you know that I don't mind, as long as they're not beneath you. However, I have just told you that I'm cursed, and you must be terribly curious what I did to get that way. Aren't you going to ask?"

He looked down at his aunt. Just a few days ago he'd thought her frail and silly, and now he didn't know what she was. He suddenly felt terribly young—big and strong but ignorant. What use was strength in the modern world anyway, unless there was a big-screen TV to mount on the wall, or heavy groceries to carry? In his ignorance, he'd thought of his aunt as almost a non-person—little more than an affluent collection of quirks and habits—and he was ashamed to realize so late that she had a rich history and that she would continue to add to it.

How many other women were out there, in their fifties or sixties—or later—who had done tremendous things, endured terrible trials, and had even more they could do, but had been ignored or dismissed by people like him? It was embarrassing.

"No," he said. "I'm not going to ask, but if you ever want to talk about it, I'll be around."

"Fair enough, but Albert, you had such an odd expression just then. What were you thinking about?"

"I'm not telling you," he answered. "And Scribe better not put it in your damn book." Marley laughed, and Albert pressed on. "I do have a different question, though: When did you know it was Evelyn?"

"From the first moment I saw her, in her office."

"Really? She tried to lie to you, didn't she? And at the restaurant, too. That's when you knew?"

"No, Albert dear. I knew from the instant we laid eyes on her in her office. Didn't you see her? She was dressed all in white, in her big chair with that big, dark, empty room all around her? And what did she have in her lap?"

"Um, a cat?"

"Exactly! A long-haired white cat, and she was stroking it thoughtfully the whole time like a Bond villain. Please! Who does she think she's kidding?"

"Um, seriously? You realized it was her because of that?" He seemed doubtful. "Have we been transported into a TV show or something?"

"People will tell you who they are, Albert, if you just pay attention. And I'm sorry I couldn't tell you, but I didn't know why she'd done it. To be honest, I'm still unsure what she's planning."

"But it has something to do with what they dug up by the river, and that chain. Whatever they are."

"Oh, I know what those are. Haven't I explained?"

"You told me not to ask."

"Oops. All right. Remember what I told you about Puget Sound, dear?"

"That it has a..." Albert could barely say the word aloud. "... Dragon in it."

"Correct. You know, dragons are powerful, but they aren't immortal.

234

What could be, in this universe of dying stars and—"

"Oh my God," Albert blurted out. "Did Evelyn dig up a dragon's egg?"

"Yes, she did."

"And the chain was to lift it out, right?"

"No, dear. The chain was to lock it up. A dragon can sense its egg, and, even when the magic in it has been shrunk down by making it real, that egg is a very, very powerful token. The chain locks the magic away, which also hides it."

"Do you think she's going to use it to cast a spell or something?"

"That would be the traditional use."

"Why? I mean, what would she use it for?"

"Even when it's made real, a dragon's egg contains a shocking amount of magical potential. Evelyn could bring someone back to life, she could create a doorway directly into the afterlife, she could do all sorts of things, but the most common thing—the one almost all of these people want, is youth and long life."

"Oh. Like Spire has."

"No, dear. Spire is cursed. Evelyn would still be able learn and grow, but she'd also be young and beautiful. She'd add approximately two hundred years to her life, barring violence or accident. It's a prize that too many people long for, I'm afraid."

"I assume the mother dragon would be a little bit upset."

"They're very protective of their young. In the past, when an egg was destroyed, the dragon swam away, never to return. We'd have to wait for a new egg to form and hatch, which might take decades."

"What happens if it leaves?"

"There are many dragons in the world. They help us maintain our sense of wonder, mystery, and most important of all, our humility. Without dragons, human beings lose control of themselves. They grow wild, proud, and violent, and the most terrible things begin to seem logical and necessary."

"That's why Evelyn's looking for that sheet of paper," Albert said.

"Because the egg is locked away and without the paper—that key—she can't get at the magic inside it. And the dragon doesn't even realize it's been stolen yet."

"I believe she entrusted the key to Aloysius; probably because she doesn't trust the gunmen she's hired. But Aloysius must have done something to alarm her—I can't imagine what—and she ordered her gunmen to collect the key and kill him. Or maybe she planned to betray him all along. But they didn't simply shoot him. They arranged his murder to look like a vampire attack. Because of me."

"Because Evelyn knows what you do."

"She thinks she does, I'm sure. There are some people in town who believe they have a handle on me, but most of them are just silly. Aloysius, for instance. He knew enough about me to seem useful to Evelyn—how to deal with ghosts or werewolves, for instance, even if his methods were hackneyed and low-rent. He also believed in magic; when Evelyn approached him about her plan, I'm sure she imagined she was getting something of an expert. And when she killed him, she knew I would be paying attention, so she tried to divert me."

"Thank you for not being fooled."

"Thank her for thinking me a fool. By God, even other grown women underestimate old women. I intend to make her regret the error."

Hours later, after sleeping for much of their flight, they stepped off the plane in Portland at three o'clock in the afternoon.

Kevin Fletcher met them at the gate, and he'd brought Marley's Jeep Cherokee, and all their things from the hotel, as requested. "I love that car!" he told them. "I wish I could have one of my own, but it stands out too much for my line of work."

"It must be hard to have to go through life without standing out from the crowd when that's what you naturally do."

Kevin laughed. "Oh, sweetie, you're my new favorite person. And that's not a professional thing to say, but I work for myself so whatevs."

"I'm told you found Stan Grabbleton?"

"Easy. But I had to tell him I was working against you, because he doesn't like you at all."

"Oh, that's just because he hasn't met us yet."

CHAPTER THIRTY-SEVEN
The Calm Before the Party

It was four in the afternoon when they found Stan Grabbleton in a nightclub called Falcon. There was a dance floor and multi-colored lights, but of course it was too early for darkness and loud music. Stan sat alone at the end of the bar, sipping a cup of coffee and chatting with the bartender, a bodybuilder with a shaved head and handlebar mustache.

He wasn't pleased to see Kevin walk in with Marley and Albert. "Oh God, this is just perfect. What a fantastic day this is turning out to be."

"Sorry, buddy," Kevin said. "This is my job."

"Lying to people is your job? Well, good for you. I hope that brings you a lifetime of happiness."

Stan had a strange, simpering way of speaking that turned his deadpan tone to intense sarcasm. Marley couldn't help but like him. "Oh, don't be so hard on him, Stan. I'm the one who needed to speak with you."

"Didn't you get my message? I don't want to talk to you. At all. I'm not interested in being your fall guy."

"Stop being dramatic, Stan. You didn't kill my nephew. You might have gone through his desk, but I know you didn't kill him."

"You know it? Sure you do. Sure. I have no alibi for the time he was killed, and at least ten people know I hated his guts." He turned to Albert. "I'm sorry for speaking ill of the dead, and I know he was your family, but he really was an awful, awful person and I despised him like..." He couldn't find the words to carry the full force of his feeling, and shuddered instead.

"You don't have to tell me," Albert said. "He was my brother."

"Then you have my sympathy, not because he's gone, but because you knew him."

Marley tried to keep her voice light and reasonable. "But Stan, it's true. I know who killed him and I'm hoping you can explain why."

"Hmm. I wonder why I don't believe you. Oh! I remember now! It's because you just walked in with Mr. Lying Is My Job."

The bartender leaned across the bar. "Stan, are these folks bothering you?"

"It's all right, I guess. Thanks, Ed. If I don't talk to them now they'll just bother me later, am I right?"

"I'm afraid so," Marley said.

"Then let's tear the Band-aid off all at once."

"I understand," Marley said, sitting beside him. Albert stood close to her.

Kevin leaned against the bar. "Do you folks want me to sit in on your conversation as a witness or something?"

Stan turned to him. "No."

"Excellent!" Kevin moved toward the other end of the bar.

The bartender nodded at Albert. "What can I get you, sweetheart?"

Albert didn't think this was the time to admit he was only twenty years old. "I'm driving."

"And you, ma'am?"

"Oh, do you have a white wine spritzer?"

The bartender gave her an Are you serious? look and set one in front of her. Then he moved to the far end of the bar to take Kevin's order.

Stan looked Marley and Albert over as though they were a large pill he was expected to swallow. "How awful is this conversation going to be?" he asked.

"Not too awful," Marley answered. "Why did you hate Aloysius?"

"Because he was Aloysius," Stan answered. "Because of how he acted and who was. Because of every word that came out of his mouth, every expression on his face, every molecule in his entire body. Everything."

"You must have loved going into the office."

"The office was hell. Your nephew made sure of it. He thought it was funny."

Albert sat beside Marley. "He was a bully?"

"Exactly," Stan answered. "And this is why I didn't want to talk to you, because you're going to think I hated him enough to do something to him, but I didn't. If I had, I certainly wouldn't have let the police arrest that poor girl. Bad enough that she dated him, but to have to go to prison for it— although I'm not sure which would be worse."

"Was he physically abusive?" Marley asked.

"That was the one thing he didn't do, although he sometimes talked about slapping me or pulling my hair, as though we were little girls. What he did was insult me every chance he got, with little digs about my weight, my medications, or my boyfriend. He did this in front of clients, too, mine and his. He used to make these awful sexual comments, as though I would do anything for him. And if I told him to shut up, he'd say things like 'Going to throw a punch at me, Stan?' "

"He did this in front of your clients?"

"Yes! And he stole from me. Nothing huge, mind you. Nothing I could file charges against him without seeming like a lunatic, but he'd take things off my desk and put them in his office. He thought it was funny that I'd have to come in and search through all his stuff."

"Oh, Stan, honestly, I had no idea he was like this."

"Very few people did. Your nephew was always trying to get control over people. With women, he wanted them in his bed. With most men, he tried to get them to like him. With me... I don't know if it's because I'm gay, or fat, or the way I talk, but he reverted to a teenage bully every time he saw me. But I couldn't break my lease and move to a new office."

"Times are tough," Marley said, but Stan didn't need much prompting at all.

"Not for me. I'm doing pretty well, and I'll be damned if I was going to be the one to move out of that office. I know your nephew was struggling—

Inez is too self-centered to help me kick him out because he acted like a psychopath, but she would if he couldn't pay his bills. But me? I'm a good lawyer. I don't have time in my schedule for all the people who want to hire me. There are three reasons why I don't have a fancy suit and a huge office." He held up his hand and counted them on his chubby fingers. "First: I refuse to ever work for anyone else, ever again. I'm my own boss. Second: for most of my professional life, my health insurance has sucked. This is the first year ever that I haven't had to pay a fortune just to cover my medications. Third: I do pro-bono work for anyone your nephew tried to sue."

Marley perked up. "So you're the one giving legal advice to the Educatorium people?"

Stan rolled his eyes. "Those people! They're idiots. But Aloysius was such a sloppy lawyer—okay, hold on, let's back up. Before Evelyn Thomas became his only client, he also handled contracts for this landlord down in Kent. The guy was a real creep. They were perfect for each other.

"He was working on these evictions—God, I don't even want to go into how shady these things were. The landlord sometimes shut off the electricity to the units on weeknights to mess with people's alarm clocks. Really disgusting stuff. And your nephew couldn't help but brag about it to Sherilynne. He actually laughed. So what I did was call the tenants and offer to go over the papers they were being served, pro bono.

"These people couldn't afford a lawyer of their own. One little old lady met me in a wheelchair with the arm pads held on with duct tape, for God's sake. And the papers they were being served lied to them about their rights and threatened rent increases if the tenants didn't go along with everything.

"So I went over everything, explained all the places where they were in violation, and sent the tenants off to court to talk to the judge."

"You didn't go to court with them?"

"With the way Aloysius was treating me? I honestly didn't have the nerve. But it didn't matter. Those tenants skated to a victory, and their landlord was hit with hefty fines. Do you know how rare that is in this state? Well, that one, since we're in Oregon now. And that wasn't even the first time. See, that's why I didn't have to kill him. I wouldn't bother. I was already ruining him."

"And then," Marley said, "he apologized to you."

Stan leaned back and crossed his arms, then uncrossed them to take a sip of his coffee. For all his talk of being framed for murder, this was the subject he was truly reluctant to broach. "He wasn't even supposed to be in the office. He never came in on Sundays; that was a day Sherilynne and I could work in peace. But there he was, and just as I was about to shut the door in his face, he said he was sorry."

"What exactly did he say, dear?"

"I'm not sure I can remember the exact words because I was so flabbergasted that I nearly fell over onto the floor. Honestly, you could have knocked me down with a hard look. The gist of it was that he realized he had been an absolute monster to me, but that it was all going to stop."

"What did you think about that?"

"That it was too good to be true! I honestly didn't believe him at first, because I figured it was some new kind of gotcha. I told him, 'I still hate you, but if it means you'll never speak to me again, then hooray.' "

Marley watched him closely. "You didn't believe him at first? What changed your mind?"

"Well, it wasn't all his talk about how sorry it was. All right. See, here's the thing. He looked like someone had... he looked as though he hated himself. I mean, skin-crawling, goose-bump revulsion."

"You don't say."

"Believe me when I tell you: I know self-loathing, and your nephew had it. It was all over his face. At one point, he looked at me and said, I understand who I am."

Marley jumped in her seat. Stan looked at her quizzically as she turned away from him and took a long drink from her spritzer.

Albert leaned close to her. "Aunt Marley? Are you all right?"

"Oh, Albert. If there was ever any single thing that proved I don't know what I'm doing, it's this. I wanted to save your brother, but I might have gotten him killed. Tell me, Stan, had Aloysius stolen anything from you recently?"

"Yes! Last Friday. I had gotten in the habit of leaving decoy keys in my desk, but somehow he figured it out and got his hands on my real ones. I searched his desk Friday night and Saturday, but it wasn't in any of the usual places."

"Could you have simply lost them?"

"He admitted he'd taken them on that Sunday morning as part of his big apology. He promised to return them the next day..."

Marley glanced up the bar at the bartender. Kevin was telling him a story about a previous case, gesturing wildly, and making him laugh. Two other men had wandered in and were edging close to the conversation. Marley took the key chain she'd found in Aloysius's bedroom and held it up. "Is this your key chain?"

"Yes!" He reached for it, but she snatched them away and dropped them back into her purse. Stan leaned toward her, his eyes wide with disbelief. "Are you mad? Those are my keys."

"Oh Stan, wake up. Aloysius had his throat cut four nights ago, then I was shot at and had my home burned down. Yesterday, someone tried to run me over, and I'm sure you heard about the incident near Pier 70?"

"The car bomb?"

"That was me, too. Even worse, one of the Educatorium people was shot last night, along with a very dear friend of mine."

"You're saying all that is because of my keys?"

"Not directly. What do these keys open?"

"Lots of things: the office building and my personal office, my file cabinet, my car, my apartment, my storage unit, my gun safe, the padlock on my front gate, and my suitcase lock."

Marley narrowed her eyes at him. "Storage unit?"

CHAPTER THIRTY-EIGHT
Not Much of a Party After All

Marley tried to convince Stan to let her and Albert go to the storage unit without him, but he wasn't having any of it. Whatever trusting instinct he might have been born with had been extinguished by years of sharing office space with Aloysius, and no matter what Marley said, he couldn't believe that a little old lady would deliberately go to a place she honestly believed to be dangerous. He refused to tell them where the unit was, but he was willing to take them to it to see if Aloysius had stashed anything there.

Kevin followed them out of the bar. "Oh my God!" he exclaimed. "I got the bartender's number! I love my job."

Stan was genuinely surprised by that, and they started talking about bartenders and the best ways to chat them up. Marley interrupted, asking if Kevin would ride back to Seattle with Stan so she and Albert could talk privately.

"Sure," Stan said. "Also, having him in my car makes it less likely I'll change my mind and ditch you in traffic."

Marley smiled. He was sharp. "That, too."

But Stan refused to start the trip immediately. It was five o'clock, he explained, and traffic would be "horrendous." All four of them went to a local restaurant, where they sat and chatted amiably for nearly two hours. It was very like an impromptu dinner party, and Marley enjoyed herself very much, encouraging Stan and Kevin to tell stories about their work.

Eventually, they prodded Albert to tell how he'd lost the index and middle fingers of his right hand. He was reluctant, but they'd already shared so much that he felt it would be unfair to hold back.

"It was last fall," he said. "We were driving through Arghandab Valley—that's in Kandahar—passing an apricot orchard on one side of the road. They aren't large trees; from the back of my M-ATV, I could have stood up and looked over the tops of them. Most of them, anyway. And the smell of all those ripening apricots was amazing. The other side of the road was just open field with wrecked irrigation ditches.

"We came upon some farmers by the side of the road. Their truck had broken down and little kids were running around, maybe four or five of them. They were just trying to get home.

"The lieutenant wanted to fix the truck for them. They only needed some tape for their radiator hose, which would be enough to get them going again.

"He was pointing to the leaking hose—the farmer's family didn't speak English and we couldn't speak Pashto, and we suddenly started taking small arms fire. The lieutenant was hit in both thighs, breaking his left femur. The farmer beside him was shot full in the... in the rear end. He was, like, seventy years old or something but he limped to the other side of the truck for cover.

"But the lieutenant was in a bad spot. Everyone was shouting and racing around, and I ran over, yanked him onto my shoulders and loaded him onto the M-ATV. Then we scooped up all the kids and the three adults and packed them in, too.

"We were ready to go. I stood on the side, holding on with my left hand and, as we pulled away, I raised my right hand in the general direction the shots were coming from and...."

"And what?" Kevin asked.

Albert sighed, then shrugged. "I flipped them the bird. Two seconds later, a bullet had taken the first two fingers from my right hand."

He held up his mangled hand for them to see. Kevin and Stan gaped at it and him. Marley leaned over and squeezed his left hand.

Kevin said, "Are you joking with this?"

"I wish. I don't think the sniper meant to do it. If he could have hit me anywhere, I'm sure he'd rather have put a bullet through my eye. It was just dumb luck. Bad luck. Anyway, that's when I became a soldier with no trigger finger."

"Did you or any of your buddies ever get the guy who shot you?"

"Oh no," Albert said. "We never even worked out his position. We just loaded up and got out of there. Nobody died that day."

"Oh my God," Kevin said, shaking his hands as though he had to air-dry them. "I could never do that."

"They wouldn't let me in even if I tried," Stan said, pressing against his large, round belly.

"Not to talk against it, if you know what I mean," Kevin continued. "I respect what you did and I'm glad we have people like you willing to do it, but I could never sign up for that. I'm not brave enough."

Stan watched Albert's expression shrewdly. "How do you feel about your service now? Was it what you wanted?"

"The Army?" Albert asked. "The Army was everything I hoped it would be. The institution, the training, the people—especially the people. They were everything I hoped they would be, and more. But I wasn't."

"Oh, Albert," Marley said. Those two words were so full of meaning that even she wasn't sure what she meant. She squeezed his uninjured hand again.

After a moment's silence, Kevin started telling another story. Within five minutes they were all laughing again.

When the clock struck seven, Stan called for the check. "I hope you saved some stories for the car, because it's a long ride."

It was a long ride—over four hours—especially since the highway through Portland and Vancouver still hadn't shed the last of its business traffic. Albert kept Stan's Touareg in sight for the whole drive

Despite what Marley had said before dinner, she did not want to talk.

Albert did. "You're not blaming yourself for Aloysius, are you?"

"Of course I am. And I should. I meddled. Again."

"I'm still not sure what you did."

245

"I threw water in his face," Marley answered. "Figuratively, I mean. I had never been happy with him, because... honestly, because he was such a self-centered, manipulative jerk. I'm sure he thought of himself as charismatic and confident, but he made my skin crawl. Ever since he was a smug teenager, I've wanted a way to shatter his self-image. And on Saturday night, when he came to my party to ask a favor, I did exactly that."

Albert was amazed that his aunt had kept this information from him, but he tried not to show it. "What favor did he ask?"

"He wanted a love potion."

"Really? That's a thing?"

Marley gave Albert a steady, watchful look. "Yes, it is, and I know how to make one. Why do you ask?"

"Because," Albert said, not taking his eyes off the road and therefore not seeing his aunt's expression, "it's creepy. I wouldn't want someone to take control of me that way. How do you protect against it?"

Albert's answer was such a relief that Marley laughed. "After all this is done, I'll show you."

"Thanks. And I still think you shouldn't blame yourself. First of all, everyone acts on the intel they have. I mean, seriously, who could have guessed Aloysius was caught up in all of this? Magic circles around his bed, giving silver bullets to werewolves, calling ghost hunters up from L.A... the guy was in over his head and everyone knew it but him."

"I should have known. This is my city, and none of this should have been going on without my knowledge."

"We know now. We're dealing with it. If Aloysius hadn't been such a jerk, he would have come to you, and you would have known sooner. More important: the person who is really responsible for his death is the one who cut his throat."

"Whoever that is, and Evelyn, because she ordered it. I hear you, Albert, and I'm grateful for the pep talk, but I'm afraid you're not going to reason me out of the guilt I'm feeling. Throwing water in his face seemed like the right thing to do at the time—"

"Like water flowing downhill."

"Well, yes, but—"

"We wouldn't have found out about the egg if you hadn't given him a change of heart. The whole thing—whatever it is—would have been over by the time you heard about it."

He looked at her, and she looked at him. "I don't like that thought, Albert. If that's true, then I really did kill him; my magic maneuvered him into getting his throat cut. For my benefit."

After a brief silence, Albert said: "Damn. And I was trying to make you feel better. That's a fail right there."

The storage center was north of Seattle, and they didn't arrive until well after eleven o'clock. The units themselves were little more than long metal sheds with battered, padlocked garage doors at one end.

Since Marley had not returned Stan's keys, Albert unlocked the front gate. Stan drove along the fence until he reached a unit well in the back. Marley and Albert pulled in behind him.

"This is it," he said, pointing.

Marley turned to Kevin. "Thank you for everything you've done. Would you like me to call you a cab? It's awfully late."

"And miss this? No way! This is too exciting."

"God, I hope not," Albert said as he unlocked the padlock and, despite the glare Stan gave him, pocketed the key chain. The unit was dark. Stan fumbled along the wall, searching for a light switch, then finally flipped it on.

"I don't see how your nephew would even know about this place. I don't talk about it. This is mostly Mitch's stuff," Stan said. "Two years ago he decided he wasn't 'centered' enough and spent three months in India. When he came back, he said his possessions were possessing him. The marionettes are mine, but those boxes are his crap that he probably won't ever want again."

"And this?" Marley asked as she took a manila envelope off a banker's box. The return address read Aloysius Pierce, Attorney at Law, followed by

Aloysius's work address. It wasn't sealed. Marley drew a single sheet of paper from it. "Cream-colored, thick like stationery," she said as she examined it.

Albert glanced at it. "With hand-written numbers in brown ink."

"DON'T MOVE!" someone shouted. It was repeated several times by several different voices, and the four of them froze in place. Gunmen in black rushed at them.

There were nine, all dressed as they had been when they kicked down Marley's door, masks included. Kevin and Stan took one look at their MP5s and began to shout "No! WAIT! HOLD ON!" until one of the men told them to shut up.

The SUV with the cracked windshield pulled up and Evelyn swaggered out. Her white clothes made her seem to glow in the ugly halogen light, although she'd left her purse and cat at home.

Behind her, moving more cautiously, were Nora, Nelson, and Audrey.

"If she reaches toward the door or one of the others," Evelyn said, "shoot the tall one."

Albert's expression didn't change. Stan raised his hands in the air. "Oh isn't this just perfect."

"Take your hand out of your pocket!" one of the gunmen yelled, his voice muffled slightly by his mask. "RIGHT NOW!" He charged at Kevin and jammed the butt of his weapon into Kevin's gut.

Kevin sprawled to the asphalt, his hand coming out of his pocket and his phone skittering across the asphalt. The gunman stamped on it.

"Hey, you know what?" Kevin yelled from the ground. "That really hurts!"

One of the gunmen shouted: "Everyone! Phones out!" Stan, Marley and Albert took their phones from their pockets. "Put them on the ground!" They did it. No one bothered to pick them up.

Evelyn came forward and held out her hand, waiting for Marley to give her what she wanted.

Marley stared at her. "How many lives will you sacrifice for your—"

"You lost," Evelyn said. "You tried to pull off a come-from-behind victory, but you lost. Deal with it. And don't talk to me about lives. You're the one palling around with vampires." She licked her lips in anticipation. "Now give me the key."

Marley placed the envelope and sheet of paper into her hand.

CHAPTER THIRTY-NINE
So Cathartic!

"We should shoot them all right now,"

It was the same gunman who'd ordered them to drop their phones. The leader? Albert tried to pick out some difference in his uniform or build to ID him later—assuming there was a later, and who would want to assume anything else?—but he couldn't spot anything obvious.

"No," Evelyn said. "I just had breakfast with Marley and Adam this morning, and then they turn up shot to death? The police would be all over me. I don't want to talk to cops again. Ever. Besides, look what happened with Al; if you'd been more patient, we could have avoided all this mess."

Marley, Albert, Stan, and Kevin were cuffed—not with zip ties, which Albert knew how to break free of—but with actual metal handcuffs. Then they were blinded with black hoods, and loaded into the back of a van. Kevin began to panic, gasping for air and sweating profusely. Stan became exhausted and listless. "I can't believe I insisted on coming along," he said.

Kevin's fear began to take control of him. "Omigod omigod omigod omigod—"

"Shut up," Audrey said. He did.

They drove for quite a while. Sitting on a bench, his back to a wall, Albert tried counting out the slow seconds and mapping their turns, but somewhere in the twelve-hundreds, he felt the cold, sharp blade of a knife press against his cheek just below his eye, and he lost count.

Whoever it was—and he was convinced it was Audrey—they didn't cut out his eye or slice him open. The knife moved away from his face and didn't plunge into some other part of his body. He could hear Stan's ragged breath over the rumble of the van, and Kevin's attempts to control his panic through deep, slow exhalations. He couldn't hear Marley at all; he hoped that meant she had vanished again, and was free and safe.

Eventually, they turned sharply to the left and jounced up a parking entrance, then went down a short ramp. Underground parking, but not too far underground. Once the van stopped, the doors were thrown open and they were all herded into an elevator, down a hall, through a doorway, then shoved onto a carpeted floor.

"Stay there," the lead gunmen said. "Whatever you're doing, we should get started right away."

"We can't," Evelyn answered. "Not at night. It's no good at night."

Marley spoke up. "What's the matter, Evelyn? Afraid of the dark?"

"Don't be absurd!" Evelyn snapped. "You don't even know what's going on, do you?"

"You've stolen a dragon's egg, dear. I assume you're trying for the usual immortality or somesuch."

Evelyn yanked Marley's hood off. The lead gunman beside her cursed and turned his back as he put his mask back on. Ignoring him, Evelyn crouched beside Marley, making sure she could see her smirk. "You're right, but only accidentally. I am going to be immortal, but not because of some spell. Psht! I have bigger plans."

Marley blinked in the light. They had been taken to a condo. All the curtains had been drawn and the furniture moved into a corner. Beyond that, the place looked utterly impersonal. There were no pictures, stacks of mail, or mementos in sight. The place was so carefully staged that it looked lifeless. "I have to admit," Marley said, "I still haven't figured them out. Not completely. You had Aloysius hold on to the key for you, presumably because you didn't trust someone who had access to your office. The gunmen?" Evelyn smirked. "Oh," Marley said, "your previous receptionist, then? Not the temp. Zoe, right? She did say Aloysius cost her a job."

"Well, Marley, that's very good! You've figured out more than I expected. Or are you guessing?"

"I'm paying attention. What happened to her?"

"I honestly don't know. I'd planned to have her killed and buried with a few pieces of luggage out in the Cascades, but she disappeared before I could arrange it. She knew the plan, of course, and if she'd managed to get hold of the key she could have done whatever she wanted with the egg. But she's gone so she doesn't matter. She was instrumental, though. She had the spell book that taught me to make the persuasion potion, and she knew about the egg, you, and your nephew."

"Just another one of Aloysius's conquests. But why did you hire him? If you hadn't, I might never have discovered you."

"I needed him, of course. A regular lawyer could never have dealt with old Amos Quigley. I needed Quigley—and everyone else—to realize he was dead so that his properties would fall into the hands of his less-tight-fisted heirs. And a regular lawyer would have been torn apart by that tree-hugging werewolf."

"Quigley's properties?" Albert asked.

"The seafood restaurant," Marley said, "where Evelyn's people released their rats."

"How...?" Albert was still not following along. "Quigley said Aloysius wanted him to sell land next to a 'brownfield,' didn't he?"

"Oh, Albert, what did I tell you about ghosts giving directions? The Unoco Brownfield has been gone a long time."

"Everyone knows that!" Evelyn interrupted, annoyed that they were talking to each other but not her. "The Sculpture Park is there now, and I still want it."

"Did you always plan to kill Aloysius?"

"Of course! Despite the fact that he didn't freak out when he was faced with the supernatural, he was a terrible lawyer. He thought he deserved thirty percent! He didn't even know what we were really up to. He thought

251

like you did, that I was some vain ninny who longed for youth and beauty. And then someone spilled the beans and he grew a conscience."

"What do you mean?"

"He called me on Sunday from his office and asked to meet with me. He said he'd realized he'd been a terrible person and he wanted to talk about setting things straight. Well, I couldn't have him ruining my plans when I was so close, so I told him to bring the key with him, and we'd have a nice long chat. But he must have been suspicious, because he brought a fake—he hid the real one very very well—and these fools killed him too quickly."

"They also staged a vampire attack in a city where all the vampires are quite domesticated. What that your idea? To throw me off your trail?"

Evelyn shrugged that off. "At least he didn't get the chance to expose our plan."

"Evelyn, you poor fool, he wasn't talking about exposing you; he probably never knew what you were planning. He was going to apologize because he used you for sex."

Evelyn quirked her head to the side. "Really? Are you sure? The sex?"

Marley said, "He spent that whole day making amends with the women in his life."

"Pft! What an idiot. Who cares about the sex? I mean, we were in the middle of this huge, complicated plan, and he calls me up and... what an idiot."

"We all make unfortunate remarks," Marley said.

"His got him killed." She stood and leaned against the counter. "I can't believe I was so worried about you. I mean, really."

"I'm only dangerous," Marley assured her, "because I know things. Such as, the last time someone cast a spell with a dragon's egg as a fuel source, they did it in the Empty Quarter, far from the water. When you unlock that egg, the dragon is going to realize it's been moved. Whatever spell you're planning will never come off. You simply won't have the time. Have you ever seen an angry dragon?"

"No," Evelyn said, smirking, "but I plan to."

252

A Key, an Egg, an Unfortunate Remark

"Oh!" Marley exclaimed. She blinked a couple of times as Evelyn's remark sunk in. "I've had you all wrong, haven't I? The dragon egg isn't the prize here, is it? It's the bait."

"Finally!" Evelyn shouted. "Finally someone gets it! We hide the egg in the basement of a building and unlock it. During the day. The dragon rises and demolishes most of the waterfront looking for it. Property values plummet and everyone wants to sell, desperately, including Amos Quigley's heirs, once I get him put to rest. The developers who've become dependent on my persuasion potion will provide the financing, and I will finally get to build my dream. All I have to do is paint some magical-looking symbols on the front door and tell everyone that they're dragon repellant. Then, once people are actually living in the space, they'll see how perfect it is, and my design will be copied on every continent. My work will be vindicated, I'll be world-renowned, and everyone will live in my buildings. That's the kind of immortality I'm after, not the peaches-and-cream perky-boobs kind!"

Evelyn laughed a little, then laid her hand on her throat. "Did I just monologue? Like, a real movie-villain monologue? Wow, I swore to myself that I never would, but when the opportunity presented itself, I simply couldn't resist! My plan is just so damn good, and I've had to hold it in for so long... Letting it out felt incredible! So cathartic!"

From his spot in the corner, Stan said, "You're all mad."

Evelyn sighed and pulled the hood back over Marley's head. "Genius is wasted on some people. Captain, have someone keep watch over them until morning, and change shifts. I don't want your men to fall asleep during the long night."

"I know how to do my job," he answered as she walked out.

Albert wasn't sure what to think. He didn't have any frame of reference for what was going on, but he hoped his aunt could provide one. "Aunt Marley? Can we get a call in to the police?"

"Absolutely not, Albert. I'm not bringing in the police. What if they shoot Evelyn or one of the gunmen?"

"Actually," Stan butted in, "I would be perfectly fine with that."

"Me, too," Kevin added. "In fact, I'd really really really like that."

None of them could see the guard, but they all heard him tell them to shut up.

"Besides, how could I?" Marley said. "They took our phones."

Albert kept his voice low. "Maybe the guard will lend you his if..."

"Be quiet for a moment, please."

* * *

In her office across town, Naima was packing her briefcase after another long day. She'd spent all afternoon trying to arrange a new blood supplier, and the whole evening assuring the vampires that they wouldn't be locked in and left to starve. The newest one was especially troublesome; she didn't have much trust in the institution, which was understandable, but still annoying. And her boyfriend! How could he have spent more than twenty years as a companion without learning how to draw blood? What had he been doing all that time?

Her phone rang. She sighed and glanced at the screen. Strangely, the display didn't show a number for the incoming caller. It didn't even show that it was from a blocked number. It rang again and she put the receiver to her ear.

The voice at the other end was Marley's. "Naima, I need you and our guests."

CHAPTER FORTY
The Spirit of Tortures Past

Unfortunately, Marley didn't know where she was, and couldn't direct Naima to an address. The only thing she could say was that she was probably somewhere near the Sculpture Park. Naima set her desk phone to forward calls to her cell, then gathered the residents into a windowless van to take up a position near the park and wait.

In the condo, Marley lowered her face to the carpet to slide her blindfold off. A gun barrel pressed against the side of her head.

"No," the gunman said.

Marley stayed perfectly still. "I'm just an old woman. You're not going to make me sit here on the carpet for hours without being able to see, are you?"

The only response was, "Shut up."

They sat that way for over an hour, forbidden to talk or take off their blindfolds. Marley and Albert grew increasingly bored and even Kevin slowly became accustomed to his situation. Only Stan seemed to be struggling. His breathing became more labored and he sounded more miserable. After a long while, he began groaning in pain.

"Excuse me," Marley said. "Can we have something for Stan to eat? A piece of candy, maybe, or some fruit? His blood sugar is crashing."

"No," the guard said. "Let it crash."

"But it's a terrible way to die. I know you're planning to kill us all, but you could at least show a little mercy."

"What's this about mercy?" a new voice asked. It was Nora. She had entered the room without a sound—Albert guessed the living room door was open.

"Who's there?" Marley called out, pretending she hadn't recognized her voice. "Who's speaking?"

"It's us," Nora answered.

"You gotta go," the guard said. "You ain't cleared to talk to the prisoners."

Audrey answered in a low, whispery voice, "I'm going to get my gloat going here, and you better not get in my way."

"We're just gonna talk," Nelson assured him.

"Are we?" Marley snapped. "I don't see any reason to chat with people who gun down innocents."

"Why don't you take a break?" Nora said, as though Marley hadn't spoken. "Your boy is just in the hall, and I noticed nobody brought you a

255

plate from downstairs."

"All right then," the gunman answered. "Leave this door open."

Albert spoke up. "Are they the ones who shot Libertad?"

"And Janet," Marley answered. "Evelyn didn't care about our blood drives, and once she had her egg she didn't give a damn about those old lefties, either. They were shot at simply because they were seen with us."

"Shot at badly, too," Albert added.

"That's how we deal with a vampire's organization," Nora said, a little annoyed. "When the head dodges us, we strike at the edges to draw them out."

"Called it," Albert said.

"Those Educatorium people aren't part of my organization!" Marley was genuinely offended. "God forbid. We spoke to them about a murder your new friend has committed. They're just average citizens, and average citizens don't even believe in vampires."

"Like us!" Kevin chimed in. "Stan and I don't believe in vampires, either. In fact, I can't even believe I'm lying here on the floor, all handcuffed."

"That's on you, Marley Jacobs," Audrey said. "You're the one who dragged them into this."

"And you're the one," Marley said, her blindfolded face turned slightly toward the sound of Audrey's voice, "who does all the nasty things these other two don't have the stomach for. You're the one who gets your hands bloody."

"That's me. I bat cleanup."

"We're not here to talk about us," Nora said.

"I can see why! It must be dreadfully embarrassing."

"We're here to talk about your organization. It's over. I know you think you were doing good by running your little rest home, but you're not going to live out the day and what do you think is going to happen then? Everything you built is going to come apart. Those vampires won't have you to look after them, and they're going to start hunting. In your city."

"Oh, go back to Memphis. You don't care about my city."

"I care about these creatures getting loose. Tell us where they're hiding. We can put them to rest before they start killing real people, and if you cooperate, we'll spare the humans protecting them."

"You can't lie to me, dear. You might want to spare the vampires' caregivers, but you can't. Your little Audrey is getting harder and harder to control—"

"Don't call me little."

"You can't promise to spare anyone, no matter how innocent they are. Look at Stan over there; he's just a man caught up in powers he doesn't even believe in, and none of you will offer a piece of candy to ease his suffering. I'll tell you, there are worse things in this world than vampires."

"Well," Audrey said, and blindfolded or not, everyone could hear by the way she spoke that she was smiling. "I do believe she's referring to me."

"Of course I am, dear. I recognized you for what you are at first glance. Vampires kill to survive. You kill for pleasure. So, no, I wouldn't make a deal with you, even if you three hadn't been foolish enough to side with Evelyn Thomas."

"You and your kind are my enemy," Nora said. "And the enemy of my enemy is my friend."

"Psh. The enemy of my enemy is my ally, dear. Not a friend."

Albert cleared his throat. "Did you know I can see the future?"

"That doesn't seem likely," Nelson said, "considering."

"But it's totally true. Listen. I'm going to tune in." He began to hum as if in meditation, then let his voice waver from screeches to hissing sounds, like a radio searching for a signal. "Wait!" he said in his best fortune teller voice, as Nora and the others shuffled their feet and exhaled in irritation. "Wait, it's becoming clear to me. Yes. Yes! Before this day is over, you're going to realize you that you have, in fact, picked the wrong side. You'll have dozens —maybe hundreds—of innocent deaths on your consciences unless you switch now."

Nora didn't like that. "You may—"

"It. Is. Your. Destiny!" Albert finished.

Marley laughed loudly and brightly. "Oh Albert, I wish I could see this side of you more often."

Nora tried again: "You may think you're funny but I... you don't have a choice here."

"That's nonsense, Nora, and it's time you acknowledged it. You think, just because we're in a tough spot, all our choices have been taken away, but that's not so. Tough spots are when your choices matter most."

No one spoke for a while. Then Albert and Marley heard the sound of a candy wrapper crinkling, and a heavy tread on the carpet. Nelson said, "Here you go, man. Open up." They heard the sound of a piece of hard candy clicking against teeth.

"What's going on?" the gunman said, having clearly just returned.

"Think about my offer," Nora said. They filed out.

"Well," Stan said, after he'd recovered a bit. "At least I won't have a tummy ache when they shoot me to death. Thanks."

"Shut up," the guard said.

The hours crawled by, and the four of them eventually fell into a fitful sleep.

Stamping feet and an approaching argument woke Marley. As she sat up, she made a point of rubbing the blindfold against the carpet to dislodge it.

She had time enough to see that dim light shone through the narrow gaps in the drapes—morning was almost here—before Evelyn burst into the room.

"This is why I didn't want you to kill her last night. Search her! Marley, did you think you could play games with me? Did you think you could do anything but waste a little bit of my time?"

Three gunmen immediately began tearing through Marley's pockets, ripping the sleeves of her jacket, yanking off her socks and shoes, and tearing the pockets of her pants. The men searched her thoroughly, but didn't find anything.

Then they searched Albert in the same rough way, then Kevin, then Stan, yanking their pockets open and pulling off their shoes and socks.

"Nothing," the captain said.

"No! That's not true! She found it in the storage unit! I saw her!"

"Either she led us to another fake, or there is no correct one, because it don't work."

Evelyn's eyes were wild and her voice raw. "I don't accept that! I can't afford another delay! The egg is in place and will be discovered if we leave it for too long. The time is now!" She rushed out of the room, returning a few seconds later with a cast-iron skillet and a bottle of expensive olive oil.

Marley turned pale.

"Aloysius warned me about you," Evelyn said. She spun the top of the bottle off and poured two fingers of oil into the skillet. "So I did some research. This is what happened to Gustavo, isn't it? Your fiancé? Someone—the police never figured out who—poured boiling oil over him, then into his screaming mouth."

"Don't do this, Evelyn."

Evelyn's voice trembled with stress. "I don't want to do it, Marley, but you're not leaving me any other options! Your nephew is going to die screaming right in front of your eyes."

"Aunt Marley!" Albert called. His voice was even shakier than Evelyn's. "Aunt Marley, it's okay. It'll only hurt a little while—"

Evelyn stood and started toward the kitchen, skillet in hand. "If that's your decision, then fine."

"Under my jacket!" Marley said. "It's under my jacket."

Evelyn dumped the skillet on the coffee table and flipped Marley's jacket open. There, folded in half and as big as life, was the envelope they'd found in Stan's storage unit.

The captain rounded on his men. "How could you have missed that?"

"They didn't," Evelyn snapped. "It wasn't there before. Haven't you been paying attention? Now guard them while we wrap this up." She turned to Marley. "If this is another fake, so help me..."

Marley couldn't meet her gaze.

Evelyn and the captain left. a few minutes later, a sudden strange feeling washed over them. It felt as though the entire universe was a guitar string, and a giant hand had plucked it.

CHAPTER FORTY-ONE
We Know the Rules

"Earthquake!" Kevin yelled.

"I only wish it were," Marley said. She rolled to her knees. Voices down the hall were shouting in alarm, and the guard raced out of the room toward the sound.

"Oh, good," Stan said, rubbing his face against the floor to push his hood off. "They're leaving us alone." The others began to do the same thing.

"Not for long," Marley told him. "They'll be coming back to kill us any moment, so let's move. Quietly! Quietly!"

She shuffled toward the kitchen on her knees. Kevin scrambled after her the same way. Stan, feeling weak and exhausted, rolled across the floor, bumping against the coffee table and couch in the corner.

Albert rolled back onto his shoulders, swept his handcuffed hands under his legs to the front of his body then rolled forward to gain his feet. "Come on, you guys." He lifted Marley off her knees, then helped Stan up.

Marley led them around the counter into the kitchen. "Crouch down." They did. "And keep quiet."

"Why are we hiding on the kitchen floor?" Kevin asked.

"To create a two-second delay in finding us, obviously," Stan answered.

"Hey." Albert's whisper was sharp. "She asked for quiet. Let her concentrate." It clearly took some effort, but Stan shut his mouth.

Marley knelt at the edge of the kitchen counter, peeking into the living room through a shelf crowded with empty glass bottles. She closed her eyes and took a deep breath. Then another. Two gunmen ran back into the room.

260

"Who told you to leave your post?"

"I heard you call for me, sir."

Audrey rushed into the room, plastic bags in her hands. She knelt on the carpet just opposite the space where Marley and the others had spent the night, then laid out her plastic bags one by one.

"It wasn't me. Now help her clean up this mess."

"Sir, we should just shoot them. This isn't decent."

Audrey turned her back on them. Her eyes were bright and her smile savage. "Bullets draw police the way dead rats draw maggots," she said. "You don't have to watch if you're squeamish."

She leaned forward, plastic bag in hand, and mimed placing it over someone's head. She pulled the drawstring with exquisite care. The bag fluttered to the carpet. She did it again, and again, and again.

"Thirty seconds to unconsciousness," she said. "Three minutes to death." Audrey's face was alive with delight, and she giggled at something only she and the guards could see.

"Sick," the guard said.

"The old ones are always the most terrified," Audrey said, unable to look away from the blank wall. "You'd think it would be the young ones, but it's not. Look at her face. None of the others are as frightened as she is." Her voice turned whispery soft. "And I'm going to be the last thing she sees."

Marley controlled her breathing and held her eyes shut tight. Creating a false image of herself was hard enough, but creating one for four people—and having them all interact with a real human being—was a serious challenge. Finally, the thirty seconds was up, and her false images didn't have to do anything but lie there, fluttering the illusory plastic bags with their illusory dying breaths. Finally, Marley made them all become still.

Audrey didn't seem to want to move, as though she was kneeling in a church service she didn't want to end.

"That's four minutes," the captain said. Audrey sighed and left the room. She was almost glowing.

The captain clapped the guard on the shoulder. "Not going to be sick, are you?"

"Of course not, sir. Still, we should have just shot them. Anything else is un-American."

The captain guffawed. "Collect the handcuffs, then we meet downstairs in the front room." He left.

The guard knelt on the floor, tiny key in hand. As he tried to uncuff the first pretend corpse, he dropped his key. Cursing at himself, he grabbed it up, unlocked and pocketed the phantom handcuffs, then walked out of the room, shutting the door behind him.

Marley concentrated for just a moment more, then opened her eyes and collapsed onto her side.

"Aunt Marley!" Albert whispered. He caught and steadied her.

"I'm all right. It's just a strain to create a large and complicated trick; I need to prepare and to recover. Get to the window, dear, and tell me where we are."

Albert did exactly that, yanking back the drapes to the french doors and staring past the balcony into the faintly glowing light. "We're several floors up, maybe four or five, too high to read the street sign, but there's a Romio's Pizza on the ground floor of the building catercorner from us. There's a lot of traffic headed south."

* * *

Out in the van, Naima's phone rang. She answered it immediately. "Hello?"

"It's Marley. We're in a condo, possibly on the fifth floor, directly catercorner from a Romio's. We need you."

"That's just down the block from here."

"One potential spell-caster all in white. Up to ten gunmen in black tactical. Three hunters."

"Hunters!"

"You know the rules."

Naima dropped the phone into her pocket and started the engine.

Behind her, the vampires fell silent in the darkness. At this very early hour, traffic was only just beginning to get heavy. She swerved away from the curb, nearly colliding with a Mazda, and raced toward the building up ahead.

Yes, she knew the rules.

* * *

Back in the condo, Marley struggled to stay upright. Albert rushed to her again, but she said, "Get the key off the floor, Albert. I made Dominic drop it."

There it was. Albert unlocked his own cuffs, then Marley's. She went to the door to peek down the hall while Albert moved to unlock Kevin's cuffs.

He fumbled it a little. The twang they had all felt, as though the whole universe had been strummed, wasn't fading. If anything, it was growing stronger and deeper.

When the cuffs came off, Albert pressed the key into Kevin's hand and rushed to Marley, who was standing impatiently beside the French doors. He opened them and she stepped out. He followed, and so did Kevin and Stan, still fussing over the last pair of handcuffs.

Marley moved to the end of the balcony, gripping the rail with white knuckles, and stared down the street toward Elliott Bay below. The sun had not yet risen, but the sky was bright enough for them to see.

"What the hell is that?" Albert blurted out.

A wake moved through the water at startling speed, as though an invisible ocean liner was crossing the bay. Then, the wake flattened, slowly losing momentum as though the unseen ship had stopped suddenly.

"What's making that?" Kevin asked. "I can't see—"

"It hasn't surfaced yet," Marley said in a flat tone.

There was a series of underwater booms, like depth charges, and the water around Pier 70 began to churn. The entire pier suddenly sagged at the far end, then began to sink into the water.

"Jesus," Albert said. "And I thought Jaws was scary."

Then the concrete holding the pier to the sidewalk broke with the sound of a detonating bomb, and the whole thing began to slide into the deep waters of the bay, sinking out of sight.

Marley's voice was full of dread. "I think… I think we're about to have a very rare experience."

As the last of the pier vanished beneath the waves, colored lights began to flash beneath the water. This was accompanied by strange clashing noises, as though huge circuit breakers were popping deep in the bay. The water roiled and bubbled…

Then the head broke the surface.

Kevin and Stan both screamed. Albert cursed, but his aunt was right: it didn't make anything better.

The dragon's head was huge—as big as a house—and the same black color as an orca's back. Its rough skin was grooved like wet hair freshly combed, but there were no scales. Its snout was short, more like a gorilla than a serpent, but still filled with long, needle-sharp teeth. There were no horns or wings in evidence.

It turned toward the piers along the waterfront, opened its mouth, and roared.

The sound was brutal and oppressive; it seemed to shake their bones in harmony with that strange universal vibration. Marley steadied herself against the railing so she wouldn't collapse under the overwhelming pressure of it.

Then the noise died away, leaving everyone trembling. Marley forced herself to stand tall, when all she really wanted was to curl up on the floor in terror. "Astonishing," she said, her voice hoarse.

The dragon began moving toward the piers, slowly rising out of the water. The beast was upright, its foreclaws curled in front of its chest. Along its back was a row of plates like a stegosaurus, but each plate was jagged like a spatter of black blood. It came closer and closer, higher out of the water with every step, and when it laid one huge hind claw on the grass of Myrtle Edwards Park, they could see it stood over a hundred and fifty feet tall.

Joggers and bicyclists in the narrow park fled as water sloughed off the dragon's body. On the roads nearby, shocked drivers lost control of their vehicles and crashed into each other. The dragon's tail swung from side to side, smashing through the Victoria Clipper building.

Albert realized that the art bench he and his aunt had walked past only the day before had been flattened beneath that giant clawed foot.

"Oh my God," Kevin said. "We're all going to die."

CHAPTER FORTY-TWO
A Worm's-Eye View

Stan and Kevin bolted toward the door, but Marley whispered "No!" and Albert caught their arms. "The gunmen are still there."

That gave both men pause.

There was a sudden terrifying noise from the waterfront, like the sound of a raging forest fire. The dragon had unleashed a jet of flame against the seafood restaurant where Marley had thrown her stone into the air. The building buckled, then exploded, showering masonry, sheet metal and burning wood into the street.

Drivers ducked out of their cars to avoid being trapped beneath the flaming debris. Horns blared at the traffic jam, and a few people jumped the curb to drive around the wreckage and abandoned vehicles. Many more fled on foot.

Then the creature turned to the north; something had caught its attention. Marley and Albert leaned out along the balcony just in time to see another jet of fire blast all the way into—and through—the globe at the top of the P-I Building. It melted like slag onto the roof below.

Goosebumps ran the length of Albert's body. "We're going to need a bigger rest home."

Kevin cried out and pointed at the lower railing of their balcony. A hand reached up from the other side of the balcony and clutched the rail. Before anyone could react, Neil pulled himself up and over the railing as though it was the easiest thing in the world.

"Hello, Neil," Marley said.

The vampire swept his hair out of his eyes. He'd traded his Nehru jacket for a pullover paisley hemp shirt and black cotton pants. His feet were bare. "Hello, Ms. Jacobs. Big one this time, huh?"

"Yes, indeed."

He turned and stooped down; Naima was holding onto his back. After she dropped to the balcony, she straightened her clothes with as much dignity as she could muster. "The sun is nearly over the horizon," she said, glancing at the sky.

"I know, dear. Inside, everyone!"

There were screams from the street, and across the way they saw two people step from their condos onto the balcony to investigate. Marley would have thought there'd be more.

"The others engaged the bulk of your problem as they tried to exit the parking garage," Naima said. "Neil and I came up here to make sure we didn't push them all the way up to you. But the sun—"

"Yes, Naima, dear. Your concern for your charges is admirable, but you don't have to keep reminding me."

Neil laid his hands on Marley and Naima's shoulders. "I can hear them in the front room, talking on their radios. I'll go take care of them…without breaking the rules."

"Wait a minute," Stan said. "How is Jim Morrison here going to 'take care of' a room full of armed men?"

"Hello there," Kevin interjected.

"What's he going to do," Stan insisted, "throw patchouli at them?"

Neil laughed, revealing a pair of fangs, then he raced through the front door so quickly they could barely see him move.

Kevin and Stan looked at each other. Stan shook his head. "I need to sit down."

There was a sudden burst of gunfire from the front room. "Well you can't," Marley said, taking his arm. "I want you to stick with Kevin. You'll be having another sugar crash soon, won't you?"

"It's already happening."

"Kevin is going to stick by you. The two of you don't have any responsibilities here except to each other. Get away and survive, all right, dears?" They nodded. "Wonderful." Marley glanced at the fires visible through the window; they were spreading. Worse, the dragon had reached the condo building beside the burning restaurant and begun to rake the exterior with its claws. The entire structure shuddered to its foundations.

Marley took Naima's elbow. They hurried down the hall, their light footsteps a counterpoint to the massive thundering tread of the dragon as it moved along the waterfront, destroying.

Neil stood by the door, three gunmen on the floor at his feet. A cart with computer equipment and a stack of pizza boxes lay on its side in the corner, and various guns, knives, and clips were scattered on the carpet. "Everything's groovy," Neil said, smiling sleepily. He glanced at Stan, then gestured to the dozen or so wounds on his torso. "See? Only bullets. They even had their own cuffs."

"Oh good, here are some more." Marley handed him the four they had worn all night, leaving the key in her pocket. "Let's get these fellows up and moving."

Albert whispered something to the gunmen about cooperation as he helped Neil haul them to their feet. There was another stupendous crash from outside. Another building was coming down.

Marley thought it best to avoid the elevators, so they hurried to the stairs. Stan and Kevin lagged behind, as Marley hoped. Neil took point, and Albert was happy to let him. Naima held her phone to her ear. "In the parking garage," she said.

But the parking garage was empty. Naima's van sat crooked in the entrance ramp, but the only other cars were a Mini Cooper and a broken-down van. There were no people in sight. Marley ran to the ramp and out onto the street, looking downhill at the destruction below.

People were still screaming and running for their lives, but there were fewer of them. The dragon had moved south along the waterfront, tearing through the Art Institute and parking garages searching for its egg. A freight train braked, squealing, but there was no way to stop so much mass in the space it had. The engine slammed into the dragon's clawed foot, jack-knifing rail cars full of coal and scrap metal all over Alaskan Way.

And there, on the corner across the street from where Marley stood, was a middle-aged woman in her jogging clothes, holding up her phone to record the whole thing.

Marley shook her head in admiration.

Albert caught her elbow. "Aunt Marley, we need you inside."

"It's incredible, isn't it? Simply incredible."

"Yes, and scary as hell. How do we stop it?"

That brought Marley back to herself. "Albert, you can't keep asking me these obvious questions. We're much too far along for that."

They went back down the ramp into the darkness of the parking garage. Kevin and Stan passed them and headed out into the street. "Good luck," Marley called as they turned onto the sidewalk and hurried away from the dragon.

Kenneth held a metal door partly open. "In here."

Marley and Albert went inside. It was a laundry room, with six washers, six dryers and no windows. All four vampires—Neil, Betty, Clive, and Spire —were there, all riddled with bullets, and all smiling. Beside them stood Kenneth and the scowling nurse from Marley's rest home. Albert suddenly realized he'd never asked the woman's name.

On the floor in the corner were the ten mercenaries. With their masks removed, they looked like ordinary men. Evelyn had been pushed to the floor beside them, also cuffed. Off to the side a bit were Nora, Nelson, and Audrey.

"Well," Marley said brightly, raising her voice to be heard over the chaos outside, "how quickly the tables turn."

Audrey gaped at them. "I killed you."

"Oh my goodness, you did, didn't you? I almost forgot." She walked over to Audrey, plucked out a few locks of her hair, then tucked them into Naima's pocket. "Albert's clothes are torn, so you'll have to hold onto these. Now! How many deaths do you think you'll have caused today, Evelyn?"

Evelyn was defiant. "Dozens? Hundreds? Thousands? I don't care!"

"Oh my sweet lord Jesus," Nelson said, letting his forehead fall to the floor. "He really can see the future."

The dragon roared again. Everyone shut their eyes except for Marley and Albert. They looked over the faces around them… at the terror, ecstasy, and raw confusion in their expressions.

"You'll kill us if you leave us here," one of the gunmen said. Albert recognized his voice. He was the captain, although he didn't look any older or tougher than the others. "When that thing digs through the building to find her egg, we'll be crushed."

"Where is the egg?"

"In the back of that broken-down van out there."

"That's fine," Marley said. "You can go."

Kenneth couldn't help himself. "What?"

"Not now, Kenneth. Evelyn, you too. Nora, go. None of you should be here when the dragon attacks."

The mercenaries rolled to their feet. The captain stepped forward. "Our handcuffs?"

"Don't push it," Marley said.

He nodded and led the others through the door. Evelyn trailed behind them, her face a strange mix of delight and triumph. She ran through the door.

Nora, Nelson, and Audrey still stood staring at Marley, Albert, and the vampires in shock. Marley turned her back on them and went into the parking garage. "Albert, bring our van down here and turn it around. We're going to have to load the egg into it."

Kenneth stepped between them. "It's no good. A bullet froze the CV joint. The wheels won't turn."

"Oh, wonderful. Spire, Neil, I need you to drag the van down the ramp and out of the way."

Neil wrung his hands and Spire bit her black-painted lips. "There's sunlight there," she said. "Right there. I can see it."

"You won't have to touch it," Marley assured her. "I chose you because you're the youngest and the bravest. We're all depending on you, darlings."

"We'll come with you," Naima said. She and Kenneth accompanied them to the ramp.

Marley led Albert, Betty, and Clive to the van. The wheels had been removed; it sat on its undercarriage. The hood stood open. Albert took one glance at the engine and said, "This will never do the job."

Marley waved at the back doors. The van was so close to the wall that there was barely room to open them, but Betty did.

There was the egg. It was at least four feet across the middle and at least six from point to bottom, and it glowed in the darkness.

CHAPTER FORTY-THREE
Another Little Drive

"Oh!" Betty exclaimed, and backed away.

"Move this away from the wall, please." Marley said.

Clive and Betty grabbed the van beneath the front bumper and dragged it away from the wall. At the same time, Neil and Susannah began dragging Naima's van down the ramp. The sound of metal grinding against concrete was terrible, but there were louder, more horrible noises coming from outside.

Sirens screamed as two police motorcycles passed the opening to the exit ramp. Sunlight reflected off the chrome, sending brief flashes of daylight into the garage. The four vampires immediately fell into a blind panic, screaming and running for the stairs so quickly they were little more than a blur.

"Clive!" Naima shouted. "Betty! Neil!"

"Go after them," Marley ordered. Naima and Kenneth ran to the stairs. "Oh well, Albert. It looks like it's just you and me now."

"We can help," Nora said. She, Nelson, and Audrey stood just a few feet away, their hands cuffed behind their backs.

"Hah!" Marley snapped at them. "I think you've helped enough. Albert, we need to transport this egg to the water and we need to do it quickly. The longer the dragon is on the land, the more thoughtless and enraged it will become. In that state the destruction might not stop for hours, and it's likely to destroy its own egg accidentally. Since both large vehicles are useless, we'll have to roll it up the ramp and down the street."

"Or you could use my truck," Nora said.

Albert turned to her. "What truck?"

Nora nodded toward the far corner of the parking garage. There was a tarp hanging by the back wall. It was nearly the same color as the concrete around it, and neither Marley nor Albert had noticed it before. "We got pulled over by the cops after...." She didn't want to continue that sentence.

"After you shot two innocent people," Marley finished for her.

Nora glanced at Audrey. It was the barest flicker, but Albert noticed it. "Yes. That's right. He gave us a ticket for a busted taillight, and we realized we had to hide the truck until we got it fixed."

Marley took the key from her pocket and uncuffed Nora. "Bring it over here and park it opposite the van." She then uncuffed Nelson and Audrey. "You two look strong. You're going to help Albert load the egg into the truck."

Marley ran to the ramp and peeked out. For as far as she could see, everything on both sides of Elliott Avenue had been destroyed. The dragon had reached—and shattered—the elevated highway far to the south, only three blocks from Pike Place Market and thousands of tourists. The city beyond was in flames, but the dragon had apparently realized it was moving farther from its egg, not closer. It turned around and started lumbering northward toward her.

"What is in this thing," Nelson said, as his considerable muscles strained to roll the egg. "Lead?"

Nora pulled the truck around the disabled van and backed it up. Marley ran toward her. "Leave it running!" she shouted, "and help them."

Marley caught the door as Nora jumped from the drivers seat and ran back toward the others. The egg really was incredibly heavy, and the four of them struggled to move it.

"Damn! Aunt Marley!" Albert gasped. "Can't you do some magic that would help us here? This is hard work!"

"Hard work is what magic aspires to be," she answered, her hand resting on the pickup's open driver door. "Hard work is the strongest magic there is."

The four of them managed to roll it out of the bed of the van, but it seemed to want to roll to the side, off the pickup. It was almost as if it was deliberately fighting them.

"Oh, Albert," Marley said. "There just isn't enough time. Darn it. Listen: the parties are important. Do you understand? You need connections and you need perspective, too. They remind you why you go to so much trouble —"

"We're losing it!" Nelson yelled.

"It's my fault!" Albert answered. "My hand..."

They groaned, shouted and strained to force the egg onto the truck bed.

"And don't become a ghost," Marley continued. "Not when you're alive, and not when you're dead. It weakens you, and you'll need to be strong."

The four of them cried out—Albert with tears running down his cheeks —and finally rolled the egg into the truck bed.

Albert dropped to his knees, clutching his right wrist. His hand throbbed. Nora and Nelson moved to check on him while Audrey slammed the gate shut.

A sudden blast of scorching hot air roared down the ramp into the garage, dust and debris knocking the four of them to the ground. The whole building trembled, and the noise it made sounded like the end of the world.

Marley slid behind the wheel of the pickup and stamped on the gas. Naima's van still partially blocked the ramp, but maybe there was room, even for someone like her, who had not driven in...

Albert forced himself to his feet. "Aunt Marley!"

There was nothing he could say to stop her. She rammed Nora's pickup between the rest-home van and a cement column, scraping both side panels as she drove up the ramp and out into the daylight.

CHAPTER FORTY-FOUR
The Trick to Catching the World's Attention

The street looked like a scene from an apocalypse movie. Huge chunks of steel and concrete lay in the intersection. Some had crushed cars beneath them; some were on fire. Papers still floated down out of the sky, and someone's awful orange loveseat lay burning atop the mailbox on the corner.

The dragon was closer—barely a block away, hunched down over a building up the street and clawing through the wreckage. Its enormous bulk took her breath away, and its long blunt tail thrashed about, slamming through the wreckage of the condos across the street.

Once, the entire street had huge condominium buildings on both sides. Now there was only shattered wreckage.

Marley spun the steering wheel and turned away from it, driving on the sidewalk. There were no pedestrians, of course, though several people stood on the trunk of an abandoned car at the end of the block, taking video with their phones. Motorcycle cops were trying to drive them off.

She glanced into the rear-view mirror to make sure the egg hadn't rolled out of the pickup bed while she'd rammed her way up the ramp.

There was a Celica on the sidewalk up ahead, its tail end smashed into a telephone pole. Someone had tried to escape on the sidewalk and, as Marley had hoped, they'd left a gap in the traffic wide enough to drive through. She turned left, hard, and passed between two Hondas, then slammed against the back panel of an Escort to force her way through. She turned sharply to the left again, jumping the curb just beside the Sculpture Park.

Suddenly, the dragon was huge in her windshield, still clawing through that city block—wreckage flying out behind it— and still moving closer to the building where Albert and the others were hiding. The sound it made was ungodly loud.

Not for much longer, she hoped. She blared the truck horn, interspersing long and short honks, but the dragon didn't look her way. She was beneath the notice of a power like that. Oh well, she'd have to do this the hard way.

She had a sudden pang of worry over the vampires cowering inside the building. How they were going to get them safely out of there in all this chaos and daylight? Marley prayed that they wouldn't die there because she'd asked for their help. Help them, Albert. She glanced at a car beside her, partially crushed by a chunk of masonry, and saw no one inside.

Marley couldn't let herself be distracted now. A ghastly brown Sedona blocked the sidewalk ahead, there was no other way through, and Marley had to get to the water. She glanced into the rear-view mirror—the egg was still there—then stamped on the accelerator.

She slammed into the Sedona with all the momentum Nora's truck could bring to bear. Her forehead slammed against the steering wheel, bringing her a blast of pain and another blare of the truck's horn.

The driver of the Sedona must have abandoned it without setting the brake because it rolled out of her way. Marley rubbed her head to clear her thoughts, surprised that there was no air bag.

She heard Albert's voice, somehow, above the clash and tumult of the digging dragon. He was calling her name.

A Key, an Egg, an Unfortunate Remark

A burning, overstuffed avocado-colored couch bounced across the sidewalk in front of her, striking the fence to the Sculpture Park. Marley stepped on the gas, knocking the couch out of the way.

She turned the corner, heading down hill toward Alaskan Way, then started honking the horn again. The cars that had clogged this part of the street had been swept away by the dragon's dragging feet and tail, so she had room to drive.

A spray of bricks smashed the cars beside her. A cabinet full of broken dishes struck the driver's door, shattering the window into her lap. A computer crashed onto the concrete in front of her and she rolled over it, taking a small bit of satisfaction in the damage it did to Nora's truck. Marley may have been a committed pacifist, but property damage wasn't violence, and damaging this truck was probably the only payback she would get for what happened to Libertad.

Sometimes the small, petty pleasures were the only ones left.

She kept blowing the horn, but the dragon still took no notice. Its tail slammed down on the street, pancaking half a dozen cars. Marley swerved left under it, heading for the water. If she couldn't get the dragon's attention, she was going to have to put the egg in the water herself. With luck, it would sense the return of its magic and go back to the depths of the Sound. That is, if it wasn't too far gone into madness and thoughtless rage.

She pulled onto Alaskan Way, the street that ran along the waterfront. Except for a few abandoned cars and the wrecked freight train, it was deserted. In the distance, she could see flashing police lights. They were, as she hoped, nothing but a road block. There was nothing an officer with a sidearm could do in this situation.

The easiest way into the water would have been from Myrtle Edwards Park, near where she and Albert had been sitting when the car bomb went off. Unfortunately, the dragon had inconveniently failed to smash the guard rail and she couldn't drive through.

The second-best option was the broken sidewalk where the pier had been torn away. There was a wide spot where the concrete had fallen partway, forming a crooked ramp into the water between the pylons.

Marley aimed the truck's grill at it, blaring her horn. Damn if the dragon hadn't even deigned to notice her as yet. She left the truck in neutral, pulled the emergency brake, then began to climb through the broken window.

The dragon's tail slammed down on the street not ten yards from her, then slammed down again and again. She could feel the frustration coming off of it in waves. She could feel its growing rage.

The driver's window was narrow, but her yoga classes had kept her limber enough to squeeze through without falling onto the glass-strewn asphalt. Her forehead ached, but she didn't think it was too serious. She honked one more time, just in case, then gave up on the idea.

The dragon was lost to its rage. She could have rammed the truck into its hind claw and it would not have seen the egg. In fact, it might easily have destroyed it.

She took a splintered length of wood and jammed it against accelerator. The engine raced but didn't engage. She leaned in through the window and released the emergency brake at the same time she wrenched the gear into drive.

The truck took off, knocking Marley to the ground. She had not forgotten her training from her fighting days and managed to roll with the impact. Her whole left arm went numb from the impact and she cut her palm on a jagged piece of broken glass, but it could have been worse.

The truck went just where she hoped it would: It raced down the concrete and plunged into the water.

Cradling her arm, Marley struggled to her feet and hurried to the water's edge. The cab of the truck bobbed in the water for a few moments, then tilted to the right and rolled over. It vanished beneath the waves.

But the egg floated as though it were made of Styrofoam. She'd hoped it would vanish, sink, or become less real right before her eyes, but there it was, bobbing along like an accused witch. The water was not taking back.

That would never catch the dragon's attention. It was time to do something more.

A Key, an Egg, an Unfortunate Remark

She turned toward the dragon and saw that it was standing upright again. It turned toward the condo where her people were hiding.

Marley closed her eyes to concentrate.

* * *

Up on the street, Albert crouched beside the fender of a delivery truck loaded with blue canisters of water. Another flock of bricks flew overhead, clanging against the truck. He needed to make his way to his aunt, but there was so much flying debris he couldn't see a safe path.

To hell with it. He was just going to have to run for it. If there was anything that felt less like water flowing downhill, this was it, but he couldn't keep hiding here, so far from his aunt and so close to the next building to be destroyed.

The flying debris suddenly stopped, which he knew was a decidedly mixed blessing. Albert didn't know if the vampire hunters were still hunkered down in the condo garage, but Naima, Kenneth, and the vampires were. If the dragon was moving to a new target—

He couldn't finish that thought because the dragon lifted its head and roared. Albert's conscious mind was overwhelmed, reduced to a desperate, animal urge to move. He staggered away from the truck, instinctively moving farther from the building. Another attack was coming, and he had no hope of surviving out in the open if the dragon unleashed a blast of fire. He felt so small, so ridiculous and so helpless—

"YOO-HOO!"

The sound of his aunt's voice cut through everything—the dragon's roar, the rubble breaking under its feet, the thrumming of the world, everything. Even the dragon was startled. It stopped what it was doing and turned toward the waterfront.

Albert gaped. "Oh my God."

There, standing in the middle of Alaskan Way, surrounded by fire and wreckage, was Marley Jacobs.

Except she was nearly two hundred feet tall.

277

She waggled her fingers at the dragon. "YOO-HOO!" her voice boomed. "LOOK WHAT I HAVE RIGHT HERE!"

The dragon's egg—or its likeness—rested in the palm of her other hand. She showed it to the dragon, then turned and gently placed it in the water behind her.

"YOU SEE? YOU HAVE YOUR EGG BACK. THERE'S NO MORE NEED FOR ALL THIS FUSS."

The dragon seemed to disagree. It opened its jaws wide and roared a challenge at her. The sound made Albert's guts feel watery and he fell onto his hands and knees. The monster charged directly at Marley, its huge feet smashing through the wreckage of the seafood restaurant.

The gigantic image of Marley popped out of existence like a bubble. Albert stumbled to his feet and raced to the corner just in time to see his aunt stagger in the ruined street, clutching at a broken streetlight for support. If the illusion of four people lying on a carpet had drained her, what he'd just seen must have—

The dragon stopped at the water's edge. Marley—the real human being, the tiny old woman—stood right beside its massive foot.

The dragon opened its jaws and poured a jet of bright fire onto her.

CHAPTER FORTY-FIVE
Only Terrible Daylight Remains

Albert screamed something. He didn't know what. In fact, he hadn't even realized he'd made a sound until much later, when he discovered that his throat was as raw as sashimi.

Marley was nothing more than a silhouette in those massive flames, and Albert saw her figure shrink even as she fell into the bay.

He ran forward, knowing already that it was too late.

A Key, an Egg, an Unfortunate Remark

The dragon leapt into the water and, as it sank beneath the waves, seeming to turn into liquid itself. It vanished as it became less real. The egg had also disappeared.

Water rushed over the broken sidewalk, pushing broken chunks of concrete and wooden beams down the street. Steam blossomed where the water touched the fires.

"Albert!" It was Naima's voice calling from behind him somewhere. He ignored her, sprinting toward the site of his aunt's death, splashing through the receding water.

He fell once as the water swept at his feet, but it was only a moment before he reached the water's edge. He found nothing. Even if his aunt had been burned down to ashes, the water would have washed them away. He leaned over the broken edge of the sidewalk—

"Albert!" Naima was running toward him as fast as her small form could move, her gray hair a rumpled mess and sweat streaming down her face. "Albert, don't!"

"I'm not going to jump," he said, moving toward her. "Where are Betty and the others?"

Naima stopped running and put her hands on her knees to catch her breath. Kenneth, Nora, and Nelson hurried down the sidewalk toward them. "They're safely inside the condo."

"We have to get them out," Albert said.

"We can't!" Naima replied. "They're too afraid, and the van won't run. They can't ride in a normal car with windows, you know."

Albert's annoyance got the better of him and his tone turned sharp. "Emergency Services are going to search every room in that building, and they're going to try to remove everyone inside. Look at it!"

They turned up the hill. The building they'd just escaped from was badly damaged on one side. Gaping holes had been punched in the walls and flames rose out of two of the windows. As they watched, a chunk of the wall near the roof fell into the street.

"If we don't get them out of there, the government is going to do it." He turned to Kenneth, who had just arrived. "Get back up the hill and find a truck with keys still inside. UPS, bakery, I don't care. Steal it and drive it up close to the building. Go!"

Kenneth ran off and Albert turned to Naima. "While I'm helping him, I need you to find some blankets for them. You're going to have to talk them into it, because it's either leave with us or with the cops. Go!"

Nora and Nelson stepped up to him. Audrey was nowhere in sight, which was probably for the best.

"What can we do?" Nora asked him.

He almost snapped at them to get the hell out of his city, but he stopped himself. "Come on. Even if Kenneth finds a truck for the guests, someone will have to clear a path for him. I'm going to need your help moving cars."

CHAPTER FORTY-SIX
Grieving Over Unwanted Treasure

Marley's funeral was a little more than a week later. Albert tried to keep it a private affair, but there were TV cameras, protesters with signs that proclaimed all sorts of crazy things, and a thousand curious onlookers. The reception afterwards took place in the safe house, which wasn't so safe anymore. The address had leaked to the media, and it was surrounded by people day and night.

The inside was almost as crowded. Weathers carried a tray of finger sandwiches. Stan Grappleton had sent a big display of flowers, but he and Kevin were rumored to be at least three states away, lying low. Libertad and Isabeau were in the kitchen, fussing with dishes, snacks, drinks, and generally showing their love for Marley by taking care of as many people as possible, always under Miss Harriet's watchful eye and stern direction.

Naima was there with Kenneth and Sylvester. Nora and Nelson had sent

280

their condolences; they hadn't left town, but they thought it best to pay their respects from a distance.

Detectives Lonagan and Garcia were also there, of course, in their dress uniforms. Albert met them at the base of the stairs and they all shook hands politely. Just beside them, Albert's mother sat snoring in a recliner chair, an empty wine bottle in her lap.

"I'm terribly sorry for your loss," Lonagan said. "I knew your aunt for many years and liked her quite a bit. Her advice, when I needed it, was invaluable. She was an amazing lady."

"Thank you. I thought so, too."

"She left everything to you?"

Albert shrugged. The question made him deeply uncomfortable. "A little was set aside for Jenny Wu—for her tuition—but yeah. She wrote her will this way when I was, like, nine years old. And before you ask, I had no idea."

"Did she say why?"

"I don't know why she did half the things she did," Albert said. "She didn't always know herself."

Detective Garcia cleared her throat. "My condolences to you and your family. I know I have seemed... I thought your aunt was a nice woman."

Albert smiled and said, with as much kindness as he could manage, "You can't lie to me, and you don't have to. I know you were trying to do the right thing. Aunt Marley knew it, too. And she certainly didn't expect to be universally loved. Anyway, that's all in the past. She would have been pleased to see you here. Thank you for coming."

"Speaking of—" Lonagan began, but a sudden outcry in the next room caught their attention.

Albert went into the den. There he found Elaine and a dozen other neighbors he'd never met standing transfixed in front of the television. On the screen a bare-chested man in an iron cage suddenly changed into a werewolf, to the gasps of the TV audience and the women in the room.

Jenny sat alone in a darkened corner, staring at the screen with an empty expression. Her parents sat beside her. All three looked pale and shattered.

"This is happening all over," Lonagan said, his voice low. "Three men on death row are claiming their victims were vampires. A family in Montana claim to be werewolves and are trying to get a wilderness preserve. Two brothers in Spokane are suing each other over their father's estate, each claiming the other one's already dead. And then there's the footage with your aunt...." Not only had the dragon been caught on video, but so had Aunt Marley's gigantic illusion of herself. "It's a mess."

"I hadn't realized," Albert said. "I've had so many people coming at me from so many directions..."

"You have your usual naysayers and skeptics," Garcia added, "but they're getting drowned out. It's like a dam burst; as soon as people were ready to believe, they had a bunch of new things to believe in. Like Charlie said: it's a mess."

"You two should be in charge. You've been closest to the craziness."

"Well, that's exactly the problem," Lonagan looked uncomfortable. "No one trusts us, because of my relationship with your aunt. And we're not really sure what happened. I mean, a fire-breathing dinosaur? A woman transforming into a giant? Evelyn Thomas is in holding and won't talk to us, but two of the mercenaries she hired spilled their guts as soon as we brought a priest into the room. What they're telling us doesn't make sense."

"You can tell us the truth, can't you?" Garcia was standing very close to Albert. "Off the record? Please?"

"All right," Albert said. "I'll give you the honest truth, off the record, but you aren't going to thank me for it. Ready?"

"We are."

"It's exactly what you think it is. It's exactly what it looks like."

"What's going on here!" Frederika interrupted. "You're not talking to these cops, are you? Haven't they already tossed this house twice? Haven't they tried to freeze all your assets?"

"Frederika, Detective Lonagan knew Aunt Marley for many years. We were just talking about how much we'll miss her."

"And it's time for us to go," Lonagan said. He and Garcia made their exit.

A Key, an Egg, an Unfortunate Remark

Albert stepped back to let Frederika get a view of the screen. "You've been doing a great job," he said. "Thank you."

She didn't look away from the TV. "I've been on national cable news shows four times! And to think I was about to drop Marley as a client."

Albert didn't have anything to say to that, so he walked into the living room. There, sitting at the bottom of the stairs, was the oldest man he had ever seen. He wore a black suit—just like the two muscle-bound men beside him—accessorized with a scarf covered with tiny pink and white checks. All three of them had deep brown skin and flat noses, but the bodyguards had long, straight black hair, while the old man was as bald as plum.

"You," the old man said with a quavering voice, "have been handling yourself very well for such a young man."

Albert took the empty wine bottle out of his mother's lap and set it on Weather's tray as he passed. "Thank you. I've been looking after myself for a while now. Plus I ask Naima and Libertad for advice."

The old man laughed a wheezy little laugh. "Always wise to consult smart women." Then, in a different tone entirely, he said, "You must show me."

Albert thought about that for a moment, then shrugged. What the hell.

The bodyguards made space for him and he started up the stairs. The old man struggled to follow. The bodyguards didn't offer to help but stayed close in case he asked for it. He didn't.

Albert led them into Marley's bedroom, and suddenly remembered the contemptuous way Libertad's family had assumed he had been Marley's bodyguard. "Are these your grandsons?" he asked the old man.

"Great-grandsons!" the man answered. "I'm older than I look!"

Albert turned to them. "Thank you for coming today. I know my aunt would have appreciated it. Be sure to have a little something before you leave. The finger sandwiches are terrific."

The brothers looked surprised to be addressed directly and politely. "Gracias," one said in a deep voice. The other added, in an even deeper voice, "I love finger sandwiches."

Marley's laptop was sitting open on her bureau. Albert moved closer to it, read these very words as they appeared on the screen, then turned it so no one else could see.

"Show me," the old man repeated.

In the corner, a white satin sheet lay over an irregular shape on the floor. Albert drew it back gently.

"I knew a guy with scuba training," he said. "And it wasn't hard to find a winch."

"How did you know to search there?"

"I didn't," Albert answered. "It just seemed like the right thing to do. Like water flowing downhill."

Laid out on the floor was a life-sized solid gold statue of Marley Jacobs. She looked as she had at the moment of her death, her arms above her head to shield her face, her expression tense with the expectation of pain.

"What are you going to do with her?" the old man asked. "Melt her down?"

Albert spun around, ready with a sharp word, but the old man's shrewd expression dissipated his anger. "I'm going to display her, of course. She wasn't one to be hidden away in a dark room somewhere. I'm going to tell people she commissioned a self-portrait, and who cares what they think."

"Display her like art, eh? What will you call it?"

Albert took a deep breath. "The Dragon's Hoard. And I don't like to be tested, especially not in my own house."

"I'll remember that. Listen, my boy: People are going to approach you now, and they're going to be angry. They'll want to blame Marley—and you! —for letting the secret out. For tricking the world with the truth. They'll say she failed and that she weakened the magic in the world by making it real.

"Don't you listen to them! She was a smart woman and she did the right thing." He turned to his great-grandsons. "Come. I like finger sandwiches, too."

They left Albert alone in the room, shutting the door behind them. He could hear the murmur of voices through the floor, but he wasn't ready to return to them yet.

A Key, an Egg, an Unfortunate Remark

Aunt Marley still lay stretched on the floor. Albert stood for a moment, staring down at her. Then, possessed of a strange impulse, he got down on his hands and knees.

"Aunt Marley?" he said, his voice hushed. He took her cold metal hand in his and squeezed it tight. "Aunt Marley? Are you in there?"

There was a sudden whine of straining metal as Marley's golden lips moved very slightly. Albert leaned close enough to hear her say, "This sucks."

Author's Note

Obviously, there is no seafood restaurant near the Sculpture Park with rats in it. I made that up, both the vermin and the establishment where the villains turn them loose. It's one thing to blow up a building (or even a whole bunch of them), but it's another to place vermin in a functioning restaurant.

About the Author

Harry Connolly lives in Seattle with his beloved wife, beloved son, and beloved library system. You can find out more about his books at www.harryjconnolly.com